Praise for *Tainted Angel*

"An exhilarating Napoleonic adventure in which no one is what they seem, including the intrepid hero and heroine. My kind of book!"

—Teresa Grant, author of *The Paris Affair*

"Espionage and passion—Regency style—burning up the pages from chapter one."

—*New York Times* bestselling author Raine Miller

"A delightful romp with as many twists and turns as Regency London's streets! Anne Cleeland re-creates a world of spies and traitors where no one is quite what they seem and the truth is only true for a moment. Is heroine Vidia Swanson working for England or France? And will her lover Carstairs save or execute her? A thrilling tale that will keep you guessing until the very last page."

—Victoria Thompson, author of *Murder in Chelsea*

TAINTED

ANNE CLEELAND

sourcebooks
landmark

Cover design by Eileen Carey
Cover image © Mohamad Itani/Arcangel Images

Published by Sourcebooks Landmark, an imprint of Sourcebooks, Inc.
P.O. Box 4410, Naperville, Illinois 60567-4410
(630) 961-3900
Fax: (630) 961-2168
www.sourcebooks.com

Library of Congress Cataloguing-in-Publication data is on file with the publisher.

Printed and bound in the United States of America.
VP 10 9 8 7 6 5 4 3 2 1

For Hannah's mom,
who wished someone would write
Regency adventure; and for all others like her.

Out of habit, Vidia ran a quick thumb over her pistol's firing mechanism and tried to remember if she had reloaded both barrels after that little incident at Seven Dials a month ago—truly, she should have checked it before now but who could have foreseen that she'd need her weapon tonight of all nights. Walking forward with a brisk step that was meant to discourage interaction, she flipped one end of her wrap over the opposite shoulder and avoided eye contact with the wretched souls who littered this particular circle of hell, although most were no doubt insensibly drunk. Her object was a notorious tavern in this notorious corner of London's underworld, but she was not dressed for discretion, having been called away from the ambassador's soirée on some undisclosed emergency. Indeed, her thin slippers were already damp from an unidentified wetness and it would be best not to contemplate the state of her hem after this assignment—and the gown one of her favorites, too; red silk satin, the décolletage too low for good taste. Red was the color of choice in her line of work in that it camouflaged the occasional bloodstain.

"Ha'penny an' yer prayers, miss." The beggar made so bold as to grasp Vidia's sleeve, pathetically hunched over and whining through his teeth with a slight whistling sound.

"Step aside, if you please." From the looks of it, there would be dirty finger marks on her poor abused gown, but such hazards came with the territory in this part of town and she hoped it would not be necessary to take stronger measures; it was always best not to draw attention before the territory could be assessed—not that she held any real hope of evading notice, dressed as she was.

The beggar gave way, but not before lifting his face so that she caught a glimpse of shrewd grey eyes beneath the brim of his greasy hat. Making a show of straightening the seams of her gloves she paused beside him, the delicate contours of her face illuminated by the low light of the gas lamps. "You need to work on your technique, methinks. You cannot expect to make a living begging unless you tell me something complimentary—insist that you've never seen a tastier piece."

The beggar leaned back into the shadowy alcove so that she could no longer see his eyes and the voice that emanated from the darkness was suddenly cultured and correct. "What point? You are immune to pretty compliments, I imagine. Better to make an appeal for pity, if one can assume a heart beats within that cold breast of yours."

Vidia tilted her head so that the shadows hid her face except for her slow, curving smile. "Lord, you'll not win a ha'penny with that kind of remark, my friend; I give you good advice—tell me I'm a pretty young thing—"

"Not so very young, after all."

"Are you quite finished?" she asked in a mild tone.

The beggar bowed with exaggerated courtesy. "Your pardon; I forget myself."

She lifted a graceful hand to check that both her diamond earbobs were secure, and continued as though she hadn't been interrupted. "Flattery should be your stock in trade—or comedy. Anything is more appealing than pitiful—take it from one who knows."

With an edge of derision, her companion openly scoffed from the recesses of the stained brick wall. "As though one such as you has ever had need to beg for anything—from anyone."

"Only from God," she assured him. "And with mixed results."

He did not respond for a moment, and she leaned forward to smooth her skirts so that she could slide her gaze toward him—she dare not linger here for long in conversation with a beggar; he would risk his cover. "To what do I owe this honor, sir?"

From his position in the shadows the beggar jerked his chin toward the tavern behind him. "Carstairs has gone out of coverage—he's in there and profoundly drunk, I'm afraid. He's like to attract trouble or start spilling state secrets—neither course is acceptable."

Carstairs. Vidia contemplated the dirty window behind him that proclaimed "The Bowman Inn" in fading gilt letters. The door opened for a moment and Vidia could hear raised drunken voices and the clatter of cheap tin cups before it closed again. Not a reputable tavern and apparently matters were urgent or she wouldn't have been summoned on such short notice—she was in coverage, herself, and he wouldn't have sent for her save as a last resort. "Poor man—there is nothing like a low place to make one feel doubly low."

But the grey-eyed beggar had little sympathy and made an impatient sound. "Spare me the excuses—he should know better. An extraction is needful; best get him out before he breaks some heads or allows a French agent to seduce him."

"Where do I deliver him?" With a twitch of silken fabric,

she turned to rearrange her wrap over her elbows so that two men heading into the tavern could not see her face as they passed.

"Back to his cover—don't take him home as yet; I will make an assessment to determine if any harm's been done. A curse on all women—"

"Sirrah," she admonished, daring to tease him.

The beggar made another exaggerated bow. "Present company excepted, then. If you need assistance you have only to signal—others stand ready but it would be best to keep a low profile."

If she thought it odd that someone as recognizable as herself would be sent on a low-profile assignment, she left the thought unsaid; after all, the grey-eyed man was the head of their organization and he was presumably no fool. All in all, she was rather surprised he had taken a direct role in this retrieval—she usually received her orders from lesser beings and had little contact with the spymaster. But no question that Carstairs was too valuable to risk; he would be involved in only the highest-level assignments, which made his current situation all the more alarming.

Reaching into her reticule, she tossed the beggar a guinea, which he caught with a swift movement at odds with his appearance. "For your troubles," she teased with her slow smile, then bowed formally as though she was still at the ambassador's soirée. The beggar made a show of biting the coin between surprisingly white, even teeth. "Thank 'ee," he rasped, his *persona* firmly back in place as he scuttled off, hunched over and limping. She was all admiration—one would never guess he stood over six foot.

As she approached the door, Vidia took a quick, assessing glance at the assorted figures that loitered outside the building in various stages of drunkenness. She had learned a hard lesson, once, about the necessity of securing one's retreat and did not care to repeat the experience. Squaring her shoulders, she pushed open the battered door to the Bowman and paused on the threshold to survey the interior, quickly estimating the size of the crowd and identifying potential exits. A hush fell almost immediately, but she hardly noticed; such a reaction to her appearance was to be expected and could be used or not used to her advantage, depending upon the assignment. If this one was to be low profile—well, she would do her best to be discreet but since one of her earbobs was worth more than anyone in the room could hope to see in a lifetime, this seemed a tall order. No matter; best get on with it.

Moving forward in a languid fashion, she quickly scanned the crowded room and spotted Carstairs leaning on his elbows at the corner of the bar, bringing a tin cup unsteadily to his lips and giving her the barest glance of disinterest. She had to give him credit—he knew better than to present his back to the room, even drunk as a sailor. There seemed little doubt he was quite drunk—small wonder the spymaster was concerned; Carstairs was the keeper of many secrets.

She advanced toward the bar and kept her eyes fixed upon her mark, hoping to extract him quickly and without inciting undue notice—or at least more than could be helped, given that she was so very noticeable. It was too much to be hoped for, however—one of the Bowman's drunken patrons made so bold as to step before her to impede her progress, glancing at his fellows so they could appreciate his temerity. With an insolent grin, he looked her up and down and pronounced, "I gots wot yer lookin' fer, me foine lady."

Pausing, she openly assessed him with an amused smile on

her lips. "That is as may be, my friend—but you don't have what I am looking for, which is fifty guineas."

The man whistled in appreciation, hitching his thumbs in his braces and glancing at the assembled men. "No one 'ere's got that much o' the ready in a twelve-month, lady—ye must be lost."

"Not I," she teased with a hand on his arm. "I am here to gather up the lost—do step aside." She softened the command with a dazzling smile and a slow wink, then gently pushed him away, hoping it was enough to allow him to back down without losing face—but ready to twist the arm behind him, if needful. Fortunately, the gambit worked; the man chuckled in appreciation and backed away with a gesture of homage, the others around him murmuring in amusement. There was no ugly undertone as yet; Vidia could feel the weight of the pistol in her pocket and hoped she wouldn't need it. She was adept at gauging the mood of a crowd and felt that at present it hung in the balance—but by this time of night there would had been heavy inroads made into the cask of Blue Ruin and reactions were therefore unpredictable.

Carstairs was contemplating the dregs of the cup he held before him as she sidled up beside him at the bar, shoulder to shoulder so that she could keep an eye on the crowd and the door. He did not lift his eyes to her but she knew he had recognized her the moment she entered the room—it was his job. He growled, "Go 'way."

"Sorry," she apologized. "I do have orders."

He lifted his head to look at her, the movement causing him to lose his equilibrium. With an effort, he focused his steel blue eyes on hers and for a brief moment she felt a breathless sensation in the vicinity of her breast. "Bullock your orders."

Laying a gentle hand on his arm she coaxed, "Be that as it

may, I'm to bring you home. Come along, my friend, before the crowd has any say in the matter."

He resumed the contemplation of his cup, unmoving, while she could feel the interested scrutiny of those who surrounded them, the combined scent of unwashed bodies and stale ale almost overpowering. With a bit more urgency she tugged on his forearm. "I shall see to it you get your own bottle, once home. You may drink yourself into a stupor with my blessing."

Those intense eyes lifted to meet hers again, slightly unfocused. "She was so—she was so beautiful."

Her heart rent by the quiet intensity of the words, Vidia squeezed the thick forearm beneath her hand. "That she was. But you must come along, now, Carstairs."

To her relief he acquiesced and straightened upright, the movement again making him a bit unsteady on his feet. Bracing him with an arm around his waist, she had to remind herself that she was on assignment and should not enjoy the contact overmuch. Once she had him balanced again, he reached into his purse with a deliberate movement to pull out a coin and contemplate it at length, as though unsure of its value.

"Here," she offered, tossing her own coin on the counter. "That should be enough."

"You should not pay," he scolded vaguely, his dark brows drawn together.

"It is my pleasure. Follow me and stay close, now—try not to speak to anyone."

With one arm remaining around his waist, she steered him through the crowd toward the door, her gaze sharp around them as she watched for weapons. Just as she thought they might escape unaccosted, one of the patrons jostled into them, causing Carstairs to stagger. Before the man could melt into the crowd with Carstairs's purse he was facing the muzzle of her pistol, an inch from his face. "I believe you have mistaken this man's purse for your own. Pray return it."

The thief, startled and then sullen, weighed his options and then complied with her request upon hearing the metallic click as the hammer drew back. Now on full alert, Vidia kept her pistol cocked and in plain view as she guided Carstairs and made a slow progress toward the tavern's swinging door. The surprised silence around them was replaced by a murmuring undertone that she could not quite like, and she was grateful Carstairs was still able to navigate; if he had gone down she would have needed reinforcements and a public donnybrook would have ensued—not precisely low profile.

Once outside she looked for a hackney cab but they were scarce in this area of town as there was more chance of robbery than gainful fare. "This way," she told Carstairs, steering him with pressure at his waist. "Up a few streets we should find a cab—quickly, now."

"Careful," he mumbled with an effort. "Men on corner."

"I see them." She was impressed that he could still make a survey, in the shape that he was—the instinct for self-preservation ran deep in their business. She closed a hand around her pistol but no heroics were necessary; the three loitering on the corner eyed the big man and his unfazed companion and decided to await an easier set of victims.

Shepherding her unsteady charge along the center of the unswept street, Vidia avoided the shadows and moved as briskly as his condition would allow. The damp soles of her satin slippers did little to shield her from the cold cobblestones, but on the other hand the cold air seemed to have a sobering effect on Carstairs; she noted he leaned a little less heavily against her as they made their way toward the next block. When she finally spotted a hackney, Vidia lifted a gloved hand and it stopped immediately—no one ever ignored her. With the aid of the jarvey, she managed to navigate Carstairs up the footstairs and he collapsed inside, his head tilted back against the cracked leather cushions and his eyes closed. His neckcloth was unbuttoned and she was forced to tear her gaze from his exposed throat as she gave his direction to the driver. Once under way, however, she allowed herself to study his sleeping form to her heart's content, now that the opportunity had been given her. A fine specimen of a man, Carstairs was—with his broad shoulders and dark chestnut hair. The late Marie Carstairs had been a very lucky woman—until this recent turn of events, of course. Poor, grieved man; and to have wound up at the Bowman of all places—he was clearly in a bad way.

He muttered something unintelligible and she took his hand to hold it between hers—it was the least she could do—as the cab jolted over the cobblestones. Her heart ached to witness his grief even as she felt an inappropriate stab of envy; to have such a man mourn one was more than any woman could ask. Mentally she shook herself for the maudlin thought—it came of never knowing from one day to the next if she would survive long enough to see her current role to its conclusion. Not much longer, now, as long as Brodie held faith—*por favor Deus*.

They arrived at Carstairs's rented rooms and she could only be thankful it had not been necessary to deposit him alone at the residence he had once shared with his late wife—he was on assignment and apparently their spymaster felt he could continue to perform his duties, despite this rather shocking lapse. Eying him in an assessing way, Vidia tried to decide if she should accompany him to his door. Anyone who saw them may leap to the wrong conclusion—given her reputation—and she wanted to spare him the gossip. In the end she was compelled to scramble to his side when he staggered from the cab and nearly fell. She steadied him once again with an arm under his coat, trying not to notice the scent of him, masculine and enticing, or the feel of the hard muscles at his waist. It had been a long, long time since she had held a man close to her side. "Up you go, then. Let me pay the jarvey."

The blue eyes focused on hers. "You must not pay; I will pay." This was evidently important.

"We will keep an account," she soothed, and tossed up a coin.

After several abortive attempts, he directed her to the correct door and when he was unable to insert the key properly, she took it from him with gentle fingers and did the honors. She had seen him drink the time they were on assignment in Flanders—he had pegged the mark at a Guildhall fête, after all—but she had never seen him staggering drunk as he was now; if ever an occasion deserved it, though, this was the one.

Once inside, she strained her eyes in the darkness, searching for a candle and a flint and trying to decide what was best to do. He continued on through the rooms, presumably to his bedroom, and she followed, barking a shin against a low table in the darkness. He paused, contrite. "Sorry," he said thickly, and turned to run his hands down the length of her arms. "Sorry."

"Quite all right," she assured him, feeling the hair on her arms stand on end. His hands were warm—the palms callused from whatever *persona* he had taken on in this latest assignment. In the dim moonlight, she managed to maneuver him into his bedroom. "Here you are—safe and sound." As she was debating whether she should attempt to remove his boots he drew his hands up and down her arms again. Unsure of his intent, she lifted her face in inquiry and instead was met with his mouth descending on hers.

Completely surprised, she was startled into submission for a moment and he kissed her roughly, making an eager sound in his throat as he did so and pulling her against him. Instinctively she began to respond before she pulled herself together. "Carstairs," she whispered, breaking her mouth away. "That's enough of that now—to bed with you."

In response he brought a hand to her jaw and held it firmly so as to kiss her again, his mouth opening on hers and his other arm drawing her hips to his. *Mãe de Deus*, she thought as she struggled to control her wayward body, I am only flesh and blood and I had forgotten what temptation feels like. His intent unmistakable, he tugged her dress from her shoulders and moved his hands to her breasts, murmuring into the side of her throat.

You must put a stop to this while you still can, *menina*, she scolded herself with no real conviction. "No, my friend." She tried to keep her tone light as she disengaged from him. "You are in no shape."

Pulling her against him with one arm, he took her hand with the other and pressed it to his groin so that she could assess his readiness—she was reminded again that Marie Carstairs had been a lucky woman.

"I stand corrected," she said against his mouth, which had once again descended hungrily upon hers, "but you mustn't, Carstairs." Her protest was only halfhearted as he began trailing slow kisses down her throat, his hands working magic as they invaded her corset. They were alone, no one would know, and it was extremely unlikely that another opportunity to share a bed with Carstairs would present itself—he could mourn Marie for years. Why, he may not even remember in the morning—he seemed that drunk—and truly, it would be a kindness; the poor man needed comfort and this would be comfort on a very elemental level.

While she deliberated, he pushed her gown to the floor and began unfastening the tapes of her petticoats with such competence that she decided there was little hope for it, and gave in to the sensations of his hands on her body and his eager mouth on hers. As soon as he sensed her acquiescence, matters escalated quickly and he pushed her down on the bed, the wonderful weight of him pressing against her as he pulled away the clothing that impeded him; his hands cradling her hips as they rocked each other into a familiar rhythm that concluded all too soon. In the aftermath, she lay with her face pressed against his throat, their breathing the only sound in the stillness.

"Sorry," he murmured, his skin damp against hers. "Too fast—couldn't be helped."

Making an effort to speak in a light tone, she ran her palms over the muscles in his back. "No apologies needed—it was all very satisfactory." Lifting up to kiss him, she whispered, "Let me get up and leave you to sleep, shall I?"

But he did not move and she was firmly pinned beneath him. "Give me a minute." He rested atop her, stroking her with his warm hands and bestowing languorous kisses that made her toes curl.

"You taste of whiskey," she teased, "and not fine whiskey by any means."

He pulled back to look at her and she had a sudden and

panicked impression that he was not so very drunk after all, but then he returned his mouth to her throat. "Sorry," he said again, his voice slightly slurred.

She smiled into the darkness, absurdly happy despite the sure knowledge she was not behaving as she ought. "So many apologies tonight; and no need, I assure you—it is only me, Carstairs."

"Marie," he whispered, and kissed her again.

Chapter 2

Vidia knew a moment's qualm; it could not be healthy to encourage the man to believe he was making love to a ghost, could it? On the other hand, he was very practiced and oh, she was so very much out of practice and what was the harm—it was not as though she would be ruined and demand marriage; she had been ruined long ago.

After an impressively short amount of time he was ready to have another go and she was not unwilling—what was another sin, on top of the first? He didn't call her by the wrong name again but on the other hand, he didn't call her by the right name either as he took his time, caressing her until she was nearly witless. I'll not worry over it, she decided, adrift in bliss; whether he thinks I am Marie or knows I am not, it hardly matters at this point—he will be comforted and I—well, I will have an all-too-brief respite from my latest and most difficult role. Tilting her head so as to allow better access to her throat, she wished she hadn't allowed the thought to intrude. Her latest role was becoming more and more dangerous with each passing day, and she knew that a reckoning was imminent—any hint of disloyalty would mean a swift and certain punishment. You have no choice, she reminded herself, and it seems this momentary foolishness with Carstairs has made you soft-headed. To take her mind off her troubles, she concentrated on pleasing her companion instead and her efforts resulted in a very satisfactory conclusion yet again.

"Now, isn't this better than drinking gin at the Bowman?" she teased, trying to gauge his coherence. In response he murmured something unintelligible into her shoulder as his weight became heavier. To sleep, then—perhaps to dream of the fair Marie. With a small sigh, she conceded that it would be for the best if he did not remember this coupling; she had been mad to allow it and he would no doubt be stung with remorse in the morning—if he remembered. Perhaps it would be best to vacate discreetly before the effects of the whiskey wore off.

With this in mind, she carefully wriggled out from beneath him and then paused, unable to resist a chance to study his profile in the dim moonlight. Not unhandsome, she decided—but on the other hand not so handsome that he was constantly noticed, as she was. Her beauty curtailed her usefulness to some extent; she had enjoyed no little success as an "angel"—a woman used as a lure to entice information—because men had an inexplicable and uncontrolled desire to boast of their secrets to a beautiful woman. However, it also meant she could not travel unnoticed—not without a disguise that obscured her exquisite face. Although when the occasion arose—she acknowledged a little grimly—she was a first-class *diabo*, hiding among the trees and shooting *bastardo*. On those occasions no one much cared what she looked like.

With a mental shake, she brought her thoughts back to the present—and what a surprising present it was; who would have thought she would have started the night trying to keep the Chief Secretary of the Treasury at arm's length and ended it in bed with Lucien Carstairs, of all men?

Apparently, life still held some surprises for her. And it was not such a monumental mistake, she reasoned, unable to resist stroking her fingertips gently over his head. And no harm was done—as long as he does not remember. I will remember, though, and I will be the better for it, I think—I have been reminded that despite everything, life does indeed hold the occasional pleasant surprise. Steeling herself to vacate the warm bed and the equally warm man, she carefully began to shift away when suddenly he stirred and muttered, "*Rochon; allons.*"

She paused, staring, and decided she must have misheard him.

"*Oui, Capitaine. L'or…pour l'Aigle…*" The words were slurred but unmistakable. *Mãe de Deus*, she thought in astonishment; Lucien Carstairs was loosing state secrets—and not necessarily those of the right state.

"Hush," she soothed, her hand gentle again on his head. "Go to sleep, Carstairs."

He fell quiet and she sat unmoving, trying to make sense of it. "*L'Aigle*"—the Eagle—a reference to bringing gold to Napoleon. And he dreamed that he spoke to Rochon, Napoleon's notorious spymaster. The obvious explanation seemed unthinkable—Carstairs was one of the Crown's more experienced agents and could not possibly be tainted—a double agent. Or could he? Biting her lip, she reflected that there was nothing like a hint of treason to disrupt an otherwise memorable evening.

The silence stretched on as she debated the best course, and then decided she should think about what was to be done whilst she made her way homeward—that should be her first concern. With escape in mind, she was mentally girding her loins to gather up her clothes and dress in the dark when Carstairs murmured again and groped for her with a hand.

Unable to resist, she abandoned her plan without a second thought and curled herself against him as he began to show unmistakable signs of arousal. Thrice, she thought in pleased anticipation, returning his caresses—Marie Carstairs must have died of conjugal bliss.

Finally, in the dawning gray light she crept out of bed, gathering up her crumpled dress and tiptoeing to the parlor before pulling it over her head, careful not to wake him. Her exit must be unobserved so as not to bring down a storm of gossip on the new widower's head, and after taking a careful survey of the street through the window she slipped outside, walking briskly in the misty air with her head ducked for a few blocks. It was cold and she rubbed her arms—she must have left her wrap in his quarters and wished she still had it to obscure the sorry fact she was clad in a well-creased evening gown. There was nothing worse, she thought in annoyance as she hailed a hackney cab and stepped within, than when the jarvey leers at one as though one were a common strumpet. I should produce my blade from my garter, and then we would behold a change in attitude.

Settling into the threadbare cushions, she made a half-hearted attempt to dredge up some remorse for throwing caution to the winds—Carstairs was a compatriot and it was never a good idea to mix business with pleasure. Then there was the alarming disclosure he had made; she would have to tread very carefully—perhaps ask Brodie for advice. Truth to tell, her first inclination was to say nothing to anyone and ignore the lapse; she was very fond of Carstairs and would not want him to risk exposure as a tainted agent, especially at this vulnerable point in his life—Vidia knew all there was to know about walking that particular tightrope. And to confront him about it would be to confess that she had taken advantage of his weakened state—although to be fair, he had instigated the liaison, thinking she was his dead wife. With a sigh, she closed her eyes and acknowledged that perhaps it had not been her finest hour—she felt as though she were seventeen again, and just as foolish.

Only the early-morning vendors were stirring as she mounted the steps into the fashionable townhouse she was given at the pleasure of Benjamin Brodie, who stood as her current protector. She had no fear of discovery; fortunately Brodie lived in his own rooms at the Merrick Hotel and had the courtesy to refrain from being constantly underfoot—an excellent trait in a protector. And an excellent protector he was, she acknowledged in all humility—she would not be alive, else. There was a time, long ago, when she had felt otherwise, but Brodie could hardly be faulted; he saw the world in terms of profit and she—well, she was a rare and valuable commodity. The leopard would not change his spots and they did have a fondness for one another.

She slid the well-oiled door open and listened for a moment; the house was quiet, which meant the night workmen had left. This was to the good—she wanted nothing more than to crawl into bed and sleep, mainly so as not to have to think of what had transpired this evening and the new set of troubles she had brought upon herself. Her ruined slippers dangling from her fingers, she padded across the luxurious rug and mounted the sweeping stairway without a candle, the rhythmic swish of her skirts the only sound in the silence. Of a necessity, there were no servants save the one—who could be trusted to be discreet—and that one would be softly snoring in her quarters at this hour, unaware that her mistress had been out misbehaving.

The dawn was glowing faintly around the edges of the

velvet curtains as she settled before her dressing table mirror and removed the remaining pins from her hair—lucky it had been dark and Carstairs hadn't seen this mad tangle. She would wait and take a brush to it tomorrow, even though the delay would only make matters worse. Napoleon's gold, Carstairs had said. In French. She paused, reviewing her reflection and noting idly that her cheeks were red from whisker burn. It may be nothing, but there was no question she would have to tell Brodie—she would have to couch it so that the means by which she had obtained the information was not revealed, although Brodie was not an easy man to fool. She was already aware that she didn't have the wherewithal to reveal to the grey-eyed man what Carstairs had let slip, whose punishment would be only slightly less severe, one would think, than that of Napoleon's spymaster. It is beyond vexing, she thought in annoyance as she slid between the silken sheets in her chemise—she couldn't even have a warm night with a willing man without international repercussions. For two pence she would pack her bags and leave it all behind; except she couldn't of course—the fate of the world hung in the balance.

On this sobering thought, she stared at the canopy overhead and tried to decide how to handle Carstairs. A warning, perhaps; discreetly given. Or even better, to tease him as though she hadn't taken the words seriously. She would think on it—it was exquisitely ironic that she was to bear the burden of Carstairs's secret, having so many of her own.

Chapter 3

It was too much to be hoped that Brodie would not appear at Vidia's doorstep at midmorning. Maisie, her maidservant, evidenced no sympathy when Vidia pulled her pillow over her head and groaned as the curtains were pushed aside and bright sunlight streamed into the room.

"Up wi' ye," the north country woman directed, tugging at the pillow. "And ye'll need to work harder to get the smell of another man off ye."

"Lord." Vidia's muffled response was tinged with resigned amusement. "You are nine-tenths foxhound, methinks."

The woman threw a towel over her shoulder and bustled over to the steaming water jug. "I'm all-tenths fashed on account o' having not a wink of sleep; the workmen were in t' cellar yet again." The woman cast Vidia a sidelong glance as she poured hot water into the wash basin. "Ye wouldn't know, as ye wasn't here."

"I hope the workmen didn't keep you awake," offered Vidia through her pillow in a mild tone. "There is nothing worse than being awakened when one wishes to sleep."

"Sounded like t' artillery in Salamanca." Maisie retrieved Vidia's discarded gown from the floor with a baleful eye. "Bangin' about, hammer and tongs."

The widow of a gunnery sergeant, Maisie had been

extricated from behind enemy lines in Portugal by Vidia, who at the time had needed a mark to pose as a dairymaid. At loose ends due to her recent bereavement, the stolid countrywoman had agreed to drive a herd of cows across the river at Fuentes de Onoro, in the teeth of enemy fire and much to the chagrin of Marshal Messena, who led the enemy forces for the French. Not only did the timely delay help Wellington's reinforcements, it allowed Vidia to escape the siege by crossing the river crouched beside a compliant cow and wading knee-deep in the murky water. Plain and stout, Maisie nevertheless was shown to have nerves of steel and had thereafter proved her mettle on many an occasion. By unspoken agreement, she had stayed on with Vidia as a general maidservant and henchwoman when the occasion warranted, oftentimes deployed to eavesdrop in situations where she could infiltrate without fear of suspicion—her unassuming appearance was her strongest asset. Despite the fact the two women had been in many a tight corner together, Maisie never asked questions nor faltered—excellent traits that were much appreciated by Vidia, who had seen her share of betrayals.

With a resigned sigh, Vidia tossed her pillow aside and propped her hands beneath her head, contemplating the gold-shot canopy overhead as it glinted in the sunlight. "Trust Mr. Brodie to make an appearance when I am longing for another hour of sleep. Do I have time to wash my hair?" The scent of smoke from the Bowman lingered faintly.

Maisie eyed her doubtfully. "Yer hair's a rare mullycrush and it'd take an hour at least—we'll use a touch o' powder, instead."

Swinging her legs over the side of the bed, Vidia stretched like a beautiful cat and then wandered barefoot over to her armoire to select a day dress. "Is Mr. Brodie looked after?"

Maisie sniffed. "He's tuckin' into the breakfast meats. He'll do."

"Dear Mr. Brodie," said Vidia in a pious tone, sliding Maisie a teasing glance.

Maisie was not fooled. "Where were ye an' who was he?"

Unable to suppress a slow smile of delight as she chose a pale blue—best to look insipid for the coming discussion—Vidia replied, "I'd rather not say, Maisie; your proper Yorkshire soul would be shocked to its core."

As was her custom, Maisie offered no advice or condemnation, but she was nonetheless moved to remark, "Ye'll have a care, missy—beneath it all yer soft as a snail wearin' a shell."

Laughing, Vidia could only agree. "I must be—to allow you to bully me constantly, and compare me to a snail."

Her handmaiden motioned for her to sit before the mirror and then began to carefully navigate the hairbrush through the tangled locks with practiced hands. "Ye'll be rememberin' Salamanca, missy, and yer foolishness in letting t' wounded man sleep in the kitchen all on account o' his handsome face."

"I do remember." Vidia's solemn tone was belied by the twinkle in her eyes. "Thank God you know how to brain a man with a fire jack; I am a sad case, Maisie."

"A word t' the wise, is all." The tangles vanquished, Maisie brushed Vidia's hair until it crackled and then began applying the powder bag judiciously.

"There are times," Vidia admitted in all honesty, "that I fear I never learn my lessons." She conjured up the memory of the moment when Carstairs had brought his mouth down upon hers. I wonder if he will remember, she thought, and I wonder if it would make any difference if he did.

Maisie's sharp gaze rested on her charge's soft expression,

reflected in the mirror. "P'haps this mystery man is t'one to settle ye down." Unaccountably, Maisie had taken to dropping hints that it was time for Vidia to retire—no doubt recent events had raised some alarm. Small blame to her, thought Vidia; I am alarmed, myself, what with the night work in the cellar and the *estupido* carrier pigeons making a racket in the attic space. She regarded her maid's reflection with amusement, a corner of her mouth quirked up at the absurdity of the idea of settling down with Lucien Carstairs. "It is hopeless, Maisie—I am afraid I am not a settler."

"Every woman's a settler," the other insisted, speaking around the pins she held in her mouth. "'Tis not as though ye couldn't start afresh—ye're good at that sort o' thing—ye can be anything t' anyone."

But Vidia disagreed, shaking a curl loose from its pin. "I am four and twenty, my friend, and firmly on the shelf. Not to mention I am no maiden, and thus ineligible."

But Maisie refused to concede as she wound the ringlet around her finger and repinned it ruthlessly in place. "There's plenty o' men who'd not mind—bonny as ye are. Plenty o' men who'd not mind a wife who knows her way 'round the bedroom."

"Men can't be trusted, Maisie—there's the rub with such a plan." Vidia raised a subtle finger to reposition the pin and ease her beleaguered scalp.

"Not all men—but some can, I'm thinkin'." There was a pause. "Perhaps ye can find yer family, now that the war's over."

"The war is never over, my friend." Vidia eyed her companion in the mirror and reflected that this was the first time Maisie had hinted she was aware that Vidia was not, in fact, English—the poor woman must indeed be shaken. To soothe her, she arched a brow, teasing. "Do you think they'd allow us to open a bakery in Yorkshire?" The reference was to a near-disastrous mishap at the Port of Calais, when the communiqué containing the key to the enemy's code was inadvertently baked into a loaf of bread, Maisie having only a rudimentary understanding of the French language.

Willing to divert the discussion, Maisie rested her chin on her chest and pretended to contemplate such a scenario. "Ye'd be of little help in the kitchen, if I may be sayin' so."

This was inarguably true and Vidia noted in all humility, "I must throw myself on your bounty, then."

"I do has me Jem's pension, I do." Maisie was well-aware that Vidia had a fortune in jewelry downstairs in the sugar box. "Enough to buy clotted cream onct a' month, I reckon." The maidservant put the finishing touches on Vidia's hair. "Off ye go."

With a last, indifferent look in the mirror, Vidia made her way down to the dining room to greet Brodie, who was reading the *Times* at the mahogany table, which could seat twenty uncrowded. He was a large, middle-aged man who had indulged himself in food and drink to the point that he was florid of face and slightly stout. An Englishman by birth, he held little loyalty to anything or anyone other than the making of money, and as a result he was rumored to be one of the richest men in the world. Upon her entrance, he set aside his newspaper to greet her.

Vidia lifted a graceful hand. "Don't get up, Benny—forgive me for keeping you waiting."

Assessing her face, he noted abruptly, "You look a fright, *Bela*."

"Impossible," she smiled in amusement. "As well you know."

"You didn't get much sleep, I'm afraid—they were noisy, last night?"

"Hammer and tongs," she replied easily, taking a slice of toast from the rack. "And no, I didn't get much sleep." Hiding a smile, she buttered her toast.

"Perhaps it will be the last time they'll be working in your cellar." He continued to assess her with a thoughtful gaze—apparently the insipid gown had not disguised the fact she was a bit the worse for wear.

"The *Argo* will launch?" She slid him a teasing glance.

"The *Argo* will launch," he affirmed, and leaned his chair on its back legs, pushing his fingers into his waistcoat pockets with a self-satisfied air. "I am the puppet master."

"You are a blowhard." She decided to help herself to blackberry jam even though it was more his favorite than hers. *Deus*, she was hungry.

He cocked his head. "You will need to marshal your strength; there will be a card party tonight—and Montagu will attend."

She shuddered delicately. "Lord, Benny—I am running out of excuses with that miserable man."

But Brodie had little sympathy. "Use any excuse you'd like—just find out when he'll be away on undisclosed business for several days; I believe it will be next week or the week after." He leaned back in his chair again, watching her. "I daresay this will be the last time you must handle Montagu, also."

Vidia found no comfort in this pronouncement and opined crossly, "How such a creature can become the Chief Secretary of the Treasury is a mystery."

"An excellent example of over-breeding, *Bela*. Fortunately for us, he is willing to let drop the days that he must supervise the gold shipments."

"*Idiota*," she pronounced with scorn.

"But a useful idiot, and lucky for us," he reminded her.

"Lucky he is stupid enough to think someone like you would be interested in someone like him."

Vidia's own opinion was that this phenomenon was not necessarily a result of the mark's stupidity as much as her own skill as an angel, but she refrained from correcting him lest she sound vain, which was to be avoided at all costs. After debating whether her figure could withstand another slice of toast and jam, she partook. "I am much heartened to hear I will not have to suffer that fool much longer."

Nodding, he contemplated his tea cup for a moment with a satisfied air. "All is in train—the snare is nearly set and very soon the rabbit will walk into it without even being aware he has been bested." He paused for a moment, then raised his eyes to hers, his tone suddenly serious. "What has happened, *Bela*?"

Trust Brodie to sense that something was amiss—in a way, he and Maisie were very much alike. "I overheard something rather alarming, I am afraid."

Watching her, her companion dropped his chair back down and leaned forward. "Tell me, then."

She chose her words carefully. "I overheard a private conversation; one of my—compatriots—made a reference to bringing gold to the Eagle."

Silent for a moment, Brodie regarded her almost kindly. "It is a trap, *Bela*."

"No," Vidia disagreed with certainty. "I only happened to overhear—I am certain it was not an attempt to trap me."

Thoughtful, Brodie tilted his head. "Are you the only one who overheard this?"

"Yes," Vidia admitted with reluctance.

"It is a trap," he repeated. "Come, *Bela*—you are wiser than this."

Knitting her brow, she regarded him and thought it over. "Perhaps," she finally admitted.

But Brodie was unfazed by this development and leaned in to pat her hand reassuringly. "It doesn't matter—I have them all over a barrel; no one dares make a move, even if they have managed to discover what is afoot."

"I am placed in a difficult position," she ventured to remind him, "if they believe I am tainted and are seeking to trap me with such a scheme."

"You have been in difficult positions before—some more difficult than others," he pointed out reasonably. "I have every confidence in you."

She had to laugh at his coolness and teased, "What if you are wrong—what if they clap you in irons, instead? Whatever would become of me, Benny?"

But her companion was unmoved. "You would have every man in the kingdom with a thousand pounds to his name on your doorstep within the hour."

With a smile, she assured him, "None can hold a candle to you."

Chuckling, he patted her hand again, which was as much a show of affection as he ever gave her. "There's not a bureaucrat alive that can outmaneuver me, *Bela*; you forget that I am the puppet master."

Vidia was forced to admit, "My spymaster appears to have taken an interest—and he is no bureaucrat."

"Has he? As well he should—we are not dealing in petty thefts, here." Brodie leaned his head back and contemplated the ceiling for a moment with a satisfied expression. "He is a worthy opponent; steel sharpens steel."

Vidia refrained from pointing out that the sharpening was apparently to be done on her nerves and assumed a helpful air. "If they do throw you in Newgate Prison, I would bake you a cake with a file hidden in it." She was thinking of Maisie's loaf of bread.

He shot her a look. "Easier for you to beguile the guards, I think—I have seen you bake."

She shrugged her shoulders in capitulation. "Then it would be best to avoid prison altogether; I cannot imagine the guards would play cards with you—let alone allow you to cheat them."

Brodie cocked his head, pretending to contemplate this unhappy scenario. "You paint a grim picture, *Bela.* But I have no intention of going to prison, where the bricks are made of—well, merely brick."

"I am reassured, then. Please pass the teapot." Pouring a cup, she reflected that he was never one to express any doubts, no matter how dire the circumstances. It had saved her life, once.

Vidia dealt another book of thirteen cards to each of the players and gave Montagu a slow glance under her lashes as she leaned over to display her impressive bosom to full advantage. The card room at Stoffer's was thick with smoke and masculine attention; it was an open secret that Brodie's relationship with Vidia was a platonic one and therefore nearly every man she met was convinced she was starved for bed sport and he was the best candidate to service her on the side. On occasions such as this, when it was well after midnight and staggering amounts of brandy had been imbibed, the competition for her favors was almost feverish and she was beginning to worry that she would not have an opportunity for private conversation with Montagu.

Glancing to Brodie, she noted he was content to stand propped in a corner, smoking a cigarillo and holding court with gentlemen who sought financial advice—the state of the Treasury was precarious and investors were nervous, what with the instability on the Continent and rumors that Napoleon was set to escape his imprisonment on the Island of Elba. They don't know the half of it, thought Vidia, as she operated the bank for the game of Basset. And Brodie is the least likely candidate to offer honest advice—more likely he will pick their pockets where they stand.

"Bring me luck, Vidia," implored Montagu, his balding head wet with perspiration and his gaze on the expanse of her exposed bosom.

"You need no more luck, my lord," teased Vidia, who had manipulated the cards so as to allow him to win. "If you win any more from me I shall be forced to beg for bread in the streets."

The gentlemen seated at the table chuckled at the unlikeliness of this as she drew the cards and called out in her low-pitched voice, "Ace wins, ten loses."

Exclamations of satisfaction or disappointment met her call, and the croupier who assisted her gathered up and paid out the bets placed on the cards. One of the players at the table was a marquess who had held her gaze with his own several times this evening, making it clear he was interested in establishing a relationship. Rather handsome, and with a deep purse, too—such a shame he was married yet had a penchant for child prostitutes. "Queen wins, king loses," she announced, smiling at him with an arched brow. There was little she didn't know about those who ran in Brodie's circles—either from Brodie himself or those in her own line of work who watched Brodie carefully.

Montagu leaned in and murmured, "I must speak with you—about what we spoke of the other night."

Although his brandied breath made her want to recoil, she leaned in to whisper, "With pleasure," touching his arm briefly with her fingertips. He had been hinting at stealing away for a tryst—honestly, did the man truly think she would favor him above the others who vied for her? Short, balding, and rather stupid—to drop hints boasting of his secret work with the Treasury so as to impress her. Out of spite, she arranged for him to lose the hand.

A merry gentleman who had lost a great deal of money with a great deal of good humor finally stood to withdraw from the game and the croupier indicated that a newcomer should sit. Dealing another hand, Vidia glanced up to find that she was looking into Carstairs's blue eyes, intent upon hers. Despite herself, she found she could not suppress a smile, and he nodded in acknowledgment. *Santos*, she thought as she shuffled the cards and looked away—he definitely remembers last night. She tried with little success to quash the butterflies in her midsection and concentrate on the game. Unkind of him to show up in this manner—not to mention he could complicate her efforts to speak with Montagu. A pox on him; unless he was here on assignment, which was always a possibility. After all, Brodie was convinced his sleep-talking was merely a means to entrap her.

"Madam," prompted the croupier in an undertone. "Your draw."

With an effort, Vidia controlled her wayward thoughts and focused on the game, deciding out of fairness that she shouldn't punish Carstairs for surprising her and so she allowed the cards to fall where they may.

After another hour, she excused herself to the others so as to take a break, fully expecting Carstairs to follow her out as she made her way with slow, graceful movements to the buffet room. He did not, however, which led her to believe that perhaps he was indeed here on assignment, only monitoring Montagu. If this was the case, it meant that her compatriots who worked for the Crown were figuring out Brodie's scheme and would be justly wondering why she hadn't figured it out herself—as she was their angel assigned to Brodie. Small wonder they think I may be tainted, she thought with an inward sigh; my chickens are coming home to roost—or I suppose more properly, my pigeons—and running a bakery in Yorkshire is beginning to sound more and more appealing.

Taking a plate from the buffet, she couldn't resist scooping up several apricot tarts and a glass of watered punch as she laughed and flirted with several regulars—a cabinet minister with an opium habit, a wealthy alderman whose wife had left him; she had studied them well and knew all their secrets.

She spied Montagu coming toward her and set down her plate with no little regret so as to hold out her hands to him in a warm greeting.

"Vidia." He kissed her cheek, his mouth rather moist and unpleasant. "Come away for a moment—I must show you something."

"For shame," she teased wickedly, feigning shock, and the others chuckled while he led her away with the air of the victor.

They strolled to a quieter corner near the smoking room, and he tucked her hand into his arm as he leaned in to murmur in her ear, "I must visit with you—privately—perhaps some afternoon when you are free for a few hours." He nearly panted in anticipation and stroked her hand where it rested on his arm.

"Do you have a place we could enjoy such a visit?" It couldn't be Brodie's house, after all, and the gentleman had a rather fearsome wife at home, whose fortune had bankrolled his political aspirations.

"I do," he breathed in excitement. "I have taken rooms in Kensington."

Vidia ducked her head, thinking how Brodie would laugh out loud at the thought of this fool thinking he could entice one such as she to rooms in Kensington. "Then I will come willingly, my lord," she murmured with her slow smile. "But I mustn't let Mr. Brodie catch wind and I am not certain when I will be free—I may need to send you a note on short notice."

"I stand at your disposal," the man assured her, his gaze on her mouth. "A moment's notice—nothing else shall take precedence—nothing."

"Any day?" she teased, "You flatter me, my lord."

Hesitating, he admitted, "I shall be away Monday and Tuesday a week from next—Treasury business, I'm afraid."

"Then I will watch for an opportunity on another day," she assured him, and wondered if she could vacate to Yorkshire in the meantime—or perhaps an excuse was no longer needed, as Brodie seemed to think this the last time she was needed to extract the gold shipment schedule from Montagu. I hope so, she thought as she listened to his assurances of devotion with half an ear. Perhaps Maisie is right; perhaps once this scheme of Brodie's is completed it will be time to look for a different life. In all honesty, Vidia had never made plans for a future because she had never imagined she would have lived this long—and truth to tell, hadn't much cared. But some strange and unnatural yearnings now resided in her breast, no doubt connected to the fact that Carstairs was now an eligible widower and she had been given a taste of what a life with a fine man in her bed would be like. Bringing herself up short, she was reminded that Carstairs was probably arranging for her downfall, and focused again on whatever it was that Montagu was saying.

"...rubies, perhaps?"

"I adore rubies," she agreed, thinking the man must surely realize that someone with her coloring should never wear rubies. *Idiota*, she thought again, and wished him away.

Her wish was unexpectedly granted as a servant approached them and bowed. "Lord Montagu, there is a gentleman by the cloakroom who wishes a word."

As Montagu made his regretful excuses, the servant then met Vidia's eyes and made an indication toward the outer hallway with his own, signaling that she was to head in that direction. Carstairs, she thought in pleased anticipation, and casually drifted through the doors. The hallway was nearly deserted at this late hour, and she took a survey but did not spy Carstairs or anyone else, for that matter. One of the doors leading out to a balcony at the end of the hallway was ajar, however, and she decided this was apparently to be her destination. Feeling those unexpected butterflies again, she made her way down the hallway and slipped through the balcony door.

To her surprise, the man who drew her into his arms in the cold night air was not Carstairs, and in the darkness she wasn't certain who he was for a moment. Closing her hand over her pistol, she drew away only to discover that her admirer was the marquess from the card table, who gently bit her shoulder, chuckling, as he brought his hands to rest on her breasts.

Her acute disappointment did not help Vidia's mood at being thus accosted; however, she had mastered her temper long ago and so only chided in a mild tone, "You forget yourself, my lord."

But he would not allow her to draw away and muttered, "Come, I shall pay whatever you wish—or perhaps you will wish to pay me, afterward." He pinned her against the balcony railing, his hand sliding into her bodice.

If I shoot him, Brodie will strangle me, she thought—he is too powerful a peer and the scandal would be horrific. I suppose I must entice him into a carriage and give him the slip somehow—unless he plans to have his way with me right here, which is unkind of him as it is far too cold.

Fortunately, no plan was needed as the balcony door suddenly opened and Carstairs brought a cosh down on the back of the marquess's head. As the man sagged against her, Vidia pushed him to the tiled floor and watched Carstairs wedge the door shut.

"I thank you," she said, straightening her bodice. "A timely rescue."

Pushing the prone man with his boot, Carstairs admitted, "I wasn't certain you sought a rescue, but I didn't want to take the chance."

Stung, she frowned at him in the dim light. "You know what he is—you cannot imagine I would seek out such a one."

"No—I beg your pardon." They stood in awkward silence for a moment, contemplating the felled marquess. "I have your wrap; I must find a way to return it."

It was too dark to read his expression, and with an effort, she controlled her reaction to his proximity and reminded herself that he was trying to trap her. "There is no hurry."

With a nod, he crouched down to place a casual hand on the man's throat, checking his pulse.

"Should we leave him locked out here?" Vidia suggested. "He never saw you and it would serve him right."

Glancing up at her, he lifted a conspiratorial brow. "We have been granted such an opportunity, though—it seems a shame to waste it."

This was intriguing, and spoke of a willingness to bend the rules—normally they were called to follow orders without improvisation and never risk bringing attention to themselves. "What do you suggest?"

"We could arrange to leave him at the brothel on Wymore."

"Oh," she breathed in admiration. "That is *diabolical*, Carstairs." The Wymore brothel catered to men who sought out boys. "See to it that the concerned proprietor summons the Watch on account of his unexplained injury."

With a nod of agreement, he pulled a length of cord from his pocket and efficiently bound the man's hands. "We must have a pact, then—this is out of coverage—agreed?"

"I'll not tell a soul," she promised.

"Another secret we'll share." He stood and met her eyes although it was too dark to see what he was thinking. Placing his hands on her waist, he drew her toward him and bent his head to kiss her but she withstood the temptation and turned her face.

"Not now, Carstairs."

Accepting the rebuff without comment, he released her and asked, "I'll need a distraction—ten minutes?"

"You shall have one," she agreed. "I have just the candidate."

"Good—I'll arrange to have him sent on his way." He paused and bent his head to hers. "May I visit you at home later? I'd like to speak with you."

So—he wanted to inveigle his way into the town house; a pox on Brodie for always—*always*—being right. Smoothly, she countered, "I shall quarrel with Brodie and you may escort me home, if you'd like—in an hour I will exit out the back in a huff."

He bowed his head in agreement and she put her ear against the door to listen for a moment, then slipped through.

Upon reentering the card room Vidia spotted Brodie, cradling a brandy snifter and idly reviewing the room. He watches Montagu and wonders what has happened to me, she thought with a twinge of remorse as she came to his side. This is exactly what happens when I allow myself to be distracted by Lucien Carstairs, who is very good at seeming smitten, I must say. As Brodie raised his glass to her in a playful salute, she leaned toward him in a flirtatious manner and murmured in an undertone, "I would ask you to quarrel with Montagu."

The smile faded from his face, and he had the look of a man who was annoyed. In a low voice he asked, "You have the information, then?"

"Monday and Tuesday, a week from next," she affirmed, tilting her head and placing a hand on his arm as though she were trying to soothe him. "But I need an excuse not to go trysting with that creature."

In a show of anger, he pulled his arm away from her hand and took a step back. In a mild undertone at odds with his actions he cautioned, "You must first assure me you are not making arrangements with Torquay, *Bela*—the man's a dirty dish."

He referred to the marquess, and Vidia was reminded that

there was little that Brodie didn't notice. Glancing around as though embarrassed by his public display of anger, she tugged on his sleeve and bent her head to his as though trying to draw him away from the crowd. "Lord, no—I need a distraction so as to dispose of him—the poor man seems to have hit his head." For reasons she did not wish to explore, she didn't mention Carstairs's involvement to Brodie.

"Where is Montagu?" demanded Brodie in a loud, belligerent voice. "By *God*, I shall demand satisfaction." He then spotted Montagu, who—like everyone else in the room—was watching their burgeoning quarrel with barely concealed interest. "You *blackguard*." Brodie then stalked toward the surprised government official with a slightly unsteady gait, as though drunk.

"Stop, Benny—you are absurd," Vidia hissed at him in an audible aside as she tugged on his arm. "You are drunk and ridiculous."

Yanking his arm away from her, Brodie advanced on the horrified Montagu as several discreet servants nervously closed on the two men. Cocking his arm, Brodie took a swing at the other man but did not connect as several of the other guests grappled him away, admonishing him to keep his head. Blustering, Montagu backed away but tipped over a lamp table as Vidia let out a small shriek to alert Carstairs that now was the time. In the ensuing ruckus, she made a show of extreme disgust and hooked her arm in the alderman's. "Come, sir—we shall play Piquet."

Although he cast a doubtful eye at the contretemps still unfolding between Brodie and Montagu, the alderman apparently decided to grasp his opportunity and damn the consequences, and willingly escorted her back into the side room. They found a quiet table and called for a deck of cards,

Vidia playing a desultory game with him and making it clear she was in no mood for conversation. A servant appeared and explained to her in a discreet tone that Mr. Brodie had been asked to leave the premises, but her only response was to make a discard and reply, "A good riddance."

After she had played cards with the alderman long enough to ensure that the story would get back to the wife who had deserted him, she rose to kiss his cheek and thank him, and then slipped out the back entrance so as to avoid the inevitable offers to escort her home.

Once outside, Vidia decided that if Carstairs didn't appear very soon she would call for a hackney because once again she was walking the streets without a wrap, her arms crossed to ward off the cold. I truly am behaving as though I am a foolish *menina* once again, she thought—I have to stop this. But her resolution was abandoned as soon as Carstairs appeared beside her, shrugging off his jacket so as to place it around her shoulders.

"Assignment completed?" she asked, glancing up.

"Completed—his reputation will be in ruins by the morn."

Chuckling, she fell into step beside him, their footsteps echoing in the empty street. It was well past midnight, which meant little to either of them—often their best work was done in the wee hours. He made no effort to shorten his stride nor did she expect him to—they could transform into society creatures if the circumstances warranted, but circumstances didn't warrant and so they were simply covering ground.

He broke the silence. "I will bring your wrap around tomorrow—you need it."

Keeping her tone light, she repeated, "There is no hurry, Carstairs." She had probably earned the right to call him by his Christian name—it had certainly seemed so, the second or third session last night—but she refrained, wishing to keep him at a mental arm's length.

"I wanted you to know I did not set out—last night—"

"I know it," she assured him, looking up with a smile. She knew no such thing, of course.

He tilted his head in a self-deprecatory gesture. "I had too much to drink—stupid of me."

Which may or may not be true; if he had not been truly drunk he had certainly fooled her, which only reminded her to be very wary. Lifting her face to his, she replied with all sincerity, "If you'd rather we didn't speak of it, we won't—it was a miserable situation for you and I don't want to add to your misery."

His gaze was suddenly intent upon hers. "I don't want to stop speaking of it, Vidia—I can't. In fact, I would like to continue to meet with you when it can be arranged."

She halted so as to face him—this was the kind of discussion one should have face-to-face; after all, and she needed to gauge his motives. She had seen the message conveyed in his eyes too many times in her life to be mistaken by its meaning, but there was every possibility it was merely playacting—that he was angling to drop more hints of his supposed treason so as to goad her into some unexplained action, and take a survey of Brodie's town house for good measure. When she made no reply, he lifted a hand to run his finger along her jaw line, and despite herself, she could feel a *frisson* of desire, remembering his hands upon her body.

He continued, "I know it cannot be every day. And I know we must not let the others know." Lifting her face with his finger, he kissed her mouth, his lips gently tracing hers. "But I must insist."

He is very good, she thought with reluctant admiration—it feels completely genuine. "Carstairs," she whispered, buying time. "This is your grief speaking."

He lifted one of her hands to kiss the palm. "No—it is not grief, I promise you."

With a mighty effort, she turned her face and stepped away when he moved to kiss her again. "You cannot think to compromise my assignment." Her assignment was to spy on Brodie to find out what he was up to—which was ironic, because she could easily tell them but then she would run the risk that they would all fall out of their chairs.

"Brodie does not live with you," he reminded her, quietly insistent. "We can contrive—we are good at that sort of thing." He then ran his hands down her arms in a gesture reminiscent of the night before as his gaze held hers, and even though she was aware it was undoubtedly a sham, she could not look away to save her life. *Deus*, but it is oh, so annoying to have obligations when one has such an attractive man opportuning one, she thought crossly, but said with gentle regret, "I don't know, Carstairs—perhaps it would be best to forget last night."

But he would not accept her gentle rebuff and redoubled his efforts, bringing his face so close to hers in the gas light that she could see where his razor did not reach the whiskers in the cleft of his chin. "This is not something out of the blue, Vidia. You knew it in Flanders—you must have been aware that I was attracted to you."

Here was a rare dose of honesty—their assignment in Flanders had nearly ended in disaster and in the euphoria that always bubbled up after death had been cheated, she had sensed that he wanted to bed her—he who was married to Marie. She had moved away from him and the moment had passed, never to reoccur. Never until last night, that was, and then it reoccurred with a vengeance—three times. *Santos*, she thought, but life is unfair.

His hands caressing her waist under his jacket, he leaned in to whisper in a teasing tone, "We were very good together."

"That we were," she agreed, and decided it was past time to grasp hold of the situation before it wobbled out of control. "Were you raised in France?"

If he was surprised by the *non sequitur*, he did not betray it. "Suffolk. Why?"

"It is the oddest thing—you speak French in your dreams," she said lightly.

His hands stilled for a moment. "Do I? I had no idea—but my nursemaid was French."

"That explains it, then." Hopefully it was just the right touch; he was now aware that she knew either he was a tainted agent—or thought she was tainted and was trying to trap her. Probably the latter, unfortunately; Brodie was right—Carstairs would no more betray his country than he would fly to the moon.

Matching her light tone he asked, "Did I say anything I oughtn't?"

With a small shrug, she sidestepped a direct answer and fingered a button on his waistcoat. "You must be careful not to call the right woman by the wrong name."

He took her hands in his, one at a time, and held them in his warm clasp. "You are the one right woman for me, and I would never mistake you for another."

Except you already have, she thought as he leaned down to kiss her, with more urgency this time. She returned his kiss long enough to allow him to believe he had persuaded her before she pulled away. "Not the time nor the place, Carstairs," she whispered. "We may be seen."

His tone intent, he urged, "Then let me come home with you and we can discuss the matter in private."

For a brief moment she toyed with the idea of having another magical night with him—what was the harm, after all? She knew what was afoot, and she was not one to give away secrets in her sleep. Reluctantly recalling the state of her cellar, and the ongoing work therein, she laid a hand on his cheek and said with some regret, "Not tonight, my friend."

He was silent as he escorted her across to a main street so as to hail a hackney, the few passersby abroad at this time of night taking little notice of the couple who had stood together in intimate conversation. As he flagged down a cab, he glanced at her. "Please think about it—I'm afraid I am going to persevere until I've changed your mind."

"Oh, I am well aware of your staying power." She gave him a wicked glance that had stopped the heart of many a man as she handed him his jacket. Chuckling, he helped her into the cab and then gave her direction to the jarvey. She watched him out the window as she pulled away, and he didn't turn to go until she was nearly out of sight.

Vidia sank back into the cushions, her brow knit as she assessed the situation. If they truly thought she was tainted, she doubted they would play such a cat-and-mouse game; she would be delivered over to some very unpleasant men whose job it would be to wring a confession from her, along with any information she could give. There would be no mercy shown—not with so much at stake. Instead, it must be as Brodie said—he had them all over a barrel, unable to make a move against him. Therefore, they either suspected or knew that she was aligned with Brodie and were testing to see if she could be turned against him. They needed a means to control Brodie—over whom they had no control—and apparently they were aware she had a weakness for Lucien Carstairs.

Sighing, she gazed out the narrow window at the deserted street without actually seeing it. It was true she cherished a *tendre* for him, despite the fact she had turned him down in Flanders. Indeed, one of the reasons she had admired him was his devotion to his wife. It was a paradox—that which made him so attractive to her also made him unattainable; her own experience with men had shown how little they valued loyalty. And now he was free—and was pretending he wanted her, with his wife barely cold in her grave. You are a foolish, foolish *menina*, she thought, closing her eyes briefly; for two pins you'd accept his offer even though you *know* he doesn't mean it.

The hackney pulled up to her residence and Vidia alighted, wondering if Maisie had stayed up to wait for her—some hot water would be welcome to wash off the loathsome marquess, not to mention the loathsome Montagu. She glanced up at the elegant town house as she ascended the stairs and then turned her gaze to the side, toward the man who watched her entry from the shadows to the left. "*Bonne nuit*," she greeted him in French.

He bowed ironically. "*Bonne nuit, mademoiselle.*"

Letting herself in, she locked the door behind her.

Chapter 6

Vidia paraded alongside Brodie on the broad sidewalk of Threadneedle Street as they prepared to make a visit to the Bank of England, her skirts sweeping the pavement and an elaborate hat perched at a reckless angle atop her curls. He had asked that she accompany him on this visit, which meant she was needed to distract—unlikely he would ask her to cast her lures at a banker, as bankers were notoriously bloodless. She eyed a pastry cart stationed on the corner as they passed, but decided with some regret that it would be too messy to indulge in one, considering the cost of her gloves. Breakfast had been an hour ago and she was unaccountably hungry again.

Lifting her face so that she could feel the sun despite the hat's wide brim, she asked, "What is it we do here, Benny? Or are we giving the poor man who watches my town house a diversion?" Brodie was well-aware her every move was being watched by agents for the French.

"I'm to be inveigled by the wretched bankers," he disclosed as he tucked her hand in his arm. "And I would ask that you do some inveigling of your own, if you would be so kind."

"A tall order, my friend." She smiled and nodded to a gentleman on the sidewalk who had stopped and was openly staring, his embarrassed wife tugging on his arm. One could hardly blame him; she did look very fine in her apricot gown with its slashed sleeves, embellished with discreet pearls so as to be appropriate for daytime. She was very fond of the soft color; it reminded her of the terra-cotta walls that had surrounded her village—before it was razed to the ground, of course.

Brodie replied, "Perhaps, perhaps not. One is a gentleman named Sundren, whose wife has been ill for a time. Lately he has taken to the occasional visit with a prostitute, poor fellow. See what you can contrive—I would like to have a line of communication with someone on the inside if it is possible."

This was rather a surprise, and she glanced at him, guessing at his reasons. "There is a Home Office plant on the inside, then? Who?"

He said kindly, as though he was speaking to a small child, "I am not yet certain, *Bela*, hence the request."

Lifting the corner of her mouth at his tone, she assured him, "I shall do my humble best, then."

"Excellent; the poor man doesn't stand a chance."

They walked in silence for a few moments while she thought over this development. He must be concerned about this or he wouldn't have asked that she act as an angel for him; normally she did not accompany him to business meetings and in any event they rarely went out together in daytime for the simple reason that she attracted too much attention—the last outing having caused a horrific collision between a dray and a milk wagon.

Brodie paused, ostensibly to admire a collection of flower pots. "We must slow down a bit; I'd like to be late."

Vidia dutifully bent to touch a flower petal and teased,

"You tempt fate, methinks; have a care lest they decide it isn't worth it and wash their hands of you."

Brodie only smiled and glanced at her. "Montagu sent 'round a note of apology—claims he had too much to drink the other night and begs my pardon."

Amused, she shook her head. "Lord, Benny—you *do* have them all over a barrel if the Treasury is forcing him to apologize."

Making a sound of derision, he nodded to an acquaintance coming the other way who had tipped his hat to Vidia, and then began walking again so as to discourage any further advances. "You have twice the backbone he does, *Bela*—I do you an injustice, having to tolerate such a pretender for your favors. He is a very dull stick."

Her eyes gleaming, she riposted, "I disagree; he thinks his stick very lively."

"*Bela*," he admonished with distaste. "Spare me, I beg of you."

"So—no more Montagu?" she asked hopefully.

"No more," he affirmed. "Very soon, all will be resolved."

This was news that was equal parts welcome and alarming. "When will the *Argo* sail? Do we have a date certain?"

There was a small pause. "I'm afraid I'd rather not tell you just yet. You'll understand."

She did, and took it in good part as they resumed their progress, the bank rising up before them. Brodie was justifiably concerned that she would be forced, by very unpleasant means, to reveal the information—after all, her spymaster was now making his own maneuvers to counter Brodie's. His next words, however, reminded her that there was little he did not notice.

"Who was the gentleman at the card table? You were acquainted, I think."

No point to pretending she didn't know who he meant. "Lucien Carstairs—a compatriot," she answered easily. "We worked together in Flanders, once."

Brodie's shrewd glance assessed her face. "Tell me of Mr. Carstairs—he seems a very capable fellow."

"I'd rather not—I'm afraid I have divided loyalties on the subject." The last thing she wanted was to inform Brodie that it was Carstairs who spoke of bringing gold to Napoleon.

But it seemed she was a step behind Brodie, and his next words indicated he had already guessed Carstairs's role. "They will try to come at me through you, you know," he noted in a matter-of-fact tone. "Be ready for it."

"I am not a fool, Benny," she responded sharply, then immediately was contrite. "My nerves are ragged—I do beg your pardon." They entered the impressive edifice, the vaulted ceilings and marble floors proclaiming the unassailable authority of the mighty Bank of England—a casual observer could be forgiven for not being aware that the bank was teetering on the edge of collapse.

Brodie laid a hand on hers where it rested on his arm. "Venice," he pronounced, tilting his head back to consider the elaborate domed ceiling. "I've a mind to go to Venice and embark on a new venture."

"I don't know where I would go," she mused beside him, grateful for the change in subject. "Somewhere quiet, methinks; and near the ocean—I would grow lilies."

"Lucky lilies, to have you tend them." He glanced at her sidelong. "Do lilies thrive in Venice?"

But she shook her head. "I find that I am rather fond of England." She was ashamed to admit that it was impossible to contemplate living in a country that did not contain Lucien Carstairs, given the fact that he was at present taking brutal advantage of her silly infatuation with him. "And I am thinking of retiring from the lists—I am not as reckless as I once was." She was almost surprised at the words, which had seemed to come out almost without conscious volition.

"You alarm me," he replied with some surprise. "Not to mention it would be a tremendous waste of talent."

"There must be something else I can do—someplace where I can simply mind my own business, as opposed to everyone else's."

"Not with that face," Brodie pronounced bluntly. "A nunnery, perhaps—although the priests would be constantly at confession. Better to come with me."

Squeezing his arm, she said sincerely, "I appreciate what you have done for me—my hand on my heart, Benny—but I find that I don't have the appetite for it any longer."

"All will be well, *Bela*. My own hand on my heart."

They were escorted into an oak-lined meeting room, where the two gentlemen who awaited them respectfully bowed upon their entrance. Brodie introduced the larger man as Mr. Sundren and the smaller man as Mr. Grant.

Mr. Grant made a gesture with his hand toward the antechamber. "If your—companion—would care to await without, I shall see to it she is served refreshments."

"I dare not," said Brodie casually as he drew out her chair. "There is no guarantee she'd still be there upon my return."

Vidia laughed merrily and threw Brodie a teasing glance as she was seated, privately regretting the loss of the refreshments.

Thus stymied, Grant tried to hide his annoyance with little success. "We were afraid, Mr. Brodie, that you had forgotten our appointment."

"My lamentable memory." Brodie spread his hands

in apology. "I remembered just as we were heading to Rundell's, and I came straightaway."

"I am most unhappy with him, and with you," Vidia teased, glancing up from beneath the wide brim of her hat; Rundell & Bridge were jewelers who catered to London's most monied residents. She then bestowed an intimate, dazzling smile on Sundren, who stared at her as though sunstruck. Vidia instantly had formed a dislike for Grant, and ignored him.

"Now, how may I help the Bank of England?" asked Brodie in a genial tone.

"You have been most generous," began Sundren in a conciliatory manner, "lending the Treasury such sums for the war effort." His gaze slid to Vidia because he could not seem to help himself.

A hint of impatience in his voice, Brodie prompted, "But the war is now over, and Napoleon sits in exile; when do you suppose my bonds shall be repaid?"

Sundren having lost his train of thought, Grant gave his cohort an impatient glance and continued, "Unfortunately, the bank is a bit shorthanded at present."

"Ah," said Brodie, nodding in understanding. "The missing gold."

"The missing gold," agreed Sundren, recalled to the conversation. "The last two shipments to the troops stationed on the Continent have gone missing—it is a major blow; the bank—and the Treasury—were dangerously depleted by the war and there is little to spare." He paused, then added in a somber tone, "And the Home Office is greatly concerned that Napoleon will attempt another conquest."

Brodie clasped his hands on the table and bent his head, considering. "That is indeed grave news. You wish me to hold off cashing in the bonds, then."

"If you would," asked Sundren humbly. "I do not exaggerate when I say it is a matter of national security."

"I am a businessman," Brodie pointed out. "I cannot be held responsible because the Treasury is careless with its gold."

"It is not only the Treasury that has suffered losses," Sundren was moved to point out. "The Continent is by no means secure—there are rumors that Napoleon's gold supplies have been stolen, also."

"Such lawlessness," exclaimed Vidia, her delicate brow knit in distress. "Why, whatever is the world coming to?" She appealed to Sundren, who looked as though he had to restrain himself from taking her into his arms.

But Brodie remained unsympathetic. "Ask Rothschild for a loan, then; he is the one who made a fortune shipping gold to Wellington during the war." Brodie continued in an aside to Vidia, "A clever man—he uses pigeons to carry messages back and forth from England to the Continent—did you know, my dear?"

"Does he indeed?" she asked in amusement. "Perhaps the pigeons know where the missing gold is."

Sundren laughed as though she had said something very clever until Grant glared at him, and he then subsided. Nevertheless, Vidia gave him a slow smile from beneath the brim of her hat as a reward.

Grant explained in a constrained voice, "I am afraid Rothschild's fortune is tied up—as are many others'—paying out insurance claims. There has been a spate of losses in India lately—bad timing, I'm afraid. We must strongly urge that you allow the bank more time before you redeem your bonds."

For the express purpose of annoying Grant, Vidia interjected, "This is not going to interfere with the diamond bracelet you promised me, is it Benny?"

While Grant barely concealed his irritation, Brodie patted her hand. "Perish the thought, my dear—I have to keep up appearances for fear you will find someone with a plumper purse."

Vidia smiled upon the two bankers, tilting her head playfully. "I am never careless with my gold."

"It is not a matter for levity, perhaps," Grant replied stiffly, and Vidia noted that a vein bulged in his forehead. Overwrought, she thought, resisting an urge to curl her lip. He takes it all too seriously—I can't imagine he'd do well before a firing squad. Not like some.

Chapter 7

You were unkind to poor Henry," noted Brodie as he tossed his hat on her table and signaled to Maisie for the tea tray.

"Who is Henry?" asked Vidia absently, hoping the tea tray would feature something substantial—Maisie had hired a cook to help out two days a week and with any luck this was one of the days.

"Henry Grant, from the bank," Brodie explained, watching out the window for a moment. "A very interesting fellow."

"He was not interesting, he was rude," pronounced Vidia. "Although you will be happy to hear that Mr. Sundren slipped me his card—I imagine it is not all he wishes to slip me."

"*Bela*," warned Brodie. "Please."

"Should I make contact? I rather felt sorry for him."

"No—no need."

This was a relief; despite her calling she didn't like to mislead decent men, and she assessed Sundren as a decent man. Indecent men were another matter, of course, and she dwelt with satisfaction on the marquess's scandal, which was currently the talk of the town. "Did the meeting go as you wished? I could not tell."

"As always," he replied in a tone that chided her for doubting it.

"I forget—you are the puppet master," she conceded with a smile. "Where is that tea tray?"

But when Maisie returned it was to inform her that the piano tuner was in the parlor. "Bein' as he says ye called for him, missy."

"Yes—I am sadly out of practice." Vidia studied her reflection in the mirror on the opposite wall for a moment. "The instrument is quite inferior, I'm afraid—perhaps I shall simply purchase a new one. I must seek his advice, Benny."

But Brodie had taken up the newspaper and didn't respond, so Vidia made her way to the parlor, carefully closing the door behind her. She was unsurprised to see the grey-eyed spymaster, dressed in a workman's outfit and unrolling a cloth that contained various tuning implements atop her piano.

Straightening at her entrance, he removed his cap, the expression in the grey eyes deferential. "Miss."

Hiding her wariness at his unexpected appearance, she walked across the room and, with graceful flourish, seated herself on the piano bench. "You are lucky I indeed have a piano."

"Nothing is left to chance." He bent to sound a tuning fork, then hit a key and grimaced.

"There is a man watching from across the street," she offered. It was likely the grey-eyed man was already aware of this fact but she thought she'd give the impression she would cooperate to the fullest—she wondered why he was here.

The grey eyes scrutinized her for a moment as he leaned over the instrument, the false eyebrows cocked. "How long?"

"A week, at least."

Her companion began testing various keys and tightening the screwing mechanisms. Plink, plunk. "Tell me what Brodie had to say to the bankers."

"Two men," she reported, "Sundren and Grant—"

"Grant is one of ours," he interrupted without lifting his head from the strings.

She stared at the top of his head. "You astonish me—if that is the best you can recruit, I despair for England." Her tone was tart because she was off-balance—they should have warned her, and the fact that they hadn't seemed ominous.

The grey eyes glanced at her again. "He is monitoring the situation."

Stretching out her arms before her, she contemplated her manicured nails. "And here I thought I was monitoring the situation."

He was amused and gave her a half smile as he bent over a wire. "He's watching from the business end—surely you don't feel threatened."

She wasn't fooled by his light tone—if he doubted her allegiance she should feel very threatened indeed. "I'd like some guidance, then—I need to know how I should interact with Grant."

Giving her a swift, assessing glance, he then reapplied himself; plink, plunk. "Not your usual interaction—he is rather a spinster."

"I am unsurprised," she said dryly, and realized that she never had the impression that the grey-eyed man was at all dazzled by her beauty; in an odd way it was almost refreshing. "But I am indeed surprised by this visit; I rather think you are here to discomfit me."

If she hoped to throw him off, she was unsuccessful. "Perhaps." Plink, plunk.

She didn't pursue it; it was enough to let him know she was aware of his suspicions and didn't appreciate them. "There was talk of the missing gold—did Grant tell you?"

"Was there? And what of the bonds?"

"They'd like Brodie to postpone calling them in until the gold is recovered or—barring that—something miraculous happens to help the Treasury recover from the war." She waited, but he asked no more questions about the meeting at the bank; instead, the next question seemed to indicate he had pieced the puzzle together.

"Are you aware there was a brawl with Montagu the other night?"

"Of course—I was its subject." She idly pressed a key with a forefinger. "Do you believe there is a connection, then—since Montagu is with the Treasury?"

Exchanging tuning forks, he tapped the new one, lifted it to his ear to listen, and didn't respond to her question. He then plucked another wire and applied his tool to tighten it. "Has Brodie been acquainted with Montagu for long? Perhaps from his days on the Continent?"

"I am not certain," she responded honestly. "But I do not believe so."

Plunk, plink. The piano tuner plucked the wires with his long fingers. "A coincidence that my people put them both near Paris last fall." He stilled his hands and turned his head to look fully at her.

Her guileless eyes registering surprise, she returned his gaze, stare for stare. "Truly? In the fall?" She shook her head. "It is indeed a coincidence, but I know nothing of it—it was before my current assignment, after all, so I knew little of Brodie's doings."

The grey eyes continued their scrutiny. "Of course, my sources may be mistaken—our operations were disrupted at that time—it was when Napoleon retreated from the Moscow debacle with such speed."

"It was chaotic," she agreed, and calmly crossed her hands on her lap.

"None would know better than you." He returned his attentions back to the tuning fork.

With a rueful smile, she readily admitted, "And I am unlikely to forget, having been forced to go to ground myself. Who would believe the Emperor could move so quickly, and after having suffered such losses at the hands of the Russians?"

"Indeed. I was most concerned when my contacts reported you missing around that time."

"It was a perilous week—forgive me for causing you concern."

The grey-eyed man said nothing for several moments, plucking wires and tightening screws while Vidia sat watching him, striving mightily to appear unconcerned and unalarmed by the tack the conversation had taken. *Mãe de Deus*, she thought; I do not have the nerves for this anymore. Thankfully, a diversion occurred in the form of Maisie, who appeared in the doorway and dropped an awkward curtsey; Maisie was not a graceful creature.

"Would ye like me to bring you a cup o' tea, missy?"

"If you would, Maisie."

She disappeared and the grey-eyed man addressed Vidia in a muffled voice, as his head was under the lid. "She is no maidservant—what is her story?"

Relieved by the change of subject, Vidia replied, "She was a stray."

He straightened up to meet her eyes. "From San Sebastian?"

Hiding her horror that he knew enough to mention it, Vidia struggled to control her features. "No," she managed to answer evenly. "Fuentes de Onoro. Her husband fell at

Almeida and she was trapped during the siege. I needed a dairymaid to create a diversion—a delay to allow for the reinforcements."

He contemplated her for a moment, his expression unreadable. She met his gaze with her own steady one and lifted her chin an inch. He knows he has thrown me a stinger, she thought, and watches for my reaction. I will not give him one.

He finally dropped his gaze to the keyboard where he began randomly picking out keys. Plunk, plunk. "Do you think she could be of use?"

Vidia considered it for only a moment. "No. She is too forthright; deception is not in her nature—she is useful only for eavesdropping." She placed her own hands on the keys and began to pick out a tune. Without hesitation, he manned the lower range keys to join her and between the two of them they played a very satisfactory duet.

At its conclusion he seemed genuinely pleased. "I had no idea you could actually play."

She replied serenely, "I imagine there are many things you do not know."

He chuckled at her daring and she felt a sense of accomplishment at evoking an unguarded reaction from him. "I could say the same. Where is Hagar with the tea?"

"Maisie," Vidia corrected him. "Her name is Maisie."

"My mistake," he apologized.

"Is there to be a temperance meeting soon?" She was concerned that she would now be excluded from the inner workings of their group, and it was important for Brodie's plan that she remained informed.

"Tonight." His implacable gaze met hers. "No rest for the wicked."

Vidia found she could make no reply.

Chapter 8

It was after ten o'clock when Vidia paused at the door to St. Michael's. The church was situated on a broad, quiet street in an ordinary-appearing residential neighborhood; unassuming and foursquare. Through its doors, however, passed some of the most influential individuals in the kingdom, even though the names they gave themselves would never be known by the populace and their work—and sometimes their deaths—would never be publicly recognized. The anonymous nature of the business was very appealing to Vidia, who chafed at constantly being put on display. I am a shrinking snail, just as Maisie said, she thought. Trust her to skewer me with an apt comparison—a good thing I didn't leave her in the river with the cows.

She held the hood of her dark cloak tightly around her face and had seen to it that she was not followed by shifting between several hackneys and then backtracking. The cloak obscured the gold-figured gown that displayed her impressive figure to advantage; they had gone to a late supper at the club as Brodie didn't want those who watched to notice anything unusual in their activities of late. He had been in a mellow mood, giving her hints of what was to come as he puffed on a cigarillo. "Our rabbit is very cautious—there are some alarming individuals lately come to town who seek his death."

"Must I be there when the *Argo* sails?" she asked. "Tell him I am away, knitting socks for Napoleon's army."

"It would be best if you were there—and grateful to him, besides," Brodie had replied. "There should be no hint that he has been double-crossed—otherwise we are back to where we started."

She nodded, seeing the wisdom in this. "What if my superiors indeed bring me in?" she had asked, thinking of the piano tuner's ominous visit. "What then?"

"We shall see," he had replied, unfazed. "One must remain flexible."

Hoping her superiors were contemplating no such thing, Vidia tapped a code on the oaken door of the church, and as it opened a shaft of light shot through the darkness outside. A young man monitored the door—perhaps sixteen, she guessed, and rather sunburnt. "Come in, please," he said. "The temperance meeting is in the basement."

"Are you a fellow victim of demon rum?" she asked in a serious tone.

"No, ma'am," he replied, not certain whether she was teasing. "I'm the sextant."

Having taken off her cloak, she handed it to him, only to note that he stood staring, his mouth agape. She gently placed a finger under his chin and closed his mouth for him as the spymaster appeared, dressed as a vicar. "That is all—you may return to the rectory," he directed the young man, who pulled himself together and departed.

"Pray do not ruin the help," the grey-eyed man cautioned as he led her to the basement stairs.

"Where is the Curate tonight?" she asked, following him. Usually her contact was the spymaster's assistant, who posed as a curate.

"The Curate is away from the parish, there being urgent matters requiring his attention. I will mentor the temperance meeting tonight."

"God save us all indeed," she remarked in a dry tone, and followed him down the stairs. He is trying to unnerve me, she thought, and is doing an excellent job. "Has anyone else arrived?"

"I fear we will have very few; the urgent matters being paramount." Bearing a candle, the grey-eyed man paused at the bottom of the basement stairs, and as Vidia passed, she glanced at his face, thinking in reluctant admiration that one would find little trace of the ragged beggar or the piano tuner. He was very good at his job, a fact she should keep in mind—overconfidence was Brodie's besetting sin.

He set the candle on a table, the candlelight flickering in the draft. The church, being a small parish, used all available space, and so the cramped room was made comfortable with chairs, a rudimentary table, and decorative hangings on the walls that exhorted the inhabitants to have faith. A little faith is useful, Vidia thought, but action should never be discounted. The meeting place had the added attraction of being windowless and surrounded by thick stone walls.

As she seated herself, Carstairs emerged into the room from the narrow stairway, and Vidia tried to decide what to say to him as she was not certain how much their spymaster knew and how much he believed she knew—*Deus*, it was all very complicated. Deciding on a safe topic, she said, "My poor Carstairs—will they not allow you a bereavement leave?"

Pulling up a chair, he replied easily, "Better to work—it keeps me out of low taverns. Thank you for your extraction the other night, Swanson."

"It was my pleasure." She was rewarded by the amused

glance he sent her behind the Vicar's back—her pleasure indeed, and more than once. "You should drown your sorrows where there are fewer pickpockets."

"I believe I owe you cab fare."

"And bar fare," she added without rancor. "If I hadn't paid your shot at the Bowman, Napoleon's army would be the least of your worries."

"How much?" He pulled out his purse, and they were settling accounts when Jenny Dokes entered, nodding to the three already present. Dokes was a plain and unassuming woman with an amazing head for numbers that in turn translated into a gift for deciphering code. Vidia, who was good with numbers herself, was all admiration for the other's abilities. "Dokes," she said with warmth, taking the other's hand. "It is good to see you again." As Dokes had no pretensions to beauty, she was one of the rare women who had no objection to Vidia; she was the nearest thing Vidia had to a female friend.

"And you—have you managed to unearth any new ciphers for me?" Dokes sounded a bit wistful; she loved a good puzzle.

With regret, Vidia admitted she hadn't. "Instead I am assigned to monitor Brodie and his money—mainly I cut a swath and listen at keyholes."

Dokes smiled her dry little smile. "Whereas I merely listen at keyholes and must avoid swaths of any kind." She was assigned to teach at a girls' *Académie* founded by French expatriates from the Continent, notably those who had fled the Terror, years before.

"I will trade with you," Vidia offered promptly.

Dokes had to chuckle at the picture thus presented. "You wouldn't last a day, I'm afraid—the headmistress is very strict in matters of propriety."

"Meaning I would not be allowed to teach the students how to rouge their bosoms."

"I imagine not." At the *Académie*, Dokes was well-positioned to hear information—salacious and otherwise—with respect to Napoleon's activities across the Channel during the war, and now that rumors of his planned escape were rampant, she could determine who was sympathetic to the former Emperor and might be tempted to render him aid. After a discreet investigation, the suspect was then either disregarded as harmless or was apprehended for crimes against the Crown. Dokes never appeared to care one way or the other—her interests were purely analytical. She had never married but always plucked up when Carstairs was about. Small blame to her, thought Vidia; or to me, for that matter—he is so very appealing. With an effort, she turned her thoughts away from the beauty of his naked chest.

Henry Grant entered and apologized to the Vicar for being late. "A wretched business—the bankers are all on end."

Cutting to the nub of the matter, the Vicar turned to Vidia. "Has Brodie indicated when he intends to cash in his bonds?"

"No," she responded readily. "He does not mention them at all—it is as though the money means little to him." This had the added benefit of being completely true.

"She wouldn't be in his confidence on such a matter." Grant made an annoyed gesture in Vidia's direction, impatient with the very idea.

But the Vicar, apparently, did not care for his tone. "You would be surprised how many secrets a man is willing to relate to a beautiful woman. Pray do not interrupt again."

Vidia kept her gaze lowered and reflected that her spymaster disliked Grant almost as much as she did. She continued as though there had not been an interruption, "Brodie conducts his business at his own rooms and I am rarely there, so I am at a disadvantage. I could attempt a search, though, if you think it necessary; I would have excuse for being on the premises."

The Vicar was thoughtful for a moment, then asked, "Tell me—has he mentioned an 'argo'?"

With a monumental effort, Vidia maintained her poise. "Not that I know." *Santos*, she thought—someone has been eavesdropping and Brodie must have a care.

Turning to Grant, the Vicar prompted, "What do you suppose it meant?"

Ah, thought Vidia with annoyance—observe the eavesdropper. I should have guessed it was this little weasel-*doninha*.

"I believe," offered Grant slowly, crossing his arms and enjoying the attention, "that the term referred in some way to the missing gold."

Her brow knit, Vidia looked from one to the other, pretending confusion. "Gold? I don't understand—what has Brodie to do with the missing gold?"

"It would do him no good to steal the gold," Dokes observed. "The gold backs the bonds and he'd be stealing from himself; he wouldn't want to degrade his own bonds."

"On the other hand, he holds a huge percentage of the Treasury's war bonds," the Vicar countered. "The Home Office is concerned that he has the ability to crash the country's finances if he attempted to cash them all at once. There is the possibility his motive is to bring down England rather than make a profit."

Soberly, they all contemplated this alarming theory. Indeed, Brodie's tendency to buy up nearly all of England's war bonds was the reason Vidia had been assigned to attach herself to him—his motives were unclear.

Worried that they'd indeed arrest Brodie for treason, Vidia offered, "I have seen no evidence of loyalty to the enemy, only loyalty to making money."

Dokes, who loved a good puzzle, was apparently struck by the code word. "Do you suppose 'argo' was actually 'argot'—referring to thieves' cant? Does he use such slang?"

"Never," said Vidia truthfully. "I think it is important to him to give the impression of gentility." The better to hoodwink all and sundry.

"Or is it '*Argo*' as in Jason and the Argonauts?" suggested Carstairs, thinking it over.

Vidia offered quickly, "He and Montagu engaged in a bout of fisticuffs at Stoffer's the other night—it was very much out of character."

His thoughtful gaze on Vidia, the Vicar sunk his chin to his chest. "Perhaps it was a falling-out among thieves—we must make certain the Treasury is not being undermined from within. Do you know if Montagu has visited Brodie at the town house?"

This seemed an odd question and Vidia allowed her surprise to show. "No—I would never willingly entertain Montagu, I assure you."

Grant, the banker, reminded her in a pointed tone, "It is Brodie's house, after all."

She wasn't certain if insult was intended, but she returned a mild answer. "No; the house stands in my name."

The Vicar whistled softly. "It is worth a pretty penny."

"As am I," agreed Vidia with a smile, and the others chuckled.

But the Vicar was not amused. "Beguile some secrets from him, then; I confess to disappointment in your efforts thus far."

It was the closest he had come to an open rebuke, and Vidia nodded, chastened.

The Vicar continued, "I would like Dokes to take a close look at the bank's funding records in light of the missing gold—the Home Office is not certain it is receiving valid information. If the situation is dire, we must know the truth."

"Shall I assist Dokes?" offered Vidia, hoping to regain his good graces and keep an eye on the assignment, for good measure.

"No," said the Vicar. "You shall not."

He then gestured toward the banker. "Grant will create the opportunity for Dokes to review the information—perhaps a night visit after hours, if needed."

With a final glance around the room, the spymaster stood. "That is all; you will be informed of any further meetings."

As they rose, Vidia noted that Grant pulled the grey-eyed man aside to speak to him in a low voice. Probably tattling on me, she thought, pulling on her gloves with a jerk. For two pence I would cosh him and dump his worthless body in the vestibule—*Deus*, but I am shaken by all this.

She noted that Dokes had made her way over to Carstairs, who was watching the banker with an unreadable expression. "I am sorry to hear of your sad loss, Carstairs."

Carstairs bowed and expressed his appreciation of her condolences while Vidia mounted the steps; she could be generous and allow Dokes a chance to interact with their compatriot—there is one advantage to having this face, she thought as she took her cloak from the hook by the door. I can always count on the fact that no matter what my circumstances, I can attract a man to care for me, if that is my desire. Other women were not as fortunate—although it was unclear if Dokes would ever consider marriage, even to Carstairs.

Contemplating whether the advantages of beauty outweighed its disadvantages, she decided she had come a long way if she was even considering the subject. I have changed, she thought with some surprise—it is past time, I think; perhaps I will even take my old name back.

As she prepared to slip out the door, the Vicar spoke to her from the stairway alcove. "Best look lively." He threw a meaningful glance toward the basement where Dokes could be heard conversing with Carstairs.

"For shame," Vidia admonished, lifting her hood over her hair. "The man's a grieving widower, after all—do your pandering elsewhere."

"If I were your panderer," he opined thoughtfully, "I would be a wealthy man."

"Better off than my piano tuner, certainly—you have missed the main chance, methinks."

The grey eyes intent upon hers, his hand closed around her arm for a moment, and she carefully hid her alarm at the unusual gesture. "I wish that I understood this better than I do."

"If wishes were horses, beggars would ride, my friend," she responded in a mild tone, meeting his eyes with her own steady gaze. "As an erstwhile beggar, you can appreciate the conceit."

"You are a cool one," he acknowledged as he released her arm. "But I am afraid pressure can be brought to bear. Revelations can be made."

"My dear sir," she protested as she smoothed down her sleeve. "I was under the impression pressure has already been brought to bear." Without further remark, she opened the door, took a careful survey of the area, and left.

As a matter of course, she took a circuitous route back to the main street and thought about what she had learned—it was not good. The Home Office was apparently starting to draw conclusions and make connections—but Brodie was Brodie, and as he had pointed out, even if they unearthed his plan there was little they could do without risking England's monetary system. She closed her eyes momentarily as she considered the Vicar's veiled warnings—that bakery in Yorkshire was beginning to sound more and more appealing, even though she hadn't awakened at dawn for many years, not since the Army. Abruptly, she decided she didn't want to think about that, and so she didn't—instead thinking of Carstairs and how he had looked in the candlelight this evening, the shared memory of their adventure at the club reflected in his gaze. I am a hopeless case, she thought with an inward sigh. I would have no trouble awakening at dawn every morning if he was beside me.

As though on cue, she heard her name whispered and slowed as to allow him to catch her.

"You didn't wait for me," Carstairs complained, chagrined and slightly out of breath.

With some surprise, she asked, "Was I supposed to?"

He tilted his head toward her, his tone intimate. "I thought you'd be as eager to speak to me as I am to speak to you."

She looked him over for a moment, then returned her gaze to the street. "I see."

They walked at a brisk pace for a few moments. "I cannot bring myself to return your wrap." His smile invited her to share in the absurdity of this weakness.

"Why would you wish to keep my wrap?" she asked, as though genuinely curious.

Raising his brows, he teased with a gleam, "I believe it is self-evident."

"No." She returned her gaze to the street. "No, in fact it is not. It is very lowering to be treated like a stupid child."

He did not respond and their footsteps echoed in the silence of the night. Deciding to make it easier for him, she asked, "Do they believe I am tainted, then?"

The role of the tender lover was quickly abandoned—much to her relief—and he gave an elliptical answer. "There is much at stake; caution is advised."

Eying him sidelong, she tried to gauge his thoughts, knowing all the while it was hopeless—he would only reveal what he wished, and if his aim was to arrest her he would reveal precious little. "Will you promise to give me one minute's warning before I am clapped in irons? I would do the same for you, you know."

"You will not be clapped in irons," he said immediately, but she noted he didn't meet her eye and hid a flare of alarm.

"No," she replied with forced lightness. "I would simply disappear, leaving you free to give my wrap to your next mark."

"Don't." He made an involuntary gesture of protest, and the blue eyes finally met hers with a fierce intensity that she could swear was genuine. "But if you know anything of these matters, Vidia, best to say and to say immediately."

"I cannot decide," she wondered aloud as they rounded the corner of her street, "whether our interlude that first night was strictly business. If it was, you did a very poor job of pressing for information as opposed to simply pressing."

He was not fooled by her tone. "You are angry and I cannot blame you. But I assure you it was not strictly business."

Coming to her town house, she wondered if she was making a monumental mistake—attempting to be honest with him. But she had decided—there on the street with his subtle insincerity grating on her nerves—that she couldn't continue as she was; not with him. Perhaps he will be my downfall, she thought. But it hardly matters anymore—I am seventeen again, and just as foolish as I was then.

Carstairs's voice broke into her troubled thoughts. "Allow me to come in; we can discuss it over coffee."

Refusing to look at him, Vidia did not disguise her annoyance. "You are persistent—I will give you honors for that."

He made an impatient sound in his throat that only served to remind her of other sounds that throat had made. "That was clumsy of me—but it was honest, Vidia. I'll not believe you if you tell me that you do not think about our night together."

"I do think about it," she admitted. Best not to mention she thought of it in terms of a potential charge of treason—his feelings may be hurt. Men were sensitive about such things.

He took her gloved hand and squeezed it, gently. "Then there is no reason to resist this attraction between us."

She sighed and ascended her front steps, digging for her key. "Come along—if you wish a search you shall have one."

He didn't miss a beat. "I am sorry. I do have orders, Vidia."

"I understand; none better."

Chapter 10

As it was just after midnight, Maisie had waited up for Vidia and dropped a surprised curtsey upon viewing her entry with an unexpected guest.

Vidia peeled off her gloves. "Maisie, this is Mr. Carstairs. He will be conducting a search of the house, and you may be off to bed once he has searched your room."

The other woman took Vidia's cloak and held her eye for a moment, wondering if there was an unspoken instruction. Shaking her head slightly, Vidia signaled that no heroics would be necessary and so the maidservant said only, "Right then, missy."

Standing in the marbled foyer, Carstairs removed his hat and gloves and set them on a side table, as Maisie hadn't remembered to take them. Vidia indicated the curving stairway with a graceful gesture and asked as though she were entertaining a guest, "May I accompany you or would you rather be unobserved?"

"Please come." He shrugged off his jacket, and she could swear he meant it.

"Is that wise?" she teased as she took the jacket and laid it beside the hat and gloves. "Perhaps I will try to distract you so that you miss evidence of my wrongdoing."

"It would be well worth it." He took a candlestick from

the hall table as he passed by. "The distracting, I mean—not the evidence."

Lifting her skirts, she followed him up the stairs, her stiff petticoats crackling with her movements. "I always prefer a search from the top down, in the event an escape is needful halfway through—and Maisie's room is on the top floor."

"The top floor, then."

There was something liberating about tossing aside the tension and the pretense, and she realized she felt much more at ease with him. "I should have worn my dusting smock."

As they ascended the second stairwell meant for the non-existent servants, he chuckled in appreciation. "I would be willing to wager any amount of money you do not possess a dusting smock."

"You would lose, my friend."

One of his dark brows shot up in surprise and he turned his head to observe her. "I did not peg you for a domestic."

She smiled, pleased that he was interested—or pretending an interest, anyway. "Oh, I have dressed many a chicken, I assure you."

"Where was this?" he asked casually as he made his way down the narrow hall toward the servants' rooms, the candlelight bouncing with his steps.

It was the casual tone—a bit too casual—that drew her up. Remember what was at stake, *menina*; it was a mistake to fall into this easy conversation with him, wretched man—although it was perilously appealing. "Malmaison," she responded, naming the residence Josephine had formerly shared with Napoleon.

"A fish tale," he pronounced. "The Empress would never have allowed one such as you to set foot on the premises."

They paused before Maisie's room. "Then ask me no questions and I will tell you no tales."

"Fair enough," he agreed, and stepped in.

She leaned against the door in the narrow room and watched as he began a thorough search, tapping on walls and floors and gauging distances between. He was very efficient, she realized, and recalculated her strategy. "Should I help?"

"Best not." He turned to give her his quick flashing smile. "This is strange, isn't it?"

"That we are honest in our dishonesty? I suppose so."

With deft movements he opened a cupboard and ran a hand along the interior, lifting clothes and tapping occasionally. "I don't think you dishonest."

Hesitating, she decided she may as well ask. "But some do?"

He glanced at her. "You know I cannot say."

Tired of standing in her heavy skirts, she crossed the small room to sit on the cot and was content to simply watch him moving about in his shirtsleeves—he showed to advantage, did Lucien Carstairs. "I suppose not. I only wish I knew what has happened to make them think I am tainted."

He had been crouching, scrutinizing the floorboards, but now he rose to stand with his hands on his hips and contemplated the wall for a long moment, debating whether to tell her. "Marie twigged you."

She wasn't certain what he meant. "Marie?"

He gave her a significant look. "Yes; Marie."

Astonished, she exclaimed, "*Your* Marie?"

She realized he was watching her reaction closely but it hardly mattered—if he had said the source was the mad King it would have been less surprising. "Yes. My Marie."

Vidia knit her brow and they regarded each other for a long moment. "What on earth did she tell them?"

Shrugging his broad shoulders, he disclaimed again, "I cannot say."

Completely bewildered, she shook her head in protest. "Carstairs, I hardly met Marie—once or twice, perhaps."

"I am aware. And her motivation has been taken into consideration."

He had turned to move to the next room and she leapt up to follow close behind, sensing an undercurrent. "What motivation was that?"

Beginning his tapping search anew, he replied, "She was not an admirer of yours."

Vidia was not surprised—few women were. "I see."

He glanced at her over his shoulder. "On the other hand, she was aware that I was an admirer."

This was of interest and pleased her enormously. "Were you? You hid it well, methinks."

Continuing in his endeavors, he ran his fingers along the window casements. "I thought you were the most beautiful woman I have ever seen."

Making a wry face, she responded in a tart tone. "Unfortunately, that is neither original nor unusual."

He paused and said simply, "For me it was true."

The sincerity rang in his voice and she was—strange as it seemed—ashamed of her cynicism. "Thank you," she offered a bit awkwardly.

He placed his hands on the window casement and hoisted himself up, a boot on the sill, to take a view of the top of the curtain box. "Flanders wasn't out of the bluc; I'd been sorely tempted well before that."

She realized that these revelations were doing an excellent job of throwing her off-balance, if that was his intent, and so she decided to inject a strong dose of reality. "You seemed so devoted to Marie."

Mention of the recently departed didn't seem to faze him,

and the blue eyes met hers. "I could dream. Not that I was able to get much sleep in Flanders—knowing you were in the next room."

"As opposed to the ambassador's maidservant," she noted in a dry tone.

Laughing, he knelt to examine the baseboards. "Unfair—that was strictly business—we had to get in, after all."

"And once we were in there was no getting out." *Deus*, it had been a heart-stopping moment when they realized their Flemish contacts had betrayed them and it was a trap.

"It was a close-run thing," he agreed as he lifted then closed the window. "But all that matters is—although you smelt of lye for days—the extraction was ultimately successful."

They had improvised by smuggling the wretched ambassador out in the laundry bag—Vidia in a mobcap and hoping no one noticed her pink satin shoes. "Remind me never to rely upon Flemish diplomats again."

"Or Flemish horseflesh," he added as he tapped on the walls.

With a smile she disagreed, shaking her head. "On the contrary; the horses did exactly as expected, being of such poor quality."

Chuckling, he leaned back on his haunches, his arms resting on his thighs as he ducked his chin for a moment. "I enjoyed every miserable moment."

Unable to argue, she admitted, "I did too," and met his gaze—there was nothing like shared peril to create a strong bond of intimacy. The room seemed to be warmer, suddenly. Mind yourself, *menina*, she thought, and dropped her gaze to the floor.

The moment passed, and he resumed his search, tapping the floorboards. "Perhaps we will work together again."

Keeping her chin lowered, she glanced up under her lashes to watch him. "That seems unlikely, if I'm to be hanged."

Ah, that struck a nerve and she noted his reaction carefully, although his expression was unreadable. "I won't let them hang you."

She offered in a teasing tone, "Well then; if you have a plan to extract me, I am all attention—as long as it does not involve a laundry bag." Although she leaned casually against the doorjamb, in truth she continued to watch him narrowly, hoping to gauge the seriousness of the situation. There was a small silence but apparently he had nothing to offer—or, more correctly, nothing he was willing to offer.

"It won't come to that," he said again. "I will see to it."

Shaking her head so that her earbobs danced, she couldn't suppress a smile. "You know, Carstairs, I have no idea whether there is a shred of truth in anything you tell me."

He laughed aloud and she had to chuckle in turn, pleased she had cracked through his defenses. Still smiling, he rose to his feet and stepped over to rest his hands at her waist and pull her toward him, bending so he kissed her, long and hard. She did not resist, but caressed his head with her hands as he drew her intimately close. He murmured into her neck, "Where is your bedchamber?"

"Would it be out of coverage?" she whispered. He paused, his hands on the sides of her breasts. "Tell me the truth, Lucien."

"No," he admitted, and with a sigh set her away from him. His warm gaze became intense as he dropped the focus of his eyes to her mouth. "But there is a powerful attraction between us, Vidia. You wish to indulge it as much as I do."

She stood quietly between his hands and spoke without thinking. "I wish we were normal people who could indulge in a little honesty, on occasion."

He regarded her for a long moment, his expression shuttered, then he stepped away and walked into the remaining upstairs room without making a reply. Apparently he didn't appreciate her attempt to pull the veil aside, and she tried to stifle the acute disappointment she felt now that he had removed his warm body from hers.

"Are you coming?" His voice could be heard.

"I am," she called out, her heart skipping a beat. *Mãe de Deus*, she thought—I never learn.

As she watched his search of the final upstairs room from the distant safety of the hallway he noted, "No one occupies any of the other rooms."

"No. I am not one who is comfortable having servants."

With a speculative expression, he glanced at her—she was equal parts relieved and disappointed to see that he had abandoned his role as seducer. "There are no other servants who live here?"

"A new cook, not much in evidence," she admitted. There was a pause while she watched him peer up the chimney. "The fewer servants, the fewer to witness those occasions when I entertain Rochon and summon the forces of darkness." The reference was to Napoleon's spymaster, the name he had muttered in his sleep. You are a flippant creature, she scolded herself; it comes of making such a clumsy call for honesty.

"Very amusing," he acknowledged easily, his voice echoing in the chimney. "What is this 'argo' to which Brodie refers—any guesses?"

"Not a clue," she answered just as easily.

Nothing more was said as he finished, brushing off his hands. "Next floor."

Stepping aside so that he could pass, she noted that he

made no attempt to touch her again. I wonder what is pretense and what is not, she thought. And I imagine he is wondering the same thing. It would all be very amusing if only I weren't in love with him—as it is, all I can do is follow him about—yearning—and guard every word I say. Such a sad little snail.

Carstairs continued his search, descending into the main quarters on the second floor while Vidia watched and made the occasional comment. With efficient movements, he went through her things and tapped on the sides and base of her armoire, then examined the slats of her canopied bed without making any more allusions to lovemaking. He spent a considerable amount of time tapping on the plastered walls, looking for a safe. "Where are your jewels?" he finally asked, perplexed.

"In the sugar box, on a kitchen shelf behind the extra tea cups," she answered without hesitation. "Pray do not seize them—they are slated for Maisie if I do not survive this latest assignment."

Glancing to her, he asked, "You have no relatives?"

"None that I would acknowledge. You?"

"A few." He smiled as he scrutinized her ceiling carefully, his head tilted back. "I don't mind acknowledging them, only because I don't see them very often."

"What do you tell them when they ask what it is that you do?" she asked, genuinely curious.

Pulling a gilt chair over, he stood upon it and began tapping on the ceiling, his linen shirt pulled tight across his shoulders. "That I am doing bureaucratic work connected with the sea trade."

"Certainly vague enough."

"If they ask too many questions, I begin to speak at length about tariffs and they quickly lose interest." He rested for a moment, his hands on his hips atop the chair. "Would you like to change out of your gown?"

He must have noticed that she had surreptitiously slid out of her shoes. "I am quite comfortable," she insisted, smoothing her skirts. "My shoes pinch, is all."

Teasing, he tilted his head. "I can help you undress again."

"Yes, you were very deft," she noted dryly. "Were you truly drunk?"

He shrugged. "No."

"You are *extraordinary*," she said in all admiration. "I didn't have a clue."

"I felt rather guilty—you were being so kind."

"But not guilty enough to call a halt."

"God, no."

She laughed and he chuckled in response, meeting her eyes from his perch on the chair. "This is better."

"I've never undergone a nicer search," she agreed.

Shaking his head, he lifted his arms to resume his overhead search. "I mean that we have a truce of sorts." Tap, tap; tap, tap. "I wish that you would trust me more than you do."

An odd comment, considering he was conducting a search of her residence. Arching a brow, she asked, "What makes you think I don't trust you?"

Pausing in his endeavors, he was silent for a moment. Ah, she thought, reading him; he regrets the remark because he let slip that he knows I have not been honest with him. Instead, as the silence stretched out, he gave an oblique answer. "If you need help—I hope you will come to me."

She had trouble finding her voice for a moment; a wild,

unnamed yearning welled up within her breast, nearly choking her. "Thank you," was all she managed to say. *Menina*, she cautioned herself a bit frantically—have a care; he seeks to beguile you and you are not one to be so easily beguiled—remember the hard lessons you have learned, and what is at stake.

They spoke no more on personal matters, and he finally descended into the wine cellar as the search neared its conclusion. Sighing, she settled in to sit on the last few steps, her skirts billowing around her stockinged feet as she stretched her arms over her head and watched him. "Does the name Hagar mean anything to you?"

He raised his brows as took a survey of the cellar. "Hagar as in the Bible?"

"Oh—is it a Bible character?" Vidia was not well-versed in matters religious.

"That would be the only Hagar I know of—why?"

Vidia decided she wouldn't tell him. "I'd heard the name, is all." As he made a circuit around the interior of the cavernous cellar with his candle, she teased, "How disappointing for you, Carstairs—nary a clue to be found."

"I have passed a very enjoyable visit," he insisted, "despite the fact the lady has had second thoughts."

"The lady wishes to avoid any more traps," she retorted with a smile. "The other night I thought I offered a kindness to a grieving man and this is how I am repaid."

But he would not be put on the defensive and responded in a mild tone as he opened the doors to one of the large wine cabinets, "I misremember, then—it did not seem such a sacrifice at the time."

She could not help laughing. "Lord—I am twigged. It was a very fine night, indeed."

"Just so we are clear." He continued rooting around the wine cabinets, tapping on the base and walls of each one. When he finally withdrew from the last, he straightened up and whistled, a bottle in his hand. "Will you look at this?"

She shrugged. "Would you like it? It is yours."

Raising his gaze to meet hers, he offered, "Share it with me—in your room tonight, and out of coverage—I promise. No one need know."

I am mightily tempted, she thought, resisting an urge to walk to him. Instead, she tilted her head in apology. "I do not drink, I am afraid."

"Oh yes—I had forgotten." He gestured with the bottle. "Here's as fine a reason as I can think of to change your mind."

"No."

The syllable was sharp and he spread his hands, contrite. "I beg your pardon—I shouldn't tease you."

She carefully unclenched her jaw. "I had a bad experience, once."

He watched her, and she knew he was surprised by her loss of composure. "I'm sorry for it; you may come pour my glass and tell me the tale, if you'd like."

Smiling, she was herself once again. "Some other time, perhaps."

He accepted the rejection with good grace and made an ironic gesture that encompassed the impressive cabinets and their contents. "Quite the collection for a teetotaler."

"It belongs to Brodie," she acknowledged. "He cannot keep it at his hotel."

Carstairs nodded and set the bottle on the floor as he closed the cabinets. "An intriguing man; his allegiances are not at all clear—although he does seem to be genuinely fond of you."

"I am a fine trophy," she agreed absently. No one knew better than she that Brodie's main allegiance was to the making of money—that and outwitting others. With some daring, she asked, "Have you a theory about what he plans? Or can you not tell me, being as I am tainted?"

He drew his hand absently along the bricks that lined the wall and she struggled to sit calmly as he did so, but his words were as alarming as his actions. "If you know anything of this, Vidia, you must report—there is a concern that you are colluding with him against the Crown, and it does not look well."

"I understand." She carefully kept her gaze away from the hand that was resting on the bricks and noted that it was the second time he had given her a warning, which seemed out of genuine concern for her. I appreciate the gesture, she thought, although I do not appreciate the meddling by his late wife, *mulher estupida*—she caught herself; I meant instead, God rest her soul.

He waited for a few silent moments, perhaps holding out hope that she would confess her treason and throw herself upon his impressive chest. She did not, but instead stood on legs made stiff by the cold. "May I make you some coffee, or would you rather just go home?"

"Coffee," he decided, and followed close behind her as she ascended the steps, struggling to control her inclination to lead him straight to her bedchamber—if he sought to seduce her for love of country or merely for himself it hardly mattered; it was a complication she did not need just now.

When they entered the foyer, they came face-to-face with Brodie, who had just come in the front door. Completely unfazed by finding a much younger man in his mistress's house well after midnight, he offered his hand.

"Hello, Benny." Vidia gestured to her companion with an easy smile. "Mr. Carstairs is a member of my temperance group at the church."

"Pleased to meet you," said Brodie affably. "And if you were to fall off the wagon, you may as well do it in style." He motioned to the wine bottle in Carstairs's hand.

The other man laughed in rueful acknowledgment. "It doesn't look well, does it? It is the Vicar's birthday, and Miss Swanson offered her cellar as he much enjoys fine wine. I assured her that heaven will hold no allure if this was his gift."

"I didn't know which to choose," Vidia demurred.

"No—she is not well-versed in matters of wine." Brodie bestowed upon Carstairs the kind of look men exchange around an untutored female.

The visitor bade them farewell and Vidia put her hand in Brodie's arm as they watched him walk down the front steps.

"Maisie couldn't decide if you needed reinforcements and came over to fetch me," Brodie said in a low voice. "Forgive me, *Bela*, if I overstepped."

Feeling her color rise, Vidia disclaimed, "It was nothing like that, Benny. I think instead he was looking for an excuse to take a survey of the house." Best not to mention she had invited him to do so.

Raising his brows at her, he closed the door. "Indeed?"

"I thought to allay suspicion, and I think I did—but he is a cool one, and difficult to read. Would you like some biscuits? I am starving."

"I would," her companion replied, and asked her no more questions although she could feel his thoughtful gaze upon her.

Vidia sat before her dressing table mirror, contemplating her reflection. Look at you, she thought. She felt as though she had not truly looked at herself in years, and now she decided that she resembled her mother more than she had in the past. The way my eyes are set, she thought—it is very similar.

"There's ocean in Yorkshire, if ye like bein' by the ocean," Maisie noted in a neutral tone as she gathered up the hairdressing tools. "Scarborough comes to mind."

Vidia met her maidservant's gaze in the mirror. "I don't think I can think about it, just yet."

Maisie nodded and said no more. Vidia's voracious appetite had disappeared as quickly as it had come, to be replaced by a complete lack of interest in anything edible—and it was becoming more and more apparent why this was. I need a plan, she thought—but I am not one for planning; I am more likely to act on impulse and then be somewhat surprised that I have managed to survive. Brodie, on the other hand, is a master planner—but I cannot tell him of this fix. Not yet, leastways.

"The Prince," Maisie remarked tones of wonder. "Ye'll be tellin' me what he says to ye."

"I've met him twice before—mainly he tries to look down the front of my dress."

"Missy," Maisie admonished her, shocked. "'Tis the Prince—ye must watch yerself." Maisie had a great admiration for the aristocracy, although Vidia surmised that if Maisie could see her monarch-in-waiting when he was in his cups she might feel a bit differently. Brodie had been invited to Carlton House for cards and Vidia had no doubt it was connected to the precarious state of the Treasury. The news had been kept quiet, but another shipment of gold bricks on its way to the Continent had been stolen between Monday and Tuesday this week. Montagu had been removed from his position, it being discovered that the carrier pigeons Rothschild used to send messages had been replaced by imposters carrying false messages. Vidia had no doubt that Brodie would be treated with kid gloves tonight—with this latest loss, his hold over the country's finances had just become stronger.

Sighing, Vidia gathered her fan and her reticule after checking as a matter of course to see that her pistol was loaded. "We'll be late, Maisie—don't wait up."

"Will the other gentleman be there?" The maid made the attempt to pretend it was a casual question, but Maisie was not well-versed in deception, which was why Vidia was careful not to tell her anything remotely confidential.

"No," said Vidia, who then added, "I assume you mean Mr. Carstairs."

"He seemed a kind man." Maisie slid her a sidelong glance.

Vidia struggled not to laugh aloud, as Maisie's only interaction with Carstairs had been to be informed that he was conducting a search. Nevertheless, it appeared Maisie had drawn a conclusion or two in that country-bred head of hers. "He is a bureaucrat, who monitors the sea trade," Vidia informed her gravely. "He knows a great deal about tariffs."

"A good, reliable man," Maisie suggested, then caught herself, "not that Mr. Brodie is not a good man…"

"Mr. Brodie is definitely not a good man, Maisie," Vidia assured her with a smile. "And lately he has been distracted—perhaps I have a rival for his affections."

Maisie colored up and dropped the subject, stepping over to the armoire to fetch Vidia's silk pelisse as Vidia smiled into the mirror. She had borrowed a Bible from the lending library—much to the bemusement of the clerk—and had discovered who Hagar was.

With a final assessment, her maid sent her on her way. "Ye look a treat, missy. See if ye can eat somethin'."

"I shall try, Maisie."

Hesitating, the other woman stood with her hands folded under her apron. "Ye'll come about, if I may say so; look on t' bright side—'tis Providence, p'haps."

But Vidia could not agree and shook her curls gently so as not to loosen any diamond-studded combs. "Lord, Maisie; you are overwrought—I cannot believe Providence takes the slightest interest in me."

She then left through her front door, nodding in a friendly fashion to the French spy in the shadows as the footman handed her into Brodie's coach. Brodie had not come to fetch her, having decided—matters being as they were—that he would rather not be out in public more than necessary. Earlier he had noted, "For purposes of self-preservation, I have made certain that no one can easily determine what will happen to my bonds if I am met with a sudden and tragic death—still, it is best to take no chances; these are desperate times."

"They do not dare murder you," Vidia had assured him. "You would only haunt them."

Nevertheless, she noted that he brought an extra outrider with him when he emerged from his hotel. "Good evening, Benny—you look very fine."

Settling into the thick cushions across from her, he smoothed down his side-whiskers, well-pleased. "It is a wonderful thing to be inveigled by a prince of the realm—I outdo myself."

"Such vanity, Benny—he only wishes your purse was more patriotic," she teased. "Perhaps he will offer you a title as an incentive."

"I wouldn't take it." He tapped his cane to signal the driver to go forward. "The aristocracy only serves as an impediment to industry."

"What will you do if they try to buttonhole you?" She was genuinely curious as the coach started forward, and she clutched at the leather strap, awaiting his answer.

But Brodie was not made anxious by the thought. "I shall stall them—the *denouement* of our little adventure is at hand and the final arrangements are being made for the *Argo* to set sail. A bit more time is all that is needed."

And I have little time before my own *denouement,* thought Vidia with an inward sigh. Aloud, she said, "Recall that you must watch your words around Henry Grant—although I doubt he'll be there."

"Yes—I'll remember. What is the world coming to when bankers serve as spies?"

"Shocking," she agreed in a grave tone, smoothing a glove. "If you can't trust the Bank of England, who can you trust?"

He laughed aloud and reached to take her hand. "It is such an excellent plan, *Bela*."

He lived for this, and she smiled to observe his extreme pleasure. "It is such a shame that no one will know of it, save you and me."

But he disclaimed and shrugged with an easy gesture. "I amuse myself, only—I do not seek recognition; such a desire is counterproductive."

Squeezing the hand in hers, she thought of the future she had once never thought to have. "I appreciate—everything, Benny; I truly do."

"*Bela*," her companion warned, "do not start weeping into your handkerchief, I beg of you."

Chuckling, she sat back into the cushions. "Well, then—I won't. If the Prince asks me to deal the bank for Basset, who should win?"

Sighing, he drummed his fingers on his knees. "Deal a fair game," he decided with deep regret. "We don't want to give anyone an excuse to lock us up."

"The Prince would not lock me up," she pointed out. "Instead he would lock you up so as to have a clear field to me."

Cocking his head, Brodie thought this over as though it was a serious matter. "So—you honestly believe beauty holds more allure than wealth?"

"It shouldn't," she agreed, "but it has been proved so many a time—it is the only reason I am successful at what I do."

"Perhaps," he acknowledged, thinking about it. "But not with respect to my little plan, surely?"

"No—here wealth has more power than beauty but only because we are not dealing with the usual man with the usual tastes." She barely refrained from a shudder.

"True," he admitted. "Perhaps you have the right of it, but we should test out your theory—in Venice, perhaps."

She had to chuckle at his persistence—she was a valuable asset and he was unwilling to give her up. "No thank you, my friend—I imagine I shall stay in England for the foreseeable future." Eight more months, certainly.

"Unless your people run out of patience, *Bela.*" Slightly shaking the hand in his, he persisted, "What then?"

"Then wealth will be called upon to rescue beauty," she replied in a light tone. "Best bake a cake."

Chuckling together, they subsided into a companionable silence as Vidia looked out the window to review the fashionable part of the city as it passed by. I have come to the end of my usefulness, it seems—Maisie is right, it is as though Providence has stepped in and taken charge, will-I or nil-I. But mainly I have to decide if I should tell Carstairs. As soon as she gave voice to the thought, she chastised herself as a coward—of course she would tell him; he had every right to know. But she would make it clear that she'd manage—and flourish—somewhere far enough away that she wouldn't embarrass him. He and Marie had no children and it may have been by choice. This news would come as a shock to any man, but under the circumstances—considering who they were and what was at stake—it would be a wonder if he didn't have a hostile reaction. She would have to handle it very carefully.

They pulled into the line of carriages that were waiting to discharge their passengers for the supper party at Carlton House, a crowd of footmen and servants hurrying between each. Brodie rubbed his hands together. "We are arrived, *Bela.* Let the games begin." He was in high spirits at the prospect of the evening ahead—he never doubted himself; never doubted that his wits would allow him to prevail. On the other hand, Vidia now had two separate but equally monumental problems driving her to distraction. She took the footman's hand as he helped her out and thought, *Mãe de Deus*—it is truly a shame I do not drink.

Chapter 13

It was well past midnight and Vidia was a bit worried as she clung to the Prince Regent's arm, laughing at his latest jest and watching the watch fobs jingle together on his impressive abdomen. The room was heavy with smoke from cigars and cigarillos, and although the scent had never bothered her before, now it did. If I cast up my accounts on the Prince I imagine I can no longer count on him to pardon me for my crimes, she thought. I'd best excuse myself before such a disaster occurs.

But the Prince was calling for Mountjoy and begging Vidia to recite the titillating story she had told him about the Prussian ambassador for the other man's amusement, so she drew a deep breath and soldiered on.

Apparently Mountjoy was just drunk enough to ask questions he oughtn't. "Vidia," he pronounced, running a gentle hand along her arm. "Brodie may be rich, but he is not as handsome as I—will you throw him over?"

The Prince threw back his head and laughed in appreciation; Mountjoy, poor man, had a face scarred from smallpox. Vidia tapped his hand with her fan, her eyes dancing. "Fie, sir," she laughed, "where would you keep me—at Craystone?" Mountjoy had famously married his ancient title to a wealthy merchant's daughter who was known to keep him on a tight leash.

"You could pose as the governess," insisted Mountjoy. "I would seek a lesson each and every day."

Again, the Prince laughed with such gusto that he began to choke, and Vidia as well as Mountjoy pounded his back as he gulped brandy. "Impossible," he gasped after he had recovered. "Brodie is richer than I am, for God's sake—even Lady Mountjoy cannot compete."

But Vidia teased, "Perhaps Lady Mountjoy would instead pay me to keep this handsome face away from hers." She softened the barb by stroking a graceful hand over Mountjoy's cheek, and he chuckled in appreciation.

"A pox on Brodie—he is driving my people mad," complained the Prince with ill humor. "Turn him up sweet, Vidia—tell him something to melt that cold heart of his." Swirling the brandy in his glass, he took another drink.

"He does have a counting-house heart," she soothed. "I shall do my best, sir." She began to play with her left earbob—her signal to Brodie that she'd like to leave, but the situation wasn't urgent. If she played with the right earbob, urgency was indicated.

"Ah, Vidia—if it were me I would do anything you asked of me—give up a hundred fortunes." Mountjoy had taken her hand and was waxing sentimental as only a man in his cups can do without appearing foolish. "Upon my honor."

"You are very sweet," Vidia said with a smile, meeting his yearning gaze with her own amused one. "A trifle well-to-go, but sweet."

"Drunk as a barrow," pronounced the Prince in a genial tone. "Be off, Mountjoy—you'll annoy Brodie and then where shall I be? I shall have to mortgage Windsor Castle."

As Mountjoy rose to bow, Brodie appeared. The two men exchanged good-natured jibes, and then Brodie leaned over Vidia, his hands on the table. "Shall we go, my dear?"

"Willingly—pending permission from my prince, of course."

"She is charged with sweetening you up," announced said prince in a sour tone. "God speed to her."

But Brodie was prepared to offer an olive branch to the heir to the Crown. "I have spoken to your minister—I need only transfer a few assets and we will rework the bonds to your satisfaction."

"Excellent," the other said in surprise, eying him with approval. Then, to Vidia, "You are hereby relieved of your duties."

"I thank you," she teased, and dropped a formal curtsey, calculated to expose her impressive cleavage to him.

"Minx." He smiled and waved a languid hand. "Take her away, Brodie, before I make a fool of myself."

"Too late," murmured Brodie as he led Vidia away.

"Hush," cautioned Vidia, stifling her laughter. "We are not out of the woods, yet."

"Certainly we are." Brodie nodded to cronies as they made a slow progress toward the door, his hand at her back. "I am the puppet master."

"Tell me, puppet master; are you truly going to rework the bonds?"

Brodie shot her a look of disbelief. "Good God, no—but I have managed to delay long enough to keep your people off our necks." He looked at the room around him with regret. "It is a shame I cannot digress from my plan; a *coterie* with more money and less sense would be hard to find."

"Behave yourself, Benny—I confess I am weary and wouldn't be fit to count the cards, anyway."

There was a line of guests awaiting their carriages on the

crowded steps out front, and Brodie's new outrider from the hotel approached and indicated that if they were agreeable, the coach had been stationed on a side street so that they could walk directly to it. Vidia agreed, hoping the cool evening air would settle her stomach, and with a deferential gesture, the man escorted them along the pavement toward the next street.

Wrapping her pelisse tighter around her, Vidia took a deep breath and felt much better. "Pray do not come early tomorrow," she suggested to Brodie. "I need to sleep."

"Sleep, then; you deserve it, after parrying such clumsy advances all evening."

"I don't think his heart is in it," she reflected with a small smile. "It's only to keep up the reputation from his youth."

"Fool," pronounced Brodie, and Vidia cast him a cautionary glance, as the outrider was listening—although they had not named the Prince outright.

As she looked up at Brodie, her slipper slid off a cobblestone and she stumbled forward slightly and clutched at the footman's arm so as not to fall. "Are you all right, miss?" he turned to ask with concern.

"Quite all right," she assured him, and wondered why he hadn't tried to steady her, as would have been natural. Taking a covert glance she saw, to her astonishment, that he held a pistol next to his breeches on the side opposite her. Halting suddenly, she looked back over her shoulder toward the Prince's residence, her expression chagrined. "I believe I have lost my right earbob," she said in dismay.

Alert, Brodie replied, "We go back then," but he stepped slightly away from Vidia and the footman. Disconcerted, the other man hesitated as he tried to decide which to follow and in an instant Vidia's hands were on the wrist holding the pistol, waiting for his reaction. He instinctively tried to break free by jerking his hand upward, and gauging her moment, she stepped in and brought her knee to his groin with all her strength.

While the man dropped to the ground in agony she wrested his pistol from him and turned her back to Brodie, who had already drawn the sword that was concealed in the hilt of his cane and was reviewing the shadows on the other side of the street. "*Tenga cuidado*," he muttered in Spanish. "There will be others."

"*Retournez*," she answered in French. "We should go back to the crowd—*rapidmente*." wary, they began to retrace their steps toward Carlton House, back to back.

"*Saisissez-la*," called out the man on the ground behind them, gasping. "*Saisissez-la*."

Alarmed, Vidia saw two men closing in from the shadows. "*Fique ao lado de mim*," she warned Brodie in Portuguese as he turned to face them with her, shoulder to shoulder.

"*Si*." Brodie circled his sword before him in a menacing manner.

"*Reculez ou je tirerai*," Vidia called to the attackers in French with as much menace as she could muster, threatening to shoot. The two hesitated as she brandished their comrade's pistol as well as her own, but urged on by the original attacker they warily began to separate and surround Vidia and Brodie so as to force her to choose a target.

Time to cause a ruckus, she decided, and drew a bead on one of the elaborate windows that lined the Prince Regent's residence. She fired, the discharge creating a very satisfying crack that was immediately followed by a horrendous noise as the huge window came crashing down on the stone pavement. Glass flew around them as the startled men retreated in disarray, and alarmed voices could be heard coming from the Prince's residence. Vidia deftly tossed the man's pistol to the pavement in the direction of their fleeing attackers and said to Brodie, "How do we play this?"

Brodie's voice was grim. "We make a scene."

A group of gentlemen and footmen quickly approached, their surprised voices raised in inquiry as they surveyed the broken glass.

"An *outrage*!" Brodie shouted, incensed and purple of face. "After them!" He pointed in the direction the attackers had taken and several pursuers took off running, although Vidia felt there was little chance of catching them. Amidst exclamations of shock and dismay, they were escorted back to the entry—Brodie loudly decrying a country where even a visit to the Prince's residence was fraught with peril. Those who surrounded them agreed with this sentiment in murmuring voices, and Vidia suddenly stilled as she recognized one of those voices. As she stood in shocked surprise, one of the younger guests with whom she was not familiar stepped forward to offer his handkerchief to her, explaining that her arm was cut and bleeding.

"Oh," she exclaimed, and saw that this was so. She was not worried—Maisie was a wizard at removing bloodstains from dress gowns—but she found she had a sudden and intense interest in removing herself from the scene. The young gentleman held his handkerchief to her arm, then offered in a gallant manner, "You are safe now, miss—allow me to escort you away from this place."

"I will do the escorting, you puppy—begone." Brodie made a show of being annoyed and grasped Vidia's other arm, but her rescuer was not going to relinquish such a chance and explained angrily that he was tending to Vidia's wound.

While the two men exchanged unfriendly barbs, Vidia sank

down on the marble steps and pronounced, "I feel a bit faint," in her best imitation of a helpless maiden. Brodie and the other man immediately ceased all hostilities, Brodie calling for water and the young man fanning her with his beaver hat.

The Prince materialized by her side and directed that Vidia be taken inside so that he could call his physicians, but she demurred, insisting that she had recovered and would rather go home. The Prince then called for one of his own carriages and in no time at all Vidia was safely within its luxurious confines, rattling over the cobblestones toward Belgrave Square with Brodie beside her.

"Do you need to be stitched?" he asked, lifting the handkerchief to review her cut dispassionately.

"I think not—a binding tape should do," said Vidia, who had dressed many a scar. "Our attackers may have some cuts, though, which would make it easier to identify them."

"We may not wish to identify them. I imagine it was your people, trying to make you doubt me."

"Yes," she agreed reluctantly. "I think you have the right of it—yet another trap." *Saisissez-la*, the man had ordered—seize *her*. Since Brodie was not their target, it could be presumed the contretemps was designed to make her think Brodie—or even Rochon—was willing to remove her from the scene so as not to jeopardize their plan. Out of fear for her life, she would then presumably repent of her many sins and ask for protection from the grey-eyed spymaster.

Brodie seemed to find it amusing. "They think you are the weak link."

Despite everything, she had to chuckle. "How annoying for them—I never behave as I ought."

"I could have warned them of that," Brodie replied with good humor.

Chapter 14

Vidia sat in her chambers, her pistol on the dressing table, debating whether to wake Maisie. She knew from long experience that it was important to tend a cut immediately so as to avoid a scar, but she was expecting a visitor and besides, she wasn't in the mood to have to explain what had happened—not until she had straightened out the story in her mind. Brodie had the right of it, but she hadn't been willing to tell him that the reason she knew that it was her compatriots who had set up the abduction attempt was because she had heard Carstairs's voice in the throng, quietly urging the young man to see to her wound. He must have been disguised as a servant, and she was surprised she hadn't spotted him; she had recognized his voice, though—even though it was only one of many. You are a hopeless case, she thought, picking at the lace on her best dressing gown. You should call Maisie, bar the door, pull on a plain cotton nightdress, and go to bed.

Instead she waited, clad in her lace dressing gown and practicing with a deck of cards—she hadn't played in a few days and it was important to keep her hands dexterous. She did not doubt that Carstairs would make an appearance, and did not doubt that he would make his way undetected past the Frenchman stationed outside and the additional guard Brodie had posted this evening.

Her patience was rewarded when she heard a tapping on her chamber door even though she had left it ajar. He didn't want to frighten her, she thought with irony. It was a bit late for such concerns.

"Come in," she said, and turned to hold her pistol on him.

Raising his hands, he stood still. "I am unarmed."

She made a derisive sound and he amended, "I am armed but I shall not draw."

As he stepped into the room they regarded each other; he was dressed in dark clothes from head to foot—the only contrast coming from the candlelight's exposure of his intense blue eyes. She thought about those eyes and did not invite him to sit.

"I wanted to see that you are recovered."

"As you see." Her tone was mild, her pistol unwavering.

He hesitated. "You were unwell, I think."

Deus, if he only knew. She smiled. "Only a feint, to stop a quarrel."

"Ah."

She waited.

His gaze traveled to the cut on her arm. "Do you need a stitch or two?"

"No," she replied in an exasperated tone. "And everyone should quit asking."

"Then where is the binding tape?"

Weighing her options, she relented and placed her pistol on the table, produced the tape, and allowed him to draw up a chair and reposition the candle so that he could see better. He examined the cut on her upper arm and met her eyes. "I sew a fine seam."

"Not on me, you don't," she retorted. "Apply the tape and begone."

He did, asking her to hold one end in place while he carefully wrapped the tape around her arm, his head bent close to her own. "I am sorry for this."

"Are you?" She made no effort to keep the bitter edge from her voice.

His eyes met hers, and she wondered, unbidden, whether the child would have his eyes. He insisted, "I am indeed sorry. And I am here out of coverage."

Watching him, she decided that perhaps this was the truth. "Do you believe me tainted?"

He thought about it for a moment. "I don't know what I believe."

Chiding him, she said, "I thought you agreed to give me warning before I was clapped in irons."

"No," he corrected her softly, his gaze on hers. "I never agreed."

Struggling to control herself, she accused, "Yes—you asked me to come to you if I needed help."

"You have not come to me," he pointed out.

Dropping her head, she felt a sudden and surprising inclination to cry. She hadn't cried in many years—not even when Rochon's man held his knife to her face, discussing which of her beautiful eyes he should remove first.

"It is a damnable situation," Carstairs said in the same soft tone. "Shall we set it aside for an hour and agree not to speak of it?"

"I suppose we can try," she agreed, calming herself. I should tell him about the baby, she thought, but could not bring herself to do it—not in this vulnerable state, so uncharacteristic of her. Instead she asked, "Would you like to play cards?"

"I would," he promptly responded. "I watched you at the club—you are a very good cheat."

It was a sincere compliment. "Thank you," she said, and began to deal.

He pulled his chair closer. "Are we playing for points or money?"

"Points," she decided, sorting the cards with a flick of her wrist. "Then I won't be tempted to cheat."

With a smile, he gathered up his hand. "Every now and then," he mused, arranging his cards before making a discard, "I get a glimpse of what lies beneath that façade."

"My snail shell," she replied, unperturbed.

His lips curved in amusement. "There; it happened again."

She pounced on his discard. "On the other hand, I am not certain I have ever been given such a glimpse."

His gaze flicked up to meet hers. "You have—you were perhaps unaware." She knew he referred to their night together and as these were dangerous waters, she made no reply.

As they continued to play, he observed, "One becomes cynical in this business; in the end it permeates every aspect—even the personal."

She turned over her cards to show she had won the hand. "But trust is always an issue, whether in business or the personal—wouldn't you agree?"

He gathered up the cards to redeal while she marked the points. They were very evenly matched, she decided, and tried to control that yearning feeling that always seemed to rise up within her when she was in his company.

Thoroughly shuffling the cards, he offered, "I agree—but that is not what I meant. We are trained not to trust anyone in order to survive, but it creates such a disadvantage—it poisons the atmosphere so that we are unwilling to take a chance on trust." He met her eyes. "Even when it means we forfeit a chance at happiness."

"Do you think it possible to trust another person to such an extent?" She was genuinely curious. "And how would one know, in any event?"

"True—we have seen so much duplicity. And it is against our natures, you and me, to be made vulnerable."

She nodded, pausing to finger the cards in her hand and thinking him very astute. "So the manner in which we live our lives has taught us that reposing trust in another person is not only foolish, but dangerous."

"It is a shame," he agreed, taking her discard. "I wonder if we could change our natures."

"You had a wife," she reminded him. It seemed an opportune time to make the reminder; she could practically feel the heat emanating from him across the table.

"I did," he agreed, and did not elaborate.

She decided that for the briefest instant she had seen beneath his façade and wanted to follow up. "Do you miss her?" The question was sincere—she had always had the impression they were a devoted couple but his willingness to pursue her—and so soon after Marie's death—didn't mesh with that impression.

Studying his hand, he chose his words with care. "Marriage is not always easy; even the most compatible couple may not have a smooth road at all times. It is hard to explain to someone who observes it only from the outside."

"You mistake the matter," she said calmly. "I am widowed, myself."

His gaze flew to hers, startled, and there was a pause. "I did not know—I am sorry."

Watching his reaction carefully, she decided his surprise was genuine. Interesting, she thought—he was not in their spymaster's confidence.

Carstairs's eyes still rested upon her, assessing this revelation. "How did he die?"

"On the Peninsula—during the war." With a monumental effort she forced herself to relax and curtailed any more questions by asking her own. "How long were you married?"

"Six years," he said. "And you?"

"Nearly two." Realizing she had bitten off the syllable, she tried to make up for her lapse of composure. "A very tumultuous time."

He nodded slowly. "I can well imagine. Will you wed again?"

"No," she answered without hesitation, drawing a card. "You?"

With gentle amusement he replied, "I regret to say it appears not."

She glanced up in surprise and met his gaze, fixed upon hers with teasing warmth. Smiling and shaking her head, she tried to control those butterflies again. "Come now, Lucien—if we were wed we would be afraid to swallow our breakfast tea and would be forced to sleep with one eye open."

"There wouldn't be much sleeping," he corrected her, "and therefore even if you poisoned my breakfast tea, I would die a happy man."

Dangerous waters, she reminded herself. Don't start thinking about being abed with him—too much is at stake.

But he had no such qualms as he reached over to take her hands in his, the cards falling to the table. "Allow me to demonstrate," he said softly, pulling her up with him as he stood and brought his mouth down to hers. I shouldn't, she thought—I have no idea if he means a word he says. But almost against her will, her mouth softened beneath his as he kissed her gently and began to untie the ribbons on her dressing gown.

"Vidia," he whispered, his mouth moving to her throat. "Sweetheart—I have wanted this ever since that first night."

Ah yes—that first night, she thought as her hands came up to caress his shoulders. I've already paid the price—there seems little point in holding him at arm's length at this late date.

The dressing gown fell to the floor as he lifted her in his arms to carry her to the bed, his head bent to hers as he traced his mouth across her cheeks. Laying her into the luxurious featherbed, he followed her down and lay atop her, shrugging out of his coat in between kisses.

"Aren't you going to take off your boots?" she whispered in bemusement.

He did not pause in his endeavors, but confessed, "I am afraid if I give you a moment to think, you will change your mind." He rested with his forearms on either side of her head and moved his mouth to her throat.

Placing a hand on his cheek, she chuckled. "I won't change my mind—may as well be comfortable."

Lifting himself off her, he sat on the edge of the bed and pulled off his boots as she knelt on the bed and embraced him from behind, nuzzling the nape of his neck and reaching around to unbutton his shirt buttons.

He seized her hands and kissed them, one at a time, then stood to peel off his shirt and breeches. Her hands tracing his ribs, she said, "You will have to tell me of your scars, sometime."

"Not now," he muttered, his need urgent as he lifted her nightdress over her head. His warm hands slid down the sides of her breasts, her waist, her hips. "You are so beautiful—and I don't care how many times you've heard it before."

Murmuring into his mouth she replied, "Then tell me again."

Chapter 15

At the appointed time, Vidia squared her shoulders and tapped the code on the church door. Earlier, a messenger had come around her house with a ciphered note, stating there would be a temperance meeting that evening. Brodie had thought there would be no harm in attending, despite the attack at the Prince's residence.

"Truly?" she had asked doubtfully as she put the note into the fire. "What if I descend into the basement never to be seen again?"

With a patient manner, he explained, "Come, *Bela*—think on it. They are trying to make you doubt your allegiance to me; the best tack for you to take is innocent outrage."

"I can do innocent outrage," she had agreed. "None better."

"Besides," he pointed out, "the Prince's supper party has softened my stance—I have agreed to rework the bonds, remember?"

"Ah—I had almost forgotten," she said dryly. "But what if instead, they are trying to get to you through me—force you to act by threatening me; have you thought of it from that angle?"

But he had discarded such a notion out of hand, "No one would even think it—I am not a sentimental man and would easily put another in your place. No; they are trying to make you doubt me."

So now she prepared to face them all down—although she did look forward to seeing Carstairs again—she hadn't heard from him since the night of their card game. While Brodie is not sentimental about me, I am definitely sentimental about Carstairs, she thought, and it's a weakness they have already attempted to exploit; foolish snail—look where it's landed you. But she couldn't regret it—there was such heat and such an attraction between them that it had been another blissful night of making love, this time interspersed with laughter and soft words. Lying in his arms, she had resolved to tell him of her condition but she had fallen asleep instead—she didn't have the stamina to stay awake anymore. In the morning, Carstairs was gone and Maisie had opened the curtains without comment, but Vidia could sense the maid knew more than she was letting on—only this time she didn't tease Vidia about it; she knew it was not a teasing matter anymore.

The church door opened to reveal the grey-eyed man posing as a vicar again, dressed in black vestments. Affecting a brash air, she surveyed him, head to foot. "You again—where is your curate? I am beginning to think you are running some sort of a rig."

"Speaks the master," he replied, and bowed.

"Am I beneath his notice, now? Should I beg for an appointment?"

The Vicar gestured her in. "He sends his apologies—a trifling matter at the Treasury; perhaps you have heard."

She removed her cloak and he took it from her and hung it on the hook. "I do hope he finds the misplaced gold."

"I imagine it is his dearest wish." He lifted the candle and led her within.

She followed him down the stairs to the basement, trying

to gauge his mood. "You must come visit—we shall play a duet again."

"My own dearest wish."

Not good, she decided. Whatever Marie Carstairs had told them, it was definitely not to her credit. Who would have thought the woman could cause so much trouble? It occurred to her that she was not aware of the circumstances surrounding the late Mrs. Carstairs's unexpected death, and resolved to ask Carstairs—that is, if they were still on speaking terms after she gave him the news tonight. She was determined to give him the news tonight; there was no sense in putting it off and apparently Brodie's plan would come to a conclusion soon—she may need to leave quickly.

"How many have we?"

"We speak of Brodie tonight and so it is Dokes, Carstairs, and Grant."

"Is Droughm back from Algiers? I thought I saw him riding in the park."

"Lord Droughm has indeed returned."

Eying his back, she subsided. Apparently he wasn't going to tell her how the assignment went in Algiers or why Droughm, of all people, had been chaperoning a schoolgirl in the park.

As she passed before him into the basement, she remarked, "I am amazed you tolerate Grant—the Bank of England must be in dire straits indeed."

His face in the shadows, the Vicar said only, "He is uniquely qualified for the position."

The others had already arrived and she greeted them, her gaze meeting Carstairs's only briefly so that she gave nothing away—they had agreed that the other night was out of coverage, but the grey-eyed man was notorious for uncovering secrets; only see how he had found out about San Sebastian.

"Swanson," Jenny Dokes greeted her with her dry smile. "How goes your life of ease?"

Vidia spoke with her for a moment, relieved. Whatever the Vicar suspected, it seemed it was not generally known among her compatriots. It doesn't truly matter, she acknowledged. I do not have the luxury of pride—not anymore.

The meeting was called to order and the Vicar began without preamble. "I needn't tell you that matters are grave; it is clear there is a breach—that supposedly secure information with respect to the gold shipments was not, in fact, secure. To counter this problem, all personnel who were privy to the information have been dismissed from their positions and there are even fewer with access."

Too little, too late, thought Vidia; Brodie has all the gold he needs, *por favor Deus*.

"Treason," pronounced Grant, his arms crossed before him in disgust. "Infamous. We can only hope those who are behind this plot are made to pay." His gaze slid to Vidia, and she barely refrained from flinging her blade at him.

But the Vicar paced across the small room thoughtfully. "There is always the possibility the perpetrators have no political motivation; recall that there are rumors Napoleon's people have also lost shipments of gold—we may be dealing with international thieves who have no particular loyalty."

"France can afford the losses even less than England," noted Dokes. "Their currency is guaranteed by gold, while England is not on the gold standard."

"Brodie has agreed to rework his bonds," offered Vidia, thinking to steer the conversation toward more productive channels. "There is that, at least."

"You are misinformed; I understand the little contretemps the other night has caused him to balk once again." The Vicar rested his unreadable gaze upon her.

Surprised, Vidia replied honestly, "I was not aware of this."

"Apparently," the Vicar answered slowly, "he was very unhappy you were injured and blames the Government to no small extent."

So; thought Vidia with interest, Brodie is not so unsentimental after all—I shall have to tease him about it.

"What contretemps?" asked Dokes.

There was a pause, and Vidia remembered she was supposed to be outraged. "We were attacked, Brodie and I, on the street outside Carlton House, of all places. The attackers were not caught but it seemed that I was their object."

"Heavens," exclaimed Dokes, her pale brows lifting in surprise. "And you were injured?"

"A scratch or two," Vidia disclaimed. "Brodie was furious that security was so lax, all things considered." She met the Vicar's eye, daring him to make a comment.

He did not disappoint, but replied in a mocking tone, "Deplorable; who would do such a thing?"

"Cowards," she flung at him.

Carstairs had remained silent to this point, but interjected, "Perhaps it was a group of common felons—after all, Brodie is famously wealthy."

Taking control of her temper, Vidia subsided. It would do no good to antagonize the spymaster, and so she followed Carstairs's lead. "Perhaps."

But apparently the Vicar was not yet done and he addressed her in a dulcet tone. "It is impossible to control such lawlessness—surely you understand?"

It seemed to Vidia that this remark was a thinly veiled

threat, but she was not one to be cowed by threats, as Rochon himself could attest. Lifting her chin, she retorted, "Indeed; many things are impossible to control." There—let him make what he would of her counterthreat.

Before blows could be exchanged, Carstairs interceded once again. "Can we look into Brodie's financial dealings for the past few months—see if everything is aboveboard? Perhaps we can discover some leverage to apply to him."

"The situation is extremely delicate," the Vicar conceded, reluctantly pulling his gaze away from Vidia's angry glare. "Brodie has done nothing unlawful—at least that we are aware. If he is mishandled it may compel exactly the behavior we are trying to prevent; it is not clear if he has any particular loyalty to England and we do not wish to create the very disloyalty we fear."

Everyone is stymied—just as Brodie said, thought Vidia; say what you will about him, you have to give the devil his due. Offering an olive branch, she asked, "Shall I conduct a search of Brodie's rooms?" She would show that she could cooperate if she wasn't being attacked by Englishmen pretending to be Frenchmen now being passed off as common felons.

"Too risky," pronounced the Vicar. "What have we discovered from the bank's records?"

"I see no major discrepancies," said Dokes. "The debts are as they appear—no worse."

"A small piece of good news," said the Vicar, nodding. "Now we need only find the missing gold."

"It is nothing short of amazing we can find no one who knows *something*," Dokes offered with a knit brow. "This much gold would be heavy and could not be easily transported or stored."

"It is indeed a mystery," said the Vicar, a slight edge to his voice. "But there has been no indication that any attempt has been made to cash it in, so we are without clues in that respect, also."

"What is the timeline?" asked Carstairs.

Nine months, Lucien—or eight, now, thought Vidia, and wished she didn't feel so nervous.

"Matters are grave," was all the Vicar would say. "Brodie can alleviate the immediate pressure if he does not seek to cash in his bonds immediately, but if he does, a financial crisis could easily ensue—a panic which could collapse the economy."

While they all absorbed this unwelcome assessment, Vidia caught Carstairs's eye briefly, then returned her attention to the Vicar as he adjourned the meeting. Hopefully he would know she wished to speak to him in private.

"Swanson," asked Dokes in a low voice as they stood to leave. "What was that all about?" she indicated the Vicar with her eyes.

Having cooled down, Vidia decided she should downplay the display of open hostility. "He is unhappy with my efforts—thinks I may be a bit too comfortable in my assignment."

"The men in this business are always doubting the resolve of the women," the other woman observed without bitterness. "They think we are easily swayed and therefore weaker, so we are held to a higher standard."

Vidia knew she was offering support and appreciated it. "I think you have the right of it, Dokes. Tell me—how is your investigation at the *Académie* coming along?" Vidia had forgotten the name of the former French aristocrat they had marked as a suspect.

"Nothing new," Dokes replied in a neutral tone. "Tell me what the Prince was like—did you speak to him at length?"

Although she was willing to allow the change of subject, Vidia noted with some dismay that even Jenny Dokes had been warned to tell her nothing.

Chapter 16

After speaking with Dokes, Vidia emerged from the church onto the quiet street and began to walk in the direction of the main crossroad, her senses surveying the surroundings for any hidden dangers. It was second nature to make such a survey and she wondered if she would shake the habit anytime soon, now that her future would entail a different kind of life altogether. I shall have to try to make friends, she realized, which was a novel idea. As Carstairs had pointed out, they had learned to stay alive by not trusting anyone, and women of her acquaintance tended not to trust her for fear their menfolk would succumb. Another disadvantage of beauty, she thought, then could not help smiling when she remembered an advantage; how Carstairs had given her such pretty compliments the other night—when he could manage to put two words together, that was.

On cue, he materialized up ahead on the pavement and waited for her to catch up to him. *Deus*, she thought. The moment is upon me.

"Thank you, Lucien," she said. "I wished to speak with you privately."

He bowed his head in acknowledgment and offered his arm. "I am at your disposal—lay into me as you will."

Chuckling at the pun, she disclaimed, "I have no intention of laying into you, one way or the other."

They began walking together. "Why are you all on end tonight? You do yourself no favors by antagonizing him."

"I am out of sorts," she acknowledged. "It comes from not being certain I would be allowed to emerge from that basement with a whole skin, I suppose." She shot him a look but he did not return it; he would give nothing away, even for her. "What on earth did Marie tell them to put me into their black books?" It had occurred to her that she should make more of an effort to discover this, as it could have a bearing on Brodie's plan.

"You can appreciate that I'd rather not say," he replied in a mild tone that nevertheless was a rebuke.

She was instantly contrite—he wouldn't be disloyal to his dead wife, and particularly to his new lover who may well be a traitoress. Acknowledging her tactlessness, she took his arm and squeezed it. "I beg your pardon, Lucien—the Vicar has made me irritable and I so wanted to be calm and rational when I spoke to you."

He gave her a searching glance as their footsteps echoed in the silent street. "This does not bode well, I think. There are to be no more card games?"

"I did enjoy the card games," she admitted, smiling at the euphemism, "but I have received the type of unsettling news that requires immediate action."

"Then let me help you." He bent his head to hers, his expression serious.

Realizing he thought she was going to confess her treason, she quickly disabused him. "You have already helped enough, my friend—I am increasing."

As the words sunk in, he stopped abruptly and she walked

on a few paces before turning to face him. They regarded each other for a long moment, their breath creating clouds in the chill air.

"I see," he finally said.

She made a wry mouth. "This is one of those conversations one does not think one will ever have, is it not? I am sorry, Lucien."

He began to walk again and when he came abreast of her, took her hand and tucked it in his arm as she fell into step beside him. "The fault is mine."

"No," she insisted, matching her pace to his as they walked forward. "The fault is mine—I should know better."

He was silent and she took a breath. "I plan to wait a month or so and then retire to Yorkshire to play a war widow—Maisie's people are in Yorkshire." Picturing it with a show of good humor, she lifted her chin and gazed into the starry sky. "I would make a very good war widow—brave and kind with just a trace of pathos, I think. I would do good works and wear kerseymere."

He struggled to ask the question she had been expecting. "Can you be certain—I mean, if the child is Brodie's, it will want for nothing."

She said simply, "Brodie and I have never had that type of relationship. I am afraid you are the sole candidate, my friend."

The silence stretched out a minute or more, which she had expected. News like this must be digested and possible avenues reviewed—it was never productive to make rash decisions or accusations in their business. She allowed him his reverie and then noted that his pace had slowed. The next question she expected was now to be asked.

"And what would you have from me?"

Turning to face him, she met his eyes in the lamplight.

"Nothing," she said with emphasis. "I have my father's pension from the Army and plenty in savings—although not at the Bank of England, which appears to be a good thing. And a small fortune in the sugar box, besides—I need nothing from you; I just thought you should know, is all. If I were a man—" To her horror, her voice started to break. Pausing, she ducked her chin for a moment to regain her equilibrium. She took a breath and her voice was steady again. "Were I a man I would want to know."

"We will marry tomorrow."

Utterly astonished, she stared at his face, which was now set in grim lines. "No, Lucien—I truly would like to go to Yorkshire and try my hand at a quiet life."

He pulled her hand through his arm again and began walking, his words clipped. "What you would like or what I would like no longer matters. We will marry tomorrow."

"I will not," she protested, thoroughly annoyed with his high-handedness. *Mãe de Deus*, but this was unexpected.

"The child needs a father."

"I had thought to look among the local gentry and find one," she assured him.

He stopped so suddenly that she stumbled, and he then pulled her around rather roughly so that she faced his anger head on. "No other man is going to raise my child."

Seeking to soothe him, she continued in an even tone, "I shall write you as often as you like, and I will not marry if it would upset you. Please, Lucien—you must see it would be for the best."

He leaned toward her, his voice tinged with accusation. "Best for whom?"

She answered calmly, "For this child, Lucien. Recall who its mother is."

This gave him pause. "You can change your identity—after all, you have done it before."

Now it was her turn to be shocked, and they stared at each other for a few moments. He turned abruptly. "I will call a hackney—you should not be walking."

Covering her eyes with her palms, she felt as though she was a player in a very bad melodrama. "Lucien. Please, please consider."

But he was implacable. "There is nothing to consider. I shall call at ten o'clock tomorrow and you will be ready to be married."

While he hailed a cab, she stood beside him in silence. Emotions were running high and she would allow him to settle—to think it through. It was complete foolishness to think that the two of them could marry and raise a child together. More than one, perhaps. Blue-eyed children. In acute dismay she reined in her unguarded thoughts and concentrated instead on her careful plan that appeared to be unraveling at the seams. She hadn't informed Brodie of it because he would almost certainly try to argue against it—now it seemed that perhaps she should have asked for his advice. Assessing Carstairs from the corner of her eye she thought, he thinks to rescue me—it is in his nature and I must assure him no rescue is required or even desired.

After handing her into the hackney, he directed the driver and settled in beside her. He must have decided he needed to calm himself because when next he addressed her the words were conciliatory. "You will not regret it, Vidia—I promise you. I shall devote myself to your happiness."

The formal words were sincere but so jarringly out of place that she couldn't help but chuckle at the absurdity.

He joined in with her and the tension was broken as they enjoyed the joke together, his hand taking hers.

"If nothing else," he teased, "we shall be abed whenever possible."

"That would be to the good—I much enjoy being abed with you."

"Then we are agreed?"

She sighed. "I only ask that you think on it, my friend. There is no need to race to the altar, after all. If you are of the same mind in a few months you may visit me at my cottage in Yorkshire in the guise of a suitor—an old Army friend of my dead husband, I think. The old biddies will weep into their handkerchiefs upon witnessing such high romance."

She could see his flashing grin in the dim light but his response remained the same. "We will marry tomorrow. I will call at ten."

She shook her head, bemused by his stubbornness. "I hope you will come to your senses before morning, Lucien. Use those senses, if you please—you do not have a special license."

"I shall have one by tomorrow."

"If you mean to procure the Vicar's services, I must warn you that I suspect he is not truly a vicar." She didn't know if Carstairs was as familiar as she was with the variety of disguises the man assumed.

"He is a vicar, as a matter of fact. But I will not procure his services—I would rather present them with a *fait accompli*; you can appreciate the concern."

Once again she covered her eyes with her palms, thinking of this mad scheme and the certain repercussions from those they worked for. "Yes. They will slay you then slay me then slay you a second time for being so foolish."

He chuckled and they rode for a moment without

speaking, the horse's hooves clattering on the cobblestones and the hackney's cab creaking in the silence. Vidia found that her resolutions were fast ebbing away and so instead she turned over possible scenarios in her mind. "Perhaps we needn't announce it—not immediately," she suggested.

"No, we will announce it immediately." He took her hand in a firm grip.

But she persisted. "If we revealed a secret marriage at a later date it would prevent everyone from counting the months on their fingers."

"Not exactly," he reminded her in a dry tone. "I am recently bereaved."

"Oh—I forgot," she breathed. "Oh, Lucien—what a tangle."

"We shall come about," he assured her. "I will not have a hole-in-corner marriage; everything will be aboveboard."

"Your assignment will be compromised," she warned. "You will be removed forthwith."

Grinning, he disagreed with a tilt of his chin. "On the contrary—I will have given my assignment my all."

She couldn't help but laugh. "Such a sacrifice—and here I thought you wouldn't even remember in the morning."

"Anything for God and country."

As he seemed disinclined to be serious, she gave it one more attempt. "Think, Lucien—you may be furloughed for this rash act; they may not trust you again."

But he was resolute and did not waver. "It cannot be helped—some things are more important than others."

Vidia wasn't sure this was one of them. "Are you certain?"

"I am," he said firmly. "Leave me to have my way in this."

She sighed in resignation. "That was what caused the problem to begin with."

Mãe de Deus, it is all of a piece, Vidia thought crossly as she held aloft her candle. "May I assist you?"

It was late at night and she stood in the cellar of her town house, facing a footman who appeared to be supremely unconcerned by his discovery in such a compromising position. Vidia had been unable to sleep—what with the momentous decision to be made—and decided to wander down to the kitchen to forage for something to eat; she had a sudden desire for brined cucumbers. Thinking she could hear Maisie stirring upstairs, she stole away to the cellar to enjoy her repast but found—much to her astonishment—that the cellar was already occupied. Setting down the candlestick, she sank down upon the step in her nightdress, the cucumbers set aside. "It is Brodie's wine, you know—you would be stealing. I have a good mind to summon the Watch."

The footman stood in the light of the lantern that he had placed on the floor, the grey eyes thoughtful. "I wondered that Brodie would keep his wine in your cellar."

So, she thought, he and Carstairs have compared notes. "There is no place at his hotel, after all—and he needn't fear that I would tipple the more expensive bottles when he was not looking."

"You do not drink?" He opened one of the wine cabinets and surveyed the interior.

"No—I learned my lesson at San Sebastian."

He glanced at her over the cabinet door, and she thought she could discern a grudging admiration in the grey depths. "You are a cool one."

"So you say," she acknowledged humbly. "What is it you seek?"

"Answers," he replied, moving bottles about. "And perhaps a fine Cabernet."

Stifling a yawn, she said, "I am of two minds; shall I go back to bed or shout for Maisie to bring my pistol?"

He raised his head and eyed her. "Not the most loyal of maidservants."

Vidia lifted her chin. "I disagree. She is exactly what she seems—a true rarity, in my experience."

"And as you do not service Brodie, you do not begrudge another the task."

"More like I do not delve into what is none of my business."

"Everything is my business," he replied without remorse. "Make no mistake."

They measured each other for a moment or two, and Vidia decided it was time to make a home thrust. "Do you believe I am working hand in glove with Rochon, then?"

If the question threw him, he betrayed no discomfiture. "What I believe is not your concern."

"I beg your pardon," she apologized. "It is cold and I thought to cut the conversation short."

Closing the doors, he moved on to the next cabinet. "I remain curious as to your unexplained disappearance in France this past fall—I believe it was three days you were out of coverage."

"I was very busy measuring the draperies for Napoleon's summer house." There it was again—as had happened at the meeting, she had a tendency to be insolent when she should be treading warily; it appeared her spymaster brought out the worst in her.

Fortunately, he chose to be amused and returned to his search within the wine cabinet. "You will be the death of me."

"God forfend," she offered piously.

A chuckle could be heard reverberating among the bottles and Vidia began to entertain cautious optimism that she might escape the cellar unscathed. To this end, she redoubled her efforts to appear calm and unfazed—he did seem to admire her coolness.

As he moved bottles and held them up to the light she watched him, saying nothing, and he seemed unconcerned that she was a witness to his search. He noted, "You managed to beguile Carstairs into an escort home—I rather thought the two of you would be occupied upstairs and I could search undetected."

"You are mistaken—I am faithful to a fault." She gave him her slow smile, daring him to find a double meaning. Although she was playing with fire, again he chose to be amused and only shook his head in appreciation.

Placing a bottle on the stone floor next to his lantern, he asked, "How did you know I was here?"

"You are very noisy—you need to work on this, methinks." It wasn't true and he knew it, but the last thing she wanted to do was tell him why she could not sleep. She watched as he opened another cabinet and surveyed the inventory. "Whose livery do you ape?"

He gave her an admonishing look. "Brodie's."

Laughing she exclaimed "Oh—is it indeed? I should know, I suppose."

Crossing his arms on the top of the cabinet door he leaned his long frame upon it and contemplated her. "I note you have no footmen to hand, yourself."

"No, only Maisie. And a cook, for those occasions when no man is plying me with fine food; in truth, I am a simple soul."

"Simple like a succubus," he noted without malice, and resumed his inspection.

Curious, she asked, "Did you leave a means of entry when you tuned the piano?"

He gave her a look over his shoulder that indicated she should know better. "I'll not reveal trade secrets."

She sighed and rubbed her cold arms. "I shall give you a key, if you'd like—it would save a lot of bother."

But he was not to be teased. "Who else has a key?"

She considered. "Brodie; other than that, no one."

"Hagar?"

Her tone suddenly sharp, Vidia retorted, "Her name is Maisie, and I'll not hear you disparage her."

"Your pardon." He straightened up to face her. "You are indeed faithful to a fault."

Vidia pressed her lips together and vowed to give him no more insights. She wished she had thought to bring a robe—her nightdress was only thin cotton. "If you would give a key to the man who watches across the street he could come in to warm himself occasionally."

"He is not mine."

Wondering if he knew, she asked, "Then whose?"

"I'd rather not say, I am afraid. It does seem that you have many admirers."

"A pox on you all," she retorted crossly. "I need my sleep."

"I do not keep you from your bed," he reminded her with a small smile. "Far from it."

Returning his smile, she acknowledged the jest. "All the more reason to catch some sleep when I may."

After standing in place for a few moments, thinking, he clasped his hands behind his back and began to pace, his manner suddenly serious. "What is Brodie's game? I cannot believe he seeks to bring down England."

"No," she agreed. "I cannot believe such a thing, either—perhaps he holds some grudge, and enjoys driving you to distraction."

The other made a sound of impatience. "No—it is not in his nature to seek attention, or even vengeance."

This was undeniably true, and Vidia was impressed by the shrewd observation. She ventured, "He does like having you all on a string, though—he much enjoys the outwitting."

Tossing her a look, he chided, "Have done—you'll not convince me he is bringing about a national crisis for the sport of it."

"No, I suppose not," she agreed in a meek tone.

With an exasperated chuckle, he repeated, "You will be the death of me."

"Or vice versa." She gauged his reaction.

"Perhaps," he agreed, matching her in coolness. "The only thing that stays my hand is that I can't imagine you would support the enemy—not with your history, Libby. When did you change your name?"

Without a tremor she confessed, "San Sebastian."

"Is that where your father was killed?"

"No," she replied. "My husband."

He nodded as if he had already guessed this. "And now you are Invidia—the goddess of vengeance."

She made no response, as it seemed none need be made. His gaze traveled about the room. "How many of the enemy did you kill?"

With a monumental effort, Vidia kept her gaze steady as he surveyed the brick-lined walls. "I do not know—not exactly. More than a few."

He approached to stand directly before her, his eyes hooded and his arms crossed. "I cannot trust you, I'm afraid, which is a drawback in this business. What am I to do with you?"

"Ordinarily," she ventured, "men do not wonder such a thing."

For the first time he lost countenance and allowed his annoyance to show, his voice rough; "Do not cast your lures at me—I know you better than you think."

Alarmed by this show of emotion, she acted to soothe him. "Then tell me how to best reassure you; I have no desire to disappear without a trace."

They regarded each other for a long moment and she had no idea what he was thinking. He finally spoke. "You are fond of Carstairs."

And I carry proof positive, she thought. "Does that create a problem?" She didn't want to make a denial; it would be disingenuous considering they were to wed the next day. *Santos*, she thought with a start; apparently I am going to marry Lucien Carstairs.

He seemed impatient with the idea. "I admit to surprise that Invidia would allow herself the indulgence."

"The snail peeps out."

"I beg your pardon?"

She smiled. "It is naught—shall I firmly quash any tender feelings for the man?"

He shrugged. "You will do as you will—there are times

that I believe it is you who has us all on a string. But I would not have you forget the lesson of Samson's first wife."

Shaking her head so that her mane tumbled around her shoulders, she said in exasperation, "I lack the wit to decipher these riddles of yours."

He turned to fetch the lantern and the bottle he had chosen. "There is nothing lacking about your wits."

As it appeared the interlude was at an end, she stood, a bit stiff. "Am I free to go then? You will not slay me and stuff my corpse in to cool with the champagne?"

He walked up the step and paused beside her, regarding her with a gleam of humor in the grey eyes. "I do not know if I could bring myself to do it, Libby—but do not tempt me."

"Never," she assured him, and wondered how he would react to the news on the morrow. "Save your powder for the enemy, my friend."

"Precisely." With no further comment, he walked past her.

When Carstairs called for her the next morning at ten, Vidia was ready. Having nothing in her wardrobe that was appropriate to wear for the occasion, she managed to pull together a more-or-less demure outfit by the strategic placement of a fichu in the *décolletage* of her least objectionable day dress. She opened the door herself, having sent Maisie on several long and unnecessary errands. The cook, as usual, was not in evidence.

"You look lovely," her bridegroom pronounced, the expression in the blue eyes very warm. He carried a nosegay of hothouse roses and handed them to her, as though she was an ordinary bride and this an ordinary wedding, which was much appreciated.

Breathing in the scent, she tried to quell her butterflies—he was the only man she had ever met who could bestow them. "Confess; you were not certain I would keep the appointment."

"I was not." He tilted his head in rueful acknowledgment. "But I am now the happiest of men."

He was dressed in a morning coat that showed his broad shoulders to advantage and he had taken care with his appearance, his hair was trimmed and his chin clean-shaven. No whisker burn tonight, she thought, suppressing more butterflies. The sight of him—so handsome and correct—brought home the realization that he was willing to dedicate his life to her, despite the circumstances that counseled against it, and it made her breath catch in her throat. It is possible, she thought cautiously, that a small measure of happiness is to be mine, *graças a Deus*.

"Shall we go?" He offered his arm and indicated the carriage waiting at the curb.

"Again, you are rushing me before I change my mind," she teased as she gathered up her reticule and gloves. "At least this time you don't have to manage around your boots."

"It seems the best strategy," he confessed as they descended the front steps, several passersby stopping to admire the handsome couple. "It is all too good to be true and so I want to have it done and quickly."

It was a sweet compliment—considering he could very well be bitterly railing against fate—and so she smiled warmly to reward him. "You make a very handsome bridegroom, Lucien." She wondered what he had worn for his first wedding; she had worn a nightdress.

"And you a beautiful bride—although you would be beautiful even after being pulled through a chimney flue."

"Let us not test your theory."

With a hand at her waist, he saw her settled into the carriage, then bent to solicitously tuck in her skirt so that it wouldn't be caught in the door. "Are you well? Have you suffered any symptoms as yet?"

"I'm afraid I've lost my appetite, but I am forcing the issue as best I can."

His brows drew together in concern. "Perhaps you should consult a physician."

She touched his arm, pleased by this husband-like display. "One traumatic event at a time, Lucien."

Smiling his teasing smile, he climbed into the carriage and sat beside her, rather than across from her, which led her to hope that there would be more kisses coming her way. "Your pardon; last night I could hardly sleep, thinking over your news—our news—and making plans."

"That is to the good—after my war widow plan was scotched I was fresh out."

He gave instruction to the driver, who then closed the door with a snap. "Your war widow plan was nothing short of alarming."

"Never say so," she protested, laughing. "I thought it an excellent plan."

With a sidelong glance, he reminded her, "The last time you wore a widow's veil you inspired a knife fight at the Guildhall in Campine."

She primmed her mouth, her eyes merry. "That was a different situation entirely, and your fault as much as mine—yours and Droughm's. And unlikely to reoccur in the wilds of Yorkshire, as there is no occupying French army to hand."

"Hopefully, we shall never know. Are you comfortable?"

As the carriage started off with a slight jerk, he held her hand in his as he had done last night and she decided it was very agreeable to have him attend her with such patent devotion. I hope this newfound devotion withstands the tests it will be put to, she thought; it would be a shame if it did not—but on the other hand it would be very much in keeping with my luck. "What is our destination?"

"St. Mary's Chapel," he replied. "It is near Greenwich, at the Old Royal Naval Hospital—quiet and simple."

Interesting that he chose a military venue for this clandestine affair, but perhaps it was the best he could do on such short notice—or perhaps he was acquainted with the celebrant. She thought about the enormity of the step they were to take and the certain repercussions when the news was revealed. "We are mad, the both of us."

"No—we are parents, the both of us." He smiled into her eyes, his manner meant to reassure, and she knew a moment's qualm—he was entirely too reconciled to the situation, was Lucien Carstairs. Surely he should have railed and doubted—or at least delayed, given her history?

He must have read her concerns because he leaned his head toward hers and said with quiet emphasis, "You take the proper course—we both do," and gently kissed her mouth. As her pulse leapt, she considered the undeniable fact she almost didn't care what consequences would follow—she knew only that she wanted to belong to the man beside her as she had never wanted anything in her life. To counter this folly she said aloud, "I did not look to take another husband."

He traced her gloved fingers with his own as they swayed along in the well-sprung carriage. "Then we have something in common—I did not look to take another wife."

"I hope you do not make a bad bargain, Lucien." Already he would have to contend with the scandal of this marriage of necessity on the heels of his first wife's death; he was not the sort of man who would appreciate being the object of whispering gossip. She, on the other hand, was well-used to it.

Raising her hand, he bestowed a kiss upon its back. "Then let me consider your merits—you are clever, not given to crochets, and sublime in the bedroom. All in all, I will take my chances."

She smiled, inordinately pleased that he had not included her appearance in his listing. "I could say the same about you, my friend."

"Then we are well-matched."

Leaning back into the cushions, she felt herself begin to relax. "Little did we know—that night we played cards—that the two of us would have little choice but to trust each other, and very soon."

He smiled and cocked his head. "The irony is not lost on me, I assure you."

"Can we, do you think?" She searched his eyes with her own, thinking she would ask nothing more than to be able to trust him. Her natural tendency to be cautious was quickly fading before the sheer exhilaration of this journey and what it meant for her future.

He thought about it—seriously—as they crossed London Bridge to the south bank of the Thames. "I think we can trust each other, given time. It will not be easy to unlearn the habits of a lifetime overnight."

She appreciated this sensible view of the issue, which was in keeping with her own concerns. "No—it will seem like a luxury to trust someone."

"Did you not trust your husband?"

Her face fell, and before she could fashion an answer, he took her hands and interrupted her. "Now, that was clumsy of me; do not answer and instead tell me how you like your eggs—I know so little about you."

With an effort, her smile returned. "Coddled."

"As do I," he pronounced and again kissed the hand in his. "An excellent omen. Coffee or tea?"

"Coffee," she decided. "As the tea may be poisoned."

"Never—poison is a woman's weapon; a man must be more forthright in murdering his wife."

She laughed, delighted with his teasing.

"Boy or girl?"

She looked at him blankly for a moment, and he lifted his brows at her confusion. "The baby."

"Oh. I hadn't considered—I am still coming to terms with the idea, I'm afraid—does it matter to you?"

"A girl," he pronounced. "With her mother's smile."

She found that she could make no rejoinder as her throat had closed with emotion. Instead she lowered her gaze and tightened her grip on his hand. *Graças a Deus*.

Observing her reaction, he bent his head and spoke to her softly. "After I recovered from the initial shock, I find—much to my surprise—that I am looking forward to fatherhood; I hadn't thought it was in my future."

Unable to suppress her curiosity, she looked up at him. "Marie did not conceive?"

"No—and apparently the fault was not mine."

She was surprised by the edge to his tone and he immediately recanted. "That was unkind—pray disregard it."

She did as she was asked but noted the tinge of bitterness he could not conceal. "Will Marie's relatives be shocked by your sudden remarriage?"

"There is no one left to be shocked; she was only survived by a sister and we have little contact. Everyone else died rather suddenly." His tone was now carefully neutral.

Interesting, she thought, as she allowed him to change the subject. Apparently I am not the only one who is steeped in secrets.

The countryside opened up as they approached the park, Queen's House visible on the hill. Rounded white clouds were scattered across the deep blue sky; the daffodils bright along the footpaths. I wonder, she thought as she reviewed the pleasing panorama, if I have should have thought this through a bit more, or at least consulted with Brodie.

"A beautiful day for a wedding," Carstairs observed, drawing her face to his own with a hand on her chin and kissing her.

"Glorious," she agreed.

Chapter 19

The chaplain of St. Mary's Chapel greeted them in a very genial manner, which made Vidia wonder how much money had crossed his palm to bring the ceremony about on such short notice. As introductions were made it did not appear as though Carstairs had a previous acquaintance with the clergyman, and so she surmised the arrangements must have been made strictly for the purpose of having a quiet, out-of-the-way ceremony. And she was heartened by the fact that the chaplain refrained from taking a covert assessment of her appearance as they were introduced—the clergy should exercise some self-restraint, after all.

They were escorted into the rectory office, the chaplain indicating they should be seated while he reviewed the special license and filled out the marriage lines. Sunlight shafted through the diamond-paned windows in the stone walls as Vidia folded her hands in her lap and awaited events. I am not nervous, she assured herself; I am never nervous.

A matronly woman who apparently served as the chaplain's housekeeper had agreed to act as witness, and she stood at the ready while the documents were reviewed. After adjusting his spectacles, the clergyman then looked up at Vidia with a twinkle, his quill poised over parchment. "Name?"

"Miss Invidia Swanson."

"Parish?"

But Carstairs interrupted the recital in a quiet voice. "Your pardon—could you allow us a moment alone, please?"

The chaplain looked with mild surprise from one to the other and rose. "Of course, of course—please signal when you wish to proceed."

He left, carefully closing the door behind him. Vidia watched him leave, then sat and contemplated Carstairs for a long moment while he returned her regard with a steady gaze. He said gently, "We are at *point non plus*, are we not? I think you must give your true name or the marriage will not be legal."

Vidia felt her midsection twist as she decided this was probably true, and could not believe she had not thought of this problem before now—she had acted hastily, and without Brodie's sound advice, and now she was not certain what was best to do. She dropped her gaze to the table, thinking.

Her bridegroom's voice, amused and tender, interrupted her thoughts. "We will have a pact—I will never mention your name to another if you will promise the same to me."

Looking up at him, she nodded, unsurprised that his operative name was not his true name—it was the way of things. But her disclosure would be one she had never made to another—not since San Sebastian.

He dragged his chair closer to hers so that he faced her, their knees almost touching. He took both her hands in his in a playful manner and bent forward as though he would hear a confession. "I am ready—do your worst."

In the silence she could hear the ticking of the mantel clock over the fireplace. Pressing her lips together, she whispered, "Catalina Ana Inacio da Silva." The soft syllables seemed to float in the room, lighter than air. It had been a long time since she had spoken her name. For a moment, she almost thought she could hear her mother's voice, saying it.

He raised his head to meet her eyes in surprise. "I understood your name was Libby."

"No," she said only.

Thinking about it, he asked, "*Portguesa*?"

Nodding, she admitted, "*Si, minha mãe era Português.*"

The blue eyes searched hers while he pondered this. "Then your father was not in the Army?"

"No," she said again, and decided she may as well tell him—or tell him as much as she was able. "My father ran a gaming house. I took the name of another girl I knew in the war after she was killed." She firmly suppressed the vision of the bloody wall that sprang to her mind's eye,; the memory of the synchronized crack of the rifles.

Rubbing his thumbs across the backs of her hands, he studied her thoughtfully. "And her name was Invidia?"

She swallowed, and said through stiff lips. "No. Her name was Libby—Libby Swanson." Lifting her gaze to the far upper corner of the room, she fought the misery that threatened to overwhelm her and carefully withdrew her hands from his. "I cannot go through with this," she said quietly. "But I appreciate the gesture, Lucien."

He was instantly contrite and placed his fingers under her chin so as to turn her face back to his, the expression in his eyes concerned and sincere. "The fault is mine—here I am, pressing when I promised I would not. Forgive me, Vidia—it matters not a whit to me and I have upset you."

She stared at him, close enough to see his long, dark eyelashes and the stubble of his beard in the cleft of his chin—it must be difficult to shave it. She could not find two thoughts to rub together.

"My own name is Luc-Damien."

This brought her from her reverie. "Is it indeed?"

He gave a rueful smile. "It is a long tradition—my ancestors came over from Normandy with William the Conqueror, but you can appreciate why I do not use it."

She could—it sounded very French, which was not a good thing, nowadays.

"Tell no one," he teased, squeezing her hands.

"My hand on my heart," she agreed absently. Impossible to think rationally whilst he sat so close.

Lifting her hand, he kissed her fingers. "Was your first marriage valid?"

She blinked. "Yes—yes it was."

"Then I believe you hold his last name, at present."

"Oh. Of course." With a monumental effort, she righted herself. "McCord, then—Catalina McCord."

His gaze intent upon hers, he said quietly, "Catalina McCord, I would very much like to marry you—if you will have me."

He means it, she thought. And if he doesn't, it hardly matters; I am lost. "I will."

And so the chaplain was duly notified that Catalina Ana McCord, an unregistered widow, was to marry Luc-Damien Michel Dessiere, a widower of Sussex. Which is strange, thought Vidia, as she stood beside him and the ceremony in the quiet chapel commenced. I could swear he told me Suffolk.

At the ceremony's conclusion he presented her with a very pretty ring, set with three small rose-cut diamonds. "Not what you are used to," he noted as he slipped it on her finger.

"But worth far more," was the sincere reply as she lifted her face for his kiss. I have married Lucien Carstairs, she thought with wonder, and could hardly credit her good luck. How fortunate that I am fertile, so as to be given the opportunity.

The chaplain congratulated them, the housekeeper signed as witness, and then they were back in the carriage and away, the towers of the Royal Naval Hospital disappearing behind them as they headed back to Belgrave. Once the deed was done, Vidia felt a rush of confidence replace all the qualms she had suffered leading up to the ceremony. As Carstairs had said, they took the proper course—she must learn not to be so wary that she imagined danger in every shadowed corner.

He kissed her soundly, a gleam of amusement lighting his eyes. "We had best get our story straight."

She had also been thinking of how to break this alarming news to those who must hear it. "The truth, I think. There would be little point to making up a tale, after all. Shall we beard the Vicar and the Curate together?"

But he shook his head. "Allow me—some awkward questions may be asked."

She leaned toward him, willing to show her support. "Are you certain? I excel at turning aside awkward questions—you need only ask the Vicar."

"Thank you, but I'd rather have my hair trimmed alone, I think. On your end, shall I leave you to break the news to Brodie—or do you wish for reinforcements?"

"Allow me," she repeated his own words back to him. "Some awkward questions may be asked."

They smiled at each other and he bent to kiss her again. Tonight, she thought, melting into his kiss, I'll be abed with him—he who is now my husband and will be abed with me on a nightly basis. She felt the stirrings of desire and asked, "Shall we plan to meet up for dinner? If I can find my new cook, I'll request something appropriate for a wedding celebration."

But her companion raised a skeptical brow. "I can't imagine Brodie will allow me to take up residence in your town house."

"He has no grounds to object," she assured him, slightly surprised by the objection. "Remember—the house is mine in fee."

There was a small silence. "I confess I would not feel comfortable living in the house that Brodie gave to you—surely you can understand." His smile was apologetic.

Hiding her dismay at confronting yet another issue she should have thought through, Vidia gave him her most beguiling smile. "I'm sorry, Lucien—but for my part I don't know if I could be comfortable in the home you shared with Marie."

He ran a finger along her cheek. "We needn't decide just yet—I had thought first to bring you to meet my family in Sussex."

Mãe de Deus, thought Vidia, I have been outmaneuvered. "That sounds lovely, Lucien. I shall look forward to it."

He was gracious in victory. "Shall I speak to Brodie as one man to another? Would that make it easier for you?"

Smiling, Vidia said, "I too shall take the trimming alone, I believe." And throw myself on Brodie's mercy, she added silently. We'll need a new plan, and quickly.

Chapter 20

Looking up at Vidia in astonishment, Brodie slowly set aside the newspaper he was reading. "Well then—allow me to call for champagne."

"None for me," she reminded him as she sank down in the chair beside him. "And there is no one to call—Maisie is from home."

They sat together in silence for a moment while she allowed him to process the startling news. "This is sudden," he observed, his benign gaze upon her.

"You have no idea—I did not know of it myself, at this time yesterday."

Upon hearing this, he leaned forward and clasped his hands between his knees, assessing her narrowly. "Was this your wish, *Bela*? Tell me the truth, if you please."

"Yes," she assured him with complete sincerity, her gaze steady upon his. "My hand on my heart, Benny."

After a careful review he nodded, satisfied. "Yes—I did have a feeling you had met your fate in our Mr. Carstairs." He rose and made his way to the sideboard to rattle the glasses. "Some cider then—we shall celebrate."

Reading him aright, she confessed, "I was afraid you'd deter me with sensible advice, so I didn't tell you."

"You were always unpredictable, *Bela.*" He poured the cider and brought over the glasses, raised his to her and toasted, "To your happiness, Mrs. Carstairs."

"It is not a trap," she said with some firmness, watching him.

But he only said mildly, "I have no doubt it is not—you would never be so foolish."

She set down her glass. "I fear I have been foolish, Benny—he wishes me to take a wedding trip to visit his family in Sussex and I hadn't considered such a possibility."

Raising his brows, he thought this over. "When would you return?"

"I shall be certain to return for the sailing of the *Argo*," she assured him. "Sussex is not so very far away—only let me know when I must be in London and I promise I will be here—by hook or by crook."

He nodded as he gazed out the window for a moment. "I am not certain it would be wise to give you any details ahead of time."

Dismayed, she stared at him for a moment and then shook her head with vehemence. "I would never tell Carstairs anything about it, Benny—you know I would not—even if I trusted him."

Brodie's hand stilled on his glass. "You do not trust him?"

She sighed, thinking there was nothing for it—Brodie needed to know. "He was involved in the attempted seizure at Carlton House."

Sinking back in his chair with a deliberate movement, Brodie did not attempt to hide his astonishment. "*Bela*, you have run mad."

Fingering her wedding ring, she met his eyes with a smile. "Not quite as mad as it appears—I am afraid it is a marriage of necessity."

After a surprised pause, his brows drew together. "Never say he took advantage of you?"

She quirked her mouth. "More like I took advantage of him."

His brow cleared. "Well then; he poor fellow did not stand a chance—my further congratulations."

He leaned forward, his glass aloft, and she tapped it with her own, grateful that he was willing to pretend she had not thrown an enormous spoke in the wheel of his carefully laid-out plans. "It is rather a shock—but it seems I am bound to retire from the lists, one way or another."

Nodding, he conceded, "It does put paid to my Venice plan—I had hope of overcoming your objections."

She ran a finger along the rim of the glass. "I was planning to go live in Yorkshire to raise the child, Benny—truly I was—but I thought I owed it to Carstairs to tell him—"

"You were always deplorably noble, *Bela.*" Brodie shook his head in disapproval.

"And he insisted we marry immediately; he hasn't even told our people as yet. I imagine they will be very unhappy with him."

Brodie lowered his gaze to the contents of his glass as he swirled the cider and made no comment.

Watching him, Vidia sighed with resignation. "What are you thinking—tell me the truth, *por favor.*"

He lifted his head to meet her gaze. "I think it very fortuitous that you are now subject to Mr. Carstairs's authority, your house will be left vacant, and you will be inaccessible to me."

But she shook her head, unable to believe the implication. "Come, Benny—he had little choice, as an honorable man. He certainly didn't plan to have a hurried wedding and an eight months baby—not with his wife just dead."

But Brodie was unconvinced and raised his glass in a mock salute. "One can only admire his initiative and flexibility."

"Benny," she protested.

"I wonder," he said thoughtfully, "if such initiative and flexibility can be used to our advantage."

"I'll not allow you to use him ill," she warned, alarmed by the tack the conversation had taken.

"*Bela*," he chided gently. "The man is your chosen husband—acquit me of wishing to use him ill. But perhaps matters may be arranged so as to bring everyone's interests to a satisfactory conclusion—including the enterprising Mr. Carstairs."

Suspicious, she eyed him. "I am given to understand you like to work alone."

He returned her gaze with a benign eye. "I do work alone. But I can be unselfish." Leaning his chair back on its legs, he contemplated the view out the window for a moment. "Go to Sussex for your bride visit—where exactly will you be?"

"I am afraid I am not certain," she confessed, feeling foolish. *Deus*, but Carstairs had taken her by surprise. "Shall I leave Maisie in the house here whilst I am away? She can man the ramparts."

But he shook his head. "No—take her; I imagine you will need reinforcements."

"I can handle any number of mothers-in-law," Vidia assured him.

His hands in his pockets, he kept his gaze fixed out the window. "It is not his relatives I am worried about."

She wouldn't argue with him anymore—he was too often right. "I shall be wary, Benny."

He brought his chair back down to the floor with a snap and changed the subject, his expression merry. "Plain Mrs.

Carstairs of Sussex—and here I thought you could look to ensnare minor European royalty at the very least."

She replied in a mild tone, "No, thank you—I do not have pleasant memories of Europe."

"No," he agreed, and they sat in silence for a moment.

Brodie set his glass down suddenly. "A wedding gift—I must think of something appropriate."

"Benny," she warned. "Pray bring no more trouble down upon me."

"*Bela*," he responded in a wounded tone. "I cannot allow the occasion to pass unacknowledged."

"You terrify me," she replied dryly. "And remember I have a husband's sensibilities to consider now."

But Brodie's eyes were alight, thinking over possibilities. "It must be something worthy of this series of blessed events you have managed to bring about."

She tilted her head in a conciliatory gesture. "I didn't have much of a hand in the managing, I'm afraid. I am sorry about this coil, Benny."

But Brodie was unflappable—as always. "Not to worry, all is in train—a pox on all warmongers for requiring such exertions of me."

"Confess," she teased him. "You enjoy the exertions—and the rewards."

His chest rising and falling, he sighed hugely. "This one shall be particularly rewarding—when this little rabbit is snared. A fouler man never walked the earth."

Sobering, she nodded in agreement. "You will be careful, Benny?"

"*Bela*," he chided in a reproachful tone, "when have you known me to be careful?"

"Forgive me," she said with a smile. "I forget myself."

He raised his glass to her again, his eyes gleaming. "Never fear—Invidia shall once more have her revenge."

Toasting him in return with a graceful tilt of her wrist, she returned, "And you shall have yet another fortune—and well-deserved."

"To your future."

A bit mistily, she confessed, "I wouldn't have one without you—do not think for a moment that I am not aware of it."

"*Bela*," he warned her with distaste. "Pray don't be maudlin."

Smiling, she offered, "Well then—to your future as well, Benny. *Saude*."

"*Saude*," he agreed, and drank.

Chapter 21

When Vidia broke the news to her maidservant the reaction was not unmixed. "He married ye?" Maisie breathed, and sat down abruptly on the dressing room chair, staring at her mistress in dismay and unconsciously twisting the corner of her apron. "Are ye sure?"

Laughing, Vidia protested, "Lord, Maisie—of course I am sure. And I have the ring to show for it." She displayed it with some pride—truly, it was a very pretty ring.

"Gar," said Maisie, much taken aback. "Yer wed."

"Indeed," agreed Vidia. "The deed was done in two shakes—he proposed immediately upon hearing my news, which was chivalrous of him and not at all what I expected."

"An' me all unknowin'." Maisie was having some trouble assimilating the change in Vidia's circumstances, her eyes fixed on the ring as though it was a venomous reptile.

"We thought it best," Vidia soothed. "We didn't want word to get out." Vidia diplomatically didn't specify who would have carried word to whom. Smiling, she teased, "So now I suppose I must learn to be respectable, and hold house."

The other woman raised her eyes to Vidia's, dubious. "Can ye, d'ye think?"

Laughing again, Vidia observed, "Well, if I can run a rig to keep the Flemish ambassador from stealing the weapons he was supposed to be sending to Wellington, I suppose I can organize linens. After all, the ambassador's extraction did involve the laundry chute."

"If ye say so," her henchwoman agreed, twisting the other corner of her apron.

"Now—here's faint praise," Vidia chided her gently. "You do not seem very happy about this turn of events, Maisie—and I thought you were urging me to find a fine husband who would appreciate me."

"I'm that happy fer ye, missy," Maisie offered in a doubtful tone.

"Missus," Vidia corrected her with a fond smile. "Mrs. Carstairs." She said it with relish; such a nice sounding name, it was.

Maisie swallowed, pale of lip.

Hiding a smile, Vidia decided to be merciful. "I have already broken the news to Mr. Brodie and he is very pleased."

Lifting her brows, Maisie sat up and was cautiously optimistic. "Is he?"

"Drank a toast to my future happiness," Vidia assured her. "I honestly believe he is relieved to have me off his hands—he is a restless soul and doesn't like to stay in one place very long." This said as a veiled warning, in the event Maisie was under any misapprehensions about Brodie's nature.

Belatedly realizing that she sat while her mistress stood, Maisie rose to her feet, folding her hands under her apron so as to consider the situation. "Are ye sure he's not hidin' a broken heart?"

Vidia was blunt. "Brodie has no heart." Best that Maisie be aware—although she did not seem the romantic sort.

But her henchwoman insisted stubbornly, "He is that fond o' ye—I am sure of it."

"Yes," Vidia agreed. "He is—I am a valuable asset."

Maisie knit her brow, not understanding her meaning, but Vidia had moved on to the next topic. "Mr. Carstairs is taking me to Sussex to meet his family and I believe he plans to leave in the morning, so best get us packed."

"Sussex," mused Maisie, thinking over the practicalities. "How long a stay?"

"No more than a week, with any luck." Vidia crossed to her armoire and, opening the doors, reviewed her extensive wardrobe. "I cannot play the blushing maiden, but I can certainly play the respectful and grateful daughter-in-law."

"If ye say," said Maisie agreeably. "Wearin' what, exactly?"

Vidia made a wry face. "*Touché*, my friend—I shall leave it to your capable talents." Maisie may not be the most satisfactory of maids but she was an excellent seamstress, having learned the skill as a necessity, patching together uniforms taken from the fallen during the war.

Thinking aloud of what needed to be done, her maidservant muttered, "I'll be needin' to buy ready-made, an' make some alterations—ye can't be respectable in yer silks and satins. And ye'd best pull that hair o' yers back tight—and wear a cap." She eyed it askance but Vidia was comforted by the knowledge that Carstairs very much enjoyed running his hands through her hair and would do so nightly from now on.

"Spend whatever is necessary and do your worst, my friend, as long as I make a good impression on his mother. I don't want Mr. Carstairs to regret this straightaway."

"Never say so; he's a lucky man to have ye," Maisie insisted, stung. "His family will think he carried off the prize, once they see ye."

"Not if they can count to nine on their fingers."

"Nowt the first time sech a thing has happened," reflected her maid, unperturbed as she began to thumb through the armoire. "And besides, who's to say whether the babe comes early—they do sometimes."

Sighing, Vidia confessed, "I thank you for your support, Maisie, but I don't think I have yet mentioned that his first wife died a few short weeks ago."

Nonplussed, Maisie turned to stare at her. "Is that so?"

With a rustle of taffeta petticoats, Vidia sank into the chair her maid had vacated. "They shall think me a Jezebel—and no help for it; I may as well wear my silks and satins and play the role with relish."

"Nonsense," retorted her maid stoutly, even though Vidia suspected she was taken aback by this disclosure. "Nowt the first time sech a thing as that has happened, either—handsome widowers are always snapped up; the menfolk dinna like to be alone."

"He is very handsome," Vidia agreed with a smile, willing to be distracted from contemplating the awkward situation ahead. "He shall come for dinner, so pray warn the cook, and I would like you to find the nightdress I wore to distract the French master-at-arms while the horses were being stolen."

"Hardly a nightdress," Maisie noted.

"But fit for the purpose—I don't think he plans to stay tonight and I hope to change his mind."

"That'll do it—if he's alive and a man." The maid bent to rummage through a wardrobe chest. "Where's he to stay, if not here?"

Vidia said airily, "It was all so spur of the moment—and since we are leaving tomorrow he thinks to put his affairs in order." Best not to mention her new husband refused to abide at her residence—one shocking revelation at a time for her beleaguered servant. “To this end, I would like a bath, if you don’t mind—and let’s perfume the water.”

Maisie was not worried about the success of these machinations as she shook out the gossamer nightdress. “He’ll never be able to resist ye—he’s yer lawful husband, after all.”

Vidia bent to unlace her shoes. “And as I am in dire need of a husband, I count my own luck. Otherwise I would have been forced to throw myself upon your mercy, Maisie—thank heaven you didn’t desert me in my hour of need.”

Placing a can of water on the hearth to warm, Maisie dragged the hip bath forward. “Of course I couldn’t desert ye—ye have no more sense than a kitten about how to care for a bairn.”

“Too true.” Vidia thought it best not to mention that Maisie, being childless, was by no means an expert.

As the water warmed, her servant also warmed to the subject, her hands on her hips. “Did I desert ye at Pamploma? An’ with me havin’ to shoot a gun an’ pretend to be a soldier in knee breeches? I should say not.”

“You did not—most would have refused such a humiliating episode.”

“An’ the fire jack incident—did I wash my hands of ye then?” Maisie tested the water’s temperature with a forefinger, a twinkle in her eye.

“I shall never forget the fire jack,” Vidia assured her, peeling off her clothes and smiling at the memory. “The poor man was addled for an hour.”

“And Calais? Did I desert ye in Calais, when I thought we was to drown fer sure—havin’ to hold our breath and hope they couldn’t see us well enough t’ shoot us in the water?”

“No,” Vidia agreed, stepping into the bath as Maisie steadied her. “It was a rare wonder—you had every incentive.”

"No more o' that kind o' life," pronounced Maisie, rinsing Vidia's hair with a ladle. "Yer a married lady now—and a mum, besides."

"Another rare wonder—I have yet to come to terms with it." Vidia closed her eyes and enjoyed the feel of the warm water cascading down her back. "What was your wedding day like, Maisie?"

Maisie paused in her ministrations and waxed thoughtful. "Quiet-like—me da had died so's it were a small weddin' breakfast." She resumed ladling the water with a steady rhythm. "'T'were a grand day, all the same."

Wonderfully grand, thought Vidia in agreement, and felt her throat close with emotion. "Was it a love match, you and your Jem?"

Maisie chuckled. "I suppose ye could say so. He loved me da's farm."

Vidia met her amused gaze. "He married you for your inheritance?"

"An' I was right grateful. I weren't a pretty thing, like yerself. I got me a fine husband and he got a fine farm."

Vidia stared at her, suddenly stricken, and said slowly, "Because as your husband, your property became his."

"The men handle the property," Maisie agreed, scrubbing with a sponge. "'Tis the way o' things."

Mãe de Deus, thought Vidia. The men own the property.

Chapter 22

Vidia was surprised by her emotions, and she hadn't thought she was capable of being surprised, which only surprised her all the more. She found that she was nervous waiting for Carstairs to arrive and unsure of how to play it—never having had an assignment that fit this particular situation.

She answered the door herself when he arrived so that Maisie wouldn't overhear them. "Lucien." She rose on her tiptoes to kiss him—which she deemed to be the appropriate conjugal gesture. After the barest hesitation, he leaned down to meet her lips with his, leading her to believe he was unsure of his own role as well. "I must give you a key," she teased. "Although I am not certain you need one."

Matching her teasing tone he replied, "Note that I come through the front door like a proper visitor this time—I am trying to make a good impression."

"I appreciate the gesture, husband, although I would welcome you through any window at any time." She cast him a wicked glance under her lashes to remind him of the lovemaking in her room that night, and wondered if they could move dinner ahead.

He kissed her once more, quickly, and then walked into the parlor to the sideboard, where he poured himself a whiskey with no further ado. Vidia watched his movements and decided he must be suffering from the same uncertainties as she; well—there was no time like the present to address them. Walking up behind him, she touched his sleeve. "This is strange, is it not? I would like to start as we mean to go on—but I'm not certain how that should be."

With relief, she saw that he knew exactly what she meant as he nodded and turned to her. "There are so many levels of deception that we are not certain how we should present to one another."

"Exactly." He stood so close; she had to curb that familiar feeling of breathlessness in his presence—at the thought of being abed with him again. "How should we go on?"

Placing his glass on the sideboard with a click, he gently held her arms above the elbows and met her gaze with his own steady one. "I suggest we attempt to be honest with each other—or as honest as we can possibly be."

"I am nervous," she confessed. "And that's the honest truth."

"You are famous for your coolness." He drew his hands down her arms and took her hands in his. "I am a bit shocked."

"I haven't been nervous in a long time—I think I haven't cared so much about anything in a long time."

His expression unreadable, he gazed into her eyes for a long moment. "It is a good sign then—your nervousness." He tilted his head. "On the other hand—I am not so much nervous as browbeaten."

"Oh—Lucien, was it terrible?"

"Worse," he admitted. "The church hierarchy is up in arms."

"Are they?" she leaned forward to hide her face in his coat and breathe in his scent. "I cannot confess to surprise. Were they furious?"

She could feel him sigh. "My judgment was called into

question in graphic terms. In particular, the Vicar puts you on a level with the Antichrist."

She lifted her face to his, trying to lighten the moment. "Surely not—I told Maisie I am more along the lines of a Jezebel."

He gestured toward the settee, indicating they should sit, and kept his arm around her as they walked across the room. "I am afraid I have orders—as do you."

Making a wry mouth, she settled on the settee. "I am ready, husband—do your worst."

His answering smile did not quite reach his eyes. "The Vicar is very unhappy that you have compromised your assignment with Brodie, and he wishes for you to stay indefinitely with my family."

She bowed her head in mock chagrin, hiding her dismay behind an easy manner. "Behold the errant bride." As Brodie had predicted, she was to be made inaccessible—it was a bit unsettling to have it confirmed. No matter—she would contrive to attend the launch of the *Argo*; Brodie felt it important that she be present and so she would be. The small matter of her husband's authority over her would have to be circumvented for the greater good.

Carstairs gently clasped her arm with his fingers and tried to soften the blow. "I think it is more an exercise in caution—as you are no longer in a condition to work, he would like you to be isolated elsewhere."

"In the event I am indeed tattling to Rochon." She watched for his reaction, but he remained matter-of-fact.

"Yes. In the event."

She kept her tone light; no need to quarrel on their wedding night. "Where is my Sussex exile?" Brodie needed to be informed before they left; they had to be certain that she could be contacted.

"Near Fairlight, which is a coastal village near Hastings in East Sussex. We leave tomorrow morning."

Mustering a smile, she assured him, "I anticipated as much—Maisie is frantically putting together a semi-suitable wardrobe; I'm afraid there's not much I can salvage from my current assignment."

The blue eyes searched hers for a moment, their expression very serious. "We are being honest with one another," he reminded her.

"We are," she agreed, and wondered if it was true.

"Are you tainted?"

Time for pound dealing, she thought, hiding her surprise at the blunt question. "No. Are you?"

"No," he replied.

"Well then—that's settled."

With a small smile, he ducked his chin. "I had to ask."

Vidia sighed. "Your late wife's legacy; Marie, you did me no favors."

With a shrug, he ventured, "Perhaps she overheard something and misunderstood."

"Or perhaps she sought to cause me trouble." After the words had come out, she realized she should temper her comments. "I beg your pardon, Lucien—I did not know her well and am judging her harshly, I'm afraid."

Gazing into the fire, he rubbed a hand absently across her shoulder. "I will tell you about her, some day—but not just yet."

She was silent, wondering if she would be called upon to speak of Sergeant Tim McCord; she sincerely hoped not.

Maisie appeared before them and bobbed her awkward curtsey. "Dinner is served."

Vidia hid a smile at Maisie's attempt at formality and asked Carstairs, "Are you hungry after your trimming?"

"I am—I feel lucky to have survived." He smiled at the maidservant. "I will eat anything you put before me, Maisie."

"Yessir." Another bob and she departed for the kitchen.

Vidia explained, "She will be less nervous when she becomes accustomed—it has been just the two of us for so long."

It could not have been more evident that Maisie was a fish out of water and as they stood he asked, "How did you come to have her?"

As this was an entertaining tale, she recited it at length through the course of their meal, Vidia warming to the ordinariness of the interaction. This is how I play this, she thought, hiding her relief. We are like any other new-married pair—putting together our routine and feeling our way toward what will soon become normal—although in very little time, normal will include a baby. And Sussex in-laws. Deciding she'd rather not think about it just now, she focused instead upon entertaining her new husband.

At the end of the tale, Carstairs leaned back in his chair and expressed his admiration for their ingenuity in stalling the French army. "Had you previous experience with cows, Maisie?"

Maisie nodded as she cleared away the dishes. "Oh, I knows me cows, sir—I be from Masham."

"And do you know your cows?" he asked Vidia with a smile.

She wondered if he was once again probing for information and so gave a light answer. "I became particularly well-acquainted with the cow I hid beside—I smelt of her for days."

"That ye did," Maisie agreed.

With good humor, Carstairs crossed his arms before him.

"For shame—you should not mock her for her service—instead Wellington should have awarded a commendation—a cow-commendation."

Laughing, Vidia replied, "I cannot disagree; she was completely uncowed by Messena's curses, and held her assignment so well I could swear she knew exactly what was at stake."

He chuckled at the pun. "I understand completely—my own horse recruited me and I had little choice in the matter."

"How was this?" She realized she was hungry to hear personal anecdotes from him and leaned forward, her elbows on the table as the candle burned low.

Carstairs reached to finger his wineglass and smiled at the memory. "It was near Burgos; my old horse had been shot out from under me, poor fellow, and I lay stunned in the snow until I felt Whistlejacket's nose prodding me back into action. He had no sympathy for my wounds and insisted I mount up and get on with it."

Vidia was delighted with the tale. "Whose was he?"

"I have no idea but I suspect he is Andalusian—I speak Spanish to him so that he doesn't realize he turned coat."

She shook her head, laughing. "Clever horse—he anticipated the future." The French had later betrayed Spain, its former ally, and the enraged Spanish had proved difficult for Napoleon's harried troops to subdue in the bloodbath that followed.

Carstairs smiled in turn. "That is true—perhaps he knew that if he threw in with me he would manage to avoid Saragossa." The reference was to an infamous battle in the streets of the Spanish town where over sixty thousand had died.

Vidia made no reply and dropped her gaze, struggling.

"What is it?" he asked, alert to her dismay. "Never say you were at Saragossa?"

"No," she replied with an effort, and raised her eyes to meet his again. "No," she said again, shaking her head and unwilling to give him any insights. "Where did Whistlejacket go instead?"

Carstairs allowed her to shift the subject. "He found himself at Cadiz; then he spent some time in the hills of the Sierra Morena."

Vidia nodded—she already knew that Carstairs had been in the thick of the *guerrilla* fighting in the southern Spanish provinces, aligned with the legendary El Halcon. The notorious *guerrilla* fighters, using ambush and stealth, had been instrumental in turning the course of the war. Not that Vidia wished to give the Spanish any credit at all—the *bastardo*; Portugal had suffered much at the hands of the Spanish and so had she.

While she was lost in her thoughts, Carstairs reached over to lay a hand on hers. "Tired?" he asked gently. "It has been a busy day."

She brightened. "Shall we go to bed, then?"

"Allow me a nightcap," he equivocated, indicating his empty wineglass.

Vidia blinked, hoping he didn't mean to send her to bed without him. "Willingly—allow me to serve." She stood to take his glass and if the movement caused her cleavage to be displayed to full advantage—well, it couldn't be helped. Unfortunately he appeared not to notice and his gaze did not linger on her breasts. *Deus*, she thought as she went to fetch the bottle; but this is a very strange wedding night.

Her legs drawn up beneath her, Vidia sat with her new husband by the firelight in the parlor and watched the shadows flicker across his face. He had been quieter than his usual, and he seemed rather tired—which was not surprising, considering the scramble to arrange for the wedding, the confrontation with their superiors, and the no doubt unwelcome news that he was soon to be a father. No matter what he told her, such a turn of events would be the last thing desired at this juncture in his life, newly bereaved and with Napoleon showing signs of rattling his sword yet again. I am so lucky, she thought, that he is a decent man—a rare breed, in my experience. She vowed to be as cooperative as possible, to show him that he would have nothing to regret. "Should I have the cook pack a box lunch for the journey tomorrow?"

He roused himself from his thoughts, and took her hand. "No—I only need to send word to the posting inn at Tunbridge Wells, which is where we will stop for luncheon. We shall stay the night at an inn near Fairlight—an historic site with an impressive prospect, situated as it is on the ocean cliffs. Then the next day we'll travel to my family's manor house, which is about ten miles farther down along the coast."

Vidia hid her alarm and tried to hold fast to her good

intentions; Brodie was right, she was to be kept isolated in the wilds—but there was no help for it and she'd best face facts. "I shall have to cashier my cook, which is just as well. He was never much in evidence; mainly he played penny-a-point with the footman next door."

Her companion seemed very much amused by this disclosure, a smile playing around his lips as he turned her hand over and ran a finger along her palm. "Yes—I'm afraid you will have to become accustomed to plain fare, and there is little need for a cook."

"I'll not complain; I ask only to gain an appetite again." Indeed, her favorite meal from childhood had been when her mother had taken a small fish and wrapped it in acacia leaves; setting it beside the fire until it nearly melted apart.

"I will contact the local physician once you are in residence—I'm afraid there are no specialists in such a rural area and he is rather elderly, but he will have to suffice."

Vidia nodded and reflected in amusement that Carstairs didn't seem aware that he was painting a rather grim picture of her future home. Small matter; she had lived very simply, once, and certainly could do so again. Of course, it was a bit unsettling to think she would be brought to childbed at his family home, away from anything familiar. And if the war re-erupted—as they all expected it would—he would be called into action and she would be left to her own devices, living among strangers. Perhaps her mother-in-law would be a kind and helpful woman to make up for the loss of her own. "I imagine your poor mother will be a bit shocked to be confronted with a new daughter-in-law so quickly."

But this seemed to be another ominous topic. Carefully choosing his words, he replied, "She will be pleased with you—how could she not, with a grandchild on the way?"

This seemed faint praise and she smiled in the hope that he would confide in her—best to know the terrain before the battle. "You are withholding information, my friend. Is your mother such a dragon, then?"

He squeezed her hand to reassure her. "No—forgive me; it is nothing like that. Instead, she is ill, and rather an invalid."

My wretched tongue, thought Vidia in contrition. "I am sorry, Lucien—I didn't mean to make light."

He let out a breath. "She cannot travel and has little stamina; indeed, I am pleased to have this excuse to make a brief visit—I have been remiss."

This was a good sign, she assured herself; that he was kind to his mother. "As long as I do not pose such a shock that her condition worsens—does she know of the baby?"

He gazed into the fire and absently fingered her hand. "Not as yet—I have only sent word that I come to visit. I thought it best to present you in person, so that there will be no anticipatory doubts."

"A wise strategy, then." Again, he didn't seem to realize he was casting a rather grim prospect, and a small doubt began to tug at the corner of her mind—it was almost as though he was purposefully presenting a daunting description of the foreseeable future. She placed a hand on his knee, thinking of how she would give anything to have her own mother back again, ill or not. "I will see to it she is well looked after."

He covered her hand with his own. "Thank you. You are very kind."

There was a small pause while the fire crackled and Vidia tried to ignore that doubt, tugging away. We are married, she finally decided, and we agreed to strive for honesty. She asked gently, "Why are you so uneasy, Lucien?"

He did not pretend to misunderstand and turned to meet her eyes, the expression in his own rather grave. "I think I am sorry for you—sorry for the sudden changes in your life, and my role in bringing them about."

This had the ring of truth, and she was almost relieved—there had been something a bit off about the conversation, about the picture he painted of his home; it was not like him to be unaware of the impact his words would have. "It is as you said—fate has stepped in, and what I want or what you want doesn't matter anymore; we take what is given us and make our lives. I promise I will have no regrets; indeed, I look forward to sinking into obscurity—it will be a novel experience for me."

He drew her to him and she rested her head upon his shoulder as they watched the fire in companionable silence. After thinking over what he had told her for a time, she decided she was tired of thinking and would put this new husband of hers to good use. "Will you excuse me for a moment?"

He rose with her and she exited the room, having decided that more direct tactics were needed to move this wedding night along. For heaven's sake, it wasn't as though the man needed to be considerate of his new bride's sensibilities—they had already spent two torrid nights together and she was rather surprised he hadn't initiated a new session then and there on the settee—he was not one to be bashful about it.

"It is time to bring in the heavy artillery," she told Maisie, who was hovering in Vidia's room. "The man is being too polite."

"He does seem very kind," offered Maisie, bringing out Vidia's nightdress. "He probably doesn't want to throw ye about—not just yet."

"Be that as it may, I am dying to throw him about, so

please make yourself scarce." Pulling on the diaphanous confection, Vidia regarded her image in the mirror with approval as the whisper-light folds fell around her body. It was nearly transparent and more than appropriate for a wedding night between two people who need no longer be coy.

Her hair falling nearly to her waist, Vidia padded in her bare feet back to the parlor, hiding a smile as she anticipated her bridegroom's reaction. Stepping softly, she saw that Carstairs was contemplating the dregs of his wineglass and appeared to be deep in thought. She casually moved into the room as though she was still wearing her day dress, and crossed before the fire to pour herself a cider at the sideboard. Sensing his gaze upon her, she felt her pulse quicken—she always loved a good diversion.

"Mrs. Carstairs," he finally said. "You would tempt a monk."

She noted he hadn't moved. "I seek to tempt my husband," she explained in a mild tone, leaning against the sideboard and bending a knee slightly so that her bare leg was exposed through the slit in the nightdress.

There was a pause while she saw that his gaze remained firmly locked on her face. "I cannot think it a good idea, I'm afraid."

"No?" She took a sip of the cider.

Shaking his head with regret he cautioned, "First we should speak with a physician—I will take no chances."

She tilted her head to one side and regarded him thoughtfully. "I believe you and I have both known girls who continue with bed sport long past the time when their bellies are evident."

But he was resolute. "I only wish to be certain—it is too important, Vidia."

Hanging her head in mock disappointment, she made a gesture with her hands. "And this my best nightdress."

He let out a pent-up breath. "I cannot argue; I hope to see it many a time."

She noted he did not approach although he was aroused—she knew the signs. A very stubborn man, it seemed; a strategic retreat was in order. Straightening up, she said in a mild tone, "I will see you on the morrow, then. Good night."

He gave her his quick, flashing smile. "I doubt I'll sleep, Mrs. Carstairs."

After returning to her chambers, Vidia pulled on a plain cotton nightdress and sat at her dressing table, staring out the window at the darkness without seeing anything, her brow knit in thought. She then rang the bell for Maisie.

After a few minutes, the maid came into the bedchamber, dressed in her own nightdress and openly expressing her surprise at finding her mistress alone. "I expected more o' the man, I must say."

But Vidia wasn't listening as she pulled out a scrap of stationery. "I am sorry to pull you out of bed, but I need you to carry a note to Mr. Brodie, if you would."

Maisie was agog. "Now?"

"Now, I'm afraid—it is important. To his hand and no other."

Maisie, bless her, asked no questions. "I'll leave out the back so's no one sees me." Unspoken was the identity of the person to be thus avoided, and Vidia knew a brief moment of disappointment so acute she resisted an impulse to begin throwing things just to have the satisfaction of violent action. She scribbled on the scrap, "We leave for Fairlight in the morning." She then added, "Beware my cook," and handed the folded note to her maid.

The next morning Vidia made ready to set out on the coming journey, her actions routine and efficient, as she had much experience in vacating on short notice. Few preparations were needed; the only modest dresses Vidia owned were left over from her recent role as a draper's widow and were inappropriately black. Maisie was to supervise the finishing of the new gowns at the dressmaker's shop and then follow in a cart with the rest of the baggage. At present, the maidservant was closing up Vidia's travel bandbox while Vidia applied a last brush of powder to her cheeks, which were a bit pale. "Lord, I hope there are dressmakers where we are going—Mr. Carstairs made it sound as though it was the end of beyond and I shall need to have something made up when my waistline disappears."

"We'll manage," said Maisie with a pragmatic air. "'Though I don't know what we're to do if that bosom of yers gets any bigger."

"I shall have to live in smocks, I suppose. Is that the bell? It must be Mr. Carstairs—finish up here, Maisie, and I'll see he has breakfast." With a light step, Vidia descended the stairs to open the door and greet her husband with a bright, gay little smile. "Good morning—did you pass a pleasant night?"

"I couldn't seem to sleep—I cannot imagine why." He

tossed his hat on the table and saluted her cheek, casually dressed for traveling in a corduroy jacket with a belcher knotted at his throat, his boots unpolished. He did look a bit tired, she thought, assessing, and decided that it served him right.

"I think it best that I try to eat something—do we have time for a quick breakfast? We'd have to fend for ourselves."

"Willingly." He stepped around the boxes and trunks that littered the entry hall. "It is the least I can do for putting you at sixes and sevens on such short notice."

She laughed, the merry sound echoing in the entry hall. "It is not as though I have never had to make a hasty departure—Flanders comes to mind." Her manner was very light as she led him into the breakfast room. "And as I recall, you were not far behind me."

"Close enough to land on top of you, in fact; we were lucky the embassy had a laundry chute and doubly lucky there was enough linen to make the landing a soft one."

They sat together at the breakfast table and reminisced about their assignment in Flanders, each insisting the other's role in its success was the more important. "Your poor little maidservant," Vidia teased with a twinkle. "She probably wonders to this day what became of you."

"Not my maidservant," he corrected, lifting a brow. "Everyone's maidservant."

"You shock me." She buttered her toast without enthusiasm—her appetite had disappeared again. "Such goings-on."

"It was hard to believe that one small embassy could house such a nest of vipers," he agreed. "Thoroughly cleaned out—thanks to your quick thinking."

"And thanks to your way with maidservants."

Trading smiles and light laughter, they finished their repast and called for the coach to come around. While her new husband saw her bandbox strapped onto the boot, Vidia stood on the front steps to tie up her bonnet and give Maisie final instructions. She then took Carstairs's proffered arm and allowed him to hand her in the traveling coach, bestowing a smile upon the coachman who was eying her instead of minding the horses. Carstairs climbed in to sit beside her—gallantly kissing her hand—and they were under way, the route south similar to the one taken the day before to their wedding.

Progress was slow as they made their way through the crowded city, and they passed the time by pointing out landmarks that had witnessed a significant episode in their clandestine business.

"The Moor's Head," Carstairs noted, "where Mezzo was captured. What a night that was."

"You were there?" asked Vidia with interest. "I heard it was a donnybrook."

"They were hauling him out in handcuffs when one of his cohorts opened fire, trying to kill him before he could talk. The tavern keeper took umbrage because Mezzo hadn't paid his bill, and the next thing you knew there was crossfire like a naval battle—you never saw so much broken glass in your life."

Vidia pronounced fondly, "There are few dens as steeped in sin as The Moor's Head."

"I don't know—I think the worst of the worst is Three Saints."

She considered this assessment fairly and then nodded. "Definitely more weapons per square inch than any other den in town—always best to give the place a wide berth."

"Unless you are ordered to go in for an extraction." Extending his arm, he pushed up the sleeve, exposing a jagged scar. "A souvenir."

She examined it with interest, even though she was already well aware his arm bore a scar. "Not a knife, surely?"

"Broken bottle. It was every man for himself."

"The melees are the worst," she agreed. "There can be no strategy or protocol when one is fighting a mob." She hiked up her skirts to brandish a stockinged leg and indicate a long, narrow scar on her calf, visible through the silk. "My worst wound, to my shame, was self-inflicted."

He ran a light finger over it. "How so?"

"I made to draw my pistol from my garter and—I was green, of course—I hit the trigger by mistake. There were two swagmen attempting to wrestle me down at the time."

He gave a low whistle. "A close call."

She lowered her skirt again. "Yes—it burned like fire and I learned my lesson; I have used a pocket instead of a garter ever since."

"Did it happen at the Saints?"

With a knit brow, she tried to remember. "No—on the Continent, during my early days. I think it was in Brussels—or perhaps Marseilles; I remember I swore in Portuguese and they backed away—terrified I was conjuring up a curse on them. A good thing, it gave me time to reload and I was so furious at myself that they retreated, probably fearing I was a madwoman."

After laughing in appreciation, he rested his head back on the cushions with a contented smile. "There will be no shortage of stories at our house."

With her own bright smile she agreed, "No—there will be no shortage of stories."

There was a long, silent pause while she could see he was trying to decide if her brittle tone was a rebuke. He then brought his head forward abruptly and exclaimed in an irritated manner, "I can't do this any longer."

She was silent, not quite willing to break role.

He leaned toward her with an intensity she had not seen since their wedding and took her hands in his. "I have caused this constraint between us. Forgive me."

She did not disagree but waited.

"They were adamant that I shouldn't bed you again."

She nodded stiffly. "I thought as much. Then you have your orders, I suppose."

He made a sound of frustration and bent his head, fingering the back of her hand. "I should have told you—you would have understood, and it would have spared us both the embarrassment." Lifting his head, he met her gaze. "Now you are behind your snail shell and I am afraid you will never come out again."

"We were supposed to try our hand at honesty." She tried with little success to keep her voice devoid of accusation.

"Forgive me," he said again, gently squeezing her hands, and she could swear he meant it.

Unable to control her annoyance, she withdrew her hands from his. "I don't understand the concern—are they afraid I will slay you in your sleep? Or that you will be made vulnerable in some way?"

Watching her, he replied with complete seriousness, "They think you may seek to become pregnant in truth."

Astonished, she stared at him. "They disbelieve it?"

He nodded. "As it came right on the heels of the attempted seizure, the Vicar believes you seek to preserve your life by the tale."

She made an angry, dismissive gesture. "Small difference it would make to him."

Carstairs said only, "You touch a nerve with him, I think."

"Yes—for two pence he would strangle me himself." She sat for a moment, absorbing this information. While she had suspected this was the case, it was disheartening to have it confirmed. At least he had finally decided to play it straight with her—although she wished he had done so last night. Better late than never.

"Are you pregnant?"

The question interrupted her thoughts, and her eyes flew to his in surprise. "Poor Lucien—do you think such a thing of your new-minted wife?"

He said almost gently, "We're to try our hand at honesty."

Nonplussed, she stared at him. "I am indeed pregnant, my friend."

Without taking his level gaze from hers, he tilted his head. "Are you? Could it be a false alarm, perhaps?" He said it in the manner of someone trying to offer an excuse so that she could save face, and strange as it seemed, she was touched by his attempt to safeguard her pride.

"No, I am certain. I have lost my appetite, and—and there are other symptoms."

He bent his head for a moment and rubbed her hands with his. "Tell me."

She made a wry mouth and hesitated, then decided that he was, after all, her husband. A doubting husband—but a husband nonetheless. "My breasts are different."

He raised his head to look into her eyes, intrigued. "Are they?"

"Yes." She made a gesture. "They are tender at the sides. And my nipples—you may not remember—"

He interrupted her. "Oh—I remember; never fear."

She had to smile, as he intended. Unbuttoning a button on her blouse she pulled the fabric to the side so that she could tug at her chemise. A nipple was exposed, formerly pink, now brown and thick. "As you see."

He looked at the flesh for a long moment, then raised his eyes to hers in abject surprise. "Holy God—you are pregnant."

"And you are the father—I swear it on the soul of my mother." She buttoned up again and watched as he bent his head to cradle it in his hands for a moment. He did not think it true, either, she thought. Now, that is of interest.

Lifting his head, he took her hands in his and kissed them, one after the other. "May we start over again?"

Bemused, she knew only that if she had any—*any*—self-respect at all she should put her blade to his throat and be done with this ridiculous game of least-in-sight she kept playing with Lucien Carstairs. Instead, she willingly tried to start over, yet again. "I suppose we have little choice—and although I shouldn't make such a confession, there is very little I wouldn't forgive when it comes to you."

Apparently, he had decided to start over again with a vengeance. "Listen, Vidia; they know that Brodie is in communication with Rochon—by pigeon. They also know that the pattern of communication seems to coincide with the missing gold shipments."

She did listen, utterly dismayed. "Oh—I see."

Watching her intently, he continued, "They also believe you know of this but made no report. That—coupled with Marie's accusations—has led to an unfortunate conclusion."

"So I have gathered—the Vicar watches me as though he was a hawk and I a very tasty mouse."

He made a wry mouth. "And here I thought you were a snail."

She sighed. "Either way, I am dinner." With a knit brow she sorted out the alarming implications. "Lord, what a tangle—am I in imminent danger of being hanged?"

He met her eyes again in all seriousness. "Let us instead say it is well that you have a ready excuse to be spirited away until all concerns are alleviated."

She studied his grave expression. "As dire as that, then?"

He nodded, but then said, "I will tell them you are indeed pregnant—it may help."

With a small smile she added, "Beg them for permission to bed me—no point in closing the stable door when the horse is well away."

He laughed and shook his head. "You must think me a very sorry fellow."

Laughing in return, she agreed, "Indeed, I do."

After the laughter subsided they sat in silence, comfortable again. "This is better." He ran his thumbs over her hands again.

"Yes—much." She didn't wish to ruin the newly reconciled mood by noting that he had not asked her outright whether she knew of any of this—it appeared he didn't want to know, which seemed strange, no matter what his feelings for her were. She would keep her own counsel and await events—she had little choice.

He continued, "They wish to keep you sequestered and unable to communicate. It is an ideal situation for them while they decide what is to be done with you—I cannot stress enough that it does not look well."

"They used the pregnancy story to their own advantage, then, and think to have turned the tables on me." Struck, she lifted her face to his. "Were you ordered to marry me?" She remembered that Brodie had intimated as much

He tugged on her hands in mock reproach. "Vi-di-a," he

drew out her name in exasperation. "I proposed the minute you told me—I am not such a sorry fellow as that."

She teased him, "It was more a demand than a proposal, as I recall—you are not one for romantic gestures."

"I will prove you wrong," he replied, his gaze on her mouth. "Now that we are playing it straight."

"Hush." She placed her fingers on his mouth. "You have your orders."

It was turning evening when they approached the Mermaid Inn near Fairlight. *Santos*, Vidia thought, watching the countryside pass by the window; this one is going to be a bit more difficult than my usual. I am in the middle of nowhere and I cannot like how events are unfolding. She glanced at her companion's profile, decided it was well worth the effort, and set her mind to the task ahead.

The inn was a few miles distant from Fairlight along the rugged coast, with woodland, heathland, and grassland alternately stretching back from the desolate cliffs. There was smuggling activity in the area and Vidia could see why this would be—the isolated area was perfect for such a pastime and she couldn't imagine what else one did with oneself in this God-forsaken place. Perhaps I should take up smuggling to pass the time, she mused—how difficult can it be? I smuggled the ambassador in the laundry bag, after all. Or perhaps I could hold card parties to keep in practice—although it probably wouldn't be seemly to cheat the neighbors. With a mental sigh, she acknowledged that she would have to become a pattern-card of respectability now that she was to be a wife and mother with a family to disgrace. This thought was almost as daunting as her present circumstances—she would bet her teeth that Carstairs was not telling her all that he knew and she would need to wrack her brains for a plan to make her way back to London when the *Argo* set sail. Pull yourself together, *menina*, she chided as the carriage lurched over the uneven road—this is nowhere near as difficult as killing off an entire company of Spaniards, one by one, with only a cart horse and a stolen pistol.

As the wheels rattled in the loose gravel, they pulled up to the inn's coach yard, and with abject gratitude Vidia alighted from the carriage, stretching and looking around her—she was unaccustomed to long carriage rides. The modest establishment was two stories, with timbered walls and a reinforced roof that probably had been thatch, originally. Young ostlers took hold of the horses as the coachman issued instruction, and Carstairs escorted Vidia toward the inn's entrance, the door a bit short as was the usual case with these ancient buildings, and topped by the wooden figure of a mermaid that was swinging in the stiff breeze. Carstairs ducked through the door and brought her into the warm interior that smelled of old wood and smoke. "We'll stay here the night, then meet my family tomorrow—I didn't want you to have to meet them after traveling all day, and it is best for your condition that we allow you to rest."

"An excellent plan," she agreed, allowing him to remove her cloak. No point in mentioning that when he made these arrangements he didn't, in fact, believe she was pregnant. They approached the innkeeper's desk, but almost immediately a servant who had been seated in the common room sprang up to intercept them.

"Joseph," said Carstairs, greeting him warmly. "It is good to see you again."

The man held his hat in his hand, his expression grave.

"I'm that sorry, sir, but I've been sent to meet you. Your mother has taken a turn and is doing poorly."

"Oh, Lucien," exclaimed Vidia softly. "I am so sorry."

Drawing the man aside, Carstairs first introduced Vidia to the startled servant. "We are newly wed and I wished to surprise everyone," he explained. "Now, tell me what has happened."

After tearing his gaze from Vidia only with some difficulty, the servant described a grave situation, with her mother-in-law in a weakened condition and attended around the clock by worried physicians. After hearing the report, Carstairs turned to Vidia. "I fear I should ride over immediately—the house is only ten miles away, and the moon is nearly full—I should be able to see the road."

"Go," she agreed without a qualm. "And Godspeed—I will await word."

He pulled on his gloves again, his expression concerned. "I am sorry to leave you here like this—"

Touching his sleeve, she assured him, "Maisie will be arriving tomorrow, and until then I shall enjoy the sea air. It is not as though I am unable to take care of myself, Lucien."

"Right," he reluctantly agreed, and went to give orders to have a fresh horse saddled and brought around for him.

Joseph remained in the parlor, standing at a deferential distance and trying to disguise the fact he was stealing covert glances at her when he thought she was not looking. She could hardly blame him; she was quite the shock—doubly so with Marie just dead. In a grave manner commensurate with the circumstances, she addressed him. "I am sorry for the situation; I understand Mrs. Dessiere has suffered in the past from a weak heart."

Bemused, the man regarded her for a moment. "I think you mean Mrs. Carstairs, ma'am."

Shaking her head, Vidia smiled and rendered a pretty, self-deprecatory shrug. "Of course—I meant Mrs. Carstairs—and I should know, certainly, as it is now my own name also. I believe she is unaware that her son has married, so you may wish to ask my husband how to handle the situation…" Here she paused delicately.

"Of course," the other nodded in ready understanding. "Mum's the word—I'll let him decide what's to be said."

"You will take good care of Lucien?" she asked in her best imitation of a concerned wife.

"I will indeed." The servant dragged his gaze from her face as Carstairs rejoined them and Vidia considered the interesting fact that the old family retainer did not know the old family's name—nor did he know that Lucien wasn't Lucien's true name, and it now appeared that she was to be left to her own devices here at the end of beyond until further notice. I'd best keep my wits about me, she thought; the whole situation is very smoky—it wants only Rochon himself, rising from the sea and hurling lightning bolts.

Revealing nothing of her unhappy thoughts, Vidia accompanied Carstairs out into the coach yard once again, and he took her elbow to draw her aside so that they could speak privately for a moment while the ostler held his horse—although he had to speak over the wind, which was blowing steadily. He bent his head to hers and hesitated, as though weighing whether or not to speak. "I would like to see you settled here but I must go straightaway—I am sorry."

"I understand, Lucien. Please do not worry—I shall contrive." That her contrivances may not be in accord with his wishes, she kept to herself.

After another pause he lifted his face to hers, the expression in the blue eyes intense as the wind blew his hair about.

"You must have a care, Vidia; you are pregnant—everything is different now."

This seemed an odd warning in light of the situation. "I will be careful, Lucien—I cannot add to your burdens."

Tempering his tone, he drew her shawl tighter around her almost absently. "I only meant you should take no chances—not with the baby on the way." He bent so that his face was close to hers and spoke with quiet emphasis. "Promise me you will err on the side of protecting yourself."

"I promise." That he was preoccupied with something other than his mother's illness seemed apparent; perhaps he was uncertain about which name he should use to address the poor woman, if she indeed existed. "What is it that worries you, my friend?"

He tried to lighten the moment while the cool wind blew and the horse moved restlessly. "Sometimes—and I say it only as a kindness, you understand—you have a tendency to be reckless. I have a very clear vision of the ambassador's chaise-and-four bearing down upon you while you faced them with a pistol."

"Unfair," she protested, smiling up at him. "What else was I to do under the circumstances? And the ambassador's odious footmen so deserving of a little gunplay—not to mention the odious horses deserving the same."

But he was adamant and reiterated with emphasis, "I'll have your promise, Vidia—wait here and do nothing reckless until I see you again."

"I will," she assured him. "I will be as prim as a nun."

With a small smile he ducked his head in amused acknowledgment. "Another memory from Flanders."

Chapter 26

Although Vidia half-expected something of consequence to occur in the nighttime, it passed peacefully and in the morning she withdrew her pistol from under her pillow and returned it to her pocket.

After breakfasting, she decided to reconnoiter the area so as to further assess her situation and potential escape routes, if necessary. She had already noted that the innkeeper and the ostlers had shown little interest in her, which was at odds with how the vast majority of the male populace normally behaved. Only Joseph hadn't received a warning not to gawk—he must be a recent recruit; he hadn't held his role very well.

Despite her suspicions, she wished Carstairs was here to spend a quiet day with her—just the two of them. It is a shame we are not an ordinary couple, living ordinary lives, she thought, and then almost immediately retreated from the thought. The reason we live as we do is that it suits us to the core—the danger and intrigue attracts us and we live for the next crisis; the next chance to risk our lives. I hope it does not bode ill for our marriage, this craving for excitement—although we are well-matched since we are uniquely able to understand the other. Nodding to the innkeeper, she wandered outside into the pale sunlight and decided to walk along the sandy track that led to the edge of the rocky cliffs; it would be pleasant to view the ocean for a while—she had heard the waves crashing last night from her bed. Making a desultory progress through the yard, she took a covert survey and noted several men who were busy with tasks but were probably charged with keeping an eye on her. Soon she left the shelter of the buildings and headed toward the cliffs, the scent of the sea sharp upon the wind. It was not as cool in the daytime, but the sea air blew her curls loose from their pins and she wished she had thought to wrap a shawl over her head—her hair would be in a rare tangle when Maisie arrived.

Looking around her, she found the prospect as unappealing as it had seemed the evening before. The low cliffs protruded over the ocean, a small inlet the only relief in the rocky shores over which the waters broke and receded. She could see why the area was infamous for smuggling; due to the war there had been an embargo on French goods and the shore was ideally situated for night landings—isolated and barren with the nearest law enforcement ten miles away. She remembered the calluses on Carstairs's hands and would not have been surprised to discover he had been on assignment as a smuggler or a deckhand of some sort. Crossing her arms before her against the chill, she continued on so as to look out over the cliffs at the sea—mainly because she was bored and there was little else to do; she didn't want to sit alone at the inn with only her suspicions to keep her company. The landscape would have some appeal if one admired the untamed and gothic but as Vidia had never been mistaken for a hardy outdoorswoman, she was unimpressed. *Santos*, but this place was forlorn and tedious. She hoped that whatever trap was to be sprung involved some creativity, at least;

Brodie was the master at springing a creative trap but the English tended to be dully predictable.

Coming right to the edge, she noted a fisherman casting a line from the rocks below and she watched his movements for a few minutes, then turned to continue her walk as her mind reeled and her hands were suddenly clammy. *Idiota*, she chastised herself, and a pox on Brodie for always—*always* being right. I never learn, she thought, struggling for control and consumed with equal parts fury and despair. The fisherman on the cliffs had not looked at her, but she recognized him nonetheless—despite the false sideburns he wore she was certain it was the chaplain who had officiated at her wedding.

Only he is not truly a chaplain and I am not truly married, she thought, nearly gnashing her teeth at this inescapable conclusion. And curse Carstairs for a liar—although he probably had little choice and indeed seemed to be teetering on the edge of confessing his many sins to her last night just before he left—it cannot be easy to believe an enemy of the Crown is the mother of one's child. *Mãe de Deus*, she thought abruptly—I must not make excuses for Carstairs but instead I must think this through and make a plan. They are monitoring me and hope to trick me into taking some action—if I tried to flee back to Brodie, I would be thwarted easily; I could disguise myself but any lone traveler would be immediately spotted in this God-forsaken area, and I cannot very well swim back to London.

Forcing herself to walk slowly and breathe evenly, she thought it over. That it was a trap seemed evident—which meant something more was planned. Brodie was right and she was a fool, but at least they didn't know she had twigged them—not yet. She had no choice but to await events and then decide what was to be done. In the meantime, caution was advised.

When she returned, she asked the kitchen if they had any fresh fish, as she had seen a fisherman on the rocks. For some reason the thought of having a fish—roasted, as she had eaten it in her childhood—sounded palatable, and comforting.

To her relief, she did indeed have an appetite for fish and was finishing her meal in her room when Maisie arrived. "Hallo, Maisie," she greeted the new arrival. "Only look—I have discovered something I can eat."

Maisie observed her mistress for a long moment, then directed that the bags be left on the floor. Closing the door with a worried frown, she asked, "What's amiss?"

"Nothing at all," replied Vidia, sucking on the remaining bones. "Why do you ask?"

Watching her, Maisie ventured, "Where's Mr. Carstairs?"

Pushing her plate away, Vidia explained the situation to her dismayed maidservant. "Indeed, he has just sent a note to inform me that his mother's condition remains grave, and that he will stay another night as it appears necessary."

"Poor woman," offered Maisie, eying her mistress with misgiving.

"Indeed," Vidia replied in a neutral tone.

After apparently deciding there was no point to asking questions, the maid inspected the linens on the truckle bed and began unpacking. "Mr. Brodie were not best pleased with your note t' him."

Vidia shook her head, a smile playing around her mouth as she gazed into the fire. "No, I imagine not. Did he send any message in return?"

"Nay, he did nowt—only told me to mind ye like I was a warden at Newgate." Reminded, she fished in her apron pocket. "I do has a note from yer seamstress though. She come fer her appointment and didn't know ye'd left all sudden-like."

"Thank you." Vidia accepted the note without betraying the fact she had scheduled no such appointment. She wondered for one wild moment if the Vicar was now masquerading as a woman but upon opening the note realized it was from Jenny Dokes. It was unsigned, but written in a cipher consisting of sequenced numbers—she and Dokes had communicated using such a cipher during their work together on last year's investment swindle.

Concentrating on the sequence, she sank down at her dressing table and puzzled it out: "*I must speak to you at your earliest convenience. Be on guard; I can say no more until we meet.*"

Vidia walked to the fire and tossed the note in while Maisie watched from the corner of her eye. As the flames burned the paper Vidia thought it over. It was so very kind of Dokes to warn her of dire events—just as kind as Carstairs, come to think of it. It was almost as though their affection for her was more important than their loyalty to king and country—how very unlike them.

"Perhaps ye should take a nap, missy," suggested Maisie, unconsciously twisting the fabric of her sleeve.

With a languid motion, Vidia stretched her arms over her head. "I am only out-of-sorts, my friend, and require some fresh air to cure these dismals; come, let us take a look 'round—unfortunately it won't take very long."

Willingly, the maid accompanied Vidia out of doors and they took a circuit of the property as the afternoon light was fading.

"Have you ever seen a more desolate prospect?" Vidia lifted her chin in the direction of the heaths. "Horrid."

"Reminds me o' parts of Yorkshire," Maisie admitted as the gravel crunched under their feet.

Vidia made a wry mouth. "You alarm me."

"Nothin' to be alarmed 'bout," Maisie's gaze was on the ground, watching where she stepped. "It is not as though ye'll ever live in Yorkshire, now." She carefully did not look to Vidia for confirmation of this observation.

Dear Maisie, thought Vidia as they walked toward the cliffs. She is aware something cataclysmic has happened but makes no demands and asks no questions—small wonder she is so appealing to Brodie. "It's a rare tangle, Maisie. You'll not like to hear that I may have to disappear and ask you to pretend I am ill in my room for a time."

As anticipated, Maisie agreed without demur. "If I must."

Alive to the nuance in her tone, Vidia took her companion's arm. "I promise—my hand on my heart—that I will be in no danger. But it will be no easy thing to escape from this place—which I imagine is the very point of dumping me here."

"We can run a rig like we did in Calais," offered the maid. Vidia had been secreted under a heap of fishing nets on the floor of a small fishing skiff, and it had worked long enough to get them away—until the fisherman panicked, the boat ran aground, and the enemy began firing.

"That rig didn't work very well," Vidia reminded her.

"It were a good idea," Maisie insisted in a stubborn tone. "The man was a glomper, is all."

Vidia raised her face to the sky for a moment, into the breeze that now was growing cold. "You are a trump, Maisie—I don't tell you near enough."

Her companion disclaimed, embarrassed by the praise. "Go on wi' ye, missy. I does what I'm told."

"You remember if anything happens to me you are to go straight to Mr. Brodie—he will see to you."

"Now, missy; I'll hear none o' yer nonsense," the other cautioned with some dismay.

"And take the sugar box—I will have your promise."

But the maid was forced to demur, "Except fer t' opals—opals are bad luck."

This was of interest and Vidia turned to regard her. "Are they indeed? And why did you not tell me earlier—it would have saved me a fistful of trouble."

Maisie chuckled and Vidia joined in, amazed that she could laugh. I will come about, she thought; I always have.

"Mayhap the babe has put ye out o' sorts," the maid suggested as they toured the area behind the boathouse.

"The babe has definitely put me off," Vidia agreed, taking a quick inventory of the boats lodged therein. "I have given my promise not to act recklessly, and I am regretting it already."

"Tea," offered Maisie. "Strong an' sweet; a spot of tea will put you t' rights."

"Of course." Vidia pretended to be much struck. "Tea will turn the trick; if only I had thought of it."

Chuckling again, Maisie directed their steps back to the inn, while Vidia carefully watched the shadows.

They came in through the kitchen door, thinking to ask for tea on their way to the common room, and found the cook in hushed conversation with another man who was seated at the kitchen table, their heads close together. All conversation ceased and both men looked up, wary, as the women nodded to them and progressed through the kitchen.

Ah, thought Vidia, hiding a smile. The trap is sprung, and I am impressed—the grey-eyed man has indeed put together something creative. He could not know, after all, that I know more than I should about the gentleman at the kitchen table—and it is a good plan. But now it is time to turn the tables.

Chapter 27

"I will need you to vacate the room, Maisie—and be much in evidence elsewhere." Vidia stood at the window, holding the lace curtain aside with her fingertips. Their room was on the second floor but she had every confidence her visitor would manage it; he was a very fine cat burglar when he wasn't smuggling—or pretending to smuggle, as the case may be. She would soon find out, being as she was a very fine discerner of plots.

"Is Mr. Carstairs to visit?" her maidservant asked with a hopeful mien.

"You never know." Vidia arched an eyebrow; best not to tell Maisie that she expected a different gentleman altogether—Maisie had enough on her plate, what with trying to relieve her mistress's case of the dismals.

Maisie gathered up her tatting and her shawl. "I'll be in the common room—should I fall asleep on a chair, do you think?"

She was probably hopeful that Carstairs would take Vidia to bed and thus restore order in the world, and Vidia was sorry to disappoint her. "I don't think it necessary—I imagine an hour or two will be sufficient. I shall come fetch you—have a pot of tea in the meantime."

Once alone, Vidia approached her mirror and unbuttoned the top two buttons of her modest bodice, then pinched some color into her cheeks. I cannot overplay this and appear too desperate, she thought. Fortunately I have been deserted by my husband, and that will support my role.

There was a soft tap at her door, and she was almost disappointed that no attempt had been made to scale the wall outside. Opening the door a few inches, she perceived the gentleman who had been conspiring with the cook earlier, grinning with delight. He was a Romany—thin, dark-haired, and handsome, his face marked with an intriguing scar.

Laughing, she pulled him inside. "Gaston; *entrez—vite.*"

He enfolded her in an embrace and lifted her off the floor for a moment. "*La belle* Vidia—I thought to fall from my chair." He set her down and held her at arm's length, openly admiring her and making a sucking sound with his mouth. "You are *une ange, chérie.*"

"And you are up to no good, I'll wager—what are you doing here? Is there a daughter of the house you seek to ruin?" She indicated he was to sit in the chair while she sat across from him on the edge of the bed, casually tucking her legs beneath her in such a way so as to reveal some lace petticoat.

Gaston made a derisive gesture with his forefinger. "Bah—there are no good women here; instead, I bring decent tobacco and the brandy to the stupid English who cannot make their own."

Vidia gave him her slow smile and leaned forward so that the unbuttoned buttons could work their magic. "So—you smuggle into the inn with a cutter moored out in the cove? You are like the hero in a gothic novel, Gaston, small wonder all the girls sigh."

He cast her a wicked glance, his eyes glinting. "Shall I take you for a sail? The moon is nearly full."

Shrugging her graceful shoulders, she sighed with regret. "*Quel dommage*; I cannot tarry with you, Gaston—I am new-married."

Incredulous, he stared at her. "*Non—incroyable*."

Laughing softly at his reaction, she bowed her head in mock contrition. "*C'est vrai*."

He chuckled. "That was fast work, *mignon*—who managed this *miracle*?"

"Lucien Carstairs—do you know of him?"

With a show of acute surprise, he made a deprecatory gesture. "Why would you marry that one? *Anglais; un tel gaspillage*."

Spreading her hands, she disclaimed, "It could not be helped; there were no Romany men to hand."

He chuckled in appreciation and raised his dark brows. "But what of the rich man?"

She leaned forward, allowing another glimpse of her cleavage—a shame her dress wasn't one of her usual—and looked at him from beneath her lashes. "I needed something more—you know me."

As his gaze lingered appreciatively on her *décolletage*, he replied, "*Hélas*—I do not but I wish I did."

She laughed softly, deep in her throat. Gaston had always had a soft spot for her—as had nearly every man she had ever met.

Gaston cocked his head at her, unable to take his gaze from her breasts. "Where is this new *Anglais* husband? He neglects you, perhaps?"

Vidia made a *moue* with her mouth. "*Oui*, he neglects me—I think he has second thoughts; he worries I'll not be faithful." With her eyes, she invited him to share in her amusement at such a thought.

Gaston stared at her in dismay for a moment. "He would not leave you, surely?"

Finding that she didn't want to discuss it, even within her role, she cut to the nub of the matter—there seemed little point in flirting for another hour. "When do you return to *la belle France, mon ami?*"

He tilted his head, making a sound of regret. "On tonight's tide—do you need money? Or a weapon with which to shoot such a man?"

"I shall come with you to France," she pronounced as though it was a simple thing and recrossed her legs, smoothing out her skirt with a lingering gesture. "We shall sail and admire the moon together."

There was a slight pause, and he replied lightly, "Do not tempt me, *ma belle*."

But Vidia became deadly serious. "The wolves are closing in, my friend—I must be away, and quickly."

Raising his brows, he regarded her narrowly for a moment. "I have no desire to have this new husband kill me."

"He is one of the wolves. That is why I must be away."

He rendered a low whistle. "You must report to Rochon?"

The question lingered in the air, a hint of challenge contained therein. "Indeed—I will meet up with Monsieur Rochon." She held his gaze without flinching.

He thought it over for a moment, then shook his head with regret. "I think I must stay away from such a plan, *chérie*."

She made an impatient gesture with her hand and chided him, "Gaston, Gaston—and here I thought you stood my friend. Have you forgotten how I distracted the angry papa in Leiden?"

He spread his own hands in a purely Gallic gesture of regret. "It is too great a risk, *ma belle*."

"One thousand pounds to get me away," she replied coolly, fingering a curl that rested atop her breast.

Giving a silent whistle, he stared at her—the sum was staggering. "You tempt me, Vidia, but if it is known I help you escape to Rochon, the English will hang me *très-vite*."

"I will tell no one, will you?"

Ducking his chin to his chest, he considered while Vidia watched him from beneath her lashes. She had little doubt of the outcome.

"*Bien*. I will do it—only for you, *belle* Vidia."

"*Très bien*. Shall I see if there is a bottle of your fine French brandy downstairs? I would hear of your adventures."

His expression changed subtly. "I no longer drink."

She thought as much; Gaston had undergone a sea change—and she could only hope his was not as hard as hers had been at San Sebastian. Aloud she teased him, "You will astonish me next, and tell me you are a holy man."

"Not this side of heaven." He relaxed again, relieved to change the subject.

She lifted her feet to rest them on his chair and clasped her knees with her hands. "Tell me a round tale, then—I am in dire need of entertainment in this God-forsaken place."

"*D'accord*—I shall tell you that my friends in Calais still swear that you are a mermaid."

Making a wry mouth, she disclaimed, "No—they only seek to conceal the fact they cannot shoot straight."

As he chuckled, she teased him with an arched brow, "Tell me, what do you hear from Renée—does she pine for you?"

He threw back his head and laughed so that she had to caution him to stay quiet. "You are cruel to remind me."

Smiling, Vidia shrugged. "How were you to know that

Renée was more properly a René? Or that he would be so smitten by your *beaux yeux?*"

"And I could not make an exit without stirring up the guards—it was a situation *intenable.*" He paused, remembering, then sobered. "Poor René met with a bad end."

Watching him carefully, she shrugged slightly. "Did he? I cannot say I am surprised—he had many dangerous friends."

Gaston nodded and threw her a significant glance. "Some more dangerous than others."

"Yes—it cannot be a comfortable existence—to hold the secrets of dangerous men."

His sharp gaze flew to her face, but she was contemplating the fire in the grate, her expression mild. "Does the counterfeiter still live—what was his name?"

Gaston shifted in his chair. "Gerard—he does; he was too useful to kill, even when Rochon discovered his treachery."

Making a wry mouth she asked, "Is he a—guest—of Monsieur Rochon nowadays?"

Gaston shrugged. "I know not." Then, with a sly smile, "You would know, better than I."

She kept her gaze upon the grate and did not react to the insinuation. "I have not been a guest myself, of late." She then moved on to more general subjects, inquiring after other acquaintances as they spoke of old times and the general injustice of the war.

After an hour, he rose. "I must go. The tide will turn at ten o'clock—can you meet me on the beach down below without being seen?"

"I will be there, my friend. How many in your crew? I do not wish any tale-bearers."

"Only one, to man the jibs. He will say nothing—especially if he is paid to stay silent."

"Good," she said. "I shall see to it."

He paused at the door. "It is not that I do not trust you, *ma belle*—but are you certain you can bring such a sum?"

"I can—but take this as a sign of good faith." She pulled off her ring with the three diamonds and handed it to him.

He examined it doubtfully. "Your wedding ring?"

"No," she assured him. "Only a trifle."

Ah, me," sighed Maisie with resignation.

"I'll disappear in London for a time." Vidia wrapped a dark shawl around her head and carefully tucked her hair in the edges. "It's best you don't know more than that."

"Yer nowt one who can disappear easy-like," Maisie cautioned. "It'll be quite a trick."

Bending over to tighten the laces on her half boots, Vidia agreed. "It's a shame I don't have the widow's weeds outfit with me—at least it has a veil."

"What do I say in the morning?"

Considering this aspect for a moment, Vidia straightened up and advised, "Stall as long as possible—and if you are asked, admit you are not certain and button your lip. I imagine there are witnesses who noted that I had a gentleman in my room last night, and you will be trying to protect my shredded reputation."

Dubious, Maisie eyed her mistress. "I'm to say such to Mr. Carstairs?"

"Especially to Mr. Carstairs." Vidia's tone was grim as she pulled her sleeves down with a jerk. With an abrupt movement, she flung the end of her shawl over the opposite shoulder. "I'll need a diversion, Maisie, as I have no desire to go out the window."

"I'll drop t' teapot on the kitchen floor; wait for it."

Before she opened the door, Vidia paused and took the woman's hands in hers for a moment. "Thank you, Maisie—I shall meet up with you as soon as I can."

"G'wan with ye," her unhappy maidservant mumbled, and left for the kitchen.

Vidia waited in the shadows at the top of the servant's stairway until she heard a crash and alarmed voices heading toward the kitchen, then she slipped out the side door and clung to the shadows, circling around wide so as to avoid detection by those who watched her—although unless she very much missed her guess, they were all well-aware of her plans for escape. I agree with Brodie, she thought, pressing her lips together in a thin line—a pox on all warmongers, everywhere, for requiring such exertions of me.

She made her way to the sandy track that wound to the beach, careful to stay to the shoulder so as not to allow her silhouette to be visible in the moonlight. If nothing else, I shall be away from this miserable, windy place, she thought as she walked along, soft-footed. Perhaps I do not wish to live by the sea, after all.

Staying to the shadows, she arrived at the cove and hovered near the cover of the cliffs, waiting for Gaston's rowboat to emerge from the sea. When she was on the crest she had spotted Gaston's cutter anchored just outside the inlet, but it was not visible from her current vantage point and so she waited with a cautious hand on her pistol, wondering who knew she waited here, and what they were expecting. There—she could see the light from a lantern on the horizon well before she heard the sound of the oars in the oarlocks as the small vessel approached, bucking about on the choppy surf. When it came within a few yards of landing, she approached the shoreline, wearing a light skirt tied up around her calves so that it would not become heavy with water when she waded out to board the boat—she had learned that lesson at Calais.

There were two men in the rowboat, Gaston and another who kept his collar up and his cap pulled low as he plied the oars. Too short to be the false chaplain, Vidia thought, and I cannot like the odds of two against one.

Gaston jumped out with a graceful movement and the other man pulled the rowboat onto the beach behind him, keeping his face averted which only convinced Vidia that she needed to have a good look at him.

"*Bonne nuit.*" Gaston's teeth flashed white in the moonlight.

"*Bonne nuit,*" she greeted in return, and then bent her head coyly to peer at his companion. "*Bonne nuit,*" she said softly in a throaty voice.

Unable to resist, the man took a quick glimpse at her face and Vidia saw it was Joseph, Carstairs's erstwhile servant, wearing an imperfect disguise. He needs a good lesson about how important it is to hold one's role, thought Vidia, and with a chopping arc brought her pistol down on the back of his head. He fell forward, face-first into the shallow water.

"*Parbleu—*" Gaston exclaimed in astonishment, gazing into the barrel of her pistol, now inches from his face.

"*Vôtre pistolet,*" she demanded in a voice of steel. "Then pull him out of the water."

"*Chérie—*"

Vidia did not respond but pulled the hammer back with a click. Quickly, the Romany man threw his pistol to the sand and then hauled Joseph up on the beach so that he was no longer in danger of drowning.

"Into the boat," directed Vidia. "We sail for London—I will man the jibs, since this man is unfortunately disabled."

In an urgent tone, Gaston implored her, "Come, *belle* Vidia—is it the money? We can negotiate."

"No, it is not the money, Gaston. I shall pay you handsomely, but we will sail to London, not France."

He bent his head as though to consider what she said, but the movement was meant to hide an urgent whisper; "*Fuyez*."

But Vidia did not flee as advised. Instead, with a sigh she lowered her pistol and waited to be seized; she had no desire for a battle, cornered here on the beach and no doubt outnumbered—and she had promised not to be reckless. She placed a hand on his arm. "I am glad to see that you are well, my friend, and I harbor no hard feelings."

Turning to see who had inspired Gaston's warning, she spied Carstairs's figure approaching along the shoreline in an unhurried manner—he must have been watching from the rocks. She hadn't guessed he was there, but overall she was not surprised. I think I am no longer surprised by anything, she thought, and stood beside a silent Gaston to await his approach as the water lapped around their feet.

He stopped an arm's length away from her. "Mr. Carstairs," she bowed, as though they were in a drawing room.

His expression unreadable in the lantern light, he regarded her for a long moment, then nudged the prone Joseph with his toe. "You are unkind."

"He could not hold his role—next time someone less kind will kill him."

They stood, the three of them in a strange tableau, with no one speaking. Vidia could feel Gaston's misery—it was not an easy thing to betray one's friends.

"She wished to go to London, instead," Gaston told Carstairs in a quiet tone. Although Vidia appreciated his attempt at a defense, she didn't feel she needed to explain her actions, and so remained silent.

"You twigged us," Carstairs concluded.

Vidia returned no response.

His chest rose as he took a deep breath. "How did you know that Gaston now works for the Home Office?"

There was a pause while she weighed her options, pulling her shawl tighter around her in the unending chilly breeze. She decided that she, at least, would hold up her end of their agreement to be honest with each other. "I would rather not say."

He turned to Gaston. "Did you tell her—give her any hint?"

"No." The other man shook his head, not meeting Vidia's eyes and obviously uncomfortable.

There was another long pause while Carstairs ducked his chin to his chest. "You do not make this easy for me," he finally said to Vidia.

As this comment seemed patently unfair she did not deign to reply, and waited.

Having come to a decision, he lifted his chin and offered, "Let's take you back to London and sort this out—we'll take the schooner."

She thought about it. "Do I have a choice?"

Turning his face to look out over the ocean, he did not answer directly. "I will tell them you did not implicate yourself—and that you are truly pregnant. I will vouch for you."

At the mention of her pregnancy, she saw Gaston glance sidelong in her direction, hiding his surprise. In a wry tone she warned Carstairs, "They will only believe you have succumbed to my wiles."

Stepping closer to her, he touched her arm and the contact made her catch her breath—foolish, to allow him to have such a hold over her. He continued in an intense tone, "Vidia, please come. I will not let them hurt you."

"Would you hold a pistol to me if I refused?" She was genuinely curious—she doubted she could do the same to him.

He thought it over. "I don't know."

She sighed. "I'd rather not find out." Moving forward, she allowed him to assist her into the boat so that she was seated in the stern. Gaston hoisted the hapless Joseph and dumped him onto the floorboards as Carstairs pushed the boat off the sand and into the water, leaping in beside Vidia and then rocking the boat from side to side as he moved to the bow. Once they were settled, Gaston began to ply the oars while Carstairs pointed out shoals and other hazards as they navigated through the inlet to head out to the open sea. Progress was slow; the swells among the rocks created a chop that tossed the boat about, and Vidia was forced to brace herself with her feet and hands against the sides of the rowboat as they made their way toward the cutter. Vidia chose her moment when Gaston and Carstairs were preoccupied with avoiding a shoal, then slipped off the stern of the boat and into the water.

Chapter 29

The cold water was a shock. Vidia was a strong swimmer and she struck out immediately under the water toward the shore for as long as she was able to hold her breath, both to evade detection and to keep warm. She emerged cautiously, took a quick breath while she assessed her position, then submerged again. Fortunately the moon was reflecting off the waves and she had already noted where the protruding rocks were located. Still, it was hard work—she hadn't calculated the effect the receding tide would have, and coupled with the weight of her skirt and boots she knew some anxious moments. She was just beginning to admit that this was—perhaps—not the best idea she had ever had when she brushed up against a moving object and fled to the surface, stifling a scream.

Gasping for breath, she whirled around to see Carstairs, his wet hair plastered against his head, doing some gasping of his own as the waves rocked them about.

"Go away," she managed.

"Hold on to my back—keep kicking."

Having made a respectable protest, she willingly grasped his shoulders and hung on to his back while he navigated them through the remaining shoals to the shore. He had removed his coat and boots and his white shirt was like a second skin; she clung to his back and tried not to impede his movements although she occasionally kicked his foot by mistake. The moonlight glistened on the roiling waves and Vidia reflected that if they weren't in such dire straits it would be an exhilarating experience between the moon, the wild sea, and hoping they wouldn't be dashed to pieces by the next swell—she always loved a good adventure.

Finally she could feel him find traction on the sand beneath his feet as he began to wade to the shore. The breakers made him unsteady and she dismounted from his back, only to find she couldn't yet stand upright against the weight of her skirts so instead she scrambled on all fours onto the sand and lay supine for a moment, panting and spent, the sand coarse against her cheek. Carstairs crawled up behind her and roughly grasped a shoulder, pulling her over to face him. He was mad as fire, and rasped, "Don't *ever* do anything so stupid again."

"*Va aos diabos*," was her own gasping reply. She pushed at him angrily but instead of the desired result he brought his arms around her and brought his mouth down hard upon hers. She resisted the kiss, keeping her lips firmly closed as she struggled against him. What was this—did he think now was the time to demonstrate his mastery over her? Or was it just the same as Flanders—they had cheated death and now he wished to mark the occasion? As she continued to resist, his mouth moved to her throat and his hands moved to her breasts, her waist, her thighs. She became aware, on some elemental level, that she wanted this as much as he did and she would have to regain her dignity at some later time. When her hands moved up to caress his back in a gesture of surrender, she heard him make a sound of satisfaction deep in his throat as he began pulling up at her sodden skirts.

Cradling his head in her hands, she arched against him,

moaning and nearly mindless with the wanting of him. He positioned her hips and drove into her while her legs clung to him as best she could, unaware of the hard beach beneath them or anything but the rightness of their lovemaking and the heat of his mouth upon hers. After a blissfully satisfying space of time he collapsed on her, spent, and she was forced to return to reality—which was cold and uncomfortable. While he recovered his breath, she gently kissed the hollow of his throat, being as it was within reach. In response, he turned his head and kissed the corner of her mouth and then her temple. "I love you, Catalina."

"Lina," she corrected on an exhaled breath. "My mother called me Lina."

He kissed her brow, his fingers stroking the hair back from her temples. "I love you, Lina."

She said without rancor, "I do not believe a word you say."

"You will." He kissed her mouth gently.

"Unlikely. Where is Gaston?"

"He will have to wait his turn," he teased.

"Is he looking for us?" She hoped they had not had an audience—her reputation for calm composure would be in tatters.

"No. I sent him on." He tugged gently at her hair in remonstrance. "You gave us both quite a scare."

"Good."

He rolled over to fasten his breeches and then helped her straighten her soggy skirts. She began to shiver uncontrollably as he pulled her to her feet, putting his arms around her. As he led her away, he took a careful glance around them. "Leave nothing behind—you have drowned."

"I have? What fresh hell is this?" She stooped to wring out her skirt and gather it up into her fist.

"We'll smuggle you into the inn and hide you there until we come up with a plan."

She brushed her wet, sandy hair from her face. "Are you out of coverage, then? I didn't think you had it in you."

With a grim smile, he ushered her onward, his arms around her. "I will keep you out of trouble—so help me God—until you are cleared, one way or another. I was already turning over the idea in my mind when you obligingly abandoned ship."

Shaking her head, she exclaimed, "*Deus*—my wiles are indeed formidable. I had no idea."

"You have never needed wiles—not with me."

Steering her into an indent in one of the rocky outcroppings, he rubbed her arms with his own cold hands as they walked on the graveled sand. "There is a tunnel which connects to the inn's cellar; it was used for smuggling in the old days." He motioned for her to stand for a moment in the sheltered area between the rocks, and she obliged, shivering, as she watched him climb lightly into a sheltered crevice. The area smelled of must and salt, and deposits of seaweed beneath her feet marked where the tide had receded. I am as foolish as I was at seventeen, she reminded herself, but decided there was nothing for it; she loved the man, and apparently—although the matter had not yet been verified—apparently he loved her in return. She watched as he groped with his fingers for a moment, then she saw the outlines of a weathered wooden door appear in the recesses of the rocks as he pulled at an iron ring handle. The ancient door creaked open, the sound echoing eerily off the rocks.

He gestured for her to come to him, but she did not move, instead raising her voice over the sound of the waves. "Give me one good reason why I should not shoot you instead."

He thought about it, poised with one leg braced against the rocks. "Your weapon is too wet."

She shook her head. "Not good enough."

He bent his head, as though seriously considering the question. "You love me."

Looking away, she fought her emotions and wished she could control her shivering—she hated to appear pathetic.

His voice continued, "My name is Lucien Jameson Carstairs Tyneburne. I hold a Baronet with an estate in Suffolk."

She assimilated this information, still unable to look at him. "And we are not wed." Her voice sounded bleak to her own ears, and again she hated sounding so weak.

"We will be."

She turned then to look at him. "I gave your *estupido* ring away."

"I know it—my first clue that we had been twigged."

With some defiance, she tossed her head. "I knew as soon as I saw Gaston, pretending to scheme with the cook."

"Lina," he said gently. "You will freeze to death."

Gathering her dignity, she relented and climbed up to pass before him into the opening, which revealed a dark, cramped, and musty tunnel hewn from the rock. "You should take the lead," she offered. "I am too cold to flee, I promise. Pending tomorrow."

Placing a guiding hand on the wall, he walked forward into the inky darkness. "How did you know that Gaston had changed sides?"

"I am Napoleon's *chère-amie*."

There was silence for a few moments as she followed him. "Sorry," he said over his shoulder.

She spoke, her voice echoing off the narrow walls as they felt their way in the darkness. "I am base-born, and from the wrong side of the blanket. My father was an itinerant gambler and my mother a very headstrong and beautiful woman."

His disembodied voice echoed back from the darkness ahead. "They produced an excellent product between them and so I can find nothing to criticize in either."

They continued in silence for a moment, and she decided she was rather enjoying herself, gauging the extent of his foolishness. "At the risk of sounding vain, I am an infamous courtesan."

But he corrected her in a level tone. "On the contrary—you are minor Portuguese nobility and every now and then your accent shows itself despite your best efforts to be as Anglicized as possible; the lapse only endears you to the neighbors."

Possibly, she thought, intrigued and turning over the role in her mind as she followed his voice. But he is a madman to even think of it. "I cannot feel my feet."

"At least you still have your shoes," he retorted.

"I did not ask you to come," she countered with some heat. "Do not complain."

"I cannot complain—the benefits thus far outweigh the detriments."

She smiled at his back, which was really quite lovely and would probably sport fingernail marks on the morrow. "That may not always be the case," she warned.

"Too late," came the answer from the darkness ahead of her. "I'm in."

"As I am already aware."

She heard him chuckle. "Mind your step—there is a stair coming up. We are almost there."

Chapter 30

Lina sat before the grate in a servant's garret under the eaves of the Mermaid Inn, wrapped in a blanket and leaning in so as to allow her hair to dry while Maisie collected her sodden clothes, muttering under her breath. Frozen feet and fingers had been thoroughly thawed out in a hot bath that was equal parts pleasure and pain, and now Lina sat content by the fire, fighting to stay awake and fully aware that the night was far from over.

Once she and Carstairs had gained access to the cellar, he had wrapped two burlap sacks around her and instructed her to wait while he reconnoitered; there was a crude stairway hidden within the walls that led to the attic, but he had to ensure it was not currently in use. This meant, Lina surmised, that their Home Office superiors used the place for other purposes throughout the year—she had noted there had been no cobwebs in the tunnel and the cellar had been swept clean recently.

Upon his return, he had rubbed her cold hands between his. "We'll tuck you in the servant's quarters under the eaves for the next few days while I enlist some local men to conduct a search. You will have to lie low for a bit."

"To what end, Lucien?" she had asked through chattering teeth.

"We'll discuss it later—after you are warmed and fed."

As this seemed a good plan, Lina asked him to send Maisie to her but he had balked, perhaps thinking of Maisie's ties to Brodie. Lina had insisted and won the point, probably because he was as aware as she that Maisie would be harder to fool than the local residents. Indeed, her maidservant did not appear to accept Lina's explanation of a boating mishap and was uncharacteristically cross as she bustled about, tidying up after the bath.

"A female in yer condition; flailin' about in the sea in the dead of night and puttin' yerself in danger without usin' a mite o' the sense God gave ye."

Slightly alarmed that her normally unflappable henchwoman appeared to be undone, Lina made an attempt to soothe her, "It was indeed foolish, Maisie—I do not know what's come over me."

But Maisie was not to be mollified as she cast an eye toward her mistress. "I knows 'xactly wot's come over ye, and ye've got to think serious-like about gettin' out from under 'im, if I may say so."

Thoughtfully, Lina turned back to face the fire. "It is not easy to explain, Maisie, but it is not Mr. Carstairs's fault and it is not my fault, either—we are each trying to sort out our loyalties, I think."

"I knows wot I know and I sees wot I see," intoned her unhappy maidservant.

Thinking to divert her thoughts, Lina teased, "Then know that I am starving, and this baby is starving, so best shake your stumps and see what you can see in the kitchen pantry."

With a final, disapproving sniff Maisie left to forage up a meal while Lina sat, arms around her knees, staring at the fire. I hope I can eat whatever Maisie brings me and I wish I knew what was best to do, she thought. And I wish I knew whom to trust—or more properly, whom to trust most. And I mustn't be dazzled by the prospect of living in Suffolk and having this fine man make love to me every night. That is, if he doesn't plan to do me in, first.

As if in answer to her thoughts, Carstairs slipped silently through the door and leaned against it to assess her in the candlelight. He had bathed and was dressed in clean clothes, which she thought was considerate as it created the illusion they wouldn't wind up in bed together even though they both knew this was not at all the case.

"Better?"

"As you see," she responded with a smile. "Maisie is downstairs finding food. I have not yet thanked you for coming to my rescue."

"Because you are not yet certain that I have." He approached and sat across from her on the edge of the cot that served as a bed, his hands clasped between his knees. The blue eyes glinted in the candlelight; his hair was damp and there was dark stubble on his chin. He was a lovely, lovely man.

She pulled up one corner of her mouth. "I am willing to concede that our sea adventure was not part of the trap and seizure plan."

"I beg of you," he said in complete seriousness. "Don't ever do that to me again—I thought my heart would burst from my chest."

"You have little right to make any demands of me, my friend."

He ducked his chin, contemplating the wooden floor. "Forgive me. There are competing interests."

"I know." It was true, she did. And as he was an honorable man, his love for her would always take second place to those interests—she could not hold it against him. "Are those competing interests planning to hang me?"

He tilted his head, unwilling to answer directly. "They saw our situation as an opportunity to expose your hand and arrest you—away from London and without Brodie's knowledge. They are certain you are tainted."

"And you?"

He thought about it, seriously. "I don't know."

She appreciated his honesty. "I see. And if I were?"

His jaw hardened as he met her eyes. "I would keep you out of trouble, one way or another."

She laid a hand on her abdomen. "Because of the baby."

Shaking his head, he gave her his half smile. "In part—but mainly because I cannot seem to help myself."

As the light flickered over his face she thought, I cannot seem to help myself, either, even though this is not the season to dally in romance—too much is at stake. They sat in silence for a few moments. "So what will you tell them?"

"I will tell them you jumped ship to avoid capture and I was unable to recover your lifeless corpse despite diligent search."

Frowning, she pointed out, "But my reanimated corpse is going to appear at some point, certainly."

"Yes, but in such a way that you are cleared of any taint."

Arching her brows, she had to shake her head slightly in disbelief. "This sounds an excellent plan, and I am all attention."

He shrugged his shoulders in rueful acknowledgment. "My plan is unfledged as yet—but it cannot hurt to have a lapse of time with no further suspicious activity on your part."

Her gaze upon the candle, she thought, ah—he is careful

not to mention Brodie and the inconvenient fact they hope to catch him red-handed in a treasonous plot. She decided she'd not bring up the subject as it seemed certain to be a point of contention and things were going along so well—she would swear that Carstairs had been completely honest with her from the time they emerged from the sea—perhaps it had not been such a bad idea to leap overboard, after all.

"First things first. Help me think of a way to bring you back to London without every man jack who sees you remembering your face."

She rested her chin on her knees and hid a smile. It pleased her that he spoke of her beauty as though it were a thing separate from herself, and an annoyance besides. "I could wear a veil."

He shook his head. "A woman wearing a veil is an object of scrutiny—we'd be no better off."

She thought of other resorts she had used. "A nursemaid? Or a nun?"

Meeting her eyes in apology, he said, "We cannot run the risk—you may have to hide in a sack."

"Like the Flemish ambassador?"

"Only without the coshing and the laundry chute. Would you do it, do you think?"

They regarded each other, both aware that she would not want to be so constrained, and thus forced to trust him. "I will think on it," she conceded.

At this point the door opened and Maisie came through, bearing a drawn-up cloth and a stoneware flagon. She paused when she saw Carstairs and made no acknowledgment to him. As this was an ominous sign, Lina said hurriedly, "Thank you, Maisie—that will be all."

The maidservant made no comment as she set the flagon down and unfolded the cloth to reveal cheese and sliced bread.

Carstairs addressed her. "Maisie, you and I must come to terms."

Lina looked from one to the other with alarm. It was best not to square off against Maisie on any subject—she was a gunnery sergeant's widow, after all.

Maisie faced him, folding her hands before her. "Permission t' speak, sir."

He nodded. "You have it. Proceed."

"Ye're nowt to put that look on 'er face again."

"Understood."

The woman turned and left, shutting the door with a click behind her, and Lina didn't know where to look. "Forgive her—she has the luxury of only one allegiance." She realized as soon as she had said the words that it may not have been the wisest thing to say to him, but he did not press her and moved down beside her on the floor so as to eat. Watching his profile in the firelight, she felt a wave of longing so strong that it nearly suffocated her. "I am not much of a courtesan, truly—despite what I said earlier."

"It doesn't matter to me, Lina." Reaching in, he held up a slice of cheese to her. "Come; you must try to eat."

"I ate a fish this afternoon." She tentatively nibbled on the cheese even though she had little appetite. Watching her, he put cheese to bread and ate with his fingers, obviously hungry. When he drank from the flagon he grimaced in disappointment. "Water."

"I do not drink, Lucien," she reminded him.

He paused and wiped his mouth with the back of his hand. "That first night," he said slowly. "You told me I tasted of cheap whiskey. It surprised me at the time—you are a notorious teetotaler."

"Yes—I remember," she hedged. *Deus*, it seemed they knew everything; well, she amended—almost everything.

He didn't press but lifted her hand to kiss it. "That was without a doubt the best assignment I have ever received."

"And well-done of you," she noted in an ironic tone. "And here I felt so guilty that you thought I was Marie."

"There is no confusing the two of you."

She nibbled on a crust and decided not to probe the undercurrent that lay beneath the last comment.

He glanced over at her. "However well-done my role was, you were not misled."

"You mistake," she disagreed in a mild tone. "It is not that I was not misled, it is that I am not tainted."

There was a pause as he stared at her, turning over what she had said. He then spoke slowly, "I would like to believe you—I would, Lina. But what is at work here, then? It makes little sense."

Her voice gentle, she replied, "I'm afraid I cannot say—leastways, not yet."

Trying to control his exasperation, he ran a hand over his head, his hair still damp from his bath. "Then I should simply trust you? Even though you cannot tell me and there is so much at stake?"

"If you would—I swear to you that England will not suffer for it."

There was a silence for a few moments. A novelty, she thought. For either of us to trust anyone an inch.

"All right," he said finally.

Emotion closed her throat as she bowed her head and thought about how foolish it was to have weaknesses, and how she would very much like to give in to this particular blue-eyed weakness and tell him of Brodie's plan.

But he had moved on to another topic. "And now I would like to hear how Lina became Invidia."

She thought about it, studying the floorboards in the small, sparse room as the fire crackled. "It is not a pretty tale," she warned.

"Nevertheless, I would like to hear it."

And so she told him.

Chapter 31

I married Tom when I was seventeen, in Spain."

He interrupted her. "How did you meet?"

She gave him a look. "I was a hostess in a gaming ken."

Brows drawn together, he regarded her intently. "How did you come to be in Spain?"

"Are you going to interrupt me every step of the way? This is not an easy tale to tell."

He leaned forward, his gaze very blue in the flickering firelight. "Could you start at the beginning, perhaps?"

She contemplated the fire, debating how much to tell him. She decided she may as well start at the very beginning—he had no one to blame but himself. "My mother had a liaison with my father, who was a traveling gambler and not one to be settling down with a family. I was born. I lived with my mother for a time, but then she married another ne'er-do-well against the advice of her relatives. He tended to drink away the money my father sent to support me." She paused. "When I was fourteen I began to avoid my stepfather as he was a bit too friendly."

She heard him make an involuntary sound of dismay, but she lifted her face to his and assured him, "I was very adept at defending myself—even then. My appearance was already beyond that of ordinary girls, and so I was forced to learn at an early age. One of our neighbors was an old man who had been a *soldado* a long time ago—when the Portuguese fought Spain." She smiled, remembering. "He taught me to fight and to use a knife. He gave me his dead wife's pistol and told me I would need it—if he was twenty years younger he would abduct me himself."

Carstairs smiled to hear it. "An ally, then."

She nodded. "Of a sort. He despised my stepfather and thought my mother a fool, but then again, he thought everyone a fool."

Gently, he asked, "Did your mother refuse to believe ill of your stepfather?"

Lina rendered a soft smile. "No, she was very protective of me. She began to bring me to work—she sold flowers, ten *reis* a dozen—at a booth at the center of town. Lilies, mostly. We discovered if I hawked the flowers to gentlemen, sales were brisk." She paused again, lost in the memory. "She told me my father had opened a gaming ken in Sevilla and was doing well—I believe she was thinking of leaving my stepfather and seeking him out. Then the invasion came."

"Where was this?"

"Guarda."

Carstairs whistled softly.

Swallowing, Lina tried to keep her voice level. "Well, you know what came next. The Portuguese army was guarding the ports and so there was literally no one to defend the villages when the French came marching through. The clergy and the old *soldado* closed the gates and mounted a defense—although it was hopeless from the first. My mother was never one to sit idly by; she hid me in the root cellar and manned a musket at the wall for a half-day before it was overrun and she was killed, as was everyone."

There was another pause while Lina gently placed a finger under her eye and drew it away, observing the tip. Why, she thought in surprise, I am weeping—how strange.

His voice gentle, he asked, "Were you able to bury your mother?"

She drew a breath. "No. The soldiers took revenge for our resistance, but fortunately the pillaging could not last for long as they were on the march. After hiding another day in the cellar, I escaped at night and made my way to the east, avoiding the roads." Impossible to describe to him the stench of the corpses that had already lain a day in the sun; or the acrid smell of gunpowder that still lingered as she picked her way through the rubble of her old neighborhood, alone and terrified of discovery.

Carstairs was quiet for a moment. "And your stepfather?"

She shook her head. "I know not—I assume he was killed also. I left for Sevilla to find my father. I had a romanticized notion that he was heroic, you see, and would rescue me from my difficulties."

"And did he?"

She shook her head, but with a smile. "No—he had not the first clue what to do with a sixteen-year-old girl. To his credit, he looked after me in his own way and taught me cards. I have a good head for numbers, as it turned out, which was very helpful. He expanded his business and we moved northward. The Allied Armies were an excellent source of gaming revenue, but Napoleon's troops were kept on a tighter string so he tended to avoid the areas occupied by the French."

"Where was this?"

"San Pablo."

He nodded.

Tracing a finger on the hearth beside her, she reflected, "It was not a bad life—I learned to read people, and to calculate odds and be patient until the odds were in my favor. And I made some friends."

"Is that how you met Tom?"

She made a wry face. "Not exactly. My father wanted to buy another building but did not have the funds. The owner was an older widower—very wealthy—and my father arranged for my marriage to him in exchange for the building. I was seventeen and very unhappy with such a plan."

"Infamous."

But Lina only shook her head. "No, not infamous, in retrospect. Marriages for worldly gain are arranged every day, and I imagine I would have been treated very well. At the time, however, it seemed the end of the world."

She paused, so he prompted, "Did you run away?"

She sighed. "No; there was no need as I was never without champions—but I was too young, as yet, to judge the quality of those champions. I was sitting on the garden wall and weeping with frustration when Tom wandered by—he was a sergeant stationed with the 59th at Corunna, and I was acquainted with him; I was acquainted with everyone in the area. He heard my story and promptly offered to elope with me."

"Lucky man, to be in the right place at the right time."

"Not so lucky—my father discovered the plan because Tom was boasting to his fellows and I was locked in my room pending my nuptials to the elderly widower."

"And then? Did Tom rescue you?"

She shrugged. "I rescued myself; I tied the sheets together in the best tradition and climbed down the wall. My father had taken my clothes away so that I wouldn't attempt an escape—as a result I turned up at the barracks in my nightdress."

Carstairs grinned in appreciation and leaned back, resting on his hands. "Holy God—I can only imagine."

Remembering the scene, she couldn't help but smile herself. "Yes—it created quite the ruckus. But we managed to find the chaplain, a romantic soul who married us on the spot."

"And your father?"

"I left with the regiment and never spoke to him. I imagine he was furious, but no more furious than I."

"Is he still alive?"

She shrugged. "As far as I know."

There was a pause while she drew her knees closer to her, and a small silence stretched out between them. Carstairs walked over to stir up the embers with the poker and place another piece of wood in the grate. He stood watching the fire for a moment in the silence, one boot resting on the fire jack. "How long did you follow the drum?" he prodded gently.

"Over a year."

There was another silent pause, which was broken when he said in a quiet tone, "If you'd rather not tell me you needn't, you know."

She ran a hand through her hair, gauging its dryness and then fingered the very tip of a curl for a moment. "We were caught behind enemy lines in San Sebastian, after the French had turned on the Spanish—a small distance from Saragossa."

This caught his interest and he turned his head toward her. "During the Spanish retreat?"

"Yes, our regiment was heading westward and didn't anticipate the extent or the speed of the retreating Spanish. Some of the regiment managed to break through but the remainder were captured and held at San Sebastian. The Spanish soldiers were fresh from the misery of their own campaign and the French betrayal; they were bitter and undisciplined."

He nodded, as they were both aware of the tumult at the time, when the French had suddenly turned on the Spaniards—their former ally—and all hell had broken loose. "Why did the Spanish bother to capture you? They should have been pelting back to Portugal to escape from the port."

She explained, "The Spanish company who captured us had become separated from the rest of their regiment and were hoping for leverage, I think, to get them through the British lines and away to the port. They were panicked; rumors flew and no one knew where the main French force was."

"It was chaos," he agreed.

She looked up at him. "Were you there?"

"Southern Spain—in the hills."

"With El Halcon," she remembered. "I would like to hear your tale."

He nodded. "Willingly—but let us finish your own, first."

Dropping her gaze again she traced her knee through the blanket as the new wood crackled in the fire. "The Spanish captain found me attractive."

"Did you shoot him?"

She met his eyes and realized he was serious, which she thought a fine compliment. "No. I wasn't given the chance—or at least not at first."

He settled in beside her on the hearth, stretching his long legs out before him. "Did he pay for his impertinence?"

She nodded and bit her lip. "Oh yes. He—and the others, they paid."

"Good." He took her hand. "Tell me."

Chapter 32

Our group was comprised of a dozen soldiers and three camp followers; Johanna and Libby were the other two women. We were captured at the Convent of Santa Isabella after a gun battle in the church; the Spanish held the altar and the sacristy at one end and we held the nave and the vestibule at the other end—it was absurd, truly. After we ran out of ammunition, we were forced to surrender, much to the relief of the Holy Sisters, who did not even wait until we were marched out before they swarmed the altar rail to begin prying the musket balls loose."

He made a sound reflecting his sympathy while Lina put her chin on her knees and continued, "We were held in the general barracks on the outskirts of the town overnight; the Spanish had sustained terrible losses and were on edge—they had been betrayed and were not certain they could escape to Portugal. They believed, I think, that they could use us to force the English to come to their aid. A soldier was sent out as a scout to discover the status of their regiment, where the French were, and whether it would be worth their while to hold us as hostages."

Carstairs interrupted her recital. "There is nothing worse than being captured—I'd as soon be wounded."

"I agree—recall how we took a swim this night." She slid him a sidelong look.

He ducked his head in acknowledgment. "*Touché.* Pray continue."

"We thought it best to try to engage the captain and prevail upon him to let us go, and Tom went to parlay. When he returned to the barracks he was in high spirits—a false heartiness, as it turned out. He reported that the captain was a reasonable man and would let us go if I came to his quarters and played cards with him over a bottle of wine." Color flooded her cheeks at the memory. "Of course, the unspoken condition was that I would let him bed me. Tom tried to make it sound as though this was a reasonable request." She realized her voice was rising and took a breath to calm herself. "I refused, and we quarreled, but at least I thought that was the end of it."

Soberly, her companion watched her in the flickering firelight. "But it wasn't?"

"No. Later in the evening the mood seemed to change—our captors were friendlier, joking with our men, and we were informed we would be released the following morning when they retreated westward. We were fed the soldiers' fare; a spicy stew with peppers and bread. The only drink was home-brewed whiskey—powerful stuff. I was unused to spirits, but our men kept toasting me, encouraging me to drink. A deal had been struck, with me unaware." She could not contain the bitterness in her voice.

Carstairs bent his head and traced a finger along the veins on the back of her hand. "It was war. He was young, and frightened; and he didn't have your steel—few do."

"You would have died first."

"A hundred times over," he agreed. "But then I would have been dead and unable to help you."

She retorted with anger, "Better to die with honor than to be slaughtered like a sheep in the courtyard the next morning."

He met her eyes, startled. "Holy God. All of them?"

"Except the women," she said in a brittle voice. "And the other two had a worse time of it than I—I was so sick from the drink that I miscarried. The soldiers looked for more appealing prey."

He pulled her head against his shoulder and she felt his lips on her hair. "Lina, I am so sorry."

"An evil day," she whispered.

"How did you escape?"

She bowed her head for a moment. "The captain's plans to keep me as a trophy were stymied by the pressing need to retreat. As I was in no shape to flee, he left me there."

"And the other women?"

"I do not know what became of Johanna—she was not a strong woman to begin with. On the other hand, Libby had convinced one of the soldiers she was fond of him long enough to wrest his pistol and kill him. She was executed in the courtyard—flinging curses and defiant. I admired her greatly."

"And took her name."

Lina was apologetic. "She had a pension from her father, you see. It seemed such a waste—she would have understood."

He was silent, absently rubbing her shoulder with his hand. "And then Invidia had her vengeance."

"Yes. I found a pistol that had been left among the corpses and stumbled down the hill to a farmstead, where I stole an old cart horse; the occupants had fled ahead of the retreating army. I managed to mount up—even though I was weak as a kitten—and stalked the *bastardo* in the best *guerrilla* tradition; you would have been proud."

"I could not be prouder."

"As they retreated I followed along the tree line and

picked them off—one by one—when the opportunity arose." She mustered up a grim smile at the memory. "They were terrified, and had no idea who tormented them."

"But the captain escaped?"

She sighed. "I finally fainted and fell off the horse near the Portuguese border."

"Bad luck."

"I suppose—although I lived to tell the tale, thanks to the kindness of a prostitute who took me in, thinking I shared her profession. At the time I truly didn't care if I lived or died."

"If the captain yet lives, I will find him and we will kill him together."

She was touched by the gesture. "Lucien—how sweet."

He rested his cheek against her temple. "A wedding gift."

Smiling, she shook her head slightly. "Oh-ho; I have been down that wedding road before, my friend, and it is not a pleasant memory."

His tone firm, he reiterated, "You will marry me, whether you will or no."

Mildly, she returned, "I would be loath to have to take my pistol to you, too."

"You wouldn't." He lifted her hand and kissed the palm. "I have been privileged to see beneath the shell."

She stared into the fire, a half smile on her lips, feeling as though a burden had been lifted from her heart. He ran his hand down her back and absently played with her hair. "Who else knows of your story?"

"The Vicar, apparently," she answered with a grimace. "Much to my dismay."

He whistled again. "Impressive, that he tracked you back through that chaos."

She corrected him, "Not precisely—remember, he believes I am Libby."

"How did you come to be in this business—were you recruited over there?"

Resting her chin on her drawn-up knees, she gazed at the fire. "Yes. I continued killing French and Spanish soldiers indiscriminately, and apparently some spymaster heard of my exploits and thought I was sufficiently reckless to be recruited. And of course it helped that I had no connections and no plans."

"And can make men witless," he added.

"That, too," she agreed. "At first, my role was constrained to that of an angel—to beguile military leaders into confessing strategy. Then I began interpreting the ciphered documents myself without having to make copies for others to interpret; my value increased and my assignments became more high profile. Then the war ended—or at least it seemed so at the time—and I moved to England to investigate those attempting to bring down the country from within; investment fraud, or embezzlement."

He nodded. "And so you were assigned to link up with Brodie, whose actions in buying up all the Treasury bonds have alarmed the Home Office."

"Yes—certainly a cause of grave concern."

Into the silence he spoke, the words all the more alarming for their quiet tenor. "They are certain Rochon has met with you personally—last fall, when you broke contact."

There was a long pause before she turned to meet his eyes. "Is that what this is about? I'm to confess, now that I've been softened up by my not-quite husband?"

He did not flinch. "I need to know how complicated my plan must be to clear you of any taint."

With a wry smile, she rested her head on his shoulder and confessed, "Complicated. I have indeed met with Rochon in the flesh, and on more than one occasion."

He was taken aback, she could tell, although he did not betray his surprise. "Yet you insist you are not tainted."

She shook her head. "I am not—*santos*, it is tiresome of you to keep asking."

With a frown, he attempted to puzzle it out. "If you are not tainted, then you must mean to betray Rochon—yet why won't you simply admit this and say what you know?"

But she would not be drawn. "Again, complicated."

He made a sound of frustration. "Who holds your allegiance, Lina?"

"You do."

She lifted her head and they stared at each other for a long moment as the fire crackled. "We will save it for another time," he pronounced in a husky voice and drew her into his arms.

Chapter 33

Lina woke the next morning, stiff from having spent an uncomfortable night. Carstairs had determined that the cot wouldn't be sturdy enough to hold their combined weight, and so the straw mattress was dragged to the floor beside the banked fire. He had then tenderly covered her with both a blanket and his own warm and wonderful body but she had been unable to fight exhaustion and so had fallen asleep during his lovemaking. Remembering, she covered her face with her hands and groaned with embarrassment.

"So ye're awake." Maisie was pouring a jug of hot water into the basin.

Lina assessed her maidservant through her fingers and decided the other's mood had improved, which was a good thing. "I could sleep the clock 'round, Maisie, and this wretched pallet reminds me of sleeping in a haystack."

"Ye can sleep later—I has me orders, I do." The other woman slung a flannel towel over her shoulder and assessed Lina with a practiced gaze, her hands on her hips.

Propping herself on an elbow, Lina swept the hair from her eyes and returned her regard with some surprise. "And who, pray tell, is giving you orders?"

But Maisie was unrepentant. "Yer man, that's who. He's nowt happy ye've never seen a doctor about the babe, and small blame t' him."

Amused, Lina contemplated the fact that her erstwhile husband knew exactly how to winkle his way back into favor. "Heavens, Maisie—what has he said to sweeten you up? Or did he bribe you?"

Ignoring the slight, her maidservant continued, "I'm to keep ye quiet today and see to it ye have eggs an' milk."

With a grimace, Lina lay back down. "Neither sounds very appetizing just now."

Considering this, Maisie suggested, "I can dip some bread in the eggs and milk so as to soak—then toast the bread."

"With jam?" Jam actually sounded rather appealing.

"I'll find some," agreed Maisie. "We'll see iffen ye can keep it down."

Lina gingerly stretched out her aching back, trying to muster up an appetite. She could hear rain tapping on the garret's window and pulled the wool blanket closer around her shoulders. "Has Mr. Carstairs eaten?"

"Hours ago—he left t' mount a search. Sech a fine horse." Maisie considered herself a fair judge of horseflesh, being from the north country.

Smiling, Lina teased her, "Ah—now I understand why you will take orders from him. Did he promise you a foal?"

But her maid continued, unashamed of her new loyalty as she laid out the linens. "He made me promise ye wouldn't try to escape t'day whilst he was away. Ye're to hide—bein' as ye've drowned an' all." Reminded, she added, "He said yer not to walk about when I'm downstairs, so no one hears you and comes to look."

Lina lay back to contemplate the rough-hewn ceiling, her hands behind her head. "You've turned coat, Maisie—I am disappointed but unsurprised."

Unfazed by this calumny, Maisie bustled out the door. "I'll

fetch yer breakfast. Iffen ye can manage to go back to sleep, I won't wake ye—it'd be better than eatin', I'm thinkin'."

Lina tried to muster up enough energy to rise and dress, the straw pallet rustling while she turned to sit up. Although she was used to sleeping in uncertain surroundings, she had not done well last night; she had dreamed of San Sebastian—probably because she had spoken of it—and woke in a cold terror, her heart pounding. Carstairs had held her and assured her in Portuguese that the baby was safe—she must have said something in her nightmare. Poor man, she thought. First I fall asleep during lovemaking and then I give him a scare for his troubles; he'll think long and hard about taking me on.

Raising her arms over her head to stretch, she could not suppress a smile because despite the fact she should not trust him an inch, it did seem—and here she was cautiously optimistic—he truly meant to take her on. Even though I am a bundle of troubles, she thought with remorse; I should help him sort them out.

To this end she spoke to Maisie while picking with little enthusiasm at the proffered toast and jam. "Do you think you can lay hands on a Bible somewhere?"

Maisie blinked. "Ye'll be studyin' the Bible now, missy?"

"I have a mind to," Lina teased with a sidelong glance. "I shall have to teach this child something other than how to nick an ace."

Dubious, Maisie offered, "I'll see if I can find one downstairs—I has t' leave at noon, though."

"Oh?" Lina raised her brows in amusement. "Do you have standing orders, then?"

Maisie lifted her eyes to the ceiling, folded her hands under her apron, and recited, "I'm to bring food t' the men who're lookin' for ye; I'm to remember to be sorrowful, and weep."

Privately, Lina hoped Maisie could pull it off; she tended to be self-conscious when she was playing a role, which is why it was a rare—and desperate—occurrence. *Deus*, she thought, I cannot take another bite to save my life, and she pushed the plate away.

Shaking her head with sympathy, Maisie gathered up the breakfast things while Lina lay back, fighting nausea. "I'll bring a Bible an' ye kin read while I'm gone. And don't forget—no movin' about."

Thus enjoined, Lina passed a tedious day watching the rain on the tiny windowsill and thumbing through the onionskin pages of the ancient Bible until she found what she was looking for—not that it eased her mind. I don't know why it's such a Good Book, she thought, staring at the fire—it does me precious little good.

In the late afternoon she heard voices and doors slamming and was sorely tempted to do some soft-footed listening, but Maisie came in just as she moving toward the door.

"Ye'll stay put, missy," the maid warned. "Yer man's back, wi' some o' the men; he says he'll offer 'em a drink and then he'll come up to see ye."

Lina brightened, pleased her abject boredom would soon be at an end. "Good—first brush out my hair and then make yourself scarce."

Maisie looked disapproving. "Best t' let the poor man rest—he's had a long day."

"He won't complain, Maisie."

And he didn't; instead he paused in the doorway for a moment, surveying her naked form with approval as she approached and twined her arms around his neck. "Poor Lucien—you look tired."

He wrapped his arms around her and spoke into her

ear. "Knackered. But recovering nicely, as I imagine you can tell."

She chuckled and trailed kisses along his throat. "Good—I have to make it up to you for falling asleep last night."

He bent to kiss her shoulder as his fingers began unfastening the buttons on his shirt. "I didn't take it personally—I just soldiered on without you."

Laughing, she kissed his chest as she helped him pull off his shirt. "I am sorry, Lucien. I meant no insult."

He enclosed her in his arms and squeezed tightly, lifting her off her feet. "I don't know—I've never had a woman lose interest as quickly as you did."

She obligingly wrapped her legs around his waist and ran her tongue along the inside of his ear, evoking a grunt of pleasure. "I am all attention, now."

"As am I—painfully so." He cupped her hips and pressed her against him as he carried her across to the fire. "Mind your head," he warned as he maneuvered them beneath the low ceiling and onto the pallet. "Someday soon," he murmured into her breasts, "we are going to do this in a decent bed."

"I shall hold you to it," she whispered, and could feel a chuckle reverberate in his chest, although he was fast becoming too serious to joke. He began to caress her while she gave in to the mindless pleasure—they were becoming accustomed to one another, and she now knew what pleased him best, as he knew her own preferences. For a moment, she was aware she would have to test their newfound trust, and soon—but she quickly quashed the thought and instead concentrated on the delightful present.

After a very satisfying session of lovemaking, Lina rested her head on his shoulder and pulled gently at the hairs on his chest. "Are you too tired to tell me what's afoot?"

"We'll see," he murmured sleepily.

"How are you playing it?"

She felt his chest rise and fall. "I am grim but resigned—I hold out little hope."

"Are you bereft?" she teased. "I would appreciate it if you were bereft."

"Only so much that I won't be suspected of doing you in. Recall that I only married you because you were pregnant."

Keeping her tone light, she asked, "Are you more bereft or less bereft than when Marie died?"

There was a small pause. "Unfair," he finally said.

"Sorry." He is good, she thought; he does not allow a distraction and his guard never comes down. Perhaps I have met my match—which may or may not be a good thing, considering this tale is not yet told and much remains to be accomplished.

"The Vicar does not believe you are dead."

Startled, she propped herself up on her elbow and looked down into his face. "The Vicar is *here*?"

Carstairs regarded her from beneath hooded lids and ran his hand over her back. "He is in close contact."

Lina was all admiration; Carstairs was much better at serving up a distraction than she was.

Chapter 34

Lina prodded, "What does our illustrious Vicar have to say on the subject?"

Carstairs's hands continued their lazy progress across her lower back. "He says we are fools to believe it, short of having your lifeless corpse before us on a slab."

Frowning, she absorbed this distressing information. "Does he suspect your complicity?"

"Not as far as I can tell."

She thought it over. "What is next?"

Tracing a finger across her lower lip, he replied, "The weather is helping; the locals tell us nothing will wash up for days—if at all—and most likely a half-mile to the south."

She teased, "Will you call off the search and take long and contemplative walks on the cliffs, thinking of what might have been?"

He lowered his chin slightly. "No—I will depart this sad place with all speed."

This was of interest, as she was slated to accompany him—although the logistics had not yet been sorted out. "Where do you go to mourn my poor dead self?"

Slowly he drew a tendril of her hair with two fingers to place it behind her ear. "Even your ears are perfect."

Impatiently, she shook his fingers away because they

tickled. "Do not change the subject, if you please. I would know where the twice-widower will reside, being as I imagine I will reside there with him."

He drew a finger along her cheek. "There is a safe house in Kensington—it will answer, and I doubt anyone will think to look for you there, with me. Only Maisie is to know," he added with emphasis, and it was clear he was warning her not to contact Brodie.

Laying her head on his chest, she said lightly, "So—you are to go home grieving, and break the news to my unknowing friends and acquaintances."

She felt him sigh in acknowledgment. "My sad charge."

There was a pause. "It's a bit rainy for a ride in a sack, Lucien."

"You are welcome to remain in this garret" was his mild reply.

She rose on her elbows again and gently punched him in the arm. "Don't even joke; I hate being cramped up in here—I've been miserable every moment."

He cupped her hips against him with his hands, smiling. "Oh?"

She chuckled and conceded, "Well, perhaps not every moment."

"I thank you." He drew her head toward him for a kiss.

After the lingering kiss, she smoothed his hair from his forehead. "I am reconciled to your plan, I suppose—how am I to be extracted?"

"Maisie will accompany me back to London, bringing your trunk and weeping into her handkerchief all the while."

With a sigh, she lowered her head again to his chest. "Just make certain I have enough air."

"That's my girl." He fingered the ends of her hair where it spilled around his ribs.

"But won't the Vicar be watching Maisie for such a trick?"

Drawing a strand of hair through his fingers, he lifted it and watched it fall. "I think not. He is preoccupied—your disappearance is not nearly as important as the disappearance of the latest gold shipment. The Treasury is in an uproar."

Lina lifted her head and met his gaze. "Are there any leads?"

In a neutral tone he disclosed, "One. A gold brick was discovered in your house."

Lina had no problem portraying her extreme surprise. "Truly? In *my* house?"

"It was under your cook's pillow."

She stared at him in horror, and then ducked her head and struggled not to smile. I cannot break role, she thought in desperation—hold steady, *menina*. Laughter welled up from within her breast, and she could not control it to save her life, so she burst into laughter until the tears came to her eyes. She had not laughed so hard in a long, long time.

He pulled her to him and laughed right along with her. "You can only imagine…"

"Oh Lucien," she gasped. "He must have been furious."

They laughed together again, then brought themselves under control, Carstairs's hand resting on her head. "How did you twig him?"

"Lucien," she protested with a smile. "I know nothing of this."

With good humor he pointed out, "But you knew it was the Curate, masquerading as your cook."

"Only because you gave him away—when I mentioned the card games with the footman next door you couldn't hold your role."

They gazed at each other a long moment and a smile still played around his lips. "Don't tell him I gave him away."

"As if I'd grass on you, wretched man—you should know better."

Chuckling, he rubbed his hand along her back. "I now see why my plan to clear your taint must be so complicated."

But she disagreed and shook her head at him with a smile. "Pray acquit me of this prank—how can I be implicated? I was safely stowed away here at the end of the earth with no friends at hand. Then I was good enough to drown."

Ducking his chin, he conceded, "Good point—all suspicion must fall on Brodie, then." His gaze was suddenly sharp upon her.

She arched a brow. "You know Brodie—perhaps he merely twists the Vicar's tail. It is not as though Brodie doesn't have his own gold bricks lying about."

Carstairs nodded in acknowledgment. "It is not enough to bring him in, certainly—and even if it was, they wouldn't dare for fear of what he'd do, and how it would look if they couldn't find proof of any wrongdoing."

"Definitely—and remember that he is unpredictable and does not always react as you would expect. Not to mention that he will have been bereaved of a very fine mistress—I'd not like to cross him just now."

"Will he grieve?" Carstairs asked, touching her face with his fingertips. He seemed genuinely curious.

Lina answered easily, "I imagine—he is very fond of me."

He traced her jaw line with a forefinger. "No more."

"No more what?" she teased.

"No more of that life."

She leaned in to bite his ear, gently. "Alas—and I have such a lovely sugar box full of jewels."

He tilted his head toward her because he was enjoying the attentions to his ear. "You won't need them in Suffolk."

She chuckled. "Lord, Suffolk will not know what to make of me."

"I will." He nibbled on her throat, then twisting, shifted himself atop her, his mouth trailing down to her abdomen. He paused and placed his hand across her trim waist for a moment, contemplating it. "It is hard to believe there is someone in there."

"I tend to forget, myself."

He propped up on an elbow and placed a palm where the baby rested. "What was your mother's name?"

She gazed at the ceiling and smiled. "Concepción."

He grinned. "Perhaps not."

"No—we shouldn't saddle this poor child with such a name."

"Constance, perhaps," he suggested.

Touched, she laid a hand against his face. "You are a wonderful, wonderful man."

He turned his head to kiss her palm and returned the compliment. "I cannot believe my good fortune—that I am here, with you."

"An amazing turn of luck." She could not suppress the undercurrent of irony and berated herself; she shouldn't undermine the bliss of the moment.

He did not respond to her tone but shifted up to lie beside her, pulling her head to rest on his shoulder. "I have to earn your trust. I understand."

They lay together in drowsy silence for a few moments while the rain pattered on the tiny window. "What if the child is a boy, Lucien?"

He tightened his arm around her. "Jameson. We have little choice, I'm afraid—every other generation is Jameson or Lucien."

With some alarm she confessed, "I am afraid to ask how many generations there have been."

"Nonsense; you are fearless."

Making a wry mouth she continued, "And I'll wager none of them has ever brought home someone like me."

"Poor souls."

Apparently he was feeling amorous again as he began to engage in the preliminaries. "Lucien," she whispered. "I'm afraid you are being foolish—to ignore such things."

He kissed her, open mouthed, and trailed kisses down her throat before he asked, "Is there any chance you will be executed for treason?" Suddenly his face was above hers, the expression in his blue eyes very serious.

"No," she said with complete sincerity. "Not the smallest chance."

"Then I don't care what they think." His face disappeared between her breasts and she decided there was nothing to be done—he was certifiable, poor man. But a master at love-making, which completely made up for the lapse. "Lucien," she gasped. "We have to stay quiet."

His busy mouth was muffled. "I am not the one who is noisy."

Writhing with pleasure, she laughed again. I could become accustomed to this, she thought. *Por favor Deus.*

Chapter 35

The next morning found Lina curled up in her trunk, listening to the sound of the rain on the lid as she rocked back and forth with the coach's movements. *Deus*, it will be nothing short of amazing if I do not become sick from the motion, she thought with resignation. If this doesn't turn the trick, nothing will.

In truth, she did feel a bit queasy but refused to dwell on this unfortunate fact and instead wriggled to place her nose and mouth a bit closer to the holes Carstairs had punched through the wall of the trunk and breathed in, smelling the scent of rain. She worked her pocket watch out of her pocket and carefully brought it before her face so that she could see the time by virtue of the light shafting through the air holes. Another hour or so; they would stop for lunch and to change the horses at Tunbridge Wells. She could hang on until then; she had been in worse straits—Rochon's lair came to mind.

As she was rocked back and forth, she thought about Carstairs, and how his skin tasted, and how much she craved him. She wondered idly about the last time he made love to Marie, perhaps only a few short weeks ago. His mention of her name that first night had been part of the trap—it was acutely annoying to think they had plotted her seduction, hoping for her own revelation of treason, and then when that hadn't worked had plotted her sham marriage with the same aim. How frustrating it must be for them that I am not cooperating, she thought with a twinge of satisfaction. By now they would have me clapped in irons so that they could root through my town house with impunity. As it is, they have spent a great deal of time and effort plotting my downfall with little to show for it.

She shifted position and tried not to think about her wayward stomach. Even if they seized her, they would still have to contend with Brodie, and he was a force to be reckoned with since he held the bonds that could bring the Treasury to its knees. Not to mention the Prince Regent was fond of Brodie since he never called in his debts—an excellent trait in a gambling crony.

And now Carstairs, by all indications, was so deeply in love with her that he was willing to risk sharing her disgrace if indeed she was tainted—unless his change of heart was merely the third of such attempts to beguile her into saying something damning. I wish I knew what was sham and what was not, she thought, breathing in deeply with her eyes closed. But I don't, and so I must plan accordingly—it seems that I have never rested easy; never had the luxury of peace, starting from that first day in Guarda when the French stormed in and the world came to an end.

Frowning, she shook herself out of her sadness, blaming it upon the current state of her stomach. She refused to rail against fate—there was no point to it, and thanks to what she had lived through she now had a prodigious strength of will; the old *soldado* would be proud. She kept breathing deeply and tried to concentrate on the task ahead.

When they finally came to a halt, it was not soon enough

for Lina. The rain had lessened but still continued in a light sprinkle; beyond the rain she could hear the bustling noises of the posting yard at the inn. She smiled to herself when she heard Carstairs's voice giving commands to the coachman and the posting boys. Soon, she thought, and mentally girded her loins. They had agreed ahead of time that Maisie would open the trunk to check on her while Carstairs diverted the stable personnel with instructions. Lina waited, flexing her fingers and her toes until the warning tap was heard and then the hasp unlocked. As the lid was lifted, Maisie's stolid face appeared. "Quick-like."

Lina needed no encouragement and hoisted herself out of the cramped trunk, her exit obscured by the raised lid in the event anyone was watching. She pulled Maisie's cloak from where it was folded under the maid's arm and climbed nimbly around to the rear of the carriage, away from the posting yard. Peering carefully around the corner of the vehicle, she saw that the coast was clear, and with one smooth movement swung down to the ground and then darted into one of the stable stalls, thankful her legs could still obey instruction. As she caught her breath, she viewed the yard through a crack between the boards and saw that no one had noticed her escape. Carstairs glanced toward the carriage to gauge Maisie's need as he finished up his conversation with the ostlers, and her maid could be seen gazing into the trunk for a few moments more before she lowered the lid and locked it up.

Quickly, Lina donned Maisie's serviceable cloak over her own and pulled the hood strings around her face as she watched Maisie walk across the courtyard to the inn. Carstairs soon followed the maid, probably anxious to hear a report on Lina. She felt a pang; she was wicked to serve him such a trick, but needs must when the devil drives, and they were dealing with the *diabo* himself.

She and Maisie had agreed that the break from the journey should be minimal so that it would be resumed as soon as possible, with Carstairs unaware that Lina no longer remained sequestered in the trunk. Once the carriage was under way again, Lina would then either steal a horse or beguile some man into lending her a mount and be on her way. She settled in to watch the yard and tentatively stretched out her legs—she hadn't ridden a horse in some time and hoped she would not disgrace herself. While she waited in the stall, she took off her gloves to blow on her fingers; the air was cold and damp as the light rain resumed.

After a short space of time, the new horses were put to and the coach was made ready for the continuation of the journey to London. Carstairs came out to inspect the harnesses while Maisie climbed into the interior, never glancing her way. Carstairs soon joined the maid inside and they were away, the wheels rattling on the gravel and Carstairs's horse tied to the boot.

Lina had already assessed the horseflesh stabled in her proximity and decided she liked the looks of a small bay mare. Moving slowly, she sidled alongside it and stroked the soft nose. "How would you like to go to London, my friend?" she whispered. The mare seemed to think the idea agreeable and nickered softly, searching for a tidbit. Taking a quick glance around, Lina began to move toward the tack room. As it was lunchtime, there were only a few hands about and she had learned long ago the best tactic when one was stealing something was to move with confidence. Hopefully no one would think to question her.

She grasped a likely looking saddle and bridle and returned to the mare only to confront Carstairs, leaning against the stall and watching her, his expression grave. Lina stood stock-still, her heart hammering. Finding that she could not lie to him, she said nothing.

"Where do you go?" he asked quietly.

She swallowed. "I must go on an errand, Lucien—I am sorry I could not say."

He dropped his gaze to the floor and said nothing for a moment. "Shall I see you again?"

She put all the sincerity she could muster into her voice. "Of course. This very evening—my hand on my heart, *querido*."

He stepped toward her and lifted the saddle from her hand so that he could saddle the mare. "It is raining, Lina."

"I will be very careful—and I think it is beginning to clear to the north." He was going to trust her, just as he had agreed. She was humbly touched, as she wasn't certain she could have done the same if she were in his position.

"Take my hat." He handed it to her and she donned it without comment, pulling the leather brim down low over her face—between the hood and the hat she wouldn't be recognizable. He tightened the mare's saddle girth. "Would you rather take Whistlejacket? He is a very steady fellow."

She considered. "I'd rather have a smaller mount in this weather, methinks. But I thank you for the offer." Unspoken was the additional fact that it wouldn't be helpful to either of them if she was spotted on his Andalusian stallion.

He cupped his hands for her boot and threw her up. She tightened the strings around her face to pull the hood close and gathered the reins. She couldn't help but ask, "How did you twig me?"

"Maisie's cloak was missing."

She smiled down at him in admiration. "Lord, you are a downy one, Mr. Tyneburne."

"Sir Lucien," he corrected her, with an apologetic tilt of his head.

Regarding him for a long moment she thought, I am a sad trial to this poor man—I must make it up to him. She leaned down and kissed him, pulling up the hat's broad brim. "I love you, Sir Lucien—never doubt it."

He did not smile. "I will not rest easy until you return."

She gathered up the reins and kicked the mare away. I shouldn't look back, she thought, or I may lose my nerve for the first time in my life.

Urging the horse into a canter, she cleared away from the posting house as quickly as she dared, the rain in her face making it difficult to see. She kept a hand on the crown of the borrowed hat, determined not to lose it to a gust of wind as it was a bit too large for her. I should have stolen a hat string, she thought; next time.

As the weather kept most other travelers indoors, she met very few on her journey, and as the mare was sure of foot, she had time to contemplate her actions. She wanted to trust Carstairs but dared not; she needed to make contact with Brodie and she needed to assess Jenny Dokes's complicity in the various plots and counterplots—that Dokes had sent her the note was alarming; Lina believed she was one of the few people capable of unraveling Brodie's careful plans and so it was important that she not be given the opportunity.

The sturdy little mare made no complaint as the miles passed. Lina continued unwell; the child within her was making his or her presence known. Jameson or Constance, she corrected, and belatedly realized that a long hard ride in the driving rain was perhaps not the best course of action for a woman in her condition. I should not tempt fate, now that happiness appears within my grasp, she thought, brushing the rain from her eyes with the back of a hand. *Mãe Maria*, please don't let me lose this child like the last one—I couldn't bear it. Even as she made the plea she realized that the memories from San Sebastian weren't as vivid; the horror not as acute. I have probed that wound, thanks to Carstairs, and have come away healed—or at least more healed than I was. Perhaps I am finished with the nightmares at last—I should work to ensure I do not replace them with an entirely new set. With renewed determination, she urged the mare forward.

Chapter 36

It is amazing the pigeons are so reliable, Lina thought idly as she watched them strutting about in their cote. They are such *passaros estupidos*.

Wrapped in Maisie's cloak, she sat on a joint stool, trying to stay warm and waiting patiently in the warehouse loft. She had dispatched one of the aforesaid pigeons as a signal to Brodie to meet with her, as any attempt to contact him directly would be observed by those who watched his every move—although the Curate probably no longer numbered among them. He was very clever at hiding his identity from me—my erstwhile cook, she thought with amusement. I wonder if he learned anything of interest other than how I like my eggs.

The pigeons stirred, flapping their wings upon feeling the air move when a door opened downstairs. Lina cocked her pistol but was reassured when she heard a soft whistle.

"Ho," said Brodie as he climbed up the narrow wooden stairs into the loft. "Well met, Mrs. Carstairs."

"Not exactly," she disclaimed from her perch on the stool, watching his approach. "You were right—it was a trap."

Pausing to catching his breath after coming up the steps, he considered this revelation with a frown. "Did you slay him?"

With her slow smile she shrugged in a self-satisfied

manner. "No; fortunately he is unable to resist me, and so at present he is trying to clear me of any taint—out of coverage, no less."

"Good man," pronounced Brodie, nodding in approval. "That he was compelled to follow orders can easily be forgiven—and his turnaround demonstrates flexibility, which is a virtue." He then belied this accolade by cocking a wary eye at her. "Did he follow you?"

"No," she assured him. "I am certain."

"Only have a care, *Bela*," he advised in a mild tone as he absently poked at the fluttering pigeons. "I believe you are smitten."

She leaned her head back against the rough boards behind her. "I am indeed smitten, and if this doesn't work out, you have permission to shoot me."

He made no comment but chuckled, looking out over the roofs of the adjacent warehouses; the loft was located in a dilapidated building that ostensibly housed goods in transit for the East India Company. The owner of record, however, did not exist. Instead the edifice served as a staging area for heavy, unmarked merchandise smuggled in under the floorboards of cargo wagons until it disappeared, little by little, into the London night. That, and as a pigeon cote for homing pigeons who seemed to spend the bulk of their time eating and preening, until they were required to fly with messages written on bank notes strapped to their legs.

"You will soon hear reports of my untimely death." Lina shifted from one hip to the other—she was already sore from the unaccustomed horse ride. "At least, I imagine they will want to tell you."

With some surprise, Brodie turned to her, his brows lifted. "Indeed? How is this?"

"I drowned off the coast of Sussex; it is part of Mr. Carstairs's plan to clear me of a taint." She decided not to mention that it was she who had flung herself into the vasty deep—no point in provoking a lecture.

Clasping his hands behind his back, Brodie rocked back on his heels and considered this. "To what end? I fail to see his intent—you are as recognizable as the Prince Regent, after all, and your compatriots will certainly take notice if you reappear at some later date."

"I am not certain," she admitted, "but I believe he is going to set up a trap for you while I am sidelined and thereby make it evident I am not involved in any of your dark doings."

Brodie's expression cleared and he nodded, thinking it over. "Rudimentary—but often the simplest plans are the best; there are not as many variables."

She cautioned him, "You must have a care, Benny; they know of the pigeons—of the communications with Rochon—and suspect the worst. They may feel they have no choice but to move in."

"I am not surprised," he replied absently. "They are not fools." He continued to review the skyline.

He was clearly preoccupied and a bit suspicious; she prodded, "What is afoot, my friend? Or am I not to be told the details just yet, being as I am smitten?"

Brodie stirred himself to walk over to the pigeons and lay a hand on the cote, watching them for a moment. "He should be rewarded for his loyalty, our Mr. Carstairs."

"Benny," she protested in mock alarm, "don't get him killed, I beg of you."

"He jeopardizes his livelihood to keep you safe," Brodie continued, warming to his subject. "He risks much on your behalf."

"No question that he is smitten," she admitted with all modesty.

Raising his gaze to meet hers, he declared, "He must have a hand in our little *denouement*—it is only fitting."

Narrowing her eyes, she watched him, not liking the look in his eye. "And here I believed I was to have a hand in our little *denouement*."

"Of course, *Bela*—you must be present and flying full colors so that our little rabbit does not suspect a trap." He said it in the tone of one having to explain to a child.

Lina knit her brow. "Then how can you have Mr. Carstairs present also? We cannot allow the rabbit to suspect my people are in any way involved; and on the other hand we cannot allow Mr. Carstairs to suspect we are working with the rabbit."

"I shall contrive." Brodie rested his thumbs in his waistcoat pockets and contemplated the skyline again. "I am the puppet master."

"I had forgotten," Lina responded in a dry tone. "Your pardon." She shifted on her stool again and decided to stand—*Deus*, it had been a long ride.

"You mock me." Brodie turned to give her a baleful look.

"Only because I have not half your wit," she soothed. "But think on it, Benny—you cannot bring Mr. Carstairs in on the *Argo* plan for fear he will seize the chance to double-cross you—and thus clear me."

"No, no; I do not dare bring him in—he is far too by-the-book."

Except when he is making rather savage love on the beach, thought Lina, but did not express this thought aloud.

Pacing beside the cote, Brodie mused, "It is a shame you are dead; you could plant a feint."

"What sort of feint?" asked Lina, intrigued. "A false lead?"

"Perhaps." He paused in his movements. "You cannot plant a feint with Mr. Carstairs—it would be too obvious. And we cannot use Mr. Grant, which is a shame as he is at the bank—which would be an excellent place to plant a false lead."

As he didn't explain himself, Lina decided to bite. "Why not Grant—aside from the fact he despises me and wouldn't believe a word I said?"

Brodie tilted his head toward her, a gleam in his eye. "His interests are not—shall we say—aligned with England's."

Utterly astonished, Lina stared at him. "Grant is tainted?"

"Tainted," he confirmed, enjoying her surprise. "Come, *Bela*—you should trust your instinct; it is rarely wrong."

Struck with a thought, Lina asked, "Do my people know this?"

"Undoubtedly." Brodie continued his pacing.

Her brow furrowed, Lina thought this over. "Then they must be planting their own false leads with Grant to pass on to Rochon."

"Indeed." He sighed hugely. "It makes my job all the more complicated—having to keep track of so many variables."

Thinking about his idea, Lina offered, "There is always Jenny Dokes—she pretended to warn me of the trap with Mr. Carstairs but I am certain she was working under orders to encourage me to flee, and thereby expose my treachery. I could pretend to believe her sincere, and reveal myself to her, asking for aid."

His brow lightening, Brodie turned to her and rubbed his hands. "The very thing—and it would serve her right for playing such a trick on you."

"I do not hold it against her," Lina protested. "She only follows orders—she knows I would understand. But she is very shrewd, Benny—you must tread warily."

But Brodie was not concerned with Jenny Dokes, and instead said to her very seriously, "Our rabbit is also very shrewd, *Bela*—you must be very careful to give him no hint of a grudge."

"Heavens, no; I shall make it clear that bygones are bygones—and at least I know for certain that I shall not be called upon to kiss him." She flashed Brodie a laughing smile and he chuckled in appreciation.

"Where do you stay?"

Making a wry mouth, she confessed, "Somewhere in Kensington—Mr. Carstairs was a little vague, probably because he fears I will tell you."

"Good man," Brodie declared again. "He shouldn't trust you an inch." He clucked his tongue. "Well, then, we shall make a preliminary plan now, and communicate only if a situation arises that would disrupt the main elements of the plan."

Lina reminded him, "It would not provoke comment if Maisie came to visit you—on account of my sad demise."

"Too risky," Brodie pronounced. "The *Argo* is too close to launch to run any risk."

"At long last. Do you think it will turn the trick?"

"*Bela*," he chided, turning to meet her gaze. "You disappoint me."

With a wary eye to him, she ventured, "I only wonder if we should have a contingency plan—as they do in the Army—in the event it does not go well."

He rested his benign gaze upon her. "The contingency plan will not include leaping from a rowboat into the sea or stealing a horse at Tunbridge Wells."

Twigged, thought Lina as she lapsed into silence. One can't put anything past Brodie.

Chapter 37

Swanson," said Jenny Dokes, her plain face lighting up with a smile that reflected equal parts pleasure and surprise. "Did I miss your note?"

Lina was seated in the other woman's sitting room where she had been patiently waiting for nearly an hour after having slipped in the servant's door. After stoking up the fire, she had spread out Maisie's cloak before it to dry. Her hair, on the other hand, was hopeless; there was nothing to be done between the rain and Carstairs's hat. After combing it out with her fingers as best she could, she settled in to wait, her cold feet thawing out on the hearth as steam rose from her half boots. Naturally she had first taken a quick search of the place and just as naturally, Dokes had left nothing of interest where a searcher could find it. The rooms were sparse and almost shabby, and Lina reflected on the general unfairness that deprived a talented woman like Jenny from having the opportunity to work for a bank or a counting house as would a man.

"No note, Dokes—I'm afraid I am out of coverage."

"I see." The other woman was unfazed by this revelation as she removed her pelisse and hat to hang them on the rack next to the door. "May I offer tea or are you in flight?"

Smiling, Lina replied with a gleam, "I would very much enjoy a cup of tea and I am more properly dead."

Dokes arched her brows as she fetched the kettle to the hearth. "Heavens; who killed you?"

Lina folded her hands and shot her a look. "No such thing—I killed myself. I drowned trying to escape."

"How shocking," the other replied, taking the tea things from the cupboard.

Lina wasn't fooled; Dokes was unshockable. In a light tone Lina asked, "You hadn't heard? I thought perhaps your ciphered note was an attempt to warn me. There was an elaborate trap and seizure in play, with my humble self as the target."

The other shook her head as she set the tray down on the table between them. "No—I know nothing of it—and the church hasn't had a meeting in more than a week. The silence is rather strange; I had the impression events were pressing." She gave Lina a dry smile as she dipped the tea strainer into the hot water. "You, on the other hand, have apparently been busy."

"You don't know the half," Lina admitted. "I won't cause you any trouble, then, Dokes. I wanted to ask you in private about your note, but I understand if you simply wish me gone."

But the other woman shook her head and smiled. "Of course I do not—you are the only sensible female of my acquaintance." As she poured out the tea she added, "Pray tell me how I may help."

Lina released her breath in relief. "Perhaps you would be so kind as to not mention you have seen me resurrected, so to speak. Arrangements must be made and I'd rather not be seized again."

"Willingly. And I suppose that this turn of events renders my own news moot."

Lina leaned forward as though curious, even though she had a very good idea of the nature of the disclosure. "What was your news?"

Dokes placed her cup carefully on its saucer, which was chipped at the edge, and gathered her thoughts for a moment. "First, I ask that you understand that men along the lines of a Carstairs are not slated for such as I—I must make do with lesser beings."

This was unexpected; carefully hiding her incredulity, Lina managed a delighted smile. "Are you to be wed, Dokes? My best wishes."

Her companion made a wry mouth. "Heavens, no. Recall that I was under orders to meet with Henry Grant at the bank; we reviewed the loan records after the bank was closed, when there was no one about."

Lina nodded in what she hoped was an encouraging manner, all the while thinking that she could not like where this was leading.

"I have been meeting him at his residence ever since." Although she said it calmly, Lina noted the other's cheeks were tinged with pink.

Suppressing her distaste, Lina instead rendered a sympathetic smile and leaned forward to touch the other's hand. "We take our pleasures where we may—I completely understand."

The other woman gave her a measuring glance. "No, I don't think you could. You have high standards and no weaknesses—I wish I could say the same. But it wasn't merely for pleasure, I assure you."

Ah—now they were coming to it and Lina feigned puzzlement. "What do you mean, Dokes?"

Dokes met her eyes with her own steady gaze. "I had a feeling—he made me uneasy."

Lina nodded. She knew those feelings well—they were the reason women who held this type of job survived. "So you inveigled him."

"Think of it—for once I could take the role of an angel." Dokes drew the corner of her mouth down at the absurdity. "It was a simple thing—he is not well-versed in deception." A tinge of contempt crept into her tone; those such as they had little patience for others less devious. She added, "He likes to boast."

"Men," Lina pronounced dryly, and both women paused to contemplate the foolishness of the sterner sex.

"He spoke very freely of you, and said it was a shame you would be hung, although he seemed to take great pleasure in thinking on it."

"They think me tainted," Lina conceded modestly. "Hence the trap and seizure."

Dokes shot her a look. "I think it is he who is tainted."

Lina stared, feigning incredulity. "Truly? Grant at the Bank of England?

The other woman nodded. "I think he is working hand in glove with Rochon." The woman observed Lina thoughtfully, as though the subject matter was quite ordinary. "I have the impression he is afraid of you—afraid you will grass on him to the others."

Lifting her delicate brows in surprise, Lina asked, "As I am acquainted with Rochon myself?"

"Or so he believes." Dokes watched Lina's reaction from beneath her lashes as she sipped her tea.

Lina laughed lightly but was not fooled—she had noted that Dokes had not inquired as to her allegiance and was giving every indication she would stand Lina's friend regardless of that presumed allegiance. In turn, Lina gave every indication that she accepted the other woman's loyalty without question even though such was not the case and indeed, both were well aware that the other knew it was all a false front. One could not hold it against Dokes, of course—she had her orders and she probably had orders to seduce Henry Grant, too, poor thing.

Lina sat back, her brow knit. "Well, this information about Grant is a wrinkle—have you reported?"

"Yes. They were unsurprised."

Lina thought it over, a tapered finger tracing the rim of the teacup. "I see; so if the church hierarchy already knows of Grant's misdeeds, perhaps he was chosen purposefully, to lay a false trail for Rochon."

"One would think," the other agreed. "It would explain why he has such responsibility." In a tone of mild contempt she pronounced, "He is no financier."

"What is your assignment?"

Dokes gave a dry smile. "I am to continue laying my own false trail."

Lina chuckled in acknowledgment at the *double entendre*. "And why did you send me my warning note?" She watched with interest to see what the other would say—she could not very well admit she was applying additional pressure so that Lina would attempt to escape with Gaston.

Her gaze sincere, Dokes replied, "I felt I should let you know what Grant was saying about you—and presumably saying to the hierarchy; although it appears the issue is now moot."

Lina agreed in an easy manner. "Yes, you are too late—I have already been seized but unfortunately I drowned in the process."

"I see." Thinking it over, the other woman continued,

"And instead of disappearing into France, you are here taking tea with me."

Lina smiled. "As you see." She then sipped her tea in the small silence that ensued.

As they had arrived at a wary impasse, Dokes apparently decided to fire a round. "The Treasury has no clue about the latest shipment of gold that went missing."

"Yes; I am aware," Lina acknowledged the apparent change of topic in a neutral tone. We are well-matched, she thought. We are each probing but neither one of us can gain an advantage.

"Napoleon has sustained a similar loss." Dokes's shrewd gaze examined her over her teacup. "An extraordinary coincidence."

Lina felt a jolt of dismay and revised her last assessment. She is rather like Brodie, Lina thought—always one step ahead.

Her companion continued, "Grant seems to think Rochon is planning to have Brodie call in his bonds while England's gold is missing—it would cause an economic panic." She paused and delicately sipped her tea. "It seems far-fetched, to assume that Rochon could control Brodie."

"Yes," Lina agreed in a steady voice. "It is unimaginable that Brodie would allow such a thing."

Absently, Dokes stared into the fire. "Of course, no matter how bad it looks for England, it is much worse for France—with its current financial situation, France cannot afford to lose any of its gold." She paused, thinking about it. "Napoleon must be livid; no one will lend him enough money to mount another war—not without gold to back it up."

Lina deemed it prudent to make no reply and stirred her tea with a desultory movement. The two women sat together in silence for a few moments.

"Where do you go now?" asked Dokes. "Would you like to stay here?"

Lina demurred smoothly, "I must try to resolve my predicament, but I will not impose upon your kindness, my friend. If it is possible, I will keep you posted."

"You will stay in town?" Her gaze was guileless.

"Of course," Lina agreed, knowing Dokes would immediately conclude no such thing was planned.

"You will be careful?"

Lina was touched; as far as she could tell, these words, at least, were sincere. "I will." She rose and set down her cup. "Thank you, Dokes—I must be off."

"My pleasure, Swanson." Dokes did not rise as Lina gathered up her cloak and made an unhurried exit, holding out hope that the other woman would not pull a pistol on her but closing her hand around her own, just in case.

Chapter 38

Weary and not at all certain who had succeeded in laying a false trail, Lina left Dokes's rooms and made her way to the agreed-upon destination; a modest Kensington row of houses where a lantern left out on one front stoop identified it as the safe house—a residence used when any of her compatriots needed a temporary place to go to ground. She signaled for the hackney to stop and drew Maisie's cloak hood tight under her chin. I must look like a cast-off from the Seven Dials district, she thought. Just as well—that way no one will attempt to peer under the brim of this oversized hat.

Alighting from the cab, she tossed a coin without raising her face, her thanks delivered in a gruff voice. She had been careful to take a circuitous route so as not to be followed by Dokes, although Dokes would certainly anticipate such a subterfuge and may not have bothered as a result. They both knew how to conserve their actions in the face of futility.

Slipping into the shrubbery beside the front stoop, Lina stood in the shadows for a few minutes, waiting for possible observers to pass by before she approached the door—no point in drawing attention at this late stage. One such passerby was a gas lighter; a tall, lean man as was suitable for his profession, carrying his torch and ambling along the pavement with a rolling gait, pausing to light the lamps in the falling dusk. A former sailor, she thought—one could always tell by the walk.

The man paused directly before her and lit a clay pipe, tamping down the tobacco and sparking a flint. In the sudden flare she caught a glimpse of grey eyes directed her way and stifled a gasp.

"Good evening," he said.

With a monumental effort, she concealed her acute dismay. "Good evening, sir."

He turned to face her, puffing a cloud of smoke from the pipe as they assessed one another for a few moments, Lina's heart pounding in her throat. He finally said, "So—you live."

She smiled serenely and wished she didn't appear so bedraggled; her beauty made a better shield. "You did not think I would make your task so easy, did you?"

He continued to puff on the pipe, regarding her. "On the contrary—I am well-pleased to behold you before me. It would be a rare tragedy were you dead."

She bowed. "I thank you."

"What the devil are you about?" He asked in the same tone he would have used to discuss the weather.

Matching his bluntness, she decided to answer honestly. "I'm afraid I cannot say. I would, but it is a matter of divided loyalties. Be assured that I am not your enemy."

He took a step toward her, thoughtful, and turned to gaze up the dark street for a moment, surveying the other people in the vicinity out of long habit. "No—you are not my enemy. Quite the contrary." He then looked down into her eyes, his own containing a message in their grey depths that she had interpreted many a time and from many a man.

She gazed up at him, unprepared to believe the implication.

Witnessing her reaction, he made a self-deprecatory gesture with his hands. "It is true—despite my best efforts, apparently I am only flesh and blood." A small smile played around his lips. "That night, when you sat in your nightdress on your cellar steps, I had half a mind to put it to the touch."

Controlling her bemusement only with an effort, she returned a mild response. "You honor me. Unfortunately for such a plan I was already pregnant at the time—and by your own contrivance, I might add."

He shook his head with regret. "You were careless, to allow such a thing to come to pass."

"No one was more surprised than I, I assure you."

He placed a boot on the railing's crossbar and contemplated it for a moment while she watched him, wary and off-balance. "And you will bear this child and stay with Carstairs?" He glanced at her, sidelong. "If you are not hanged, that is."

Nodding in acknowledgment, she agreed, "That is my plan—if I am not hanged."

He glanced up the street again, gathering himself to speak. Lina very much hoped her spymaster was not going to declare his undying devotion—it would be beyond surreal.

But instead he said only, "If it does not work out—for any reason—I will have your promise that you will give me the right of first refusal."

Frowning at him, she seriously thought about it. She then decided if she couldn't have Carstairs, she may as well have this one. "Agreed—but I have a condition."

"Name it." The grey eyes were intent upon hers.

In a level tone, she continued, "If anything untoward happens to Carstairs—even if he is hit by a dray while crossing the street—I shall never speak to you again."

He leaned back his head and chuckled, contemplating the starry sky. "You overestimate your attraction."

"I believe," she countered, "that you and I are well-suited because we understand one another very well."

He sobered and contemplated her. "My promise on it, then." He offered his hand and she took it, his clasp warm, firm, and brief.

They stood together in silence while he plied his pipe and leaned against the railing. Lina breathed in the night air and thought, I have managed another in a long string of lucky escapes, thanks to my formidable wiles. Although to be accurate I have never practiced said wiles upon this particular man—unless you count the duet at the piano, I suppose.

She also noted with interest that they were now comfortable together—as though they were old companions, neither willing to break off the interlude. In the past, there had been a tension that she had attributed to his unswerving suspicion. Now that she was aware of the true source of the tension, she was almost disappointed—he had been the one man who had seemed impervious to her beauty. Studying his averted face, she decided it was just as well they would not be together—she would never have any idea of his thoughts. "What will you do now?"

He did not hesitate in his answer. "I will be on a knifepoint of agony wondering if I should have killed you outright."

She chuckled. "No need, certainly—I am true."

"But to whom?" He shot her a look, no longer warm.

Teasing, she asked, "Is there anything you do not know?"

"No." He leaned to tap out his pipe on the railing.

"Did you know of Grant?"

Amused, he chided her. "Please—how could I not? He is an amateur."

"He is loathsome," she retorted with revulsion.

Her companion straightened up and spoke seriously. "You of all people should know not to allow your emotions to color your judgment."

Her mouth curved in amusement. "As you would never do such a thing."

Bowing his head in acknowledgment at the irony, he replied, "Then don't make the same mistake as I—I will no doubt live to regret it."

"You will not. And perhaps someday we will repose somewhere together, you and I, and laughingly remember your doubts."

He bowed. "My fondest wish."

Reminded, she sighed. "You and your wretched Bible—I spent many an unhappy hour searching for your reference."

Making a sound of annoyance, he tilted his head in contrition. "It was petty of me, and self-serving; I beg your pardon and shall say no more."

She nodded, and he lifted his lighting torch and turned as if to continue on his way. Placing a hand on his arm, she stayed him. "If I wanted the truth from you, and I asked you to swear, what would you swear by?"

"My country," he answered without hesitation, the grey eyes upon hers.

"Well then; on the honor of your country, tell me whether Carstairs told you I was yet alive and that you would find me here."

He met her gaze without wavering. "He did not. Which is disquieting in its own right."

With a fond smile, she tilted her head. "He thinks to resolve all problems neatly, and to clear me of my taint."

"Good luck to him," he riposted in a sour tone, and she chuckled in response.

His sharp gaze was upon hers once again. "I should perhaps mention that I nonetheless believe he will not put his regard for you above the interests of England."

She met his eyes calmly. "Nor should he—he will not be put to such a test."

"You reassure me."

She chuckled again at his dry tone. "Do you have an assignment for me?"

He blew out a breath. "I have no idea. I will await events."

She hesitated, then offered with all sincerity, "Shall we be friends? If I am not hanged, that is."

He cocked his head to the side and studied her. "Allow me to think on it—it may be too much of a distraction."

"Well, then." She bowed, and he bowed in return. She turned to mount the steps into the safe house and did not look back.

Chapter 39

Lina pulled her cloak around her face and tapped the knocker. She wasn't sure if there would be servants and so she invented a plausible tale in the event—although there were few available to explain an unaccompanied female visiting a widower's quarters. Thank heaven for the temperance group.

As it turned out a tale wasn't needed; Carstairs himself answered the door and pulled her inside with little ado. She walked into his arms and he held her tightly, then kissed her. "Thank God."

"Let me take off Maisie's cloak—I am heartily sick of it. And I did not lose your hat."

"Good." He took it and set it aside. "I am fond of that hat." Nevertheless she could sense his underlying anxiety as he took the cloak from her while giving her an assessing glance. "You are well?"

"Perfectly," she assured him, cradling his face with her hands. "Forgive me for my abrupt departure, Lucien—it could not be helped and I shall tell you the whole."

"I felt guilty enough to pay for the stolen horse," he admitted, lifting her hand to kiss it.

She laughed. "Then we are out of pocket—I arranged to have her sent back. We are honorable thieves, it seems."

Leaning into him, she breathed his wonderful scent, feeling as though she had arrived home at long last even though she had never been to this place before.

He put an arm around her waist and walked with her to the stairway. "Would you prefer to eat or wash first?"

She grimaced. "I have not been very hungry today."

He bent and placed his forehead against hers, pulling her gently into his arms. "Constance. Or Jameson."

"Yes; Constance or Jameson."

"Then wash first. We'll put together some tea and toast and hope for the best."

"Is Maisie about?" Maisie would know what to do with the mass of tangles that currently constituted her hair.

He tilted his head in apology. "I sent her on home—it would look strange, otherwise."

With a teasing look she began unbuttoning her bodice. "I may need some assistance, then—with the bath." There was a tried-and-true method by which she could ease his mind, and the spirit was willing even though the flesh was exhausted.

With a smile, he kissed her again, lingeringly. "I will assist—although I may need some instruction."

Twining her arms around his neck, she murmured, "Then I will show you where everything is." She had the satisfaction of hearing him chuckle against her temple; she had treated him ill this day and wanted nothing more than to make it up to him.

As was expected, the bath soon evolved into a very satisfying and vigorous lovemaking session, and at its conclusion they sat propped up in his bed, she leaning back against him, wrapped in a voluminous robe while he coaxed her to eat.

"I do feel much better—I believe you have found the cure."

He kissed the back of her neck and stole a triangle of

toast from her lap. "The cure is the same as the cause, then—how ironic."

She said without preamble, "I went to see Jenny Dokes. She had sent me a cipher and wanted to warn me of something." Best not to mention the visit with Brodie at the warehouse; Carstairs would send her straight back to Sussex.

Leaning forward, he pressed his cheek against her temple so that his mouth was near to her ear. "Dokes sent you a note out of coverage?"

Lina pretended to consider, although she had little doubt that Carstairs knew of the whole subterfuge—it had been his trap and seizure, after all. "She said she wished only to advise me of what she had learned about Henry Grant, and of his suspicions about me." She turned her head so as to see his face. "Did you know Grant was tainted?"

"Yes," he said, and offered nothing more.

She turned around again and nestled into him. "*Mãe de Deus*," she expostulated mildly. "No one trusts me anymore." She ran her fingers along the muscles in his forearms, clasped around her. "Speaking of which, how goes your plan to clear my taint?"

"It is aborning."

"Ah."

He gently nipped at her neck. "You must stay hidden while I arrange the details. You continue dead."

"As does Marie. You must have a care, Lucien, or you will acquire a reputation—quite the Bluebeard. Or Samson, from the Bible."

He stilled, and a small silence stretched out while she could feel his breath on her neck. "Should I tell you of Marie?"

She gently squeezed his wrists, where her hands rested. "If you would—I'd as lief not sleep with one eye open."

His tone was grim. “Mine is also not a pretty tale.”

But she shook her head slightly. “Oh-ho, my friend—mine trumps yours, surely.”

After a moment, he spoke slowly from behind her head. “Marie did die at my hands; but there were extenuating circumstances.”

She traced a finger along his capable hands, wondering if he had strangled pretty Marie. “I am all attention, then.”

He began his tale, and Lina could hear the constraint in his voice as he tried to give the report without emotion. “Marie was born Marie D’Amberre. Her father was a vicomte in Normandy, and had a large estate along the coast. Her father and her brother were executed during the Terror but not before her father arranged to smuggle her mother and the two daughters to England. Her mother later remarried a fellow expatriate.” He paused.

“An ordinary tale, thus far,” Lina prompted. “Well—not ordinary, but certainly not unusual.”

He continued, choosing his words carefully as he played with her fingers on the coverlet. “Marie was old enough to remember her life before the Terror. They were very wealthy but had to leave it all behind when they fled to England; the new stepfather was penniless. Her mother—” Here he paused for a moment. “Her mother was affected by the tragedies and was an unstable woman. She bitterly resented her reduced circumstances, and her attitude infected Marie, even after I married her and was able to provide for all of them. They could not come to terms with the blow that fate had delivered upon them.” He paused again, remembering. “They were constantly recalling their former situation, and nothing was ever enough.”

Poor man, Lina thought with sympathy—in the unfortunate

role of trying to please the unpleasable. She could guess the rest. "And so Marie had a weakness."

"Yes. She was susceptible to bribery."

Lina shook her head in genuine bewilderment. "It is incomprehensible to me—there is not enough money in the world to tempt me to aid Napoleon."

There was a pause while she could feel his chest rise and fall as he took a deep breath. "I am glad to hear of it."

She smiled at the irony in his tone. "You may believe me or not as you choose, but it is the truth. Pray continue—did you attempt to rehabilitate her as you do me? You have a calling, methinks."

But he was in no mood to joke. "I caught her once; she was copying the key to a cipher I kept in the safe. She wept and disclaimed, and I didn't want to believe it, but the evidence was there, right before my eyes. I kept her on a very short string from then on, and our marriage suffered greatly as a result."

"Another disloyal spouse," commented Lina, struggling to conceal her revulsion. "We were unlucky, the two of us." *Santos*, but she'd rather have a weak and frightened husband willing to barter his wife to save his life than a treacherous wife willing to ruin the country that took her in for nothing more than greed.

"I reported her actions to the church hierarchy—how could I not?"

"You had little choice." Lina remembered how the Vicar had just warned her that Carstairs would not put his personal loyalties before his loyalty to England. There had been a precedent, then.

"The Vicar was very unhappy; he believed she was the one who provided a list of our operatives on the Continent to Rochon last fall—I had kept a copy in my safe."

Lina carefully controlled her reaction. "Did she indeed?" *Mãe de Deus—Mãe doce de Deus*—the irony was thick on the ground; indeed, one did not know whether to laugh or to cry; it was Marie, of all people, who had betrayed her to Rochon.

Carstairs continued, "The Vicar thought to put her to use; to double-cross her and use her to plant false information, but I refused to allow it. In hindsight perhaps I should have, to let her atone for her treachery—albeit unknowingly—and to let her suffer the consequences when the French eventually discovered her information was faulty. Whatever allegiance I had to her had been irrevocably destroyed."

"But you could not allow it, of course—you are loyal to the bone, my friend."

"Perhaps," he admitted reluctantly, his arms tightening around her. "It was a damnable situation."

"And then?" Lina sensed he was avoiding the completion of the tale and wanted him to get on with it; she was sleepy after her long ride and the session of lovemaking in the bath.

"I'm afraid I was inveigled."

Lina clasped his hand between hers. "You are certainly not the first man and you shall certainly not be the last." She knew of what she spoke—being a master inveigler herself.

He sighed. "One night she detained me as I left for a church meeting. She made a tearful plea that I stay with her—that we try to reestablish our marriage."

Lina was surprised by the stab of jealousy she felt at the idea of Carstairs abed with his late wife. "So you stayed."

"No; I carried important information to the Vicar and could not tarry with her. Instead I left on a promise that upon my return we would discuss it over a glass of wine." He paused. "I was nearly to the church before I realized she had lifted the document when she embraced me."

"Oh, Lucien—how miserable for you." Lina was truly shocked; Marie had not seemed capable of such cunning, but one never knew, in this business.

His voice roughened, remembering. "I raced to return and found her in the garden speaking with the Comte deFabry."

Lina nodded—he was the aristocrat whose name she couldn't remember, the one whom Jenny Dokes had mentioned as a suspect.

"I shouted and they broke apart—the comte sprinting for his horse tied at the back gate; I couldn't allow my stupidity to result in any more deaths, and so I leveled my pistol and fired. In the darkness I hit Marie—she must have turned to shield him."

He was quiet for a moment, and Lina lifted his hand to gently place it against her lips. "I am so sorry, *querido*." Privately, she thought it unlikely that a renowned sharpshooter like Carstairs could so badly mistake his target—his prowess had been legendary among the *guerrillas*, after all. "But the comte managed to escape?"

"He did; I carried Marie to the house and shouted for the servants, but it was too late. I discovered she still held the papers tucked in her bodice; I imagine she was demanding more money."

Or tarrying with the comte, thought Lina, but did not say it aloud. They sat together in silence for a few minutes, her head against his shoulder as she watched the fire and thought about what he had told her. Brodie was right—the war was indeed wretched. It allowed any flaws or weaknesses in one's character to be laid bare; flaws that may have never been revealed but for the exigent events the war inspired—the difficult choices of loyalty and allegiance, of life and death.

"You and your dead wives," she commented. "You must

have a care or you will raise an unhealthy suspicion in the Bow Street magistrate's breast."

"He believes Marie died of a brain fever. And although you are missing, you are not, in fact, dead." He bent his head forward so as to speak in her ear. "Although I have been toying with the idea of Vidia's presumed death just before a new and different person named Lina arrives on the scene to attract my grieving attention."

"*Deus*," she observed. "You go through wives like other men go through cravats."

"I think it could work," he insisted stubbornly.

Brutally, she scotched any such plan. "It won't work; I have been told I am as recognizable as the Prince Regent."

"The snail could shed the shell; adjustments could be made—and those who know your true identity are unlikely to grass on you."

She sighed and sank down lower in the bed. "This sounds complicated and I am too sleepy to follow."

"All right; we will speak of it later. However, I'm afraid Brodie must be allowed to think you have drowned—at least for the time being."

"Did you tell Maisie not to tell him? She is the weak link, here."

"I did ask her to keep it quiet. Do you think she will?"

"She will follow orders," Lina assured him, and smiled to herself. "Dear Maisie."

He chuckled at her tone. "Will she come with us to Suffolk?"

"I would assume so—I am a continuing project for her."

"And for me." His mouth was warm against the nape of her neck. "I would like to marry you tomorrow morning, if you are available."

There was a small silence as his lips paused on her neck.

He raised his head and pressed his cheek to hers. "Come, then. Tell me."

"I do not have fond memories of marrying you, Lucien."

His arms tightened around her. "It would be done quietly—just you, me, and the Church of England—to correct the improprieties of the first ceremony."

"Not just yet," she repeated.

He was surprised, she could feel it. He said carefully, "If you were married to a peer, you would have certain protections."

She sighed. "Poor Lucien—you are also on a knifepoint of agony."

"Pardon?"

Turning around to face him, she twined her arms around his neck and embraced him tenderly. "Never you mind—I love you and I cannot imagine loving another and I shall marry you; my hand on my heart. Only not just yet."

He thought about it, his hands stroking her back. "All right."

She was nearly undone by a wave of affection. He was not going to press her—he was a fine, fine man—despite the occasional uxoricide. She had best see to it that all plots were resolved in a satisfactory manner, and soon.

Chapter 40

Maisie was attempting to coddle eggs in the Kensington house kitchen with little success. Cringing, Lina reflected that the language that spewed from her red-faced companion could peel the wallpaper from the walls.

"Honestly, Maisie—it is not as though anyone truly expects you to cook. Have done."

The maid regarded the broken eggs scorching on the stone hearth with a fulminating eye. "Mr. Carstairs wants ye to eat eggs."

Maisie had lately been hired by Carstairs as a housekeeper so as to give her access to Lina, although the charade would not hold together for a moment if anyone could witness the maid's ineptitude in matters culinary. Amused, Lina rose and approached her. "How anyone could have followed the drum for as long as you did and not know how crack an egg or two is beyond me. Here, let me do it."

Ceding the pot, Maisie stepped aside to allow Lina access to the grate. "I was needed to drive the oxen," the other explained, folding her hands with dignity under her apron. "Bein' as how t' drivers kept gettin' shot up."

Lina expertly broke the eggs into the boiling water in rapid succession with one hand. "Then I must beg your pardon, Maisie—yours was the greater service."

"Another for yerself—yer t'eat eggs, he says—eggs and milk."

Lina complied without demur as she actually had an appetite this morning. "Are the two of you conniving behind my back again?"

Maisie gave her an assessing look. "Yer gettin' skinny."

"I've been skinnier, I assure you." She leaned forward to monitor the eggs. "Ugh, the ashes haven't been cleaned out in months. Have we any toast?"

Reminded, Maisie placed bread in the toasting rack and set it before the fire. "How soon before we go to the country? A bit o' fresh air will put some color in yer cheeks."

Lina contemplated the fire for a moment, aware that Maisie was uneasy with the unnatural inactivity of the past two days. "It's a delicate matter, Maisie. There are double-crossings to consider, which hopefully do not include your own."

"I'll stand bluff, don't you fret." Maisie turned the toast rack to the other side. "I'm just sayin' ye need to start thinkin' about the babe, is all."

With a smile Lina disclosed, "Then plan for three days out—Mr. Brodie has a scheme and I believe it is a good one."

Maisie arched her brows in surprise, although she didn't take her watchful gaze from the toast. "That soon? What's to do?"

Lina rose and removed the eggs with a wooden spoon, ladling them into teacups for want of any other dishware. "A masquerade ball, my friend—which is always such an excellent diversion. Do you remember when I played the Condesa de la Torres in Barcelona?"

"Ah me," sighed Maisie. "Are ye plannin' fer the menfolk to have another duel?"

"Such a simple way to arrange for the removal of a problem," Lina reminisced with a fond smile. "But no—I bring it to mind only because I shall need that costume again, so you'll have to visit the town house to pack up some of my clothes and smuggle that outfit to me here. And a mask—I shall need a mask that will obscure my face."

"Aye, missy," Maisie agreed as she removed the rack from the hearth. "I know just the one."

"Don't forget to be unhappy, being as I have died," Lina reminded her, sliding the egg onto the hot toast and carefully taking a bite. "In the event you are observed on your visit."

"Who is doin' the observin'?" Maisie eyed her with alarm as she sat down to her own breakfast.

"Never you mind; but this next is very important, Maisie, so listen carefully. You are also to visit Mr. Brodie at his hotel, to be paid. He will give you a wrinkled bank note that has some letters written on it in ink. Do you follow so far?"

"I'm not daft," noted Maisie without rancor as she buttered her toast. "Then what?"

"Bring it here; Mr. Carstairs is to see you trying to decide whether there is something wrong with the bill, due to the writing on it. If necessary, you must ask him if the bank will take it in its current condition, to encourage him to examine it." The letters would be in a difficult cipher, but Lina had every confidence that Carstairs would quietly pass it on and Jenny Dokes would manage to crack it.

"Am I to say it's from Mr. Brodie?"

Lina smiled. "Only if he asks, and I doubt he will—he is quick on the uptake, is Mr. Carstairs. If he has seen the bank note, you must turn the tea canister around backward as a sign to me—then we don't have to discuss it again."

Pausing, Maisie considered the merits of this particular task with a frown. "I'm not so very good at this sort o' thing—lyin' to the man an' all."

But Lina reminded her, "You won't be lying, Maisie, and that is exactly why I am asking you to do it—he won't think I put you up to it."

"Iffen ye say so," ventured the maid in a doubtful tone.

"I do say so." Lina wiped her fingers on Maisie's apron. "And pray don't be concerned; we act to Mr. Carstairs's benefit. Mr. Brodie is the master at turning the tables."

"He's not yer master anymore," Maisie reminded her, picking up the dishes and taking them to the wash basin.

"He never was, my friend," Lina riposted with relish. "But one must give the devil his due."

"Ah, me," intoned Maisie, shaking her head as she began the washing. "I dinna like this talk o' devils."

"We entertain the devil himself in three days," Lina remarked in a cheerful tone. "Say your prayers." She was feeling considerably better now that the *denouement* was at hand; the anticipation of action always raised her spirits, particularly as she had been constrained to the house for several days. Tapping her slender fingers on the table, she thought out loud. "I must speak to Dokes again—your talk of the duel in Barcelona reminds me that I have a favor to ask of her. And it cannot hurt to draw more attention to the situation so as to put Mr. Carstairs's discovery of your note in proper context." She considered her options with a knit brow. "Another comfortable coze between two old friends is probably out of the question—I cannot risk another visit; the first one took her by surprise but she would be ready for me, now."

"There be trouble brewin'," noted Maisie to no one in particular as she reached to place the teacups back on the shelf.

Lina laughed. "Now Maisie—we are already hip deep in trouble, after all. Have some faith; have I not brought us about, time after time?"

"'Cept the one time, in Paris," Maisie reminded her heavily.

With a graceful shrug, Lina admitted, "Well—yes. But all wrongs will soon be righted, and so deftly that those who are hoodwinked will remain unaware."

"As ye say."

Smiling, Lina teased her, "And I am dying for one last gambit before I am forced by motherhood to settle down."

Maisie made a skeptical sound. "Will ye, d'ye think?"

Her eyes dancing, Lina confirmed in a solemn tone, "Indeed. Will you?"

Maisie made a gesture that portrayed long suffering. "I must; ye haven't the first idea what to do wi' a bairn."

Bowing her head with mock gravity, Lina pronounced, "A new leaf, then; for the both of us—staid householders, for our sins."

"He's a good man," noted Maisie, wiping her hands on her apron.

"No argument here." She gave the other a teasing glance. "Mr. Brodie will miss you."

Maisie was philosophical as she came back to sit on her stool. "He'll be by, I reckon. But he's nowt one t' be buildin' a nest."

Lina nodded, relieved that the maid had no illusions. "Definitely not. He's already looking to the next adventure—the proverbial rolling stone."

The two sat together in silence for a few minutes until Maisie rose and said, "I'll best be on me errands, then."

Lina responded with a gleam of amusement in her eye. "Can you also bring my costume from the Guildhall in Campine?"

If this request for the widow's weeds caused Maisie any alarm, she hid it well and only shook her head slightly. "I'll be needin' to find a new veil—the last one was torn when that Frenchman started tossin' 'is fancy knives about."

"And wasn't that a nasty surprise? Remind me never to hire a cook who hasn't been thoroughly vetted." Much struck by her own remark she added, "Although now that I think on it, I'm afraid that horse has already run—I'm not one to learn a lesson, methinks."

"I'll be fetchin' a new veil in t'afternoon," Maisie assured her.

"No matter, Maisie—stitch it up as best you can; I'm to use it today."

With a worried frown, the maid asked, "And what am I to tell Mr. Carstairs iffen he wonders where ye've gone to?"

"No need, unless I miss my guess, he has his own mysterious errands to commission this day and should be from home for most of it—which is why your bank note is going to be of such interest when you arrange for him to see it. I imagine it will inspire yet more activity on his part, in fact. If he does ask after me, simply admit you are not certain where I've gone, as you were out on your errands."

Maisie nodded. "Aye, then—I'm to fetch t' clothes and visit Mr. Brodie."

Her spirits high, Lina teased, "And pray follow instructions so as not to bring the militia down upon my head as you did in Naples."

Stung, Maisie protested, "The prelate couldn't understand what I was sayin' as he weren't a proper Englishman, and popish besides."

"My fault," Lina soothed. "I shouldn't have entrusted a Northumbrian with a message for an Italian. Small wonder he thought you were a *bandito*—I would have thought the same myself."

"No harm were done," insisted Maisie, who continued nettled. "It were all straightened out wi' everyone merry in the end; lucky ye can charm the birds offen the trees."

Lina suppressed a shudder. "Hard work; I have no fond memories of militia men."

"Nor they of ye." Maisie gave her a glance.

"I'll have none of your sauce," Lina warned her.

"Ah, me," Maisie said with resignation, shaking her head.

Chapter 41

"Would you buy a nosegay, miss? It's to support the Widows and Orphans Fund." Lina addressed Jenny Dokes as the woman passed her on the sidewalk outside the *Académie*.

Jenny examined the proffered bundles with a dubious eye. "Lily of the valley? Your profit margin must be minuscule. Small wonder the widows and orphans are in such dire straits."

"I thought them pretty." Lina was dressed in widow's weeds, the hastily repaired veil hiding her face. "And these were the only lilies I could find."

"Credibility is everything," Dokes reminded her, and fished in her reticule for a penny.

"Tuppence," Lina prompted. "And at the risk of sounding vain, there's little I don't know about selling flowers—I've made two shillings in twenty minutes."

"Less your cost," the other ruthlessly reminded her.

"No cost—Brodie stood the ready. Pure profit, I assure you."

Dokes made a show of admiring the flowers on the small chance they were being observed. "What's afoot?"

"I need your help, if you are willing. I am going to speak privately with Henry Grant, to discover why he believes what he does of me. Otherwise I shall never have my life back again."

As she breathed in the scent of the bouquet, Dokes considered this. "You are trying to clear your name?"

Lina nodded, watching the other woman from behind her veil. "I have set up a meeting in a public place where we could speak with no one the wiser—you must tell no one, Dokes; I beg of you—I will never be allowed to escape again."

"And what is it you wish me to do?"

"I ask that you neutralize his weapon—I will take no chances."

After a small silence, the other woman asked, "Who knows of this?"

"No one. But it is my best chance to eradicate my taint." The story, of course, was inherently implausible and Dokes would be furiously trying to figure out the true object. Good luck to her, thought Lina, as there is no true object—other than to put her compatriots on notice that something was afoot, and soon. That, and it certainly couldn't hurt to have Grant's weapon neutralized, as everyone seemed to think he was tainted.

Dokes lifted her head to make a covert survey of the immediate area. "I confess that I am uneasy, Swanson."

"You will have no active role, other than neutralizing his weapon," Lina assured her.

Her companion smiled her dry smile. "His weapon needs little neutralization—such as it is."

Both women chuckled.

With a small nod Dokes came to a decision. "I shall do it—on account of our friendship." Lilies in hand, she continued on her way.

Lina sold flowers for another quarter hour and then

gathered up the few remaining bouquets. She made her way down the sidewalk in the waning twilight, careful to assess whether she was being followed—she did not believe so; Dokes had been caught unawares. Still, she made a few twists and turns to double back on her route and saw no familiar figures—although it was possible the grey-eyed man had already informed her compatriots of her presence at the Kensington residence and there was no need for such strategies. She could not be certain, but she felt he would not have revealed it to any of the others; their meeting on the street was personal in nature and besides, he would have some difficulty explaining his own restraint if he confessed that he knew where she was. He is like Carstairs, she decided—if he truly believed that I was working to bring down England, he would regretfully shoot me himself without a moment's hesitation. I must be careful to give neither of them incentive.

Eventually she deposited her profits and the remaining nosegays with a flower seller on the corner—to the girl's stammered thanks—and returned to the Kensington safe house. Slipping in by the servant's door, she listened to the silence and looked to the tea canister—which was indeed turned around. Releasing a relieved breath, Lina hurriedly doffed her clothes, bundling the widow's weeds into the back of the wardrobe. Maisie had gone home and they would be quite alone so with a smile, Lina delved into the drawers, pulling on one of Carstairs's crisp linen shirts and rolling up the sleeves. She wore nothing else and arranged herself on the settee in the drawing room to await his entry.

Her patience was rewarded by the smile he bestowed upon her as he stood in the foyer, removing his hat and gloves. "Lady Tyneburne—you are a sight."

"Not Lady Tyneburne," she corrected him with her slow smile.

He approached and climbed atop her on the settee, boots and all. "Lady Tyneburne," he repeated firmly, his mouth buried in the side of her throat. "You'll not be wriggling out of it."

"I do like to wriggle." She suited word to action as he pulled aside the shirt and moved his mouth to the peak of her breast. Yes, she thought, reading him aright—there is a suppressed excitement about him; undoubtedly he is returning from a visit with the church hierarchy to tell them of what he has learned from the bank note.

With a half-growl, he began to unfasten his breeches while she arched against him, caressing the muscles of his back beneath his shirt. I will never tire of this if I live to be a hundred, she thought in a haze of passion—hopefully I will survive the next two days.

There was a knock at the door.

Without a sound she rolled to the side as Carstairs stood up and quickly straightened his clothes. Stepping behind the damask curtain, she watched, twitching aside the fabric as he went to open the front door, calm and correct. "Yes?"

"Mr. Carstairs? Message for you, sir."

He took the note and tipped the messenger, then closed the door with a deliberate motion and smiled at her. Lina chuckled as she came out from her hiding place, "I thought it was the Vicar for certain."

He drew her back into his arms, his mouth moving along her shoulder. "I do like the looks of you in my shirt."

"Better than my wedding nightdress?" She tilted her head so as to allow him better access to her neck.

He thought about it, bestowing slow kisses along the side

of her throat, his hands caressing the contours of her breasts. "I shall have to see it again to compare."

As she laughed, he lifted her in his arms. "Let's go upstairs—my heart cannot withstand another surprise."

"Are you certain it is your heart that most concerns you?" she teased him.

"Behave yourself," he said against her mouth.

He carried her up the narrow stairs, angling her feet so as not to scrape the wall. "Aren't you going to read your note?" She had a good guess as to what the note said and knew with a certainty that he would not allow her to see it.

"Not for the next twenty minutes or so."

They made languorous love and at its conclusion she lay in his arms, wishing they had paused long enough to light a fire, as it was cold. "Have you eaten?" he asked.

"No. You?"

"No. Bring the blanket—let's forage."

They made their way downstairs, and she sat wrapped in the blanket at the kitchen table, watching him as he looked through the pantry by the light of a candle. "There is bread and jam but little else—we ate all the eggs."

"I will eat anything at this point, believe me."

She did not bother to ask him where he had been or what he had been doing; there was little point. He was bare-chested and she admired his torso in the flickering candlelight. "*Deus*, but you have a fine body, Lucien—it is a shame you must walk about wearing clothes."

His muffled voice could be heard from within the confines of the pantry as he rooted around. "I cannot hold a candle to you."

"You see past it, though."

His head emerged and he smiled at her. "I much prefer the snail to the shell."

"I know it—which is why I will never let you go."

He produced a salt-cured ham and a brick of old cheese, then pulled his blade from his boot and sat beside her. "Good. Let us marry tomorrow."

There was a good reason why he was hoping to marry her sooner rather than later, depending upon whether the *denouement* revealed her treason—she would probably avoid execution if she were married to a peer. "Soon," she soothed. "First you must feed me."

They ate their potluck meal in the candlelight, she sharing her blanket with him against the chill. Thinking of the note he didn't want her to see, she asked, "May I hear of your plan?"

He considered as he sawed off a sliver of ham. "I'd rather not."

She picked the proffered piece off his knife with her fingers. "Does it involve pulling the wool over my eyes yet again?"

"No—we are to make an attempt at honesty, remember? I will hold faith with you—as long as I have the choice."

She regarded him thoughtfully and made no response. He added with some shrewdness, "You—on the other hand—are not to that point as yet."

Lowering her gaze, she confessed, "The memory of Sussex is still very fresh."

"Understood. I must re-earn your trust." He added with some deliberation, "But I am not operating under whatever constraints you are—my object is to clear you of any taint."

She eyed him thoughtfully. "Come what may?"

"Come what may."

Ah, she thought. He hints that he means to sacrifice Brodie to the wolves—just so that I am aware—and small blame to him. How fortunate that there is a much better counterplan, and the wolves will devour themselves. Aloud, she said, "I do appreciate it—I'd rather not birth this poor child in prison."

"You will be safely tucked away in Suffolk for the birth or I will know the reason why." He played with the knife, his long fingers nimbly turning it this way and that in a practiced manner. "If it is Constance, would you wish her to have your face?"

"No," she said immediately.

He thought about it. "It could be an asset."

Smiling, she disagreed and made a playful grab at the knife while he deftly kept it away. "I am like a freak at Astley's Circus—people point and stare."

He saw she was teasing and countered, "Doors will open—she could marry a duke. At the very least she would never have to pay the penny post."

"Not at all worth it," she assured him. "Pay the penny and have a normal life, instead."

But he shook his head in disagreement, and with a quick movement flipped the knife, point first, so that it quivered in the tabletop. "You would never have been content with a normal life."

She sighed with pleasure at this keen insight. "And that is why I will never let you go."

How do I look?"

Maisie stepped back, nodding in approval. "A rare treat."

Standing before the mirror, Lina turned to the side to admire the black silk gown that showed her impressive bosom and creamy shoulders to advantage. A tortoiseshell comb was secured in the dark curls of her wig—a recent gift from an anonymous admirer—and a mantilla of fine black lace was secured to it. In her hand she held a black lace-edged mask. "Help me tie the fan around my wrist; I may need to drop it so as to draw my pistol. Or perhaps I can attempt to wield the fan left-handed." She experimented and decided this was the better tack.

"If push comes to shove, ye kin always poke an eye out wi' yer fan," her maid suggested helpfully. "Remember Barcelona."

"Unnecessary—I have a very fine dagger in my garter." Lina tied her mask over her face and reviewed her disguise once more, a soft smile playing around her rouged lips. "Would you know me?"

Maisie gave an honest assessment. "I'd know ye anywhere, missy. But t'others won't."

Lina nodded, satisfied. "The dark wig is unfortunate but necessary—I look like a saracen."

"Ye look a treat," Maisie repeated, twisting the corner of her apron in her hand.

It was always the way of it, thought Lina, adjusting her mask. Maisie nervous and me, well—I am positively steeped in excitement. In deference to her maid's nerves, she soothed, "It is only a party, Maisie—do not worry overmuch."

But her maidservant only shook her head with resignation. "I seen that look in yer eye afore, if I may be sayin' so."

"But never again," Lina reminded her. "We will go off to abide in Suffolk and you will teach me to herd cows."

"Ye'll be cuttin' a rig—cows or no; it bein' in yer blood."

Laughing, Lina glanced at her as she arranged the mantilla over her shoulders. "You sound remarkably like Mr. Carstairs, but I assure you, if I never hear of Napoleon, or his gold, or his spymaster, or his counterfeiter ever again, I swear I shall die a happy woman."

"There's t' be no talk o' dyin', missy," Maisie cautioned her superstitiously.

Lina pulled her pistol from the pocket sewn into her gown and checked the firing mechanism with a practiced gesture. "Nevertheless, you'll not forget what I told you?"

"Nay."

"Good—it is only a contingency, Maisie, but it is best to have it settled. Don't take the opals if they're indeed bad luck—perhaps I should send them to the bottom of the sea, too."

Maisie's brow wrinkled in concern. "Never say ye'll be jumpin' into the sea agin?"

"Perish the thought. Now—off I go." She could not leave without taking the other woman's hands in her own. "Take care, Maisie."

Maisie stifled her alarm. "I'll wait up."

Laughing, Lina replied, "Don't bother—you'll only be asleep in the hall chair as you were in Prague when half the Royal Army walked right past you."

Maisie bristled, Lina laughed again, and then she was out the servant's door, throwing her embroidered silk wrap around her shoulders and walking quickly down the mews, keeping to the shadows. The night was clear, the moon nearly full, and the stars just beginning to appear as she took a quick glance around and moved across the alley to avoid a maidservant walking out with a beau. Turning onto the street, she hailed a hackney immediately; she would only draw attention if she walked any distance, dressed as she was.

She raised her face only enough to relay the message and otherwise kept her face averted. "The pier at Westminster," she directed with a Spanish accent. If the jarvey thought his fare unusual, he hid it well and only touched his finger to his cap in acknowledgment. His business is rather like our business, she thought in amusement as she climbed in the cab; he has seen it all and nothing can surprise him anymore.

Sinking back into the cushions, she went over the protocol once again in her mind. It was a good plan, with Brodie anticipating many of the variables—although one must remain flexible and well-armed, besides. All it needed was for everyone to react as they should and it was nearly foolproof; Brodie would have a fortune for his troubles, Napoleon would not, the despicable Grant would be arrested while Carstairs would be covered in glory, and England would have its gold again. A very good night's work, all in all.

Arriving at the pier, she dismounted from the cab, holding her fan before her face as she surveyed the barge that

Brodie had dubbed the *Argo*. It rocked gently against the dock, alight with torches and waiting to ferry a party over to the Vauxhall Pleasure Gardens, located on the opposite bank of the Thames. The popular flat-bottomed vessels were painted and decorated, oftentimes to resemble a Cleopatran barge, and this one was no exception, being gilded and decorated with lotus blossom patterns in a fanciful design. Personally, Lina could not understand the fascination that the English had with all things Egyptian; it had been sparked by Napoleon's conquest of the area, and therefore she could see no merit to it.

The torches illuminated the guests already on deck, and Lina could easily recognize Brodie since he eschewed any costume. He stood amidst a group of masked and dominoed cronies, entertaining them with some tale that kept them all enrapt, occasionally laughing at something he said. That is the merit to being overly rich, thought Lina cynically; one can always find a willing audience—it is rather like being overly beautiful. She reviewed the other guests and recognized Henry Grant, escorting a well-dressed woman and standing off to the side, observing Brodie and his group. Unable to resist, she searched out another figure—a man in a black domino, neither tall nor short, stout nor thin, and on the whole, unremarkable. Nevertheless, she would recognize him anywhere and felt the gooseflesh rise on her arms.

A string quartet played on the foredeck while servants circulated, carrying trays with drinks and offerings of food. Her gaze rested for a moment on the wooden lifeboat, suspended between two davits at the stern, a canvas stretched over its interior. Pressing her shoulders back and lifting her chin, she plied her fan before her face and began an unhurried progress toward the gangway, her hips swaying.

One of the watermen who was coiling a rope on the pier suddenly stepped before her, blocking her way. "Go home," the man said in a low voice, and when he glanced up she found she was looking into Carstairs's blue eyes.

With an outward show of calm she looked at him, puzzled. "*Perdon?*"

"It won't wash, Lina—you will go home before anyone else recognizes you." He continued to coil the rope, looping it over his shoulder.

"Twigged," she sighed with resignation. In truth, she was not surprised to see him, it being the whole point of Maisie's bank note. Carstairs would be here but none of the others would be, Brodie desiring to give Carstairs the role of the hero.

"You will leave before you are recognized if I have to cosh you and carry you." His hands stilled and he turned his head toward her, his expression grim.

This was unexpected and would cause no end of disruption to Brodie's plan. I believe it is time for pound dealing, she thought, and hoped she could trust him. "You must allow me to pass; I'm afraid my life depends upon it."

His eyes narrowing, he stared at her. "How is this?"

"Well—to begin with, Brodie is my father."

Ah—this was a complete surprise, she could see, and he stared at her, speechless. Unfortunately, further conversation was curtailed by the approach of Brodie and his group, who called out a greeting and came to meet her on the gangway. Smiling at them, Lina lifted her fan and murmured in an undertone to Carstairs, "And the situation is not at all what it seems."

She moved onboard to greet Brodie and the others flirtatiously, steering them away from Carstairs, who had thankfully reconsidered his coshing plan. Brodie lifted her hand to kiss it. "*Buenas noches, bella senorita.*"

She laughed and gave him an arch look as she tapped his arm with her fan. "*Encanto.*"

He pulled her hand into his elbow as they walked along the deck of the barge, her smile slow and seductive as she murmured into his ear in her native language, "Success—Mr. Carstairs is here and is undoubtedly of the opinion that the bank note about this meeting was a false lead."

"Of course it was—as if I would ever be so clumsy, or Maisie any good at subterfuge," Brodie commented in the same tongue, unperturbed. "I have every confidence your people are out in force on the East India Company docks, watching for any suspicious transfers of heavy cargo while we are vainly trying to distract them with our merry party."

Complacent, Lina plied her fan. "Except for Mr. Carstairs."

Brodie nodded. "Also as we expected—he is more concerned that someone will note your reappearance from the dead than any paltry gold—which is why he shall be the only agent on site when our rabbit is exposed, and the arrest will be his and his alone."

Although Brodie's predictions had come true thus far, Lina could not be easy and warned, "Don't let him get hurt, Benny."

"Come, *Bela*—he seems very capable and able to take care of himself." He turned and took a curious glance around him. "Which one is he? I should ask him about his prospects, and that sort of thing."

Despite her concerns, she couldn't help but smile at the image this remark presented. "It is a bit late for that, my friend—and apparently I'm to be a baronetess in Suffolk."

He threw back his head and laughed, genuinely amused,

while other guests in the immediate area looked on with interest.

"Lower your voice, pray—you will bring the *gendarmes* down upon us." Lina was unable to resist laughing herself; truly, it was ironic that one such as she would wind up holding a title.

His merriment subsiding, Brodie looked upon her with an indulgent eye. "A baronetess, of all things; I can recall the first time I saw you, *Bela*, grubby and barefoot but with a face that shone like an angel come to earth."

"An asset," she agreed, "all in all."

"Not as great an asset as your pluck." He covered her hand with his. "Inherited from your mother."

She cast a sideways look at him, her eyes gleaming with amusement through her mask. "I believe I inherited equal amounts of pluck from my father—observe the events of this evening."

Pleased, he chuckled. "We shall see."

"Shall we bait our rabbit?" Lina asked in a desultory fashion as though she hadn't a care in the world.

"By all means—I imagine he is in a fever of impatience to be away from here—there is a Dutchman in town he is seeking to avoid."

As they walked in a leisurely manner toward the stern, Lina squeezed his arm and offered, "I shall miss you, Benny—my hand on my heart."

"A baronetess!" he exclaimed, and laughed again.

Chapter 43

Brodie asked in a genial tone, "You are acquainted with the Condesa, I believe?"

The gentleman in the black domino turned to regard Lina, his dark eyes glittering through his mask as he bowed. "Condesa; it has been far too long." He took her hand and bowed over it, the expression in his eyes cold as a reptile's.

As she bowed her head gracefully in return, a pleasant smile played around Lina's lips. "*Senor*; I recall our time together with great fondness."

Amused by her temerity, Rochon condescended to offer a thin smile in return. "I understand your aid has been instrumental in accomplishing our objective this night." He stood against the gunwale near the stern, the mask obscuring his face and the light from the torches casting an uncertain light—he was not a man who invited attention. The memory of his face was branded in her mind, however—he had impassively watched his henchman apply a strap to sharpen his flaying tool as Lina sat bound to a chair before them, refusing to give information. I don't know how long I would have held out, she thought; Brodie's arrival was a timely one, *agradeca Deus*.

Hoping that Carstairs was not listening, she bowed her head in acknowledgment. "*De nada*; it was little enough."

The dark eyes hardened. "However, I also understand a concern has been raised—the genuineness of the bonds is in doubt." As he turned to face Brodie, the domino billowed out as it was caught by the breeze. The French spymaster's tone was mild and his stance was unthreatening; nevertheless the overall effect was very menacing indeed.

Brodie paused, as though surprised that Rochon would know of this rumor, then crossed his arms across his chest and chose his words with care, bowing his head in acknowledgment. "I have heard the claim that the bonds do not bear the appropriate watermark—it may mean nothing."

Rochon was not one who displayed any emotion, but Lina was nevertheless aware that he was most unhappy with this bit of information. The spymaster leaned forward and ventured in a dulcet tone, "The British have duped you, perhaps, and saw to it you were sold false bonds instead of genuine ones."

Brodie was seen to bristle, drawing himself up and giving the impression that he barely kept his temper in check. "They would not dare—not me, by God; why, I could ruin them in a day, and I am not such a fool that I don't recognize a counterfeit when I see it."

As though alarmed by this outburst, Lina stroked Brodie's arm to soothe him, all the while thinking he would have been a fine actor had he not decided to make a fortune with gambling kens.

However well done, Brodie's protestations did little to move Rochon, and his measured words were cold. "I cannot take the chance; the last thing I need is to have suspicions raised when the bonds are cashed in. If they have indeed been faked by the British, they are no doubt setting up a trap to arrest anyone attempting to cash them in for passing false documents."

Red of face and unwilling to concede the point, Brodie

blustered, "Then the bonds need not be redeemed at the bank—instead they can be sold to the unknowing. If I could be fooled, certainly others can be fooled into buying them."

"The point," Rochon reminded him coldly, "is to create an unsustainable run at the bank, with no gold to back up the bonds. It does me no good to sell them quietly to third parties."

As this was irrefutably true, Brodie instead retreated to his original argument, and appeared to bring himself under control with a visible effort. "You are overcautious; I cannot imagine the British would purposefully sell me forgeries—it is only a rumor put forth to plague me."

Rochon held up a gloved hand. "There is no point to this discussion until I make an examination of the bonds, and that will have to wait until the guests have disembarked."

As though he was annoyed and on the defensive, Brodie muttered, "At least the gold is genuine—that much is certain."

"And very much needed," Rochon replied in a grim tone. "I have been forced to assign additional men to investigate our latest theft and I can ill afford the lack of personnel—or the loss of the product. We will conclude our transaction with all speed, if you please—I cannot linger." He turned to bow over Lina's hand again, glancing up at her sidelong. "You understand."

"But, of course," she said pleasantly, all the while imagining driving her blade between his eyes. *Diabo*, she thought—he seeks to discomfit me but we shall see who is discomfited before this fine evening is over.

Recognizing the danger signs, Brodie steered her away. The breeze picked up as they strolled down the deck toward the quartet, the strains of a waltz floating out over the water. They were silent for a few moments as they walked, Lina's silk skirts swishing on the deck and Brodie's head bent intimately close to hers to discourage others from approaching. Behind her mask Lina was contemplating this latest encounter with the man who had captured her last fall and then had planned to kill her, and not kindly.

Brodie remarked, "To think that I was taken in by counterfeit bonds."

Lina was not fooled by his solemn tone and knew he was trying to tease her out of her temper. "You are a rascal, Benny. It is a shame he is never to know you have duped him—perhaps it would break through his famed *sangfroid* and he would have a frothing apoplexy." She imagined the event with great satisfaction.

"Cannot be allowed, *Bela*," he advised her without regret. "It is enough that you and I know the truth."

She squeezed his arm. "I thank you—I had little hope when he captured me last fall; you are a master negotiator."

"A life worth saving." He patted her hand.

She lifted her face to the starry sky, thinking how wonderful it was to be alive. "You are fortunate Gerard the counterfeiter has no loyalty to anyone."

"Except the god of money," Brodie corrected her. "And I am the next best thing."

Lina nodded, thinking of the Romany man who counterfeited French and English currency to assist Napoleon in his current economic troubles. She had made Gerard's acquaintance when she was imprisoned, and Brodie had later persuaded him to take a princely sum to serve him—even as the counterfeiter continued to serve Napoleon. "And your money was well spent; not only did Gerard create a counterfeit bond for us, he also advised me that Gaston had turned coat and was now working for the British."

Brodie glanced at her, curious. "How did he know about Gaston?"

Lina smiled. "They are brothers, Gerard and Gaston—Romanies from Brittany."

Brodie laughed aloud again; to all appearances it seemed as though he was truly enjoying himself this evening. "Oh-ho—I can only imagine the table conversation Christmas next."

Their progress was halted at the bow end of the barge where they leaned against the wood-carved lotus blossoms that decorated the railing, Lina waving her fan in a desultory manner. "Speaking of which, I discovered who was tainted—who betrayed me so that I was captured by Rochon last fall."

He met her eyes, his brows raised in inquiry.

Lina made a wry face. "Marie Carstairs, of all people—Mr. Carstairs's dead wife. She was bribed to hand over his list of the operatives on the Continent."

Brodie mulled this over, his chin tucked into his chest. "I see; it is all rather symmetrical, in a strange way."

"Yes, it is." Best not to mention that said treasonous wife had died at Carstairs's hand. Poor man—he could not be faulted for believing that he would have to repeat the experience with his wayward second wife after this little episode. When this is over I shall be a pattern-card of respectability, she vowed—barring those times when I will run some sort of rig just to keep him on his toes—I cannot allow him to become bored with me, after all.

"Ah, we are under way." Brodie observed the movement with satisfaction as they walked to the railing to watch as the barge began to drift away from the Westminster Pier, the oarsmen plying their oars and the sails lifted to catch the evening breeze. Breathing in the sea air, Lina scanned the figures but wasn't certain which was Carstairs and decided she shouldn't openly search him out—she had little doubt he would remain close by. Instead she stood at the rail with Brodie as the vessel began its slow progress down the Thames to the Pleasure Gardens. The barges could be hired by the well-to-do to transport a party of merry-goers to the Vauxhall stairs and back again after the festivities, which in this case was a masquerade ball at the famous Pavilion. It was the perfect opportunity to make the transfer of the gold; Brodie had indicated he wished a public place to ensure his own safety but the masked nature of the festivities allowed Rochon to participate unnoticed.

"Will you meet my friends, *Bela?*" Brodie indicated his group of gentlemen who stood at a distance and did not bother to conceal their extreme interest in her identity, one of them raising a glass to her.

Lina bestowed a sultry smile in their direction but said to him, "Allow me to stand here alone for a moment—perhaps Mr. Carstairs will seek a private word." Her erstwhile husband was probably in a fever wondering when they would find a chance to continue their conversation, now that she had made the revelation about her father. I hope he does not have second thoughts, she thought—Yorkshire no longer has any appeal and neither Maisie nor I could truly run a bakery.

Brodie bowed and departed; Lina idly watched him take a proffered drink and engage in hearty conversation with the group, none of whom she recognized.

Adjusting her mask, Lina figured they would arrive at the Pleasure Gardens shortly. The black lace that edged the mask made her nose itch and she was trying to scratch it unobtrusively when she was interrupted.

"May I offer you champagne?" The tall, grey-eyed gentleman wore a voluminous silk domino and a suit of clothes that identified him as a Pink of the Ton, the swallow-tailed coat molded to his torso and nipped in tight with a wasp waist; his neckcloth impossibly high and intricately arranged. He proffered a glass with a well-manicured hand, which she accepted with a slow smile, her heart beating in her throat at this unexpected and unwelcome turn of events. "*Gracias*."

The drawl disappeared and his tone was intent. "If I wanted the truth from you, what would I have you swear by?"

She considered. "The soul of my mother, who died defending the wall at Guarda."

The grey eyes behind the mask regarded her for a moment, the serious expression at odds with his frivolous appearance. Ah, she thought—here is something he didn't know.

"Then on the soul of your mother, tell me you are not bringing about the ruination of England."

Leaning in toward him, she wielded her fan to show her eyes to advantage. "I do so swear."

He bent his head as though embarked on an intimate flirtation. "I thought it very clumsy of Brodie—and you—to reveal to Carstairs and Dokes such an obviously false lead, but then I decided the clumsiness of the false lead was actually a stroke of genius."

She smiled up into his eyes, thinking with some dismay that Brodie had met his match. "And I imagine we are now surrounded by law enforcement."

He bent his head and ran a finger along her forearm. "Indeed. But tell me; what should my role be, here?"

Relieved, she noted that it seemed he was willing to take a wait-and-see attitude rather than disrupt Brodie's carefully laid plans outright. She tapped his wandering hand in a playful fashion with her fan. "Nothing is what it seems—can you wait until Rochon is in the lifeboat before you move in? It is oh—so very important."

Studying her while his fingers caressed her bare arm above her glove, he countered, "I must be allowed to take him in, though."

"You may with my blessing," she assured him. "Thank you."

Leaning in, he whispered into her ear, "You will be the death of me."

She turned her head to gently kiss his mouth and could sense his loss of composure. "Not at all—instead I am going to bestow upon you a fortune in gold."

And to what purpose, exactly, was that display?"

"He fancies me," Lina replied with some complacency, straightening the seams on her black gloves.

"Everyone fancies you," Carstairs observed in a dry tone. "But not everyone kisses you." He had materialized at her side within seconds after the spymaster had sauntered off and Lina was well-pleased by this show of jealousy.

"More like I kissed him," Lina confessed. "I needed to distract him—he is too shrewd by half."

"No more distractions, Lina," he warned as he made a show of adjusting a cleated rope. "I can't very well call him out."

"We are not yet wed," she teased him. "Perhaps you are well rid of me."

"We will wed tomorrow," he insisted, "if we survive this night."

"The day after," she compromised.

Pleased, he shot her a look as he retightened the stay he had already tightened twice. "Do you mean it?"

"My hand on my heart, *querido*."

He turned his head away to hide a smile that he could not suppress. "Tell me about Brodie."

Lina leaned on her arms against the railing and watched the lights of the City of London recede. "He reappeared into my life—a heroic figure, after all—when I was captured by Rochon in the fall. Don't ask me how he knew—he must have been keeping track of me over the years. Indeed, it has occurred to me more than once that perhaps my meeting Maisie was not so very accidental, truth be told. He negotiated for my life—the scheme to ruin England's monetary system in return for my release. Brodie has no loyalty to England and convinced Rochon that he would speculate on England's financial collapse and make his own fortune in the process. Rochon was so dazzled by the prospect that he believed him, and set me free to do his bidding."

"But it's a rig, I hope."

"Yes, it is a rig—an elaborate one." Lina took a glance around to ensure their spymaster was not lingering nearby. "But there are parts of it that cannot withstand the light of day and hence my hands are tied. I can't betray Brodie—not after what he has done for me. Suffice it to say that Rochon will not acquire the gold but he must be made to believe that Brodie and I are not at fault for its loss—otherwise, he will have gained a terrible enemy and my life will be forfeit."

Carstairs nodded and straightened upright, having already spent too much time speaking with a guest. "You will stay out of harm's way, Lina."

She turned to watch the barge's approach to the Vauxhall stairs. "Is that an order, sailor?"

But his mood remained serious. "This is not only about you anymore—and my wishes should be just as important as Brodie's."

"A thousand times more," she assured him. "But only Brodie can pull the wool over Rochon's eyes—and destroy Napoleon in the process."

"Holy God," he said softly, watching her in surprise. "Is that what is afoot?"

"You have only to watch events unfold." She touched his hand briefly. "And try not to interfere—no matter how it appears."

"No more kissing," he cautioned her.

"I can see," she said thoughtfully, "that marriage is going to require more compromises than I had originally anticipated."

"*Diabla*," he remarked, and walked away.

Lina watched him go and then casually crossed the deck to rejoin Brodie and his group. *Deus*, she thought crossly; this event is not going forward as planned and I must make Benny aware—a pox on all clever men who live only to outwit one another.

Brodie was drinking champagne with the others and watching as the barge came to a rest at the docking area. She was introduced to his friends, and parried some teasing proposals and good-natured flirtations for a few moments until she had a chance to murmur to Brodie in Portuguese, "My compatriots did not follow the false lead—or I suppose more properly, they did—and they are here in abundance."

Rocking back on his heels, he digested this unwelcome piece of news while one of the other men attempted to engage her in Spanish conversation. He was fairly fluent, and she laughed and spoke with him at some length so as to allow Brodie time to reassess his plan. She had invented a wild tale of hidden treasure at a Spanish *palacio* before Brodie rejoined the conversation and said, apropos of nothing, "We must obtain the main object, *Bela*—everything else is superfluous."

"*Si, senor*," she teased with a roguish smile, and noted with interest that his companions did not seem to find the disjointed conversation unusual. Brodie had the right of it—the main object was to have the rabbit believe he had lost his fortune through no fault of theirs—and as long as this aim was accomplished, nothing else mattered even if Carstairs was not to be the one to make the arrest. She hoped the grey-eyed man would wait, as she had requested; otherwise, their own double-cross could be exposed and one did not double-cross Rochon and survive.

The revelers began to disembark up the stairs to Vauxhall, some already showing the effects of the free-flowing champagne. The group of men who came with Brodie, however, stayed behind and entered into a lively debate about the greenest odds-maker at Newmarket and how best to fleece him. Lina was therefore given to understand the men were not cronies at all, but instead hired bravos here to protect them—Brodie would leave nothing to chance.

Almost imperceptibly, the barge began to move out toward the river again. Lina wondered if her spymaster was still close to hand—he was not in evidence, and it made her uneasy that she did not know where he was or what he did. There was nothing for it though; it was time to set events in motion. "We head out to sea," she commented to Brodie when there was a break in the conversation.

He paused in his discussion and set down his glass. "Shall we go astern, *Bela*? I have a desire to view the lights."

She placed her fingers on his proffered arm, and as they walked away she noted that the other gentlemen casually trailed at a discreet distance behind them—hopefully they were armed, although the last thing to be desired was a gun battle breaking out between the three different factions aboard.

Lina and Brodie paused at the stern of the barge to admire the view of London, illuminated by the new gas lanterns that lined the embankment. Lina offered, "You will be well-pleased to depart this place, methinks."

He made a deprecatory gesture with his hands. "It was not such a hardship, *Bela*. But my talents are more suited to Venice where the world is not quite so buttoned-up. Curse Napoleon and this next war, which will undoubtedly keep most of the young fools from my gaming kens."

She leaned into him fondly. "You were always the master at fleecing the poor young fools."

"Only because they were all besotted and couldn't keep their eyes off you—I never could find another hostess with half your charm—not to mention your head for numbers."

"Perhaps you will have to wait out the war with me in Suffolk, tending the cows."

But he predicted, "Napoleon will escape, but any attempt at a conquest will be short-lived—there is no war without funding, no matter how dedicated the cause or how shrewd the leadership."

"I believe that makes you a patriot," she teased, "as you are depriving the former Emperor of his funding. Who would have thought you would condescend to serve your country in such a way?"

"It is a strange, strange world, *Bela*," he agreed, and she wrapped her hand around his arm, chuckling.

They continued to gaze out over the water, nothing in either demeanor to suggest that the next few minutes would be in any way unusual. Lina commented, "It is indeed a strange world—now I'm to be respectable."

"And I'm to be grandfather to a peer of the realm."

They looked at each other and laughed, and were still merry when Rochon joined them, his expression impassive. "You are remarkably carefree for a man who has been duped."

"We plan to leave this miserable place and go to Prague," Brodie promptly explained. "There are many amusements in Prague—I shall regain my fortune, never fear."

"There are many wantons in Prague." Rochon's eyes slid toward Lina under his mask.

"Indeed," she agreed, impervious to insult. "Of both sexes."

Rochon's glittering eyes were suddenly sharp upon hers but she continued in a mild tone, "Although a new war will keep the soldiers occupied."

"We shall contrive." Brodie nodded to Rochon. "You must come visit—I will see that you are well-entertained."

But Rochon was not to be flattered and responded coldly, "I will be well-entertained when I see the gold."

"Certainly." Brodie spread his hands in apology for the digression. "No more delay." With a gesture, he stepped forward to direct a waterman to remove the canvas cover from the lifeboat and as the man stepped forward to obey, Lina recognized Carstairs. She could only trust that his aim was to help her rather than conspire in her arrest, but it was too late for such concerns now.

They stood and watched as Carstairs folded the tarp back, exposing what appeared to be ordinary bricks stacked, row upon row, on the floorboard within the suspended lifeboat.

The expressionless Rochon allowed himself a sigh of satisfaction. "Excellent."

Brodie pulled a packet of documents out of his waistcoat. "The bonds," he insisted in a tone that held an edge of defiance.

Taking the packet, Rochon gestured to Henry Grant, who had been standing at a distance, awaiting such a summons. I should have some compassion for him, thought Lina as she watched the banker approach. Either he will be arrested for treason by the Home Office, or he will hold Rochon's secrets; in either case he will be dead very, very shortly.

The woman who accompanied Grant tilted her head with a small movement in Lina's direction, and Lina gave her a quick, dismissive glance only to stifle a gasp and reconsider. *Mãe de Deus*, she thought in surprise—Jenny Dokes. Only Dokes's face was hidden by a mask and she was dressed in a very fashionable and low-cut confection of a dress, her hair piled high off her forehead. Their eyes met, and Lina imagined that the other woman sent her a look of apology while Lina attempted to convey her own acknowledgment of Dokes's obligations. We understand each other, she thought—we each do what we must, which is exactly what I anticipated when I went to see her in the first place. Unfortunately I hadn't foreseen that Dokes would see through Brodie's gambit and every spare agent for miles around would be joining us aboard the *Argo*.

Rochon stepped forward to gaze over Grant's shoulder at the stack of bonds as the banker pulled them from the packet. Grant held the first one to the light of a torch and scrutinized it carefully. "A good rendition," he pronounced. "But a fake, nevertheless."

Rochon was unsurprised, but Brodie affected a sound of extreme annoyance. "Taken in like a flat," he exclaimed, as though trying to bring himself under control. "*Peste*—someone will pay for this."

"You can withstand the loss," Rochon said without sympathy. "And let this be a lesson—you should have realized they were letting you buy up all the bonds because they were fake."

As though he could not contain his bitterness, Brodie retorted, "You have no reason to be so cool—it is your loss also; the Treasury is no longer vulnerable." Pretending alarm, Lina again placed a calming hand on his arm as a reminder to monitor his words before the man he addressed.

But Rochon, as always, was not shaken. "The gold is my priority now—there is no point in bringing down England if France cannot stand." With a curt command, he indicated that the lifeboat should be lowered to the sea, and Carstairs and another waterman obliged by unwinding the ropes from the davits. Rochon stepped forward to supervise, cautioning the men to be careful so as not to allow the lifeboat to become unbalanced on its descent.

As the French spymaster was thus engaged, Jenny Dokes tilted her head in puzzlement. "Gold?" she asked Grant. "What gold?"

Filled with importance, Grant indicated the bricks piled within the lifeboat. "There—a king's ransom in English gold, painted to look like ordinary bricks."

Dokes eyed the lifeboat and the wooden davits by which it was being lowered from the back of the barge. "I don't know what that boat contains, but it cannot be gold."

"Dokes," Lina bit off angrily as she suddenly sprang between the woman and Grant. "It is you—how dare you show your face to me, *cadela*."

Startled, the other woman attempted to look around Lina to view the lifeboat, murmuring, "But it makes no sense, Swanson; each brick—if it were indeed gold—should weigh at least four hundred ounces—there are well over one hundred bricks and the rope can't be more than forty pound test. Not to mention that a single tackle block could not sustain such a weight—"

Staring at Dokes, Brodie breathed, "Who *are* you?"

Fortunately Rochon had been paying close attention to the

cargo's descent to the surface of the river and had not overheard the conversation between the women. Nevertheless, with a swift movement Lina brought the butt of her pistol down on Dokes's head. "Foul *cadela*," she exclaimed loudly as the other woman sank to the deck. At her words, Rochon turned to them in surprise.

"She is a Home Office agent," Lina breathlessly explained to the French spymaster. "I recognized her voice—you must take the gold and flee with all speed."

Chapter 45

Rochon betrayed no reaction to Lina's startling announcement but reviewed Dokes's inanimate form for a moment. Raising his gaze to Lina, he directed, "See to it that she is thrown over the side, *s'il vous plait*." He then turned to Grant and asked, "Did you know of this?" His tone was neutral but the underlying menace was unmistakable.

"Yes—but she is in love with me and would not betray me," Grant insisted, his voice quavering a bit. "Indeed she has been willing to help me decipher communications from the British."

Rochon considered the unconscious woman dispassionately but was unmoved. "I will not take any chances; it may be a trap." With a jerk of his head, he indicated to Lina, "See to it."

Grant made an involuntary sound of protest as Lina gestured to Carstairs, "You there—help me carry her."

He bent to lift Dokes and hoist her over his shoulder while Lina led him away from the stern. As soon as they were out of earshot Lina hissed, "Bind her and for heaven's sake give her a gag. I will find a sail bag for her—*Mãe de Deus* but this entire event is a disaster, start to finish."

"So—not the gold," he concluded under his breath. "Cinder bricks?"

Lina dared not look around but said in an undertone, "Where is the Vicar? Did he hear what she said?"

There was a pause before Carstairs responded in a neutral tone, "I do not think so."

Meeting his eyes in desperation, she implored him under her breath, "Don't tell him, Lucien; it is very important that no one know it is not the gold—" She realized it was a request that required him to choose an allegiance with precious little information and struggled to decide what to say.

He carefully laid Dokes on the deck behind the wheelhouse, out of sight, and glanced around toward the figures gathered around the lifeboat at the stern. "Where is the gold, Lina?"

"England will have it back—well, most of it," she temporized. "Please, Lucien—you must trust me in this." She met his eyes, willing him to believe her.

"Fetch a sail bag, then—there's nowhere to hide her." He tore off a piece of Dokes's petticoat to fashion a gag.

Thinking this a good sign, Lina procured a sail bag and between them they worked it down over the unconscious woman's head. "Quickly," she urged. "I must see if Brodie needs assistance."

"At least she isn't fat, like the Flemish ambassador." He glanced up at her as he pulled the strings to secure the bag's end. "I was mad for you, even then."

"You were also married," she reminded him as they pushed the sail bag against the wheelhouse and out of the way. "Married people should be loyal to each other."

"Sorry." He placed a hand over hers for a moment. "A sore subject."

Pausing in her movements, she lifted her face to his and offered, "For you, also—let us each hope to have better luck this time."

"*Bela.*" He leaned in to kiss her, mask and all.

At his use of Brodie's pet name she accused, "You have been eavesdropping, my friend."

"It is so appropriate—Portuguese for 'beautiful.'"

"The first and only time Brodie has ever been straightforward," she noted in a dry tone. "Now, let's hurry back and see if we can salvage this miserable plot."

When they returned to the others, it was to see Rochon and Henry Grant preparing to descend to the lifeboat on a rope ladder that had been cast over the side—the waves were making the small vessel toss about because the river had turned rough where it had widened, away from the city. Scanning downriver, Lina could make out the dark shape of an unlit ship that bore no flag, waiting silently to secure its cargo and return to France.

Pausing at the railing, Rochon unbuttoned his coat so as to make his descent, his satisfaction evident. "*Adieu, mes amis.*" He reached to put an arm around Lina and pull her to him. "I thank you for your assistance, *ma belle.* Perhaps you should come along with me so that I can show you how thankful I am."

She didn't resist and gave every appearance of enjoying the attention as she slid her hands under his coat and around his waist to embrace him. He had not appreciated her veiled reference to his sexual preferences and now sought to make it clear she was mistaken—Napoleon had little tolerance for such. Men are so predictable, she thought—now he is going to maul me about, just to prove the point.

She smiled into his eyes, opaque and hard like a snake's behind his mask. "Another time, *mon bravo.*"

He bent and kissed her mouth and she returned the salute in full measure, hoping this was to be the final distraction before she retired to Suffolk—Carstairs was no doubt fit to be tied.

With a thin smile, Rochon released her and threw a leg over the gunwale to descend the rope ladder into the lifeboat. The boat tossed and bucked as he carefully stepped over the bricks, awaiting Grant's descent.

The Vicar, however, had other plans. Leaping to the barge's forecastle, he raised a pistol to aim it at his rival spymaster. "Halt," he shouted. "You are under arrest in the name of the Crown."

With a rapid movement Rochon drew for the pistol at his waist but as it now rested in Lina's hand, he came up empty. The familiar sound of the cocking of firearms could be heard from various vantage points on the deck, and Rochon, quickly calculating, drew himself up, the picture of innocent outrage as he braced himself aboard the rocking vessel. "What is the meaning of this? What is my crime?"

The Vicar, still dressed as a dandy, addressed him coolly from where he stood amidships. "You are absconding with gold that has been stolen from the Treasury. Surrender, and be taken peaceably."

"You mistake," Rochon answered with calm assurance. "These are but ordinary bricks, as you can see."

"Bring him in," commanded the Vicar. "We shall discover the truth."

The watermen began hauling on the davit ropes and after only a moment's reflection, Rochon took the only course available to him. With a curse, he grasped one of the bricks and hove it with some force at the floorboard of the lifeboat.

"Stop him," the Vicar shouted, striding toward the gunwale. "He must not sink it."

But Rochon continued with his forceful bashing of the

floorboard and barked a command at Grant, still on deck. "Shoot at the hull."

Lina knew a moment's regret that the man's pistol had been neutralized by Dokes as the Home Office agents frantically pulled on the ropes, hand over hand, while Rochon pounded at the floorboards in a desperate race to sink the boat before it was recovered. Just as it looked as though the boat would be hoisted from the water, a shot rang out from the ship, hitting the hull of the lifeboat just below the waterline and creating a geyser of water that soon broke into a torrent. While the Vicar cursed roundly, they watched the vessel break in two, its cargo and its occupant sliding ignominiously into the choppy waters of the Thames.

Lina stood quietly beside Carstairs and hoped that no one else had noticed that Grant's gun had not discharged and that Carstairs's pistol had burnt a hole in the folds of her skirt. My sharpshooter, she thought a bit mistily—and there is no longer a question of loyalty, apparently; no need to sleep with one eye open.

A tense silence prevailed for a few moments as those watching contemplated the fortune that was now making its way to the bottom of the sea.

"Pull him in," directed the Vicar in a grim tone.

In a matter of minutes the two spymasters faced one another on deck, Rochon's dignity not at all affected by his bedraggled appearance. "You have nothing on me," he pronounced coolly.

But the Vicar disagreed. "I believe you have in your possession a fortune in bonds; it is illegal for a foreign national to hold English bonds."

"You mistake the matter; the bonds are forgeries and worthless," countered Rochon.

The Vicar hesitated for only a second. "Then you will be charged with possession of forged documents with an intent to defraud."

Checkmate, thought Lina, and awaited events.

But Rochon was not to be outmaneuvered, and with a quick movement he took the packet from his jacket pocket and flung it over the side. With a curse, the Vicar strode to the railing and watched the bonds follow the gold to the bottom of the sea.

Lina stood beside Brodie and Jenny Dokes at the rail of the barge and watched the activity on the Westminster pier as Rochon and Henry Grant were escorted, hands bound behind them, into the waiting prison transport.

"I'm sorry about your head, Dokes," Lina offered.

Leaning on her elbows, the other woman shrugged in an amicable fashion. "No matter; my own fault for not holding my role."

Lina reflected that Dokes was not one to hold a grudge and neither was she, for that matter—the two of them would continue on as though there had not been multiple double-crossings or violent blows to the back of the head. It was a relief, in a way, not to have to worry about hurt feelings.

"An excellent night's work, all in all," Brodie commented with satisfaction as the transport cart lumbered away. "Not precisely as planned, but one must remain flexible." He pulled a cigarillo from his vest pocket and lit it with a lucifer, his hand shielding it from the river breeze. With a casual gesture, Dokes slid her fingers into his pocket and pulled out another for herself, which Brodie lit for her as though it were the merest commonplace.

Lina watched this display in bemusement and shook her head. "We were flexible as we hung on for our lives; it was a close-run thing, Benny—confess."

"*Bela*," he chided, tossing the lucifer over the side. "We needed only to have the cargo sunk and Rochon unaware that it wasn't the gold after all; that the plan did not go as originally drawn up is neither here nor there."

Drawing on her cigarillo, Dokes offered, "I think it exceeded all expectations—my remains needn't be fished out of the river and Rochon is in custody—although perhaps it would have been better had you arranged for him to be coshed and thrown overboard, instead."

"Allow me to know my limitations," Brodie replied in a mild tone. "Assassination is not in my line."

"A *provocateur*, then." The woman eyed Brodie with a small smile and lifted her head to exhale a cloud of smoke. "Managing from behind the scenes."

Rocking back on his heels, Brodie pronounced, "The best rigs are those done for one's own amusement—too many get caught up in the need to be admired."

As Dokes tilted her head in agreement, Lina had to hide a smile at Brodie's uncharacteristic attempt at modesty. As soon as Dokes had been revived, he had been unrelenting in his insistence that the woman come to work for him in Venice. This was unexpected—a less likely gambling hostess could hardly be imagined—but Brodie was Brodie and presumably knew a good thing when he saw it. Lina could not help but note that the two were behaving in a manner bordering on the flirtatious and managed to hide her incredulity only with an effort—perhaps the blow to Dokes's head accounted for it.

"Come with me," Brodie said bluntly. "I shall make it well worth your while."

Dokes blew out a cloud and made a gesture toward the dock. "And leave this? I am saving the kingdom, here."

But Brodie shook his head. "The war will not last—it cannot; you know it as well as I. Then what will you do? Catch counterfeiters for the Treasury, or track insurance fraud for Lloyd's of London? It will be mighty dull fare, after this."

His companion tapped an ash and noted dryly, "Whereas running a gambling ken should be my heart's desire?"

"You would travel," he urged, and Lina surmised that Brodie had shrewdly guessed which aspect would be most appealing to Dokes. "Wherever you'd like and in the first level of comfort; our establishments must be set up where the moneyed classes reside. You'd need to dress the part, of course—credibility is everything."

Considering this, the other woman bent her head to study the water lapping against the hull. "How much of the take?"

"Five percent," offered Brodie promptly.

Dokes turned her head to regard him with an unblinking gaze. "Net or gross?"

Brodie hesitated only a second. "Gross."

"Take it, Dokes," suggested Lina, arching her brows. "I believe he is drunk."

"Would we have a faro table?" Dokes persisted. "The odds most favor the house."

There was a small pause. "I must marry you," Brodie declared in all seriousness. "And as soon as possible."

While Lina struggled to conceal her astonishment, Dokes drew on the cigarillo and considered the offer as though it were an ordinary suggestion. She then threw the stub into the river. "Agreed."

Brodie turned to Lina with an apologetic air. "We'll need some privacy to discuss terms, *Bela*—you understand."

Having been thus dismissed, Lina made her way toward the gangway and saw Carstairs speaking quietly with the

Vicar, no doubt debriefing the spymaster on some version of what had transpired this fine evening—Lina did not begrudge it; as Brodie has said, one must remain flexible and there were still some loose ends to tie up. Both men looked up as she approached.

"My new stepmama." Lina indicated the couple now deep in conversation with a nod of her head.

This announcement was met with the astonished silence it deserved. "A formidable pairing," conceded the Vicar, his hands clasped behind him. "Napoleon should look to his Treasury."

With a gleam, Lina teased, "Will you not protest? You will miss her talent, methinks; perhaps you should offer for her yourself."

"Alas, I am unable to make such a commitment," the Vicar replied, his thoughtful gaze on the couple, "having a previous understanding with another." He offered Carstairs a cigar, and the men stood with Lina, smoking and contemplating the recent events as they looked out over the docks, now quiet. The Vicar rested his grey gaze on Lina for a moment. "As amazing as it seems, my faith in you has not been shaken."

"That is indeed amazing; perhaps it is unshakable."

He held out his hand. "Allow me his weapon as a souvenir."

"Willingly." With a smile she handed Rochon's pistol over to him.

He inspected it, weighing its heft. "You have provided me with a new and very useful bit of information. How did you discover it?"

Lina knew he referred to Rochon's sexual preferences and thought of René. "I met a man who was very kind to me when I was captured last fall. He is now dead, unfortunately."

Leaning his head back, the Vicar blew a cloud. "Excellent—I will see to it that Rochon finds a new *bel ami*."

Brodie's voice could be heard from behind them as he and Dokes approached the group. "Better you cultivate a counterfeiter named Gerard—he excels at creating false bonds and false currency, and being a Romany, he can be bought."

Bowing in appreciation, the spymaster noted in an ironic tone, "You are a font of useful information this night, Mr. Brodie. I am nearly driven to forgive you for the May dance you've led me."

With a dismissive gesture, Brodie protested, "All has worked out to everyone's satisfaction, I believe. No need for recriminations."

The Vicar drew on his cigar, eyeing the other man. "And I imagine—as you say—Napoleon will be reduced to counterfeiting. He has no choice; he cannot go off the gold standard, but much of his gold has disappeared."

"A terrible turn of events," observed Brodie, his pensive gaze on the distant city lights. "There is no war without a war chest."

The economics of war, thought Lina as they all stood in silence for a moment; every bit as important as the artillery.

Suddenly, the Vicar threw back his head and laughed aloud, the sound unexpected and startling. "The *Argo*," he exclaimed with an uncharacteristically broad smile. "In search of the golden fleece. Well done."

"One must have one's private jest," Brodie demurred with a show of modesty. "And I have always admired the classics."

"Fleeced indeed. I wonder," the Vicar mused aloud as he lit another cigar, "where Napoleon's gold has gone?"

But Brodie had reached the limit of his helpfulness and said no more, instead turning to engage in a murmured conversation with Jenny Dokes.

Lina decided it was past time to reward the Vicar, who had practiced a restraint in her case that had not gone unappreciated and who—after all—could wind up being husband number three. "I'd like to make a gift of my town house to the Home Office, methinks. You may do with it as you wish—I shall be abiding in Suffolk and learning how to hold house." She turned her head to smile at Carstairs. "I must make the gift tomorrow, before I marry."

The Vicar exhaled in satisfaction. "The gold is in the cellar, I am convinced—is there a hidden trapdoor?"

She gave him her slow smile. "No; the very bricks that line the walls are not what they seem."

He met her gaze, the expression in his grey eyes amused. "Ah. Another ten minutes and I would have twigged it."

"I think not," she disagreed. "You were diverted—I have not been an angel lo, these many years for nothing."

He chuckled aloud and Lina could hear Carstairs make a soft sound of disapproval. She squeezed his arm to soothe him.

The Vicar continued, "England—and the Treasury—thank you for your gift, then. Is it the French gold or the English gold?" Lina noted he was careful not to include Brodie in the question and so she answered vaguely, "Most of both." It went without saying that Brodie would have rewarded himself for his troubles. And hers, too—she imagined the new Lady Tyneburne would be given a prodigiously heavy wedding gift.

With an air of satisfaction the Vicar concluded, "Excellent; it would seem all that is left is to negotiate with you, Mr. Brodie, on a schedule for redeeming the true bonds—wherever you have hidden them."

"Too late," replied Brodie carelessly, flicking an ash from his lapel. "The true bonds are at the bottom of the sea."

As the Vicar arched his brows in surprise, Lina explained, "Only the first one was a forgery, meant to mislead Rochon; all the others were genuine."

After a moment's pause, once again the Vicar bowed in appreciation, this time without a hint of irony. "Masterfully done; you did a fine thing for England and at the same time came out from under Rochon's grip—and with him all unknowing."

Brodie shrugged. "On to the next venture." He slanted a glance at Dokes, who returned her own version of Lina's slow smile.

"I can arrange for a commendation, if you'd like." The spymaster's voice was sincere with gratitude. "From the Prince himself."

Brodie attempted to hide his revulsion with little success. "Pray resist the impulse."

After shared laughter, the party stood for a moment, basking in the success of the assignment and unwilling to allow the evening to end. "What will happen to Rochon?" Lina asked the Vicar.

The other considered, his arms crossed and the cigar smoke drifting upward. "We could attempt to hold him until an investigation is completed, but I would be very much surprised if he was not traded in exchange for other high-level prisoners."

Dokes made a sympathetic gesture. "Frustrating for you, certainly."

The Vicar tossed away his cigar butt. "On the contrary, I would expect the same courtesy were I captured—it is the way of it."

"I could not hold your job." Lina thought of her ordeal at Rochon's hands. "I could not be so complacent."

The grey eyes slid toward hers. "No, Invidia, goddess of vengeance; I imagine you could not."

"Lina," she corrected him in a mild tone. "I am retiring from the vengeance business, all debts having been satisfactorily settled." She laid a gentle hand on Carstairs's arm in acknowledgment, thinking of how San Sebastian now seemed a distant memory—as though it had happened to someone else a long, long time ago.

The gesture was not lost on the spymaster. "I shall try to see to it that this husband of yours maintains a whole skin." As she met his eyes Lina could discern a reference to their bargain.

"I would appreciate it—and pray give him no more assignments where the object is seduction."

The Vicar shrugged and smiled. "He is of little use, else."

Carstairs chuckled and Lina protested, "Then teach him an honest trade; I'll not risk losing him to the next tainted angel."

"Not to worry—he has already carried off the palm; there will certainly be no one to match you." The Vicar gave her a mock salute. "He was bested despite all efforts."

"Like Rochon," she agreed, thinking on it with a great deal of satisfaction.

Chapter 47

"Maisie," Lina cautioned. "Pull yourself together, if you please, or I will be forced to brain you with the nearest fire jack." The threat was needful; Maisie's eyes were red-rimmed with suppressed tears, and if her stalwart maidservant were to start weeping, Lina would never be able to hold her role.

That worthy pronounced in an unsteady voice, "Ye make a bonny, bonny bride."

"Stay out of the champagne," Lina scolded. They were in the drawing room of her former town house where a few short minutes before Catalina McCord had quietly become Lady Tyneburne before a duly commissioned representative of the Church of England. As a sign of her faith in her new husband, Lina did not demand that the officiant present his *bona fides*.

She had stood beside her bridegroom and listened to his voice, steady and sincere, answering the age-old questions. *Agradeca Deus*, she thought as she fought tears. *Mama, desejo estavo aqui*; I have had a long journey to this moment.

And now she accepted congratulatory wishes and planned for the next phase of that journey—a laying down of arms, so to speak. She knew not what to expect, but it didn't much matter; Suffolk could only be less tumultuous than the

Peninsular War, and childbirth could only be less harrowing than having Rochon's knife at her throat. Or one would think, anyway.

It was an intimate gathering; Lina wore a traveling dress in lavender silk as they meant to get under way as soon as possible. Carstairs would be needed to return to service, there being ominous signs accruing from the Mediterranean.

"A pretty posy," Maisie offered doubtfully, indicating the bouquet Lina still held tightly in her hand. Before the ceremony Carstairs had presented her with a humble bouquet of lilies, which she had contemplated silently for a few moments, unable to find her voice. He had put his arms around her and kissed her temple in a gesture of understanding as Maisie admonished him; saying it was bad luck to kiss her before the ceremony.

"Nonsense, Maisie," he had responded. "Her luck has turned."

Perhaps it has, Lina thought with caution as she watched him thank the clergyman. There seems little chance I'm to be hauled to the Tower on a charge of treason or that the wretched Marie will make a reappearance from the grave.

Brodie interrupted her reverie to bestow a kiss on her cheek, the first such gesture she had ever received from him. He and Dokes were duly present but he was in a fever of impatience to be away, having made vague references to the need to purchase a wooden dray containing a false bottom in Nice.

"Riveted," he pronounced to Lina with great satisfaction, clasping his hands behind his back. He was referring to himself; he and Jenny were wed the day before by special license.

"You will behave yourself," Lina warned him. "Dokes is not someone to be trifled with."

"On the contrary—I well know that one does not trifle with resourceful women. I shall do nothing that would prevail upon her to escape out the window with the bed sheets."

"I will see to him," Dokes assured her in her quiet voice, leaning forward to plant a dry kiss on Lina's cheek. "We plan to spend the next few months in the south of France, if the coming war permits."

"Casinos," Brodie explained. "Mrs. Brodie believes I should target a more upscale clientele."

"A larger profit margin, after the initial investment," Dokes added. "We should be turning a profit within a year—unless the monetary system collapses, of course."

"Excellent," Lina replied, and prudently did not wonder aloud if the Vicar's desires were behind the idea to relocate the irreplaceable Dokes to the south of France. That gentleman had declined an invitation to Lina's nuptials, citing pressing matters.

She could not suppress a smile as Carstairs approached and drew her aside. "Let us away," she whispered on tiptoe into his ear. "Or at least find a quiet garret somewhere."

With a gleam, he gently chided her, "Not just yet—some decorum is called for, and if I bring your wedding nightdress to mind I am lost."

She reached to intertwine her fingers with his, in the folds of her skirt. "This wedding trip bodes to be superior to the last."

He bent his head to hers. "That first night at the inn, I had to restrain myself from revealing all and advising you to flee."

With a smile she squeezed his hand. "Poor Lucien; torn between duty and a tainted, pregnant, faux wife."

He lifted a corner of his mouth at the memory. "You may mock me now, but at the time it was damnable."

"And what if I had heeded your advice and made my way back to Rochon's lair? What then?"

The blue eyes held hers. "I would have come for you, somehow."

Smiling tenderly, she decided she may as well believe him—it would be a novel experience for her. "All right, we are truly married; now, how do we play this?"

He contemplated her, a soft smile playing around his lips. "Should we attempt the truth?"

"*Santos*, Lucien—that is not amusing."

He persisted. "You are a Portuguese refugee, having faithfully served Wellington's Army on the Peninsula."

She fingered a button on his waistcoat, thinking it over. It had the benefit of being more or less the truth. "How did we meet?" she countered, arching a brow at him.

He knit his own brow. "How *did* we meet? Was it on the docks in Southwark?"

"You don't remember," she accused him with mock outrage.

With a bent head, he thought about it. "I should know this."

"Yes—you should." There was a small pause while she could see that he had drawn a blank. "I shall give you a hint: Calais."

His brow cleared. "Oh."

She couldn't help but laugh. "We can't very well explain that we met in a brothel."

"No," he agreed. "Although it was an excellent extraction."

"I loved you the moment I saw you," she confessed, smiling happily into his eyes. "Even though at the time I was holding the Field Marshal at knifepoint and dressed in nothing but a bustier and a petticoat."

"I couldn't concentrate." He enfolded her in his arms, his

chin resting on her head. "I couldn't believe you weren't a delightful vision."

"With a blade," she added.

"Even better—it was every man's fantasy come true."

Laughing, they shared a long moment of mutual reminiscence. "I believe we will need to concoct a story," he conceded.

"I would like to be minor Portuguese nobility, though—that does sound appealing."

"You will, then." He pressed a cheek against her temple, thinking on it. "We met during the war—after Marie died, I heard you were to be forced into a political marriage so as to transfer your holdings..."

"My vast holdings," she interrupted.

"Your vast holdings to one of Napoleon's puppets."

"A Spanish or a French puppet?"

"You choose," he offered generously.

"Spanish," she decided. That would please the old *soldado*. "And you stole me away in the dead of the night."

"And had to marry you forthwith to save you and your holdings."

She nodded, picturing it in her mind and very pleased with the role. "Was there any swordplay?"

He lifted his brows. "By me or by you?"

She laughed. "All right—I overreach. But it is a good tale."

He continued, "It will become clear that after the marriage I fell in love with you despite my grief. We will hint that there is more to the story—"

"As we embellish it."

His arms tightened around her. "I love you."

"And I love you, *querido*. Although I do not look forward to the long carriage ride—this child is making his or her presence known. We may have to travel in stages."

"Then I shall have to administer the cure, and often."

She laid a hand on his shirtfront. "It is no more than your duty, husband."

"I have always put my duty first." He bent to kiss her, long and hard, even though the guests were witness to this shocking display.

"Lucien," she whispered into his mouth. "You are not to mistake me for Marie again."

The steel blue eyes met hers. "I didn't—and in any event you were so avid for me you didn't care."

Twigged, she thought. *Mãe de Deus*.

Read on for an excerpt from
Anne Cleeland's

Daughter of the God-King

Available November 2013 from Sourcebooks Landmark

Hattie Blackhouse was aware that she had—regrettably—something of a temper, and that this trait often led to impetuous decisions that were not always thought out in a rational manner. Fortunately, because she had lived a solitary life in the Cornish countryside, few had experienced either her temper or her impetuosity, and she had thus far avoided embarrassing herself in public. Until now, of course.

"Have you a card of invitation?" asked the respectful under-footman. He asked in English, which meant he had taken one look at their clothes and concluded they were either impoverished refugees or English, as the Parisian ladies around them were very much *à la mode.*

"We do not," she replied evenly, and lifted her chin. Now that she saw how grand it all was she conceded that it had been—perhaps—not the best idea to show up here at such a place uninvited and that she may indeed wind up as a public spectacle, but she had no one to blame but herself. Her old governess—the traitorous Swansea—had been a gentle, indulgent woman who had only interfered that one time when Hattie had taken a crop to the gardener's boy after he tied a can to the Tremaine dog's tail, and even then the distraught governess had apologized for curbing Hattie's impulse to beat the boy soundly, but the gardener was a good one and good gardeners were apparently few and far between. I must remind Robbie that I did a good deed for Sophie, Hattie thought as she squared her shoulders on the threshold of the Prussian embassy. I have a feeling he may not be best pleased when I make my appearance; but truly, coming here seemed such a good idea at the time, and I was sick to *death* of being exiled in Cornwall.

"Perhaps we should have sent a card 'round to your fiancé, first." Bing's tone was dry and deferential, but Hattie was given the uneasy feeling that Bing was well aware this was all a hoax. Even more reason not to tell her freshly minted companion that she had shoved an intruder down the back stairs of their Parisian townhouse less than an hour ago. Although the jury was still out, Bing seemed the sort of person who may have felt it necessary to notify the *gendarmes*, and Hattie didn't have the time, just now; she was going to confront Robbie—another traitor in what seemed to be an unending list.

"I'm afraid we haven't any calling cards, Bing; and we are gate-crashers of the first order."

"Very well," said Bing, unruffled. "It is a good thing I am armed, then."

Hattie hid a smile as they stepped forward in the line to be announced at the Ambassador's *soirée*—fortunately it hadn't been a ball, as Hattie didn't own a ball gown. Truth to tell, she didn't own anything suitable for a Parisian *soirée*, either, but this was the least of her concerns; as she was preparing for this outing at her parents' townhouse, she had heard a noise coming from the back stairwell and after flinging open the door, had been astonished to confront an intruder, equally astonished in beholding her before him. On instinct, she had shoved him as hard as she was able and he had tumbled backward down the stairs as she slammed the door shut and bolted the lock. A burglar, she assured herself; someone who thought the place was still empty and unaware that they had lately taken up residence. Although he hadn't seemed like a burglar and had stared at her in such an odd way; as though he was seeing a ghost.

She moved forward another step, frowning in distraction. She hoped Robbie was here at the embassy, as she may have need of reinforcements—there was the other man lurking on the corner of the street yesterday, also. For pity's sake, it was as though no one had ever seen a girl from Cornwall before, and her clothes were not *that* bad, surely.

"Hathor," Bing prompted under her breath, and Hattie brightened to bestow a smile on the footman at the door, resplendent in his livery. The man looked over her head for parents or presenters—no hard task as she was rather short in stature—and then seemed surprised to behold no one there. But Hattie had successfully shoved the intruder down the stairs, and buoyed by this thought, she announced with confidence, "I am Miss Blackhouse; I am here with my companion, Miss Bing."

Understandably nonplussed, the footman inquired in a discreet tone, "You have no card of invitation, mademoiselle?"

At this juncture, Bing, who was tall and spare and very correct, offered in a shocked tone, "Perhaps you do not recognize the name, my good man. This is Miss *Blackhouse*, the daughter of the famous Blackhouses; the Ambassador will be thrilled she has chosen his *soirée* over all the others."

Although she was half inclined to laugh out loud, Hattie made an attempt to look famous as the footman's eyes widened and he quickly passed her along to the host after murmuring an apology. "Miss Blackhouse and her companion, Miss Ding."

"*Bing*," Hattie interjected impatiently. "Miss *Bing*."

But her correction was swallowed up in the reaction of the Prussian Ambassador, a large, rather burly man with a gray goatee and an impressive array of medals displayed along his blue sash, which was itself impressive due to his girth. "Miss Blackhouse," he exclaimed in astonishment, and lifted a monocle to his eye. "Welcome—why, indeed; welcome."

Hoping that the footman was paying attention, Hattie took his hand with a sense of relief that she was not to be shown the door, and then was forced to stand as he clasped her hand in both of his with no indication he would release her anytime soon. "The tomb of the god-king's daughter," he pronounced in tones of deep emotion as the candlelight glinted off his monocle. "An amazing find—it quite takes one's breath away. Tell me, do your parents know the identity of the princess as yet?"

Another fervent Egyptologist, she thought with resignation; she had met his type before and unfortunately they were thick on the ground nowadays, with everyone mad for all things Egyptian and the world's fancy being caught by the tombs currently being uncovered in the Valley of the Kings.

"I believe not," she equivocated. Best not to mention that she rarely heard from either of her negligent parents; her information instead was gleaned from the local newspapers—or Bing, who was well informed due to her late brother. Reminded, Hattie offered, "There does seem to be a curse, though." As soon as she said it, she inwardly winced—she was thoughtless to mention it in front of poor Bing, who still wore mourning black.

But Bing did not falter, and added, "Indeed; several lives have been lost under unexplained circumstances."

The Ambassador's eyes widened and he glanced to those still waiting in the receiving line, clearly torn between his duties as host and his burning desire to buttonhole Hattie and quiz her about this fascinating bit of information. He called out, "Monsieur le Baron; your aid, if you please."

Hattie turned to meet the newcomer, tamping down her impatience. She had used her connection with her parents to crash this party and it was only fair that she pay the piper for a few minutes before she went off in search of Robbie. He wouldn't fail her, although she fully anticipated a dressing-down later in private. Hopefully it wouldn't be as bad as when she'd gotten lost on the Tor back home—and *truly*, that had not been her fault.

The Baron was revealed as an elegant, silver-haired man who approached with his hands clasped behind his back. "Yes? Might I be of assistance?"

With barely suppressed exultation, the Ambassador introduced him to Hattie. "Baron du Pays, my dear." And then, with a great deal of significance, "Monsieur le Baron, if you would entertain Miss Blackhouse while I attend to my duties here—she brings the latest news from the excavations."

The Baron could be seen to go quite still for a moment, his gaze fixed upon Hattie's, until he found his voice and bowed over her hand in the elegant manner known only to Frenchmen. "*Enchanté*, Mademoiselle Blackhouse." The pale blue eyes then fixed upon hers again with an expression she could not quite interpret—assessing, or calculating, or—or something. "I was so fortunate as to have met your parents once; extraordinary people." He looked up to a companion, who approached to join him. "Monsieur Chauvelin; come meet Mademoiselle Blackhouse."

But Hattie was astonished to recognize her former

intruder, and coldly riposted with a great deal of meaning, "I believe we have already met, monsieur."

She could hear Bing's soft intake of breath at her tone, but the man only shook his head and gravely disclaimed, "I do not recall such a felicity, mademoiselle."

"If you will excuse us," Hattie said with a curt bow and then turned away, a surprised Bing in her wake. In her abrupt movement, she met the eye of a man who appeared to be watching her from the side, although he quickly turned away and melted into the crowd. He appeared to be a civil servant of some stripe; his manner unprepossessing, his dress understated. But something in his bearing—his cool assurance, perhaps—belied his appearance and made her wonder why he watched her. This is a very strange sort of *soirée*, she thought; in Cornwall we may not be *à la mode*, but everyone certainly has better manners.

"Do we seek out Mr. Tremaine, Hathor?" Bing walked along beside her as though her charge had not just snubbed two distinguished gentlemen for no apparent reason.

"We do, Bing. And I am heartily sick of the tedious god-king and his equally tedious daughter."

"As you say," Bing replied.

Robbie was tall, and so she quickly scanned the assembly, looking for his blond head and wishing she could whistle for him. In the process, her gaze rested upon the self-assured civil servant, who had managed to stay parallel with her despite the crowded quarters. Lifting her chin, she gave him a quelling look just so that he was aware she was on to him, and then at long last spotted Robbie's form at a small distance in the crowd. He was surrounded by a group of people, and bent his head for a moment to listen to a blond woman, who was trying to speak to him over the noise of the throng. "I see him, Bing—and not a moment too soon. Come along."

But before she could squeeze in his direction, Hattie was confronted by the Prussian Ambassador himself, who gallantly handed her a glass of punch and indicated he would like to speak to her in a quieter corner. Short of pulling her hand from his and pushing yet another one bodily to the floor, she had little choice but to comply, and followed him to a less-crowded area near the windows, taking a quick glance to mark Robbie's location in the process.

"Did you enjoy speaking with Baron du Pays, Miss Blackhouse? He is the French vice-consul in Egypt."

"Oh—is he indeed?" It wanted only this; Hattie had probably launched an international incident by her snub, but surely a vice-consul shouldn't be consorting with burglars. As if on cue, the vice-consul came over to join them, although this time he was not accompanied by the aforesaid burglar which was just as well, as Hattie may have felt it necessary to dress him down and she was *truly* trying to control her temper.

With an air of extreme interest, her host crossed his arms over his be-medaled chest and rocked back on his heels. "If you would, Miss Blackhouse, tell me more of the curse; could it be the wrath of the ancients, visited upon those who disturb their legacy?"

"One can only wonder," Hattie replied, as diplomatically as she was able. She barely refrained from muttering a curse herself—one that Robbie himself had taught her. How anyone could believe that lifeless objects could be "cursed" was beyond her comprehension but the superstitious were a stubborn breed and—apparently—could be found at the highest levels of diplomacy, which told its own tale. She glanced sidelong at Robbie, and saw that he was conferring with the self-assured gentleman who had been watching her; Robbie then lifting his head to glance with surprise in her direction. Which was rather strange; why would the gentleman know that it was Robbie she sought out? Bing surreptitiously touched her elbow to draw her attention back to the conversation, and with an effort, Hattie pulled her gaze back to the Ambassador's magnified eye.

"...and the tomb with no clue as to the princess's identity. Extraordinary."

For two pins, Hattie would have asked why any rational person would feel this topic was of the least importance, but so as not to embarrass poor Bing she attempted to re-focus; after all, the Ambassador was her host and she should not allow Robbie to think she was incapable of deporting herself in diplomatic circles. Although it was a dull group, truth be told, and it was hard to believe the intrepid boy next door had willingly chosen this sort of life. "It is believed she was the daughter of some famous pharaoh," offered Hattie vaguely, stealing a glance toward Robbie as he made his way toward her. Oddly enough, he had the blond woman in tow—she was quite old—at least thirty, if she was a day. Perhaps the woman required his support due to her advanced age.

"Seti," murmured Bing behind her in an undertone.

"The Great Seti," added Hattie smoothly. "The god-king; presumably her father."

The Ambassador leaned forward, his expression avid at having gleaned such an intriguing scrap of information to tout to his fellow aficionados. "Indeed? And have your parents discovered why a princess's tomb was found in the Valley of the Kings? The only female to be found—most unusual."

At this juncture, Robbie arrived and greeted her with

astonishment. "Hattie, by all that's holy—however did you come to be here?" As he turned to explain their acquaintanceship to their host, Hattie realized she couldn't very well confess that she had come to Paris for the express purpose of trying to convince him to marry her, and with this in mind she retreated to a less-crazed explanation. "I came to visit my parents, Robbie."

The reaction to this disclosure was a rather heavy silence, with the Baron lowering his gaze to the floor and Robbie's expression suddenly shuttered. Hattie looked from one to the other in surprise, but was forced to acknowledge the blond woman with Robbie because she offered with a doubtful smile, "Here—in Paris? But I recently left your parents in Thebes."

"Did you indeed?" Hattie was very much afraid her tone may have indicated her displeasure at having been shown to be equivocating, not to mention it was of all things annoying that this too-tall blond knew more about her parents than she did. She hastily added, "I thought they would be here in Paris, instead; I meant to surprise them, you see."

The Baron took the opportunity to interject, "A coincidence; I have recently journeyed from Thebes, myself."

Again, there was a tense silence in response to this observation and the woman did not acknowledge this remark with even a glance in his direction. Hattie, alive to the undercurrent, wondered why they had all converged upon her when they didn't seem to like each other very much and half-hoped for an open quarrel so that she could use the opportunity to speak privately with Robbie. Not to mention the self-assured gentleman was now standing at the vice-consul's back, pretending to converse with a woman wielding a flirtatious fan even though Hattie was well aware he was eavesdropping on their conversation. Why, every man-jack on the premises appears to be prodigiously interested in my doings, she thought with surprise; it is all very strange.

The Ambassador informed the newcomers, "We were discussing the latest Blackhouse discovery—the tomb of the god-king's daughter."

"Extraordinary," agreed the Baron. "Indeed, the artifacts uncovered include the sacred sword *Shefrh Lelmelwek*—the Glory of Kings, bestowed by the gods on the pharaoh himself."

Hattie didn't need to look at Bing to feel her companion's surprise. It appeared the vice-consul was indeed lately come from the excavation at Thebes, and he was very well informed. Bing's brother had indicated in his letters that the discovery of the mythical sword was a well-kept secret.

With an attitude that bordered on the rapturous, the Ambassador looked to Hattie, wide of eye. "Such a mystery! How could such a wonder have been bestowed upon a mere female? And how could she have warranted a tomb in the Valley of the Kings?"

Hattie did her best to come up with an answer, wishing she had paid more attention when Bing was speaking of such things. "We must suppose that she some performed some extraordinary service so as to be a heroine in the eyes of the Eighteenth Dynasty."

Bing made a small sound behind her which indicated Hattie was mixing her dynasties again—but honestly, who could keep them straight? It was three thousand years ago, for the *love* of *heaven*. But correction was to come from the blond woman, who announced in an indulgent tone, "Seti was Nineteenth Dynasty, I believe."

Curbing an urgent desire to make a cutting remark,

Hattie recalled her circumstances and subsided. "Yes—yes I am sorry; I misspoke." She then caught the self-assured gentleman's gaze upon her again and realized he was amused. Why, he is *laughing* at me, the wretch; I should spill my punch on him, just to show how little I appreciate being the object of his amusement—or being exposed as ignorant in matters Egyptian. The man turned away as Hattie sipped her punch, thinking that this was an odd sort of party—and Robbie was making no effort to have a private word, which was perplexing in itself; if nothing else, he should want to take her aside to give her a bear-garden jawing for surprising him in such a way.

But he had his own surprise that, as it turned out, would trump hers. Robbie turned to the woman in warm approval, and pulled her hand through his arm. "Madame Auguste knows a great deal about the excavations—she lived in Egypt for years."

"No more," she laughed. "Now I will be an Englishwoman."

"England's gain," offered the Ambassador gallantly, and sketched a small bow.

With a smile that bordered on the patronizing, the woman addressed Hattie. "Only think, Mademoiselle Blackhouse, we shall be neighbors, you and I."

With dawning horror, Hattie found she was having trouble putting together a coherent thought. "Is that so?" she managed, and almost dispassionately noted that she could now hear her heartbeat in her ears—never a good sign.

"Wish me happy, Hattie," Robbie revealed with his easy smile. "Madame has agreed to marry me, and I am the luckiest of men."

About the Author

Anne Cleeland holds a degree in English from UCLA as well as a law degree from Pepperdine University and is a member of the California State Bar. She writes historical fiction set in the Regency period and contemporary mystery. A member of the Historical Novel Society, she lives on Balboa Island, California, and has four children. *Tainted Angel* is her first novel.